"*The Realms Thereunder* is a fantastically compelling novel mixing the best of fantasy, adventure, and intrigue. It's one of those can't-put-down tales you'll be thinking about long after turning the last page. Fans of C.S. Lewis, the Inkheart Trilogy, and of course Stephen Lawhead will find much to enjoy in this well-crafted read."

—C.J. DARLINGTON, TITLETRAKK.COM;
AUTHOR OF *BOUND BY GUILT*

"With beautiful imagery, thoughtful imagination, and a touch of humor, *The Realms Thereunder* is an excellent beginning to an insightful and exciting new fantasy series."

—MELISSA WILLIS, THECHRISTIANMANIFESTO.COM

"For lovers of Stephen Lawhead, his influence shines through in this story of fantasy, reality and everything in between!"

—LORI TWICHELL, RADIANTLIT.COM

THE ANCIENT EARTH TRILOGY

BOOK ONE:

THE REALMS THEREUNDER

ROSS LAWHEAD

THOMAS NELSON
Since 1798

NASHVILLE DALLAS MEXICO CITY RIO DE JANEIRO

FOR DRAKE—
WHO HAS BEEN ON OVER A HUNDRED
HEROIC QUESTS WITH ME.

Published in Nashville, Tennessee, by Thomas Nelson. Thomas Nelson is a registered trademark of Thomas Nelson, Inc.

Page design by Mandi Cofer.

Thomas Nelson, Inc., titles may be purchased in bulk for educational, business, fund-raising, or sales promotional use. For information, please e-mail SpecialMarkets@ThomasNelson.com.

Library of Congress Cataloging-in-Publication Data

Lawhead, Ross.
  The realms thereunder / by Ross Lawhead.
    p. cm. -- (The elder earth trilogy ; bk. 1)
  ISBN 978-1-59554-909-9 (trade paper)
  I. Title.
  PS3562.A864R43 2011
  813'.54--dc22

                              2011021276

Printed in the United States of America

11 12 13 14 15 16 QG 6 5 4 3 2 1

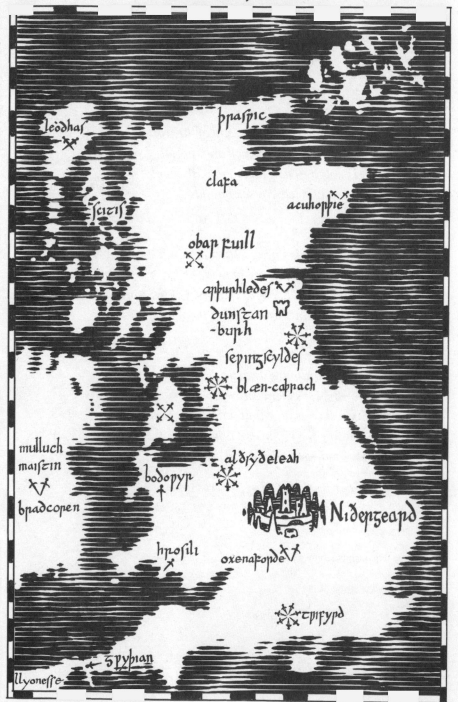

"But whatso hap at the end of the world,
Where Nothing is struck and sounds,
It is not, by Thor, these monkish men
These humbled Wessex hounds—

"Not this pale line of Christian hinds
This one white string of men,
Shall keep us back from the end of the world,
And the things that happen then.

"It is not Alfred's dwarfish sword,
Nor Egbert's pigmy crown,
Shall stay us now that descend in thunder,
Rending the realms and the realms thereunder,
Down through the world and down."

—THE BALLAD OF THE WHITE HORSE:
  VI - THE SLAYING OF THE CHIEFS,
  G. K. CHESTERTON

PROLOGUE

---------------------------------- 1 ----------------------------------

20th April, 1524

"And I say that you're a fool, Addison Fletcher!" the brawny man declared, striking his ale mug against the bare wooden table for emphasis.

"God smite me where I sit if I tell a lie, Coll Dawson!" Addison protested, his eyes flicking heavenward for the briefest of moments.

"Ah, *but*—did you not say," declared Coll, cocking an eyebrow and pointing a finger. "Did you not say that you got this account from another—"

"From Rob Fuller," piped a voice from the end of the table.

"Aye, from Rob Fuller. And who's to say that a tale told by Rob Fuller is true or false? Swearing oaths upon secondhand tales is not wise."

"Then tell me, is it wisdom or foolishness to trust honourable

1

men? I've known Rob this last twenty year and judge him to be a straight and honest man."

"Even so," continued Coll expansively. "An honest man may—"

"Enough!" came a shout from the table next to theirs. "You bicker like a pair of divinity scholars. I would hear the rest of the tale and judge for myself!"

"Aye, the tale!" came another shout from behind Addison, and the chorus was picked up by all of those in the tavern who were in earshot of the two men.

"Alright! Alright!" Addison banged his ale mug on the table. When a reasonable silence fell on the room, he drew breath to speak. "Where had I gotten to?"

"'The blacksmith was working late on a moonless night when a man walked in . . . ,'" a helpful listener prompted.

"Aye, aye, just so. And full old he was—with a beard, white as a cloud, down to his waist, and a red—"

"You described him already!" came a cry from another table.

"And a red robe!" Addison Fletcher shouted. "A red robe that was bordered with all manner of delicate and intricate designs! *Alright?*"

There was chuckling among the crowd.

"Anyhow," Addison continued, quieter. "This old gent comes up to the blacksmith—Sam, the blacksmith's name is—and bids him good evening. Sam bids him likewise and asks what service he can give the old man. The old man without saying a word hands him a bar of gold this big." Addison held his hands apart.

"'What's this?' asks Sam.

"'I need you to make a shoe from this strip of gold that would fit a warhorse,' says the stranger, and gives him the size, which is large enough for a destrier. The blacksmith sets to work and—it being no especially hard task to shape gold—he soon has the shoe made. He hands it over to the old man along with the parts of the gold bar that he hasn't used. He does this thinking that he'll get some of the gold in return and more of it if he's honest. For in working with the stuff, he's judged it to be proof pure.

"But the gent merely puts the gold scraps in a pouch he carries on his belt and asks the smith to pick up his shoeing tools and follow him.

"'Where are we going?' asks Sam, and the old man answers that the job isn't finished until the horse itself is shod. With assurance that he'll be compensated for his time, Sam falls in step alongside him.

"Well, to hear Sam tell of it, they walk out of the town proper—this was all happening in Reading, by the way—and along the river Kennet past the abandoned abbey grounds and into the forest. They go about a mile inwards, until they reach a cave in the side of a cliff. The old man ducks his head and walks in without pausing and Sam's right behind him trying not to lose sight of him in the dark.

"It's not too long before they come to a small room carved out in the rock in the corner of which is a large pile of jewels—rubies, emeralds, diamonds, garnets, sapphires, and the like. There are two grand archways in this small room leading to two large halls like feasting halls. In one of them he can see men, warriors, all done up head to foot in armour, and sleeping, each laid out on the floor shoulder to shoulder, toe to toe.

"In the other room are horses, massive warhorses, all of them likewise asleep but upright and covered in fine blankets under which they wear armour. And each one of them is shod with four golden horseshoes.

"The old man enters this second room, but Sam is told to stay where he is, and not to touch the pile of jewels. As he waits Sam takes in all he can about the place. He ends up by counting the horses and reckons there to be about seventy or so.

3

"Well, the old man reappears, leading a listing horse down the centre of the hall and into the smaller chamber.

"Sam is told by the old man to shoe the horse and so he does, all the while eyeing the pile of jewels and asking questions—questions about where he is, who the knights are, and how the horses have been kept—but the old man doesn't say a word, as if he can't hear Sam.

"Well, Sam eventually finishes his work and puts his tools away. The old man studies his work, praises his handicraft, and then hands Sam a leather pouch. Sam opens it and finds it empty. He asks the old man what it is.

"'You may fill this pouch with whatever gemstones you wish from the pile,' the old man answers. 'But do not put anything of value in your shirt, tool satchel, or anywhere on your person, else the knights will wake up and surely kill you. Fill it as much as you can but make sure that you are able to draw the strings shut, for if you leave with it open the knights will wake up and surely kill you and I won't stop them.'

"So Sam goes over to the pile as the old man leads the horse away and he starts cramming the bag full of precious stones. He's sufficiently scared of the old man's tale about the knights killing him to not put anything on his person. But also he's thinking that he'll make a return trip here the next morning with the same pouch and carry even more away.

"Sam packs the pouch tight enough to just be able to pull the strings together, and the old man leads him out of the cave.

"Once outside the old man turns to him and says that he may return to his forge, but he is not to tell anyone of what he has done this evening. The old man then goes back into the cave and Sam walks home.

"Now anyone who knows Sam knows that it only takes a prod to start his tongue wagging and scarce has he crossed his own door's threshold then he's gabbing to his wife about all that's just happened to him. She finds this all hard to believe—"

"She's not the only one," Coll Dawson said to the man sitting next to him.

"*But*," continued Addison, "he's got the bag full of gemstones that he carried out with him. He throws this on the table and says, 'Here's the proof.'

"The wife opens the bag and sticks her hand in and pulls out something small and hard and then lets go of both it and the bag. 'What is this? A joke?' she asks, angry.

"Sam goes over to the bag and tips out the contents onto the table. Instead of all his diamonds, rubies, and such, there's just a pouchful of old dried-up horse droppings. Sam tries to tell the tale again, but his wife has lost patience with him and makes him sleep that night in the forge."

"Women are unreasonable like that," said a man at the next table.

"The next day," Addison continued peevishly, "Sam goes back into the forest to look for the cave but he can't find it. He finds a cliff face that he thinks is the same place, but it is just a blank wall of stone. He keeps hunting around and finds a few caves but none of them go back very far.

"He's gone back every day since, sometimes in the morning, sometimes in the night, but he has never found the chambers of the sleeping knights again."

Addison Fletcher had finished his tale and marked it by taking a long drink of his ale. "So now," he said, wiping his moustache. "What do you say to that?"

"I've heard it before, told just that way," said one man from the back of the crowd.

Addison's face brightened. "Yeah?"

"Yeah, only it wasn't just an old man in red, it was Merlin

himself!" Addison's face fell. "And it wasn't just any knights the blacksmith saw, but the Knights of the Round Table. Waitin' for judgment, they were."

"When I was on tour in the Freincs' lands," said a grizzled man at the next table, "I heard a man tell it as with Charlemagne who needed a golden spear. But he was sleeping under this famous mountain, like."

"Lies, that is. It's *dragons* that live in mountains."

"But what about *my*—" Addison tried to break in.

"Nay, ye daft bugger, they lie on top o' them," argued the war veteran. "They fly about above the clouds in the day and sleep atop a mountain of nights."

And they all fell about to arguing over these and related matters until the bell rang for closing.

CHAPTER ONE

Oxford Is Not Safe

FOUND!

Manhunt for missing kids ends in Scotland.

Daniel Tully and Freya Reynolds, the two schoolchildren who went missing 72 days ago, have been found near Kilmarnock, in East Ayreshire, Scotland. Alex Simpson, the son of a farm owner, discovered them yesterday at 5:04 p.m. Both were covered in mud and displayed signs of severe shock and were disturbed mentally but were otherwise in good health when examined at St. Bride's Hospital by Peter Tavish, MD. No statement has yet been made by the children. A joint statement by the parents and the police describe themselves as "joyful and relieved" at the return of the children, who will be driven to Glasgow to undergo further examination.

Daniel Tully, 13, and Freya Reynolds, also 13, went missing

on a class trip to a church in Abbingdon in the British Midlands over two months ago. Criminal experts are at a loss to explain.

(continued on page 5)

2

Now . . .

Daniel Tully sat unmoving and unnoticed—just another gargoyle on Broad Street. A paper cup in front of him held fifty-six pence in small coins and there were two pounds in his pocket. That meant either a proper meal or a bed in the night shelter. He really wanted both. He could try blagging his way into the homeless café—the Gatehouse—even though he was too young at only twenty years old. That would give him a meal and he could buy the bed and keep the fifty-six pence for tomorrow.

"Spare change, mate?" he asked a pair of business trousers.

The legs continued without breaking stride. Two other pairs of legs coming the other way stopped in front of him and he looked up.

Two girls, students, stood in front of him and one of them was digging around in her purse. She hastily fished out a couple of coins—her friend gazing sourly at her all the while—and dropped them into his cup.

"God bless you," Daniel said. "Both of you, God bless you."

They hurried away, the sour one berating her friend for—what, exactly? Daniel sat stoically until they dashed between the columns of the Bodleian Library. Then he leaned forward and inspected the latest windfall. There looked to be seventy-eight pence now. That meant she only gave him twenty-two.

Sighing, he got up, shouldered his overstuffed rucksack, and started walking to St. Michael's Street. The bodies in front of him shifted, opened, and closed in their usual manner. And through the ebb and flow, a figure was suddenly revealed and then hidden again—a small, lean, heavily tattooed figure that walked with an animalistic gait, wide and lurching.

Daniel froze, his heart racing. He pushed his breath out in a low whistle, his hand instinctively rising and clutching at an object hanging under his jacket along his rib cage. He gripped it so hard that his knuckles went white.

With an effort he opened his fist and started walking again.

He strode quickly this time, weaving deftly through the crowd, trying to close the gap between himself and the tattooed head. He still had not caught sight of it by the time he stood underneath Carfax Tower, the intersection of the town's busiest foot traffic. He stood, turning slightly as he rapidly scanned the faces of those approaching from four directions, hoping—but dreading—to see the squat, hairless head.

Underneath Carfax Tower was another homeless man selling magazines—Scouse Phil. Daniel approached him with a nod. "Alright, Phil?"

"Eee, our Dan. How's yourself?"

"Yeah, not bad, not bad. You ain't seen a short bloke, kind of thin, shaved head, tattoos, that kind of thing? Passed by about ten minutes ago?"

"That who you were looking for over there? Can't say I've seen him that recently, but yeah, I've seen him about. Tattoos all swirly like, but with lots of edges. Nasty business he is. Largin' himself up, throwin' it around like God Almighty. Violent. Got thrown out of the Gatehouse a few times. You got business with him?"

"Not as such. He was at the Gatehouse? He's on the streets? Where does he hang out?"

"Dunno. I've seen him a few times around the canals down near Hythe Bridge Street. Doesn't keep regular with any company I know. Independent like."

"Name?"

"Don't know a name. Best left well alone in my opinion. Wide berth, Danny, wide berth. Listen, if it's some *horse* you want—"

"Nah, see you around, Phil. Cheers."

"Cheers, then. Be well."

Daniel turned and joined the crowd. A glance up at the clock tower showed the time to be twenty to five. The Gatehouse would be open now. He stroked his beard and turned his feet in that direction.

It was the busiest time of the day. People crisscrossed in front of him, ducking into shops, doing after-work errands before going back to their homes and dinners with their loved ones. Groups of tourists—students on school trips, all of them with matching yellow backpacks—stood in clusters outside the fast food restaurants, yelling at and flirting with each other. And for the second time that day Daniel caught a glimpse from within the swarm of faces of someone he recognised.

He stopped in his tracks. "It can't be . . ."

He turned and looked at the sea of people. She wasn't there anymore; the tide had closed. Lurching forward, he ducked into Ship Street, a long, narrow, fairly empty side road. There were two people at the far end and a solitary one walking away from him. This person was young—his age—female, slender, with black hair that was tied up loosely—and she carried a bag that looked to be bulging with books. A student, then. One hand dangled at her side and he could see that it was a light creamy brown.

He found his voice and shouted, "Freya!"

She didn't turn around or even break her stride but kept walking. He shouted her name again.

"Freya, come back!"

Without turning around she broke into a run, sprinting away from him.

He chased after her. He was only halfway down the street when she had reached the end, and by the time he finally made it to Turl Street, she was out of sight.

For the second time that day—that hour—he stood bewildered, searching the faces in the crowd. He wasn't surprised that she ran. If she was a student, then it may not be too hard to find her again, but what did it mean? First one of those creatures, and now Freya—two people he'd nearly given up ever seeing again. The fingers of his right hand stroked the edge of a notebook that was tucked in his jacket pocket. He would have to record these incidents later. No time now.

He retraced his steps and cautiously approached the Gatehouse, spending a futile ten minutes trying to convince the lady at the door that he was over twenty-five when they both knew he wasn't. In the end he asked for a plastic bottle he had to be filled with water and then he went across the street and waited, slunk against a low brick wall. He passed the time by trying to get his nerves under control but was unsuccessful in doing anything more than slowing his breathing.

The Gatehouse closed at six, its patrons trickling out singly or in pairs. If the tattooed man was in there, Daniel knew that he would be noticed but almost certainly not recognised. He hoped that would be enough of an edge.

Fewer and fewer people were coming out now and Daniel was about to get up himself when the tattooed man appeared. He got a good, clear look at him this time. Hairless, dressed in a loose-fitting T-shirt and black leather trousers. It didn't look like he was carrying any weapons except perhaps a knife in his pocket. Swathes of ink covered his body so broadly it was possible to think that he was naturally blackish-blue with only patches of white. His face was lumpy and swollen in the way that a continual scrapper's usually are; his features doughy and slightly formless. His lips were curled into a thin, cruel line and his ears were ragged, torn. He wore sunglasses that comically humanised him, like a dressed-up pet; for there was now no doubt in Daniel's mind about the creature's true identity.

It walked towards him on the opposite side of the street. Although Daniel couldn't see its eyes, it must have spotted him, though it gave no sign. It continued walking and turned the corner.

"Okay, okay . . ." Daniel rose and followed but kept to his side of the street. He didn't know how ruthless the creature would be, how heedful of public places it would be, so it was best to keep his distance for now.

He caught sight of his quarry again as it turned down George Street, towards the canals that led to Jericho. Daniel followed, lagging far enough behind to keep the thing in sight, not caring if he was seen. Although it never turned or threw a glance behind, *it knew* it was being tailed.

The sky had dimmed but it was not yet dark. This was a time of the day that excited Daniel, but he willed himself to stay calm. He tried to turn that nervous energy into a taut, controlled tension and awareness. If it was to be now, then it was to be now. Whatever must follow, must.

He stepped into the doorway of a boarded-up corner shop to quickly adjust his clothing. He unzipped his coat so it was just done up about an inch and hung loosely together in front of him. He pulled his arm out of its sleeve, which he tucked into its outer pocket. Shrugging and hunching forward, he tucked his forearm into his stomach and gripped the handle of the thin, cold object that hung at his side.

If he walked carefully enough, he'd give the impression of having both hands tucked into his jacket pockets. It wouldn't fool anyone who looked closely, but it would do for someone who was only giving him the briefest of looks.

Stepping out from behind the abandoned shop, he saw the shadow creature crossing the bridge ahead of him, still en route to the canals. He walked as quickly as he could without giving himself away, briskly crossing the street and cresting Hythe Bridge.

He was just in time to see the thing take a right turn along the canal, passing through a cycle gate. It took him some time to get across, due to traffic, and when he did, the tattooed man was nowhere in sight.

He slowed his pace and scanned the area. The canal ran just a few feet to his left. Houseboats were moored intermittently along the side, and to the right was wild scrubland, not very deep, but thick enough with brambles and tall grass to adequately hide someone in this low light undetectably. Right now Daniel's best shot was to keep himself out in the open and wait to be attacked. He kept walking.

"Steady," he whispered. "Steady now." As he inched forward, he tried to hide his fear, but then decided that it would be better for the one hunting him if he didn't hide it. He tried to keep his breath even.

The seconds dragged on until he heard, with a relief that nearly chilled him, a faint scuffle on the path behind him. He turned carefully, keeping his left shoulder most visible, and saw the creature standing off at a distance of about thirty feet. It had discarded its sunglasses and T-shirt and was crouching on the footpath, half naked and wreathed in shadows, leering at him.

"Lonely little light," it said. "Dim light, faint light. All alone in a city of one hundred and fifty thousand. A fraction so infinitesimally small, it's hardly worth expressing. Statistically insignificant, equivalent to nothing."

Daniel wanted to reply, to try to deflate its gloating pride, but he was depending on the creature's conceit to survive the fight—he had to play the role of unsuspecting prey. He set his jaw and narrowed his eyes, bracing himself for the attack.

The thing opened its lips in a sneer, revealing teeth sharpened into spikes. "It has been eighty-one days," it said, "since I've had a decent meal." It raised its hands to show that it gripped two spring-loaded knives in its hands. "Eleven and a half weeks; one thousand nine hundred and forty-four hours. I will savor you, I guarantee."

It licked its lips and then broke into a low, frantic run. Daniel crouched, waiting for it to leap. It had to leap; they always leapt. If it didn't leap, he wasn't sure of his chances.

Daniel crouched even lower as the creature drew closer, and just when he thought it was too late, it pounced nearly twice its own height up into the air where it arced perfectly, on course to land right on top of him.

He waited until it reached its peak, perfectly silhouetted against the evening sky, and then with a smooth, lightening-fast motion, Daniel's right arm came up through his open jacket, grasping the hilt of a sword with a wide blade just a few feet long. It stuck in the air, unwavering, perfectly placed to pierce the creature's chest as it fell.

The thing had only a fraction of a second before it descended upon the blade. Its eyes widened in surprise while its mouth was still twisted in hate. As the sharp, thin metal penetrated its torso, the beast spasmed and dropped its knives. In a smooth movement Daniel brought his left hand up and struck the creature on the pelvis, using its own momentum to carry it up and over his head, flipping it over onto the pathway behind him.

It fell squarely on its back, and as it fell, Daniel moved his arm in such a way that his sword was pulled automatically out the thing's chest. He held it poised for another strike but one was not necessary. There was a gaping, steaming wound in the thing's chest that gurgled and spewed thick, black lifeblood. Its throat worked, desperately trying to breathe. Its eyes gazed distantly into the sky.

Daniel kicked it in the head with his foot and then crouched down, pressing his left hand on the side of its skull and putting his mouth near the creature's tattered ear.

"Listen to me carefully," Daniel said in an even, clear voice. "If, when you reach the dark, smoky pit where you will surely burn in unending agony, you are able to send a message to your friends through whatever infernal back passages exist, tell your vile brethren this:

"Oxford *is not safe*."

He stood and with his free hand grabbed his slain victim's leg, dragging the body into the tall grass, far enough so that it almost certainly wouldn't be discovered until the next day, if not much later. Once hidden he bent and slit its throat, just to be certain. He wiped his sword as much as he could on the weeds around him—he'd have to go into a toilet somewhere and clean it more thoroughly when he had the chance—and replaced it in its sheath underneath his shirt. Then he went back and kicked around the dirt and gravel on the footpath to mask the blood.

All that done, he walked briskly back the way he came, feeling himself still glowing with adrenaline and triumph. Not too far from where the killing took place, he found the thing's discarded T-shirt and sunglasses, which he casually kicked into the dark waters of the canal. Then he stepped out onto the busy pavement and the flickering yellow light of the street lamps, which were just coming on.

When the body was discovered, he thought, they would not be able to identify it, "it" having no identity. The weapon that made the wounds upon the body was odd enough to be unique, and unknown to anyone but himself, so no one could possibly connect him to it. The business looked fairly airtight.

Still, it was prudent to keep a low profile the next few days and perhaps steer clear from the night shelter, where enquiring minds usually dropped by at some point. His stride broke slightly as he recalled that he had talked to Scouse Phil about the thing, and he chided himself. But there was little he could do about that now.

A man coming towards him on the pavement fixed an odd stare at Daniel's forehead as they passed, and then quickened his step. Daniel slowed and put a hand up to his face, then held it out.

Blood. Not his, but the creature's.

He turned to the wall and rubbed every inch of his face with his palms, drying them in his hair, until he judged that he had probably removed as much of it as he could, or at least smeared it to a thin red film. Yet another reason to find a stall in a toilet soon.

Then he had to find a place to sleep that night.

Then he had to find Freya.

And above him, from the rooftops, dark eyes that had seen the city when it was just a wooden fortress and a church watched—cold and passionless.

3

She used the glove trick to get into the coffee shop. The practiced motion of pulling her hand out of her pocket to push the door open brought Freya's woollen out as well. She went through the door anyway—pass one—and then put her hand back in her pocket. Her face registered puzzlement for a moment and then she turned and saw her gloves. She went back outside—pass two—bent down and grabbed a glove without really looking, pushed back hurriedly through the door—pass three—looked down to her hand and realised she had only picked up one glove, went back outside—four—picked up the second glove, and came back inside—five.

Five passes were enough in a place like this with lots of people, but there were some places she tried very hard to avoid and some streets that she wouldn't even walk down. Being back in Oxford made her nervous. There were too many old doorways and arches. The bricked-up ones she came across—in her college's hallways, in the sides of buildings and churches—made her especially nervous and she gave them a wide berth. She was going through her medication faster than she'd like. She'd have to talk to her psychiatrist about that, but that would have to wait five weeks until the end of term. What would she do if she ran out before then?

She ordered a latte and took a seat. It was overcast outside and she couldn't see the sun—definitely a day to be cautious. Her watch said she had about forty minutes until the lecture. She had started chapter five of her *Introduction to Moral Philosophy* book three times. Her mind kept racing ahead to the lecture at ten a.m., and she hoped she could control herself this time. The medication would take the edge off at least. Maybe.

Leaving places was fairly safe, especially with a lot of other people milling around, so she didn't have to test the doorway leaving the coffee shop like she had to when she entered it. From St. Aldate's it was a short walk down Blue Boar Street to Merton Street and then into the exam schools. She circled around and entered via the main doors on High Street, which meant that she only had to deal with one set of doors to get into the building and then one more set to get into the room the lecture was in. For both of these, she pretended that she was waiting for someone to meet her; checking her phone and looking around allowed her to repeatedly duck in and out of the doorways. People would think she was lost, maybe, or a little ditzy, but they wouldn't think that she was crazy at least.

The monitor in the entrance hall informed her that Textual Histories of Pre-Arthurian Britain was in the large lecture theater called "South Schools." She followed the signs that led her up a wide stone staircase with a bannister made of rose marble. Then she took a right into a large wood-paneled, L-shaped room and found a seat, third row from the back. Scanning the room as students continued to file in, she didn't find a single familiar face. Eventually the lecturer, a fortysomething woman dressed completely in black, came to the podium and cleared her throat, a cough that reverberated from the speakers and echoed off the walls.

"Good morning, everyone. I'm Dr. Fowler," she said when the chatter had died down. "We've got a lot to cover this morning, so let's get started.

"'The Matter of Britain' is the name that we give to the works that form up the early pseudo-histories of Britain, as told by the Anglo-Saxon settlers, orally, and recorded by monks in the ninth and tenth centuries. It should be noted as being separate from Celtic legends—in this context predominantly Welsh, Irish, or otherwise Gaelic legends, although there was quite a lot of crossover, as we shall see."

The professor tapped a few keys on her laptop and the board behind her displayed an image of an ancient piece of paper with nearly indecipherable text printed on it. "This," she continued, "is the first page of the *Historia Brittonum* written around 870 Common Era by the scribe Nennius. It is perhaps the oldest English account of the settling of the British Isles—and the origi- nator, perhaps, of a lot of the confused and conflated myths traditionally associated with the settlement of Britain, myths that initially branched out of the Trojan tales of Greece, which were also very popular in Rome. It is thought that the work was created for wealthy Welsh families in the fifth century as a way to justify their claim to nobility and to cement their position as a ruling class—and obviously has little relation to objective fact. The tales centre around the legendary Brut, a son of—yes?"

Freya's arm was in the air. Her heart was pounding partly with anxiety and partly with anger. "Wouldn't it be more reasonable to assume that those accounts are objectively true? Seeing as no other accounts disagree with them?"

Dr. Fowler shrugged. Interruptions were rare in this type of lecture, but she was professional enough to take it in her stride. "There may be certain grains of truth within the various accounts, but were you to read them closely—as I'm sure your tutor will insist you do—then the appallingly fabricated fantasies within them will show quite apparently.

"Now, this Brut," Fowler continued, "was a hero of Troy—"

"I'm sorry," Freya said amid a swell of groans from those around her. "We know that Britain must have been settled at *some* point. Why is it unreasonable to believe the tales which state that it was a group of exiled soldiers—veterans of the Trojan wars—and their families?"

"I thought *I* was scheduled to give this lecture," the professor replied. The other students in the auditorium chuckled pointedly. "I'll gladly change places with you—I did quite a lot of this during my doctoral thesis so it's old hat to me."

"But why not take the account at face value?"

"Because it's completely unverifiable—fanciful even. Why—"

"Just because something cannot be *proven* true doesn't mean it *isn't* true—even if its claim to truth is unlikely. In fact, it's more likely that an improbable truth would be recorded than a probable one." This provoked more groans, and more than one request to "shut up."

"But, *reasonably*, it is unlikely that an account of settlement could have survived two and a half thousand years to be recorded by an obscure Welsh monk."

"If there *were* an accurate relation of settlement," Freya said, her voice rising, "how else would you expect it to be recorded? Besides, the fact that there are many other surviving, corroborating, independent reports—"

"Not independent—*derivative.*"

"You say that they're derivative of a lost source because they're similar, but why can't they be similar because they're all true?"

The professor sighed and took a moment to collect herself. She shouldn't have allowed herself to be drawn in; she was falling behind schedule. Was this some sort of gag? "It makes no sense to spar with me about veracity when I have an entire section dedicated to authorial 'tricks' or 'stunts' of authenticity. You've obviously read some of the material, but if you *understood* half of what you *know*, then you would realise how outlandish your claims are.

"Why," the professor continued plaintively, "on the same grounds, you could argue the case that Britain was populated by giants as was also popularly believed and recorded."

"I *do* argue the case on the same grounds," Freya said. This brought shouts of derision from the other students, and a couple of them slipped out of the hall to fetch the porter. "The history of giants in Britain is too independently supported to argue credibly against. Accounts of giant occupation are recorded in nearly all of the Brut legends, as well as Irish tales and sagas, such as the Fenian Cycle's *Acallam na Senórach*, and Scandinavian histories like the Vatnsdal Saga—let alone those recorded in the Bible and other Middle Eastern histories as well as Slavic traditions."

Dr. Fowler snorted and then smiled. "This is a joke . . . ," she murmured.

"I'm talking about human interaction with giants in each of these cases," Freya continued. "Not creation myths or rationalisations about the acts of nature. These are one-on-one encounters."

A man in a blue uniform was now standing at the end of Freya's row, beckoning furiously at her. The class had dissolved into noise—much of it directed at Freya. The professor seemed to be in a mild form of shock. The porter leaned into the row and called to her. "Miss, could you come with me please?"

"If giants *had* existed," Freya continued defiantly, "in the way that they are reported to have been, they would have left *exactly* such an imprint on history. There are too many disparate sources, all with the same interior logic."

"No, it's impossible," the professor replied, closing her eyes and shaking her head. "There is no archaeological evidence for—"

"That's irrelevant!" Freya shouted. "There's no archaeological evidence for anything until someone finds it! Absence of evidence isn't the same thing as—"

"Miss," the porter urged. He had now come partway into the row and placed a hand on her shoulder. "I *must* insist that you come with me!"

Freya gathered her bag and rose. "That's no argument at all! If we were having this conversation two hundred years ago, you'd say that Troy didn't exist either, but they found *that*, didn't they? Then they thought twice about the so-called Myths of Troy!"

The professor stood silently and patiently as Freya was led out of the room in the company of the porter, and then she resumed her lecture with the legend of Brut. She had to run very quickly through, rather ironically, textual variants in Monmouth's *Historia Regum Britanniae*, but she came through the ordeal in the end.

Outside, Freya was enduring another stern and predictable talk that referred to the student code of conduct and the privileges and responsibilities of studying at Oxford. Her mind was racing and she was angry, though mostly at herself. Idiots. They didn't understand. Things weren't "true" or "not true" just because they wanted them to be. History didn't follow the rule "the most convenient is true." But it was impossible to explain to anyone who didn't want to listen. Why did she even try?

That was the real question: why did she even try?

"This is your second warning," the porter was saying, not unkindly. "The next time I come in to remove you may be the last.

This is the sort of discussion that you should be having with your tutor."

Freya nodded. That was something else they wouldn't understand. She couldn't talk to her tutor because her tutor wouldn't know what Freya was talking about. She wasn't reading English. She was reading philosophy and theology.

"Okay," the porter continued. "I can allow you back in if you promise not to talk or make a fuss. Can you do that?"

Freya turned without saying a word and went outside. She was so wrapped up in her thoughts that she was a good way down High Street before she realised that she'd only gone through the doorway once on her way outside. She stopped immediately, paralysed by a building tidal wave of panic. She braced herself against the wall and watched the people pass her on the pavement and the traffic rattling up and down the street, oblivious of the terrible chaos that engulfed them—that existed in all things.

She needed order; she needed to know that things could make sense, that she could enforce her will upon the storm of existence. She crossed the street twice, and then four more times. This calmed her and she kept crossing the street as she made her way into town.

Why did she do it? What did it matter what people thought and believed, even if it was a lie? What right did she have to burst the fragile bubble of unreality that people surround themselves with? So long as they live happily, what does it matter if they live a lie? Ignorance is a blessing. It was futile to try to wake people up, so *why did she do it?*

Freya sighed. She knew exactly why she did it.

She was so wrapped up in these thoughts that she almost walked right into Daniel Tully, the one person in the whole city she was deliberately trying to avoid. She held her breath and saw that he seemed to be so wrapped up in his own thoughts that he didn't notice her either. She walked closely by him, very nearly brushing his shoulder, and then took an immediate turn down a side street.

She forced herself not to break into an immediate run. If he didn't notice her by now, he didn't have a reason to come after her. Freya's heart felt like breaking, though, seeing him like that, clearly living off the street. She had spotted him yesterday, sitting outside the Sheldonian Theater, begging. She was in a bookshop café across the street and must have stared at him for almost an hour, not sure if she should go to him or leave him alone. If she did, what would she say? What could she say? Did it matter if she said anything, and if it didn't, then why should she put herself or him through the torture of awkwardness. And so she just sat there, oscillating between action and inaction, and doing nothing, on the verge of tears.

"Freya!" came a shout from behind her. It was definitely his voice even though it was deeper—a man's voice now but unmistakably his.

Her heart nearly stopped but she kept walking.

"Freya, come back!"

That was too much for her; she broke into a flat-out run. She made it to the end of the street and did a quick turn left and then right, not stopping until she reached the Bodleian Library, which was students only—they wouldn't allow him in there. She managed to keep herself together until she found an unoccupied study desk, sank into it, head in her arms, and started sobbing silently.

4

Alex Simpson of the Northern Constabulary pulled out of the Muir of Ord police station and started the drive back. He was tired to the bone, but there was an electric ball of energy in his gut that pushed him on. He had changed out of his uniform, naturally, but he had pocketed his notebook. It lay on the passenger's seat next to him almost radiating weight and importance.

He pulled into the small driveway of his small cottage and let himself in, going straight into his back study and sliding the elastic band off the cover of the black notebook. He thumbed to the last page of writing. He studied it for a few moments and then turned to the wall map. It showed all of Scotland, took up most of the wall, and had cost a fair penny. Today it would be working for him.

For the first time in several months he had managed to get some time alone on one of the office computers, where he could access the NC's intranet. Until today, he had been unable to peruse Scotland's crime and misdemeanor reports for anything that looked—well, suspicious. Suspicious to him, that is. And finally he had found something. Missing livestock, even killed and mangled livestock, was no novelty in the highlands, but that, coupled with a 27 percent bump in area crime, and a 300 percent rise in unnatural deaths in the last nine months—that was suspicious and worth sticking on the map.

Running his eyes over the blue pins already spread across the wall, he started to put red pins into the map around the Highlands Council area. Seven sheep reported missing and remains found on the farm of Robert Corbet near Kildonan. With no information on where the animals were found or known to be missing from, he stuck three pins around the farmstead. Two cattle killed and found near the farm of Mactire at Braemore—two pins. Nineteen more reports in the last four months—a couple dozen more red pins.

Next, violent crimes and robberies. A couple hundred of these, in black pins. It took the better part of an hour to mark them all. Next, suicides. Perhaps the most depressing. And again, far more common than one would hope in rural Scotland. In the last six months, *forty*. Fifteen minutes later forty more pins, these ones yellow, stuck in the map.

It was certainly painting a picture. Stepping back, he looked at the nebulous whole of incidents spread pretty much at random—except for a massive cluster of pins to the northeast, in Caithness. It was a sparsely populated area, which made the number of crimes even more remarkable. The haze of red, black, and yellow—at least half of the yellow pins—were clustered there, around a mountain called Morven, which had a bright-blue pin sticking in it. Alarm bells rang in his head.

He phoned his associate and asked him to come over. It was important. His associate was also a member of the Highland Constabulary and the only man in the world besides his father—who was now very old and of diminishing faculties—whom he could speak to about these matters.

He put the kettle on and had just made a pot of tea when his associate knocked on the door and let himself in, walking straight through to the kitchen.

"Ah, tea," he said. "The drink of the English, of my people—right? What have you got to show me?"

Alex took him through and showed him the map on the wall and briefly explained the pins.

"Then it is clear," his associate said gravely. "You must go and investigate. Make sure you go fully equipped. It could be any-thing—remember that cellar full of hobgoblins we found?"

"*I* must go? But you're coming with me?"

"No, I must go south. I may already be too late. But call me if you really need my assistance. I don't think you shall."

And that settled it. He had four more days until his break, but he might be able to move that up. He would have to call the sergeant tonight.

And he would have to get an early start.

CHAPTER TWO

The Sleeping Knights

---------- 1 ----------

Eight Years Before . . .

At seven thirty a.m. the clock radio dragged Daniel Tully out of a deep sleep. Just another ordinary day. Ordinary and dreadful.

No, today was different—something happened today. It was his birthday. This woke him up. He turned off the radio alarm and climbed out of bed. Hunting around his room, he searched for the cleanest and least-wrinkled shirt and trousers he could find and put them on. Then he pulled his school jumper over them and went downstairs.

He was the only one awake, as usual, and the kitchen table— where he had once seen presents piled on top of each other several years earlier—was empty. He wandered into the living room and saw nothing on the small dining table either. He went back to the kitchen, kicking his feet.

He put some bread in the toaster and started making coffee.

Wrinkling his nose at the earthy smell as he spooned the raw, dirt-coloured grounds into the percolator, he vowed once more to never drink coffee as long as he lived. He flicked the power button on, wondering if his mum would think about him when she drank it and if she would remember what today was. Maybe he'd get some extra presents out of guilt. It was possible, but unlikely.

He ate his toast and looked out of the kitchen window into the tiny sliver of a garden. It was still quite dark. He didn't like this time of year—he had to go to school in the dark, and also come home in the dark.

It's not fair, he thought. And then, because he could and he knew it'd make him feel better, he said the words out loud. "It's not fair."

He wondered what sort of day it was going to be. And then, with a flash of dread, he realised that today was also the field trip. He also realised that he hadn't handed in his permission slip.

He went into the hall and rummaged around on the side table. It must be here—he remembered seeing it. Yes, stuck underneath a strata of bills and junk mail was the blue, wrinkled permission slip with a blank space where his mum's signature should be. He hurried back into the kitchen and looked at the clock on the oven. He had about five minutes. Plucking a pen from the mug on the counter, he rushed back upstairs and stood in front of his mother's door and listened. He could hear faint breathing. He gently knocked on the door, which was open slightly.

"Mum?" he said.

There was no reply.

"Mum?" he said, louder.

There was a very muffled and tired moan. "Whuh 'zit?"

"Mum, I need your signature on something for school. There's a class trip today."

Silence.

"Mum?"

"L've it d'nstairs. Uh'll sign it when uh get up."

Daniel stood quietly for a moment. He needed the signature now, not later. He thought about the first of the two options now before him. He really didn't want to go into the bedroom and try to persuade his mother to sign the slip now. He would probably have to actually push the pen into her hand and if he didn't handle it right, there would be a "scene." Also, he was starting to think that there was someone lying next to her.

No, it was far easier to do the second thing. He hurried back downstairs and put the slip on the kitchen counter, then uncapped the pen he was holding. He looked at the paper for a second and then exhaled. In a quick, confident burst of motion, he wrote his mother's name in a suitably grown-up and illegible manner: *Elaine Tully*. He regarded the slip. Not his best work perhaps, but it would do. The trick was not in trying to make it look exactly like her real signature, but in making it confident.

He folded up the paper and put it in his pocket. No, he reflected, the real trick isn't the signature—it's in making all the teachers believe that you were the sort of boy who would never even *think* about faking his mum's signature. And that meant, as so many things in life, keeping your head down.

He picked up his school bag, fished out his gym clothes (wouldn't need those), and thought about signatures and permission slips. Where did they all go? What happened to them? Were they all put in a file somewhere? Did anyone really check them? Would this little scrap of paper be scrutinised against all the others—checked for authenticity by a man in a white coat with a giant magnifying glass in a brightly lit room? By now there must be more of his fake signatures on all these different slips and documents than his mother's real one. To the school office his forgeries were more authentic than the genuine article.

He was just checking that his keys were in his pocket when his eyes fell on something unusual. He and his mum didn't get a lot of mail other than bills, but there, on the floor beneath the front door, was a red envelope. He was so surprised that he actually took a half step back and then bent down to pick it up.

He turned it over and looked at who it was addressed to—it was to him. Someone had remembered his birthday.

There wasn't any sender's address on the envelope, and he didn't recognise the block capital handwriting on it. Quickly, he thrust it into his jacket. It felt like a secret, and he wanted to keep it to himself as long as possible.

All the way to school he thought about the envelope. It might be from Nan, his mum's mum, but she didn't really go in for that sort of thing—she was more forgetful than his own mother. It could be from Grandma and Grandpa Tully, but he hadn't seen them in three or four years, since the separation.

He could see that the coach was already waiting when he got to school. He sighed. He'd actually prefer a day of the ordinary routine rather than having to navigate the chaos of a field trip. For a moment he considered not going, but last time that meant he'd had to join another class for a day—a dangerous and unknown social minefield. He handed his permission slip to Miss Singh and got on the bus, sitting down in the first pair of seats that weren't occupied and sliding over by the window.

He sat there unmoving, trying to be a part of the background, holding his breath when anyone passed by. Eventually the coach was nearly full and he thought he'd gotten away with it, but just as Miss Singh had crossed the last name off her list, a group of girls—who had already passed him—came back up the aisle and stood at his seat.

"Look," said one of them. "If we get *him* to move, we can all sit together. Hey, Daniel."

He pretended not to hear.

"*Daniel!*"

He turned and saw Callie Johnson bending towards him. "Hi, do you mind moving so that we can all sit together?"

"Where to?" he asked, playing for time.

"I don't care, you little freak," Callie said in a low voice, leaning towards him. "Just leave." The girls behind her giggled. He heard one of them mutter the word "outrageous."

Daniel wasn't fazed. "I'm fine here," he said.

"Find a seat, girls," Miss Singh called down the aisle.

Callie Johnson leaned closer into Daniel. "Move," she growled, "or I'll sit next to you and pinch your arm till it falls off."

Daniel turned to look out the window.

"Girls, find a seat," said Miss Singh, coming towards them.

"*Move!*" Callie growled under her breath.

He didn't. Callie couldn't do anything else until Miss Singh reached them. Her last chance would be to protest the unjustness of Daniel's attitude and try to make the teacher move him—which she might.

However, as Callie turned towards the advancing Miss Singh, someone pushed past her and slid into the seat beside Daniel.

"This seat free? Mind if I take it? Thanks."

"Freya?" said Callie, appalled. "What the—? *I* was going to sit there!"

"If you were going to, you would have already," Freya replied curtly.

Miss Singh had reached them. "Okay, girls, find a seat. Now."

With no hope of being able to shift *two* people from their seats, the group of four was forced to disperse with groans of annoyance.

"Thanks," said Daniel to Freya, once the coach had started and they were on their way.

"No problem," said Freya. "Callie and her posse are acting like real cows these days. I can't stand them. Besides," she said, giving him a wide smile, "I know a secret."

"I know you do," said Daniel.

"It's your birthday," Freya said in a low voice.

"I know."

"Do you know how I know?"

"Yes."

"Because it's my birthday too," Freya said, her smile widening even further.

"Happy birthday," Daniel said miserably.

"Remember when we were in First Year together and they threw us both a party?"

"Barely."

"Well, I remember it." She smiled. "Did you get anything nice?"

"Sure, lots of stuff."

"Did you bring anything with you?"

"No, of course not."

"I did. Look . . ." Freya pulled a silver necklace with a teardrop-shaped pendant out from beneath her school jumper.

"It's nice," Daniel said.

"Thanks. It's from Mum and Dad. What did you get?"

"What is this all of a sudden? You haven't talked to me in a year, and now we're best friends?"

"If you don't want me here, I'll switch seats with Callie . . ."

"No, it's fine. I'm just saying . . ."

"So what did you get?"

"I told you, lots of stuff. Look." Daniel pulled out the red envelope from his jacket pocket.

"Who's it from?"

"Don't know," said Daniel. "Haven't opened it."

"Well, go on then. What are you waiting for?"

Daniel shrugged. "You do it," he said, chucking the card into her lap.

"Okay," she said, sliding her finger underneath the envelope's flap and ripping it open.

Daniel watched as she pulled out a shiny card that had a brightly coloured picture of a dancing clown on it. It was a kid's card, not a card for someone who'd just turned thirteen.

"Do you want to read it or shall I?" Freya held the card up, and Daniel watched a crinkled slip of heavy, rectangular paper slide out the bottom of it and onto her lap. She picked it up and passed it to Daniel. It was a ten-pound note.

"You read it," he said, folding the money and sliding it into his shirt pocket. Freya opened the card.

"'To Daniel,'" she read. "'Happy birthday, from your dad.'"

"That's it?" Daniel said, leaning towards her.

Freya handed the card to him. "Doesn't say much, does he?"

Daniel gave a jerky shrug. "The last time I heard from him was three years ago. Today he sends me a card with some money in it."

Daniel heard himself say those words and felt wretchedly sorry for himself. Three years—three whole years, and then what? Ten pounds and a crappy card with a stupid clown on it with a mocking, leering laugh. His hands clenched and he tore up the card, dropping its twisted pieces on the floor beneath his feet.

He turned his face to the window, eyes hot, tears threatening to drip down his face.

Freya sat quietly next to him and didn't say a word until they reached the church.

2

Daniel turned and walked down the church aisle, stopping at a short wooden railing that ran wall to wall just before the altar. His head was tilted as far back as it would go so that he could stare straight up at the ceiling. Behind him he could hear Miss Singh droning on about some stained glass window just around the corner—no one could see him here.

There were stone carvings everywhere—on the walls, on the ceiling, on the arches, around doorways, along the columns—carvings of animals, plants, people, and mythical creatures. The arches leading up to the chancel were lined with dozens of carvings of sunflowers—stacked row upon row like strings of rising suns. On the large archway over the church entrance there were a mermaid with a sword, two battling centaurs, a roaring lion, a king with a crown, a face with a leaf in its mouth, weird zigzag patterns, and other bewildering designs.

Daniel walked up the aisle towards the altar. He felt peaceful here. The anxiety and emotional chafing of the bus ride was becoming less painful, gradually washing away. Marveling at this amazing building, he felt part of something much, much bigger than himself, and he knew he was the only one who felt it. It was like he understood what the church was feeling—an old, proud indifference to the chattering, squabbling children who were walking inside of it. It was as though all the shoving and pushing and jockeying for attention and importance—all these things that affected him so much—were irrelevant to the enormous, beautiful building. It was created for something else.

Behind the altar there was a small arch, partially hidden in the shadows. For a moment he thought there was a passageway underneath it, and hearing the call to adventure, he intended to follow it, but when he got closer he saw that it spanned just a blank wall of stone.

The archway oozed antiquity and was crammed with interesting figures. It must have been a doorway to something at some point. On one side there was a knight wearing a pointed helmet and a thick beard. In his left hand he held a round shield, and in his right was a large axe with a long straight edge. Underneath him was a horse, a dragon, a lion, and an ox. Opposite him, on the other side of the arch, was another knight, a lot like the first, but this one held a spear. Beneath him was something that looked like a dog, or maybe a lamb, a woman with a staff, and then an eagle and an angel.

He sat down in an uncomfortable wooden chair beside the altar, opened his sketchbook to a clean page, and started drawing the figures on the arch. He had just finished tracing the shape of the axe in his book when he heard a rustling sound behind him, like the flapping of a flag. A shadow fell across him and then quickly lifted. Startled, he twisted around and looked up into a plain gothic window. Something had passed next to it—flickered across it from outside. But it was gone now. He turned back to his sketch.

The light in the church was growing dimmer. The December sun was setting now, even though it wasn't very late at all. He finished drawing the first knight and quickly moved on to the other. He heard his class moving across the church—probably to another window—and slouched back closer to the altar so no one would see him.

"What are you doing?" a voice asked him, making him jump. He twisted around, his eyes wide.

"Freya!" he exclaimed in a whisper. "Flip! Don't sneak up on people like that!"

"Sorry," Freya answered automatically. "What are you doing?"

"Nothing," Daniel said, moving his pencil carefully across the page. "What does it look like I'm doing?"

"You'll get in trouble for wandering off," Freya said, coming to stand behind Daniel.

"Yeah? Then so will you. Why are you hanging around me so much?"

She ignored him. "Not bad," Freya complimented. "You're good at that."

"I'm not, really," Daniel said. "It's just that I like knights. I draw them all the time."

"You've got the arm wrong just there."

"It's fine, just a little long, that's all," he said, reaching for his eraser. "Anyway, that's what it looks like on the arch."

Freya sniffed and straightened up. "Where does the tunnel lead to?"

"What tunnel?"

"Haven't you looked down it?"

"What are you talking about?"

"That tunnel, there." She pointed. "Where does it go?"

"There's no—" Daniel looked up and then jerked his head back in surprise. There *was* a tunnel underneath the arch. "That wasn't there before."

"Good artists need to notice everything," Freya said crisply. She walked up and poked her head through the arch. "The wall's curved, I can't see around it. It's odd, though, usually churches from this period don't have catacombs. We should ask Miss. I wonder if it may have been made—wait."

Daniel brushed past her, having packed up his sketchbook, and walked into the tunnel.

"Where are you going?"

"It sort of spirals downwards," he said, stopping a short distance in. "There's some kind of light coming from farther on. A glow." He took a couple more steps forward.

"I don't think we should go down there. It don't think it's allowed."

"I don't care," Daniel said. "I want to explore." He took a few more steps and put his hand up to the cold stony wall.

"Daniel, stop," Freya said, moving towards the dusty archway. "It's getting dark—we'll be leaving soon."

"One more reason to check it out—when are we ever going to come back?" Daniel said. He turned to Freya and saw her worried expression. "Come on, it'll just take a second."

Freya ducked under the small archway and they both started down the long sloping tunnel.

The walls were solid rock with little divots in them, evidence they were made with a chisel.

"We've been slowly circling around," he said when they had been walking for a while. "If we go much farther, we'll end up right underneath the church."

"It doesn't smell old or musty," said Freya. "It's sort of cool and fresh."

"The ceiling's getting higher," Daniel said. "And the walls are moving out. Feels like we're shrinking."

Freya forced a short laugh. "Come on, let's go back."

"But we don't even know—hey, look at that."

Freya leaned closer to Daniel to see around the bend. On a ledge on the cave wall was a silver lamp that emitted a pale, bluish light. It was thin and cylindrical with a wide round aperture. Freya gave it a tap. "Where's its fuel?"

"It's electric."

"No, there's no cord."

"Battery then. Come on, there's an archway up ahead."

"There's writing on it," Freya said.

Daniel tilted his head back and saw carved above the archway the words:

> Ic wordcenne æt Niðergeard
> Giefe a ælch wha boga niðeweard
> Gifu sprecan freolice
> If beo he soþlice freondlice

"Do you think it's Latin?" Daniel asked. "It's really old looking."

"No, my sister's studying that. This looks nothing like Latin. Those two letters—the *p* looking thing, and the *d* with the line through it—I've never seen them before."

They gazed at the words, trying to puzzle them out, and as they did Daniel was aware of a soft sound that he hadn't heard before—a gentle rhythmic sigh, the sound of breathing. "Do you hear that?" he whispered.

"What?"

"Shh." Gathering his courage, Daniel stepped through the arch and found himself in a perfectly square room with a very high ceiling made of rough natural rock. In the centre of the room stood a stone dais holding half a dozen of the silver lamps.

And what the lamps threw their light upon made Daniel's jaw drop. In the centre of the room lay two low, stone slabs and lying on top of each was a knight in full battle gear—not carvings this time, but genuine, authentic, larger-than-life men encased head to foot in armour.

They were dressed exactly as the knights from the archway in the church behind the altar. In their left hands they held round shields made from some sort of animal hide stretched over wood; in their right they gripped weapons—one held a spear, the other an axe. Each knight was dressed in a chain-mail shirt with long sleeves that fell low to cover the upper legs just above the knees; each shirt was cinched at the waist by a stout leather belt from which hung a short but wide sword. Their lower legs were wrapped in rough cloth and skins, joining dark, coarse-woven breeches at the top of their shins. Pointed helmets, polished to a shine, crested their heads and long beards flowed down almost past their belt buckles.

"Wow!" Daniel exclaimed.

Freya gazed around the chamber with wide eyes. "What *is* this place?" she asked. She walked closer, between two of the figures.

"I don't know," Daniel said. "It looks like some sort of display."

Freya stared hard at one of the knights. "Their faces look really real—really lifelike. I can see the pores. Are—are they dead?"

"No chance," Daniel said, looking down at the knight in front of him. "Nah, they're just models. Got to be."

"They're really good, though. Look really authentic."

"Maybe they're for a movie, like *Lord of the Rings*. They made models like this for that. I saw the special features."

Bending closer, Daniel gazed at the one with the reddish-brown beard and the axe, looking closely at his nose and mouth. He thought he saw the whiskers tremble around the nose. Stooping closer, Daniel reached out a hand and touched the sword at the knight's side. It was cold, like it was made of actual metal.

"Come on," said Freya, taking a step towards the archway. "We've had a look around, so let's go back now."

Daniel was still hunched over the knight.

"Daniel, come on." She moved towards him and put a hand on his shoulder to try to pull him around. "Let's go."

"Alright," Daniel said reluctantly. He knew that they were pushing it now. This was definitely flying in the face of "keeping your head down." He turned to leave.

"Look, what's that?" he said. Hanging on the wall was something he hadn't noticed when they came in—a curved horn with an ornate silver mouthpiece.

Freya rolled her eyes. "Daniel, come on . . ."

"Hold on, I just want to give it a toot."

"No, leave it."

"Freya, you have no sense of adventure." Daniel went to the wall and pulled the horn off of the hook it was hanging on. He pressed his lips together, put them to the mouthpiece, and gave a strong blow.

The horn let out a thin, drawn-out *parp* and had no other

immediate effect other than to turn Daniel's face red. The reedy buzz knocked around the chamber, echoing, reluctant to die. Daniel and Freya froze—waiting expectantly. But for what, they didn't know. Maybe for some caretaker to come and tell them off.

"Satisfied?" Freya asked. "Can we go now?"

"Yes, fine," Daniel said, sighing. He placed the horn back on the hook.

"Strange . . . ," he said, "sounds like it's still going. No, hold up—"

There was another sound in the chamber—one that was growing. A deep, rumbling groan.

"What is it?" asked Freya nervously.

Daniel crossed back over to one of the knights. It must have been a trick of his eyes, or the light, or something, but it looked like it was breathing. He raised his arm and was just about to brush his fingertips against its cheek—which looked more than just "lifelike"—when the knight's eyelids snapped open.

Daniel was so startled that he let out a shout and jumped backwards, colliding into Freya, who also screamed. With a creaking of leather, a rattling of metal, and a groan, the knight sat up and turned his head stiffly towards them. Dust cascaded from his chest, billowing into a cloud.

Daniel felt something snake around his wrist and then tighten. He looked down and saw that the hand of the knight behind him was gripping his arm. He leapt away, trying to jerk out of its grasp, but it felt like it was made of iron. "Freya! Help me!" he cried.

Terrified, Freya backed into the corner by the archway. She opened her mouth to call for help, but no sound came out. Then the first knight rose from his plinth.

The knight holding Daniel's arm shook his head and turned to the other knight. "Cól þe, cnihtas. Liss," he said. "Cól þe."

The other knight said something in more strange words, and Daniel felt his wrist come free. But before he could make a move or even draw a breath, the knight lurched forward and hefted himself to his feet. Daniel, startled, lost his balance and fell backwards. "Don't hurt me!" he blurted, and began scooting his way closer to Freya.

The knight took a gigantic step forward and now stood directly above them.

The towering knight stretched out his hand. "Calm yourselves, children," he said in a clear, commanding voice. "Peace!"

3

Daniel and Freya, frozen in terror, could only stare at the knight. He, in turn, gazed down at them cautiously and curiously, as if they were cornered birds that might fly away at the slightest movement.

The knight with the axe, still sitting on his bier, lay down his weapon, removed his helmet, and put it to one side, bending his neck first one way and then the other. "Faith, it's enough to wake the dead, their screaming," he said, rubbing his head, his voice a soft rumble. "Oh, *Meotodes Meahte*, my blessed bones," he muttered. His joints popped and cracked as he let out a bellowing roar. "*Ngya-aa-argh!* Has one ever been so stiff?" He patted himself down and coughed a few deep coughs as clouds of dust billowed around him.

"*Hweat, broðor!*" The knight with the spear spoke, reading Daniel's and Freya's terrified expressions. "Would you kill them with fright?"

"Beg pardon, brother," said the axe-knight, stretching his arms back to expand his chest, which caused a loud popping sound. "I am thoughtless on waking."

The spear-knight took a very small step backwards and also removed his helmet. "Ah, there now, children," he said, relaxing slightly. He leaned towards Daniel on the shaft of his lance. "Now, lad, there's a good lad. Tell me, what might your name be?"

Daniel struggled to find his voice. "D–Daniel, sir," he managed to stammer. "Daniel Tully."

"A fine name, boy," he said. "Very fine."

"Aye," said the other knight, swinging his legs around and off the plinth. "A name for a boy to grow into." With a heave and a loud grunt, he stood up.

"And my little lady," the spear-knight said, turning his head to address Freya. "Your name, please."

"Freya Reynolds," she replied quietly.

"A beautiful name, for one who will quite clearly grow into a beautiful woman. If it would please you, *æðelingas*," the spear-knight said with a smile, "would you speak to us the year?"

"You want to know the date?"

"If it would please you."

Daniel told him.

The knight broke into a wide grin. "Ah, do you see, Ecgbryt?" he said, addressing the other. "We have slept past the second thousand. You owe me your mother's golden gyrdel."

"When I have found my mother . . . ," the other replied, examining his long beard disapprovingly, "and asked it of her, it is yours, Swiðgar."

They both broke into deep, bellowing laughter at this, and after roughly combing through their beards with their fingers, they started to plait their frazzled hair into more manageable strips. As they did, they recited a poem in a gentle singsong rhythm.

> "Where goes you, little æðeling,
> In uncle's leather shoes?
> 'To see a holy man in Rome
> And hear a prophecy.'

"Where goes you, little æðeling,
With brother's golden crown?
'To talk to the men of the borderlands,
And share their Winter's ale.'

"Where goes you, little æðeling,
With hammer and with line?
'To build a wall in Somerset
To keep the north wind out.'

"Where goes you, little æðeling,
With father's rusty sword?
'To split the head of a tow-haired man
Who gave and broke his word.'

"Where com'st thou, great and mighty king,
With glory, might, and peace?
'From Wessex on the Mighty Isle,
And I rule upon my knees.'"

The song seemed very strange to Daniel and Freya, but the tune was happy and light, and the knights' easy laughter and joy at the verses put them more at ease.

"What's an 'æðeling'?" Freya asked, charmed by the song.

"Why, a young noble person, like yourself," answered Swiðgar with a chuckle. "You are both æðelingas!"

"Oh," said Freya. And then, "Who *are* you two?"

"Forgive me," said the brown-bearded knight, picking up his axe and shield. He knelt creakily in front of Daniel and Freya. "I am Ecgbryt."

"Etch-brut?" echoed Daniel.

"Aye, Ecgbryt—the name given to me by our warband's

heafod. It means 'shining edge.' I am called that for the reason that in battle, it is all that friend or foe will see of me—the blade of my weapon, twinkling in the battle-sun as it rises and falls upon the heads of my enemy." He whacked the side of his axe against the steel rim of his shield, making a loud *crack!*

"And my name," said the other knight, kneeling also, "is Swiðgar." He whacked his lance against his shield. "It means 'strong spear.' My battle-brother and I have seen more fighting than many a war-chief will see in a life, even were he to live it many times over." He raised his chin proudly and jerked it towards his weapon. "Yet the spear I hold has never been broken, nor lost to an enemy. I found this wooden shaft myself and shaped it with my two hands—it is my dearest possession."

"Sooth," agreed Ecgbryt. "It is no boast to tell that of all nobles alive in our age there were none better against a more bitter foe— it is simple truth. The evidence for those words is that we stand before you, for it is why we were chosen. Is it not so?"

"A plain fact," confirmed Swiðgar with a nod. "Though we are cousins, they called us brothers—we are that much alike in war. Blood could not make us closer."

"An aye to that!"

"H—how," Daniel blurted, "how long have you been here?"

Swiðgar began stroking his beard. "Hmm. We were laid to sleep in the same year in which Ælfred the Geatolic died . . . which would be . . ."

"Ah, Blessed Ælfred," Ecgbryt sighed, his eyes shifting focus. "England's shepherd and dearling. He was the greatest king since Arthur, Bear of Britain. So wise was Ælfred, it was said that even the elves sought his council. And more than this, he brought all of the *Anglecynn* under one banner."

"We fought with him against the North-men, the terrible Dane *jarls* from their lands of ice." The knights leaned in eagerly, their earnest faces now close to Daniel's and Freya's. "Though on occasion defeated in the field, we were not defeated in spirit, and our spirits lent strength to our arms—"

"—and our hands fell the faster in battle because of it."

Swiðgar stood up. "But to put a number to your question, I reckon we have been lying here more than five times two hundred years."

"One thousand years?" Freya exclaimed. "But that's impossible!"

"Not impossible," Ecgbryt replied and stood up next to Swiðgar. "Just very uncommon. And difficult—especially in full battle dress and stretched on a cold stone." He looked from Freya to Daniel. "It makes a body a mite stiff."

"An aye to that."

"What are you going to do now?" Freya asked.

"Well, that depends on you, young æðelingas," Swiðgar answered. "What are *you* to do now?"

Freya and Daniel looked at each other. "We need to get back to our class," Freya said. "They'll be leaving now—"

"Is that so?" said Swiðgar in an odd voice. "Back to your 'class,' eh? Back to those you belong to, or who belong to you. Yes, I suppose you could leave, if you could find your way back . . ."

Swiðgar stepped aside and revealed the archway through which Daniel and Freya had walked.

It was completely sealed up.

"No," Freya moaned. They both rushed forward and pressed their hands against the stone, which was now under the bevelled archway, as if it had always been there. They tried to find a crack or seam that ran along the edge that might suggest it was actually a stone door that had closed or slid shut. They pushed it, banged it, tapped it, thumped it, and kicked it, but it did not respond in the slightest. It was cold, solid, and immovable.

"You'll not be going back that way," Ecgbryt said.

"When did—*how* did this happen?" Freya gasped. "There was a passage here, a tunnel! Where did it go?"

"The sun will have set by now," Swiðgar said. "That is a special wall; it only opens at a certain time, and for certain people."

"I don't understand," Freya said.

"When the sun has just gone below the earth, but there are not yet any stars out, that is the time when the wall may open—under certain circumstances."

"We need—we have to get out," Freya said, starting to panic. "I have to get home."

"Calm yourself, little æðeling," Ecgbryt soothed. "That is not the only way out."

Ecgbryt stepped aside to reveal a plain tunnel that had opened in the wall opposite. Daniel and Freya dashed over to it. There was no archway, just a gap in the wall about the height and width of one of the knights. "That wasn't there before," Freya stated.

"Are you so sure?"

"Yes!"

"Where does it lead?" asked Daniel.

"It leads to the underground city of Niðergeard," Swiðgar said. He moved close and placed a large, heavy hand on Daniel's shoulder. "It is the only portal you'll find here. The only way out. We must take you there, young Daniel and young Freya."

"Aye," agreed Ecgbryt, pulling a burning log from the brazier, holding it like a torch. "And it's past time we started to cover ground."

CHAPTER THREE

That Time We Saved the World

—————————— 1 ——————————

Now . . .

Daniel was walking down Walton Street—there were police officers at the canal. It was cold and drizzly, and their high-visibility coats stood out like beacons. They stood huddled together just outside of a small marquee-style tent, warming their hands on paper cups of coffee and tea. Inside the tent, they were presumably studying the body Daniel had killed.

He'd kept his pace and turned his head to show what he felt was the expected amount of interest for a passerby to give a crime scene. Then he took a turn down Hollybrush Road, another at St. Thomas's Street, and then up Worcester Street. He wondered where it would be best for him to lay low. The police kept a pretty accurate and up-to-date social map of the Oxford indigent community, he knew. It was starting to look like a cold sleep in Port Meadow tonight. Maybe then he'd think about walking up to Abbingdon, or even Reading.

But it was while walking down Walton Street that he noticed a couple of officers were following him—at least, he felt like they were following him. They were walking the same street as he was, which was long and busy. It could be a coincidence, he thought. Or perhaps not.

He was just re-plotting a route that would take him out of their direction when he heard a familiar voice call his name. He turned and saw Freya waving at him. She wasn't wearing a coat or jacket. Daniel backtracked and came to stand near her.

"Hi, um," she said, wrapping her arms around her chest and huddling against the cold. "I've got a table in there." Freya motioned to a café with red trim and large-paned windows. "Can I buy you a drink?"

Daniel looked past her at the two policemen walking leisurely up the street and nodded. Freya smiled at him. "Good."

They entered and went up to the counter. "What would you like?"

"Tea. Hot tea."

"Anything to eat?"

Daniel shrugged. He was famished but didn't want her to know that.

"The toasted sandwiches are good. How about one of those? Ham and cheese?"

Daniel nodded.

"Cool. Why don't you sit down? I'm over there." She pointed to a table near the window. Daniel turned and went to the table. He pulled out one of the rickety wooden chairs and lowered himself onto it.

There was a pile of books stacked haphazardly next to an open laptop. He looked at their spines. When was the last time he'd read a book? He picked up the one lying on top. It was a thin, small white book—an untranslated study edition of *The Wanderer*. He opened it, paged past the introduction, and started to read the poem.

Freya joined him shortly, bringing a large mug of steaming tea with her. She placed it in front of Daniel. "They'll bring the sandwich to us when it's ready. So," she said uncertainly, closing her laptop. "How've you been?"

Daniel looked at the pile of books on the table. "What are you studying?"

"Uh, philosophy and theology. At Pembroke."

"Which is this?" Daniel said, flipping through the booklet. "Philosophy or theology?"

Freya's brow tightened. "That's—just for me."

Daniel nodded and put the book back on the pile and focused on his tea. He poured some milk into it from a small pitcher on the table. Then he started adding sugar.

Freya leaned forward and put her chin in her hands. They sat in silence for a little while, Freya looking at the table, Daniel sipping from his tea until it was cool enough to take large gulps from.

The sandwich arrived and Freya shifted things on the table to give Daniel room to eat. He asked for some mustard and the waiter brought it.

"So," she said. "I've seen you on the street."

"I called to you once."

"I heard you, but . . . I wasn't ready to see you."

Daniel nodded and took a bite of his sandwich.

"What happened?" she asked.

Daniel chewed for a moment. "Things got kind of rough with Mum. Me being missing was really hard on her. Things were better when I got back . . . and then they got worse. I think, in a way, she really enjoyed the attention she got when I was gone—she's still got the newspapers with all the headlines from that time. And when we turned up again, she was overjoyed—there were interviews and photo shoots for a couple weeks, and then they—the newspapers—stopped calling. And a couple days after that, they stopped returning her calls. She went through her first wave of depression then. I learned to stay out of her way. Nothing I could do would make her happy. She'd start things with guys she'd meet from—anywhere, I guess. Those never ended well. Then, as you know, I did an apprenticeship instead of A levels—I wanted to start making money so I could get out of there.

"That fell through and I couldn't get any more work. I joined the army, the regular army, for a year or so. That was a problem for me. I left and I've been on the streets for about . . . six months now?"

Freya couldn't look at Daniel. She was finding it work enough to breathe past the lump in her throat. "I'm sorry," she said. "I had no idea, all that time."

"It's alright. You couldn't have done anything. It's like what they say about falling through the cracks—except it felt like I fell through one huge crack that I had no way of getting across. I'll get out again, somehow." Daniel finished one half of the sandwich and picked up the other. "So, how have you been?"

Freya drew a deep breath and leaned back in her chair. "Oh, you know. Can't complain."

Daniel laughed, a free and easy laugh. "No, seriously . . ."

"Seriously, not much. I did my A levels—history, religious studies, and philosophy—and managed to get into Oxford. I took a year out and earned some money so that I could travel, mostly around France. And . . . that's it."

Daniel nodded and finished eating his sandwich.

"You ever think about it?" Daniel asked with a grin. "That time we saved the world?"

Freya frowned. "I try not to."

"Why?"

"It'd be different if I could talk to someone about it, but as I can't—I've got to keep everything inside of myself. I'm still in . . . therapy, for my"—she drew another deep breath—"habits."

"Why?"

Freya looked up, locking her eyes with his. "That wasn't a happy time of my life. It was probably the worst thing I've ever gone through."

Daniel wiped his lips with a paper napkin and put it in his pocket. "It was the best time of my life. It's been all downhill after that."

"Well, I'm sorry for you, then," Freya said, pushing back and wrapping her arms around herself. "Or happy for you. Whatever."

"Freya," Daniel said, "do you ever think of going back?"

She tried to answer, but her lips clamped down, immovable, like concrete. She shook her head.

"I have, lots of times. I've been back to that church we visited—lots of times. I've poked around, in the evening, dawn—and nothing. But it's important that we try to get back. I've been thinking, and I think something's happening—something to do with what we did. I've been seeing, I don't know, *signs*. If we went back, we could ask what they mean." Daniel leaned in. In a low voice he said, "I killed a . . . a *you-know-what* two weeks ago. I think I've seen more of them around. I think I'm being followed. I've seen shapes on rooftops."

Daniel studied Freya's face for a reaction. There wasn't one— she was still frowning—but her face seemed harder somehow, stiffer. "That's not funny."

"Freya . . . I think—I think there are things still left to do. We're not done. Look," he said, drawing his notebook out of his jacket pocket. "Remember what Modwyn said about evil invading the country? I've been keeping a log of the bad things that have happened in Oxford—just in Oxford—in the last eight weeks. See, look at this chart."

Freya closed her eyes. Her stomach was queasy. She felt like she was in a very small space with tall walls that were quickly deteriorating, and behind those walls, an ocean of fear that would come flooding through at any moment. She knew Daniel was still talking, but she couldn't hear what he was saying. He had to stop—he *had* to.

"Shut up," she said, in a small voice.

"—where we came out. That wasn't an enchanted site. We find Alexander Simpson again—"

"Shut up—shut up. I said SHUT UP!" Freya violently slapped the table several times with the palm of her hand. Then she leaned over the table, buried her face in her hands, and started sobbing.

Daniel fell silent, as did the entire café. Eyes turned towards them, concerned.

Daniel looked around and smiled. The manager scowled at him from behind the counter. His look said that although a homeless man was tolerated here, so long as he paid—homeless men who disturbed his customers most certainly were not. Palms outwards, Daniel slowly pushed his chair back and rose.

"You know," Daniel said as he slid past Freya, "if you ever wanted anyone to talk to, you could have talked to me."

Daniel pushed through the door and headed out into the evening rain.

Freya sat guiltily, fidgeting with one of her books. Then she abruptly stood and chased after Daniel.

"I'm sorry," she said. "I didn't mean to yell. It just all came back really quickly." She stood there, shivering in the sleet without her jacket. Her arms were wrapped around her stomach, as she hunched her shoulders against the cold. The gentle shower fell on her face, making it slick, wet. She lifted a hand to brush a bead of water from her brow.

"That's alright," Daniel said. "I'm sorry I upset you."

"Listen, I've got to do something tomorrow. Do you mind if we meet the day after? We can talk about whatever you want to then."

"I suppose that would be alright."

"There's a church in Summertown near where I live—St. Michael and All Angels. Can you be there at four? So we can miss the twilight?"

"Yes, okay. I'll see you then."

"Okay, see you then."

Freya left and entered the coffee shop again, hardly aware that her compulsions seemed to leave her when she was around Daniel.

2

Robin Ploughwright, Lord of the Boggy Marshes and eighteenth Earl of Shotover Hill—a portly, rotund figure—pulled a pocket watch from his large purple waistcoat and marked the time. Even though the sky was overcast, light from the setting sun reflected upon the casing and threw a ray of golden-red upon his round face. He squinted one eye at it, then closed the antique up and deposited it back into his pocket.

Not much longer now. The street that he stood on did not technically have a name but had appropriated the title "George Street Mews." Although a public right of way, it was rarely used; too small for cars to enter, and too winding to be a shortcut between two places that few people wanted to go to anyway. His sharp hearing didn't detect anyone at either end of the long passageway. He wouldn't be disturbed.

He allowed himself a smile. He was happy to be back in

Oxfordshire—even if he did have to wear a different skin. The place always comforted him. It was little more than a swampy basin, really, even after all these years. Because of the hills surrounding it, the sun set early, and because of the built-up marshland, covered rivers and hidden canals flowed through many amusing areas of the city.

And then there were the people—a tidal force in themselves. Half of the year, the population swelled with the arrival of the students. When those left, the tourists descended from the skies. And always throughout there was the steady pulse of ordinary people trying to scratch out an existence. Living and dying, ebbing and flowing, it was a city of flux—always moving from one state into another, and so never really changing at all. A town rife with opportunities.

Robin's smile twisted into a frown. Come now, surely it was time. How much longer did he have to—

Ah, there it was. The stone face in front of him shifted soundlessly to reveal a door—plain, ordinary, and painted blue. It bore the number 141b above a cast-iron knocker, a small flap for letters, and a worn stone step. Apart from the fact that it hadn't been there eight seconds ago, it was completely unremarkable.

Robin produced a key and opened the door, which admitted entry not into a building but into a sparse courtyard containing a hill.

The high, blank stone walls crowded the hill, which might properly be described as no more than a mound, except that there was a luscious covering of bright green grass that was dotted with bluebells and buttercups. From the far side, a dead, withered tree protruded. It had grown once but had not bloomed in several thousand years.

Robin Ploughwright, Lord of the Boggy Marshes and eighteenth Earl of Shotover Hill, shut the door up behind him and turned to the hill, which was growing blue and cold in the falling twilight.

He found its entrance easily and went in.

The air inside the hill was musty and wet—it obviously hadn't been aired recently. Still, he wasn't setting up a guesthouse; he was here on business.

The way was dirty and he had to dodge many low-hanging roots before he came, with obvious relief, to the meeting hall. A small bonfire had been prepared and he drew near it, trying to hide his trepidation. He swallowed a mouth of bitter saliva and turned his eyes to the platform.

The throne was occupied. He flashed a smile and tried to will himself to stop twitching, sweating, and mumbling, his eyes flicking rapidly to and from the four armed guards surrounding the seated figure who blended perfectly into the shadows. This unassuming person was dressed in a casual white shirt unbuttoned at the top, a blue suit jacket, jeans, and brown loafers. His hair was white and flowing, but his skin was uncreased.

Robin bowed hastily. "Greetings, glorious grinner," he said, smiling.

The man in the throne shifted his weight. "Ploughwright," he acknowledged. "What news?"

"I have proceeded as you instructed—as we agreed. All is in place. I await your word."

"I give that word now. Put the plan into action."

Ploughwright turned his head slightly and regarded the man on the throne. He was obviously in earnest—he was always so drearily in earnest. "Very well, it will be as you say."

The man on the throne made a gesture, permitting him to leave.

Robin had walked a few steps when he turned. "With respect," he said, "I know I shouldn't question—never have before, but I must ask . . . why not simply kill them or detain them in a more conventional manner?" He held his breath to await reply—or punishment—from perhaps the only man in the world whom he truly feared.

The man on the throne raised a hand to his chin. Robin nearly flinched at the action. "Really, Robin," he said. "Is that any way to treat a friend?"

Robin bowed and turned. He didn't expect an answer anyway. He never should have said anything.

He retraced his steps quickly and drew the watch out of his pocket once more. Good, the door would still be open. No need to make other arrangements.

Exiting the hill, he swiftly made his way through the blue door and back into George Street Mews. And since there was still no one in sight, he stretched out his arms and scaled the wall. Slinking along the rooftops, he made his way back to the rooms he occupied where he lived under the disguise of a human.

3

At a quarter past two, Freya started off for her tutorial. She left the coffee shop and made her way to her tutor's room using the most populated streets. She ran into Julie, the other student she was to take her tutorial with, just outside the college. Freya was angry with herself for arriving on time; if she were just a little earlier, she would have been able to enter and reenter the doors and arches. The arches especially upset her.

Fighting anxiety, Freya mounted the stairs ahead of Julie. Reaching the door of the tutor's room, she knocked and reached into her bag for her tutorial gown. She pulled it out, deliberately bringing some papers with it. She bent down to collect them as they heard, "Come in, please," from inside the room.

"You go ahead," Freya said to Julie, deliberately picking her bag up the wrong way around to spill some of her books onto the floor.

"I'll help," Julie said, bending down.

"No! That's fine, I've got it," Freya said, harsher than she had meant.

Julie nodded, stood, and entered.

Freya stuffed the books in her bag and then took a bottle of pills out of an inner pocket. She dry-swallowed a couple and then went to a window in the hallway. Where was the sun? The sky had become overcast, but it wouldn't set until around five thirty this time of year. Surely the tutorial wouldn't drag on that long . . . but it might.

She took a deep breath. One crisis at a time. She opened the door and went in and out of it as fast and as silently as she could, seven times. That did absolutely nothing to calm her—she had gone through too many arches already. The only thing that could help was if she went back to the street and started again fresh. She closed her eyes and started to massage her forehead.

The door clicked shut behind her, making her jump.

"I'm sorry, did I startle you?"

"A little . . ." Freya saw Professor Stowe, her tutor, standing just inside the doorway.

His face was concerned. "It's okay. I'm a little anxious because I thought I would be late."

"No, dead on time, as usual. Shall we start?" He gestured to the sitting room where Julie was already settling herself.

Freya bustled into the next room and sat on a small, uncomfortable wooden chair next to Julie, facing Professor Stowe's leather wing-backed chair.

The next fifty minutes were dedicated to the discussion of Freya's and Julie's essays on determinism. Julie got high praise for hers, while Freya had all the flaws and bad reasoning pointed out in hers. She stopped taking notes when he started critiquing her sentence structure. Eventually, Stowe got down to the end of the paper and paused long enough for her to assume that he'd finished.

"Alright," she said, her voice quavering just slightly, feeling very much under attack. "You've told me all the things I shouldn't do, what are the things that I *should* do?"

The professor smiled at her. "Address the essay title," he said, tossing her back her essay. It was creased and glossed over completely in red ink. "Stay focused, be relevant. Do better."

Freya was fuming. She ostentatiously checked her watch.

"Yes, you're right," Stowe said. "We're finished now." He set the reading and essay titles for next week and rose from his chair as Julie and Freya packed up.

"Freya, if I could have a word in private with you."

The two students made eye contact.

"I'll wait for you outside," Julie said and left.

"I just wanted to say," Professor Stowe said, standing behind his wing-backed chair and leaning forward on it, "that you are, without a doubt, one of the smartest students in your current year—perhaps *the* smartest—and *that* is why I was so tough on you."

"I don't understand."

Professor Stowe turned his head rather theatrically to gaze out of the window and said, "The problem with your essays is that you are trying to advance the reasoning of the field, trying to arrive at some conclusion, whereas your only goal is to display an evidence of having read the material and, to some degree, retained it and understood it. We're not looking for a breakthrough. We don't want to revolutionise the field"—he slid his eyes away from the window and back to her—"just yet."

Freya considered this. "So . . . ?"

"So for now, you need to toe the line. I never want to discourage original thought, but the truth is that this is the wrong forum for that. You'll want to save all that for your doctoral thesis. But in order to get there, you need to finish your graduate degree, and for that you'll need to, barbaric as it sounds, simply follow the herd—or lead it, if you can. This isn't the time for individual thought—it is the place for it, but not the time, yet. Do you follow?"

"That's an ironic comment to come out of an essay on determinism."

Professor Stowe laughed, his eyes creasing merrily. "See, you're obviously brilliant. All things in their places, that's all I'm saying." Professor Stowe straightened and went to stand by the window. "I believe you've got a shining career ahead of you—you've an excellent academic mind, but you have to maintain distance. We're scholars of philosophy and theology, not practitioners, after all. You must maintain the perspective of the outsider."

Freya didn't agree with this at all and opened her mouth to protest, but Professor Stowe held up a hand and turned his face to the window.

"Now, the other thing I wanted to talk to you about—come over here for a second, please. Look down there."

Freya cautiously crossed the room to the window that looked down on the street.

"See that man opposite us, sitting on the pavement?"

Freya craned her neck. There was a form huddled against the wall of the house across from them that looked to be . . . Daniel.

"Do you know him?"

Freya nodded. "Yes, that's . . . an old friend of mine I was at school with."

"His name is Daniel, correct?"

"Yes."

"Did you know he was following you?"

"No."

"I first noticed him sitting outside here three weeks ago. He's quite a notorious figure in Oxford. I used to volunteer at the night shelter a few years ago. He was banned for violent behavior. A couple weeks ago I saw him walking down the street with blood on his face. Has he approached you?"

"Yes. Like I said, we were at school together."

"I would never advise a student on their personal life, but I would ask you to consider your involvement with him very carefully and treat him with great trepidation. There is little doubt in my mind that he will want to exploit your past friendship. It won't seem like that initially—he'll want to earn your confidence at first—but gradually he'll make more and more demands of you, which you'll find increasingly difficult to refuse."

Freya felt anxious. She thought about her agreement to meet Daniel later on that day.

"If you like, I can ring the police and have them caution him."

"No," Freya said. "That's fine. I'll—keep an eye on him."

"Have you planned to meet him again?"

Freya was going to deny that she had but then felt childish. She nodded her head. "We arranged to meet in a church . . . St. Michael's in Summertown."

"I don't think that's wrong but if I might advise you—miss the appointment. Just this once, to let him know that you have your own schedule."

"Okay, I'll consider that."

"Good. I just want you to be safe, that's all."

"I know, thanks." Freya shouldered her bag and moved to the door. She waved good-bye and then joined Julie outside in the hallway.

"What was that about?" she asked.

"Nothing, he just wanted to give me a little more feedback."

"More? He was pretty harsh in there."

"No, he's okay, really."

They walked off into the Oxford gloom.

4

Daniel spied the police officers when he was already mostly down St. Michael's Street. They were standing outside of the Gatehouse, and although that wasn't a common sight, it wasn't particularly rare either—it just meant that he wouldn't be able to nag the staff about getting in.

The coppers were talking to some of the guests while the staff stood in the doorway. Someone turned—Daniel now recognised him as Scouse Phil—and called out.

"Johnny! Johnny Boy! Wait up!"

Daniel slowed and looked behind him. There was no one around him, but Phil was definitely talking, and walking, directly to him.

"Keep walking," Phil said in a lower voice once he was nearer. "Don't look around, just smile and greet me."

Daniel jerked his head upwards and slapped Phil on the arm as he came to walk alongside him. One of the police officers turned her head to study Daniel and Phil. Her face registered them disinterestedly and then turned back to the group.

"Are you in trouble, like, Danny? Those officers there want to talk to ya. Thought ya'd want to be told. Have ya done anything any of us should know about?"

Daniel only frowned and shook his head.

"We's got to stick together, right? I wouldn't tell them about you—just like you wouldn't tell them about me, right? I scratch your back, and we wash each other's hands, right?"

"Of course," Daniel said, trying to sound reassuring.

"Champion. Well, best lay low awhile, and stay out of the usual haunts, just for a few days—that's as long as the pigs usually stay interested."

"Sure. Cheers, Phil."

"Be seein' ya, Danny Boy."

They had reached the end of the street and they split. Daniel headed towards George Street, planning a route of escape, and then realised with a start that today was the day he had arranged to meet Freya. He had to make his way up to Summertown and dodge the police that were prowling for a vagrant matching his description. At all costs he would have to avoid the canal where he'd made his kill, which would have been an ideal route otherwise. That left Jericho as a possibility, though not a great one. He was just going to have to stick to the side roads and chance it.

A couple nerve-racking hours later, he made it. He tried to stick to streets with a lot of parked cars on them for cover. Of course that thinned out the farther he went into affluent North Oxford, but there was more street parking as soon as he crossed Marston Ferry Road into Summertown.

Now he pushed open the wooden lych-gate of the church of St. Michael and All Angels and stepped into the churchyard. Passing row after row of worn, weathered tombstones, he thought, *All these people came before me, with lives nearly as big as my own . . .*

He twisted the oversized iron ring that hung on the large double doors of the church, which responded with a half turn and a sharp *clack*. Pushing the door open, he stepped inside.

The church was rather plain, as churches go. He was still cold, but warmer for being out of the wind and the rain. He slid into a pew and closed his eyes. He was tired and began to nod off.

There was the thump of something flat hitting the stone floor. Daniel turned and saw a thin old man with dusty grey hair standing near the door of the church. He clutched a handful of narrow slips of paper and was inserting them into a stack of order of service books. He smiled, made an apologetic face, and bent to pick up the book he'd dropped.

Daniel studied him for a moment. Was this man going to make

him leave, or was he just keeping an ostentatious eye on him? This man could make trouble for him if he wanted to. Perhaps it would be better to wait for Freya outside.

He stood and started to make his way out. To do so, he passed the old gentleman, who looked up, smiling. "Can I help you?"

"I'm just leaving," Daniel said.

"That's not what I asked. I said, can I help you?"

"No, I'm fine," Daniel said, and turned to go.

"Hold up a bit," the old man said, reaching into his back pocket. He withdrew a wide leather wallet, removed a bank note, and gave it to Daniel.

"No thanks, I'm fine," Daniel said, looking at the square of paper.

The old man took Daniel's wrist and shoved the money between his fingers. Daniel kept his eyes on it—there was something odd about the way it looked.

"Is there anything else?"

"What?" Daniel asked.

"You didn't come in here to ask for money."

Daniel couldn't work out if the note was for five pounds or ten. The colours, in this low light, seemed to be somewhere between. Was it for fifty? The man's words registered then. "Sorry?"

"What did you come here for?"

"I was waiting for someone."

"Oh, do they attend this church?"

Daniel examined the note more closely. The shapes didn't seem to add up. He pulled it tight and held it steady.

"I don't know."

"What is their name?"

There was something wrong with what he was holding. His arm stiffened as he thrust the money back at the man. "Here, take this, I don't want it."

"But you asked me for it."

"No, I don't need it. It's too much."

"Too much? I don't understand . . ."

"Take your money!" Daniel yelled at the old man.

"But I didn't give you money."

"What?" Daniel looked down at his hand. He was holding one of the slips of paper—a notice sheet—that the man had been inserting into the books. "Oh." He tried to read it but couldn't.

"Come back and see me if you like. I'll be here."

"Okay—thanks." Daniel shoved the paper in his pocket and left. He hurried down the church path, towards the street. He looked past the wooden lych-gate and to the street. There was a familiar figure approaching him—Freya. He raised a hand to greet her and saw a shape slide out from behind a privet hedge behind her.

"No!" Daniel shouted, breaking into a run. He barrelled through the wooden gate and suddenly felt himself falling forward. The ground was no longer where it should have been. He didn't fall far, but landed with a jolt that knocked the air from his lungs.

When he raised his head, he saw that the sky was clear now and the sun was shining, not a cloud in the sky. He was lying in the middle of a wide field of green grass and there wasn't a building in sight.

CHAPTER FOUR

The Knights of Niðergeard

1

Before . . .

"I'm not going," said Freya, gazing into the dark, fathomless, anonymous blackness that stretched in front of her. "You can't make me."

Daniel looked into the new opening and licked his lips. He saw a fantastic opportunity before him. This was escape—he could run away with these two . . . knights, or whatever they really were. He felt the pull in his chest—the tug of adventure, of the unknown, of danger—and it was exciting to him. He turned to Freya.

"What other choice do we have?" he asked her in a meek yet reasonable voice. "I think we have to go with them," Daniel coaxed, taking her arm and pulling her along through the gap in the wall and into deeper, darker tunnels. She felt dread from the very first heavy foot that she put forward. Each step was a step further into darkness and uncertainty. Each step was a step into fear.

"Where are you two from?" Daniel asked. "Are you Vikings?"

"God's teeth," moaned Ecgbryt. "That he would call me such!"

"What makes you ask if we are Vikings?" asked Swiðgar.

"Well . . . ," said Daniel slowly, "you speak strangely; the weapons, your hair . . . you don't seem English."

"We are the very flesh of England!" Ecgbryt exploded. "The dust of the land is in our blood just as our blood is in its dirt! We are its arms, its teeth!"

"Much will have changed since we were put to rest," Swiðgar said, in a more measured fashion. "But we were born here and have lived all our lives without stepping a foot off Britain's shores."

"How come we can understand you?" Freya asked. "Shouldn't you be talking a different type of English?"

"And so we are," said Ecgbryt.

"So, how . . . ?"

"It is one of Ealdstan's devices. There was an arch that you passed under which read:

> I, the word-worker of Niðergeard,
> Give to all who pass beneath this arch
> The gift of free speech—
> If he be truly friendly.

"The enchantment was such that all who pass beneath it would not be hindered in understanding of our words due to ignorance of our language. Now wait, what is this here?"

They had come to a crossroad and stopped. The tunnel had narrowed and now split off into three different directions. Ecgbryt held a hand up to Daniel and went to Swiðgar. "What's wrong?" Daniel asked. "Are you lost?"

"Not yet. Be patient, please."

Freya crept closer to Daniel and whispered to him, "Where are they taking us?"

"I don't know. I can't remember what he said. Nither-something, I think. Nither-gard?"

"Daniel, we have to go back. I'm going to tell them that I'm going back."

"You can't go back, there's no way through there anymore."

"I don't care. I'll stay in the chamber. I'll stay there until the archway opens again. I don't want to be in these tunnels anymore. Everyone will be worried about us."

"Okay, when they come back I'll talk to them."

"Thanks," Freya said in relief.

The knights conferred a little longer and then called Daniel and Freya over. "This way, æðelingas," said Swiðgar. "Not far now."

"I think Freya's scared. She wants to go back, but I told her that this is the only way to go. That's true, right?"

"Daniel!" Freya hissed.

Swiðgar at least acted with more sensitivity. He came over and knelt before Freya, his face sympathetic. "I am sorry that it must be like this," he said. "But we must continue on."

"That's okay," Freya said. Looking into the ancient knight's face, with its creases and scars, she felt her argument start to evaporate. "But it's just that I really don't mind going back and waiting in the room for the doorway to open again. You wouldn't have to wait with me—I'm pretty sure I could find my own way back. It's just that I'm pretty tired and—and a little scared—and I really don't mind waiting. I'd prefer waiting, in fact, instead of, um . . ." She trailed off, having said everything she wanted to say. Swiðgar continued to look at her, so she added, "Please?"

"I am sorry, æðeling, but that is not possible," he said, standing up. "We continue our journey in this direction."

"But you said," Freya said, hurrying after him, "that the wall opened up at a special time, when the sun—"

"At a certain time," Swiðgar agreed, with a nod of his head, "and for a certain person. You have already started your journey and you may not stop now. You must continue or fail."

"I don't understand," said Freya.

"The moment at which you found us was no time at all; it was what is called a 'time between times.' It was the evening—the 'even-time'—when light and dark are equal. It is a sacred time. It has a strong pull to a certain type of person. The place you found us could be called a 'place between places,' and you yourself are a person between destinies. You have started along a path that you cannot go back on." He smiled at her. "But there will be more paths to choose from and soon. Perhaps one of those will lead you to the place you seek, perhaps somewhere better," he said. "Come."

Freya became conscious of her steps; her feet falling one in front of the other seemed heavy, jarring her.

"When the time, place, and person are all in an *efenheort*," Swiðgar continued as he walked, like a teacher giving a lesson, "which is a sort of unstable harmony—then fantastic things can happen. One must be careful when one finds oneself at a place between places, say a beach or a crossroads, during either dawn or dusk. If his soul is at a spiritual crossroads, his mind lost, and his body wandering—what we might call a 'person between persons'—then he may pass through the barriers between worlds as a pillar of smoke passes through a field of mist."

"There are many instances," Ecgbryt, from behind, informed them. "A restless fisherboy, with conflicting thoughts in his head and dreams churning in his heart, will cast off his bark into the sea before sunrise, when the wind sweeps the spray off the waves. Soon he finds himself far and away on distant adventures with thieves who live beneath the waves, pirate kings, and magic treasure."

"A young princess, not a girl, nor yet a queen," Swiðgar continued, "riding at dawn in the forest strays along deer paths and comes to the foot of a hill where the trees thin and finds the entrance to an Elfin court. She will rule there for many years and then return to our realm, still but a young girl, though wiser, and with many mystical virtues and gifts."

"A wandering rhymer," Ecgbryt rejoined, "old, and in the twilight of his own life, will come to a crossed road and converse with a mysterious gentleman who reveals himself to be the devil. They pass the night riddling under the gallows, and at dawn—at the even-time—the winner will demand a prize from the loser."

"Such is the universe," Swiðgar resumed. "A vast multitude of spheres all spinning and dancing in the most intricate and bewildering patterns. At the right time, and in the right place, when the spheres are close enough, a man can step from one to the other, as easily as crossing a brook.

"So it is vitally important to be aware of those times of 'evening' in your life," he said gravely, "and to consider carefully which path you decide to take, for the path will change not just you but your entire world."

Daniel's eyes were wide. These were thoughts that he had not thought before, could never have thought before.

"Of course," said Ecgbryt, "there are places that are more enchanted than others. Take the Scot's land, for instance, or the Norsemen's land. There are entire seasons of even-times, and complete holdings and folds that belong neither wholly to earth, sea, air, or ice. All manner of unnatural and magical acts have flowed from those places like water from a spring. And as for the Eire folk—well! Their entire race, land, and history is ensorcelled from one end of time to the other!"

The scraping of their footsteps continued uninterrupted for a short while. Daniel threw a look to Freya, who still appeared miserable. "Well," she huffed in a low, pained voice. "Someone might have warned us that this sort of thing could happen."

"What?" said Ecgbryt. "Does no one tell stories of such things happening anymore?"

"So when we went through the arch," Daniel said slowly, "we actually entered another world?"

"Not exactly, no," Swiðgar replied. "The place where we slept was not in one world nor another. Imagine a tide pool set in the shore of the universe alongside the sea of time—an eddy where time spins in upon itself. In such a place we remained as we were when we were first laid to rest. All who cross from one world to the next must, by necessity, pass through one of these pools. That is why, when you hear of people returning from one of those other worlds, they have sometimes been gone a day, sometimes a hundred years. There is little accounting for it, but even so there is reason—"

Swiðgar's explanation was cut short by a loud, piercing scream that rattled down the tunnel, knocking against the walls. The group halted immediately.

"What was—" Daniel's question was smothered out of him by Swiðgar's massive hand on his chest as it pushed him against the wall. Freya was pulled over and pressed next to him.

"Here, lifiendes, take this," Swiðgar said, pressing his round shield into Daniel's arms. "Stay behind it." Daniel hoisted it up in front of Freya and himself. They poked the top of their heads up from behind the rim, their eyes large and fearful.

"What's happening?" Freya asked.

Ecgbryt dropped his torch; it still burned, casting oversized shadows on the walls of the tunnel. He drew his axe from his belt and swung his shield from his back to his arm. Swiðgar likewise dropped his torch and raised his spear, gripping it with both hands. They stood, waiting, for long seconds that felt like minutes.

Another scream came from behind them—human, but wild, savage. Swiðgar swung his spear around and faced the sound. Daniel had read about banshees—spirits that wailed on rooftops when someone was about to die. *I bet it sounds the same*, he thought, shuddering.

Just then, Ecgbryt leapt into the darkness, his axe glimmering momentarily in the torchlight. There was the sound of a scuffle and a shriek and then silence.

"*Hwæt*, brother, is it well?" Swiðgar asked without turning his head. Before an answer could come, there was a snarl from the tunnel beyond the tall knight, and a dark figure sprang into the torchlight. It seemed to hang in the air for a long, fear-filled moment and then descend. It was dark and human-shaped, though thin and wiry. Its arms and elbows were like knotted ropes. Its legs were thick and shaggy, its hands raised; long, sharp fingers curled into talons. Its mouth was open in a snarl showing black gums from which sprouted thin, needle-like teeth.

Faster than they were able to follow, Swiðgar thrust his spear at the terrible shape. There was a howl and Freya felt a spray of blood on her face. The creature dropped, clutching the spear, now caught in its chest. Another leapt from behind it and crouched low, next to the torch. Daniel could see its hairless head, pale and white, face fixed in a snarl of rage, a feral hate burning in its eyes. It sprung high up in the air just as Swiðgar yanked his spear from the first beast. He spun the shaft around in his hands so that the blunt end crashed down on the creature's head.

Swiðgar drew his short sword from its scabbard and raised it high. Daniel saw it gleam against the black wall and watched it fall upon the stunned beast, hacking at the thing's shoulder and back. Neither Daniel nor Freya could stand to watch and looked away quickly.

Stepping away, Swiðgar swung his spear around in his right hand, lifting his sword in his left. Still staring into the blackness that had expelled the creatures, he called again, "Ho, brother!"

"I am here," came a reply. "All are defeated."

"What count have you?"

"Three. And you?"

"Two only."

Ecgbryt appeared again, edging slowly backwards into the torch light, sticky blood dripping from the end of his axe onto the pressed dirt floor. The two knights stood, watching and waiting for a time, but there came no more sounds or attackers.

"That appears to be all," Ecgbryt announced. He shouldered his shield and picked up the torch. "Let us see what we've killed, shall we?"

Daniel handed Swiðgar's shield back to him as Freya quickly wiped as much of the blood as she could from her face. It was thick and brown and sticky. She wiped her hands on the cold wall, trying not to touch her school clothes.

They all advanced up the tunnel to where Ecgbryt's victims lay in a mangled heap. Using the blade of his axe, he nudged the bodies apart from each other. "*Yfelgópes*," Ecgbryt said, "of a kind—yet I have never seen a sort as twisted before."

In the light of the torch, they could see the creatures clearer. Their skin was pale, almost milky white. Dark, ghastly blue veins showed through the thin skin. All were mostly naked, but their groins and upper legs were covered with rough black skins tied together with a tough, stringy material that looked like animal hide or maybe dried entrails. Parts of the creatures' torsos were tattooed or stained, but not with patterns or designs. Blotches and irregular stripes were simply dyed a deep solid black or brown. Freya took a few steps backwards and looked away, disgusted.

"Did you say ifel-gop-es?" Daniel asked.

"It is a name we give to all the twisted ones who live in the deep underground," Swiðgar said. "But I've never seen one with such a face."

The faces were terrifying. Daniel shivered as he leaned forward for a closer view of one of the corpses. Its eyes were very far apart and its nose was snubbed. Its gaping mouth showed small, needle-like teeth.

"But . . . they're human, aren't they?" Freya asked, almost surprised. "They acted like animals, but . . ."

"Aye, they're human," Ecgbryt answered her. "But nearly as foul as a man can go. Nearly. Look at this." He tapped his axe against the yfelgóp's dead hand. The thing was wearing some sort of glove made of bone, the fingers of which protruded beyond its own. The ends had been filed sharp. "A strange weapon," Ecgbryt commented.

"Aye," agreed Swiðgar. "Bring a head," he said after a moment's pause. "And a hand," he added finally.

Ecgbryt raised a corpse by its thin hair and began chopping at it. "It's unhappy work for my axe, though—and what I wouldn't give for something to wipe my blade against."

Freya stood hunched over, suddenly feeling very cold and very, very afraid. "Daniel," she said in a whisper. "What's going on?"

Daniel watched as the knights heaped the dead bodies on top of each other and cleaned their weapons. He could feel his blood pump through his body, charged, as if every cell was filled with electricity. His head spun as a wave of euphoria washed over him. He had never felt this way in his real life. They had been attacked, and the knights, because of their weapons and skill, had saved them all and come away without a scratch.

"I don't know what's going on," he said. "But I'm getting one of those swords."

2

They walked for some time, tense and wary, alert to the slightest sound that might give away the presence of something following them. Swiðgar walked in front this time, his spear at the ready and torch held high. Ecgbryt walked behind them, which Freya thought just as well since even thinking of the hideous head and ugly dangling hand tied to Ecgbryt's belt made her stomach turn over.

"Where are we going again?" Daniel asked.

"Niðergeard," Ecgbryt answered in a voice strong with pride. "It is a vast holding beneath the skin of the earth. Its boundaries are not marked, and it sits upon the gates of three hidden worlds. It is the grandest of all earthly cities, yet known to only a few. Its dark spires are seen only by those who are great and dream of a larger greatness."

"It's an underground kingdom?" Daniel asked with awe.

"It would be," the knight behind him replied, "but there is no king or queen to rule it. It is governed by Modwyn the Fair and overseen by Ealdstan the Long-Lived."

"Who are they?"

"Modwyn is Niðergeard's ward—able and cunning. Ealdstan is very old and very wise—the oldest and the wisest, in fact. By now he would be almost seventeen hundred years old, I suppose. It was he who laid us to rest, as he did the others."

"Others?" Daniel repeated, his voice rising. "There are more like you?"

"Aye. There are sleeping knights tucked away up and down the isle. A mighty force, all lying in wait."

"Waiting for what?" Daniel asked.

Ecgbryt considered the question for a moment. "For the greatest battle in history. More than that, I cannot say. Ealdstan may wish to tell you more."

"Ealdstan," Freya repeated the name to herself.

"Now," said Swiðgar. "We have told you much about our world, and now we would know about yours. What is life like on the surface in this century?"

Freya glanced at Daniel, unsure how to respond. "It's hard to say. We don't really have anything to compare it to."

"It's pretty busy," Daniel said. "At least, that's what everyone says about it. There's a lot of bustle and hurrying everywhere."

"Busy is good," said Ecgbryt. "Idleness is the cause of a great many ills, especially in great ones and rulers."

"I don't think that's a problem," said Freya. "The government is full of people who work really hard."

"What do you mean by 'hurrying'?" Swiðgar asked.

"Well, lots of people are always going places. Like, to work, to the stores to buy things, to meet people . . . that kind of thing. They're always, you know, zipping around in cars and buses."

"'Cars'?"

Daniel felt awkward. He'd watched shows on TV and read in stories about people trying to explain modern life to aliens or time travelers or primitive savages or people like that, but he never thought that he'd actually have to do it himself. "Um . . . cars are like carts that move without horses. See, you put this sort of fuel into a machine that's inside of it and, sort of, set fire to it—the fuel—and that makes it go. Buses are like that too, uh, but just bigger."

He didn't know what the knights would make of this explanation, but they seemed to accept it without any further questions. He wondered if he should try to explain airplanes as well. He decided that might be too complicated.

"So traveling is easier, then?"

"Yes," said Daniel. "Much easier. You can go anywhere in the world that you want to. Some ways of traveling are so fast that you can get clear to the other side of the world in a day. People have been everywhere in the world—including the highest mountain and the hottest desert. There's nowhere in the world that hasn't been discovered." He paused again and wondered if he should tell them about people landing on the moon. That was probably too much.

"People can go anywhere," Swiðgar said. "But are they where they want to be?"

"I suppose so," said Freya. "I think most of them are, yes."

"A lot of them aren't, though," Daniel said glumly.

"*Swa swa*," said Swiðgar. "So, people can move about quickly. What else is new?"

Freya remembered a class project she had prepared about modern life. "There's communication too," she said. "We have phones and e-mail on computers, which means that you can talk to anyone anywhere in the world anytime you want to."

"That truly is marvelous," said Swiðgar, and Ecgbryt made an admiring noise. "What do people say when they talk across the world?"

"Um . . . not much, I suppose. But it means that you can keep in touch with your loved ones wherever they are. You can speak to them, even see them at the same time."

"Ah, what a wonder that is. I would dearly love to see such a thing."

"There's information too," said Freya. "We have machines so that you can find out about any book ever written or any person living or how things work or what happened in history —anything!"

"I remember," said Ecgbryt, "that King Ælfred considered knowledge a valuable gift—one which he never denied any he thought worthy of it . . . That said, I can't recall a time he refused teaching to anyone who asked it from him."

"These days," said Freya, "everyone is educated. People without any money can know as much as kings and queens. Pretty much."

"Remarkable," said Ecgbryt. "Yes, that was Ælfred's dream."

"So, tell me," said Swiðgar, "with all of these machines and abilities—are people happy?"

"I think so," said Freya. "Yes, happier than if they didn't have all these things."

"Are they kind? Do they treat each other with honour?"

"Maybe not as much as they could," Daniel said. "Maybe not much at all, actually."

"They still fight, then? There are wars? People are hungry? They hate each other?"

"So what?" Freya said. "Were things any better in your time, whenever that was?"

"Hmm," Swiðgar grunted. "In faith, no, they were not. There were constant wars and many battles in our lifetime, as well as hunger and hate and hardship. This only serves to prove what none from my time wanted to admit to themselves—that men and women of any type, of any nation, of any advantage, at any time, will always war with, steal from, and take advantage of each other, no matter what is done to try to help them improve their lives. No matter what the advantages—education, riches, comfort—men will still tend towards evil."

"Do you think there's anything that can stop that?" Daniel asked.

"It seems not," said Swiðgar. "It seems that people carry corruption around inside of them wherever they go."

"You mean we can't do anything?"

"I mean that we must do everything, but that even that may not be enough."

They walked in silence for a while, contemplating the pessimism in that statement.

"Is it much farther?" Daniel asked after a time.

"Not at all," Swiðgar replied, and he was shortly proven to be right. Within a few hundred paces, branching tunnels started to join their own, widening their way, not dividing it. The path they were walking on grew wider and the ceiling gradually rose higher, giving them that odd shrinking sensation again. The echo of their footsteps gradually faded away and then disappeared altogether and the walls around them grew darker as they became more distant.

Swiðgar and Ecgbryt slowed, obviously cautious. They moved from the centre of the tunnel to the side, walking along the right-hand wall. Eventually they stopped and lowered their torches.

"What is it?" asked Freya, suddenly fearful again.

"Shh! *Liss*," Ecgbryt breathed, motioning them to stop.

Daniel and Freya strained to hear. Coming from the blackness in front of them they heard a faint scrabbling noise.

As they strained to see what might be making this sound, they realised they were staring into nothingness. Looking up, they could just trace the outline of the edge of the natural archway that opened into an unknowably large area. Cold, stale air swept over them in a chilling wave. "Where are we?" Daniel asked in an awed voice.

"At the mouth to one of the entrances to the Niðerland."

"Are we still underground?"

"Yes. It is a large plain—mostly flat—supported by large natural pillars. Now, silence."

As Daniel and Freya squinted, they made out a line of faint, pale-yellow pinpricks of light running straight across their field of vision. The lights were extremely dim and noticeable only if you did not look directly at them. They could hear distant voices arguing and shouting.

Daniel and Freya felt sick with anticipation now. "What's going on?" Daniel whispered.

It was a few moments before Swiðgar answered in a low voice, "I know not, but now we must move in silence and darkness, not to be seen or heard." To Ecgbryt he commanded, "We will extinguish the torches here, *broðor*."

They did so, plunging everything into such an empty darkness that Daniel and Freya gave quiet gasps. Then each of them felt one of the knight's hands on their back, and they were pushed forward.

For a time Daniel and Freya felt as if they were walking in nothingness. It was completely dark except for the fallen starfield of campfire lights. As their eyes adjusted to the almost tangible darkness, they started to distinguish the dim shapes of landscape that lay flat on the top of each other, broken by pillars of stone rising up on either side, reaching up and vanishing towards an unseen ceiling.

In the distance was a dim glow—an arc of faint light like a misty haze. Freya, who had spent some time camping up north, knew that this was the light that cities often gave out at nighttime. That must be where Niðergeard was.

As they went farther, they found that the ground wasn't as flat as they had thought—there were slight rises and falls and chasms that spewed cold air that had been spanned by bridges. Stalagmites rose ahead and to either side of them with bases larger than tree trunks and tops that vanished into the darkness.

The curious scrabbling sound grew louder and the individual noises became separate and more distinct. There was a low chattering noise, a dusty scraping, and some intermittent clanking. The pinpricks of light that ran in a line across the landscape gradually grew larger, but not much brighter, as they approached them. Freya and Daniel soon discovered they were pale campfires, burning with a dirty flame. The travelers proceeded with slow caution from stalagmite to stalagmite. Crouching close to one column, they saw shapes flicker in front of them—fast, darting shapes, very similar to those that had attacked them in the tunnels. Rasping voices could just be heard. Daniel strained his ears but could make out only a few phrases, but those phrases didn't make any sense.

". . . and three more spoon measures make twenty pebbles' worth for the final measure," explained a grating voice.

"Eight twenties make one and sixty; from two hundreds and twenty, that leaves sixty," came a creaky reply. This comment was met with a few grunts of annoyance.

"Between eight," continued the second voice, straining slightly, "that's another seven pebbles' worth each, at least! Too mean, too mean by far!" There was a slap of a palm against the bare ground and a chorus of voices rumbling with indignation. "Weigh again! Weigh again, and rats take your toes! I'm so hungry my teeth tingle!" There were further odd curses and then a rattling clank.

"To my ear and eye," whispered Ecgbryt, withdrawing slightly, "they are the kith and kind of the creature whose head and hand I have in my belt."

"Agreed," said Swiðgar. "And likely as friendly. We need a path through."

"I fear they have the whole plain surrounded. We could charge them and try to break through the weakest point," Ecgbryt suggested.

"Even without the lifiendes, I would fear . . ." Swiðgar's voice drifted off. "No," he decided, "we should investigate the Neothstream. Its waters run beneath the city. We may gain entry that way."

Ecgbryt was silent for a time and then replied, "Very well. Be it so."

"This way, æðelingas," Swiðgar commanded. "Follow me. Do not talk; the price of an overheard word may be our lives. There might be guards or patrols at any point, especially as we near the water's head."

They turned and crept through the dark, hunching low to the ground. Freya wondered what time it was in the real world. How long had they been walking? Was it as dark up there as it was under here?

She doubted it. There were no stars here, no street lamps, no houselights, only the dingy little campfires of those disgusting creatures. Her breath became short and erratic as her emotions were pulled deeper and deeper into a whirlpool of worry. She wasn't afraid of the dark but couldn't help wondering what things there were in the darkness that she couldn't see, or wouldn't want to see, or couldn't even imagine. She felt her eyes grow hot. She blinked a couple times, and then tears were flowing.

She kept her sobbing quiet—sometimes choking back her cries, sometimes drawing breath in wide gulps, but always being careful to move forward at the same pace.

After a few minutes, the worst had passed and she was wiping her wet cheeks with the palm of her hand and drawing in deep gasps. As she swallowed her third deep breath, she realised that there was another sound, a low, subtle sound that she had been hearing for some time without knowing it, a sound that had been growing in the distance. She concentrated on it, trying to tune out the quiet shuffle of their footsteps as they trudged into the darkness.

She spent a fair amount of time guessing before the answer came to her: water. There was no liquid hissing or crashing to the sound, just the gentle, playful gurgle and burble of water sliding along smooth rocks. It was such a pleasant, beautiful sound. She focused her attention on it, letting the sound fill her head and trickle down her spine in a pleasant rush that reminded her of hikes in hills, of bright skies and fresh air.

The sound grew. They were obviously approaching the source. The knights slowed and proceeded more cautiously. There was the faint glow of two dim campfires up ahead that illuminated a wet patch of rocks where the trickle of water spilled down over a series of large, water-rounded stones to swirl in a deep pool. This pool then drained into a wide and slow-moving river.

Daniel and Freya stared, trying to take in as much as they could in the poor light. They thought they could see the forms of two yfelgópes sitting slumped against short pikestaffs in a way that reminded Daniel of bored security guards. The knights motioned to Daniel and Freya, and the four of them headed along the river and away from the guards.

There was more activity farther down the river. Shouts and

squabbles drifted towards them above the gurgle of the water. The lights grew brighter, the campfires closer together. Foul, burnt smells wafted towards them, accompanied by ugly cackles and squawks.

The knights paused and crouched down; Daniel and Freya drew in close to them. "We must take to the water now," Swiðgar told them. "Be careful—the river is cold and dark and the bed will be slippery. A short distance along the river there is a rock shelf that divides the waters. It creates an underground stream that feeds many wells of the city. If we dive underneath that opening, and swim on ahead, there will be air on the other side. We will be able to climb into the city through the Western Well. Do you understand?"

"Yes," said Daniel.

"I think so," answered Freya. "But how will you do it in your armour?"

"The river and its underground passage are shallow enough for Ecgbryt and me to stand at any point, though you two may have to swim. Now, I shall go first. Ecgbryt, you will come last."

"Stay, broðor. Is it known what awaits us in the city?"

"No, but I do not believe it has fallen. I wist we would have known if that had come to pass."

"That is much trust without reason."

"An aye to that. Although I do not think the yfelgóp would be entrenched in such a fashion if they had climbed the walls. Judging from their clustered encampments, so close to the wall, this seems a siege."

"But what of the beacon?" Ecgbryt asked. "If all was well, we would be seeing by its light right now."

"I know not," said Swiðgar, a note of anxiety settling into his voice. "We are bound to investigate the city and discover its fate. It is to be hoped that things are not as dark within as without, but to find that we must take the river and enter through the Western Well."

"Then be it so," Ecgbryt returned. "I trust your advice."

3

The water was very cold, but quite shallow, coming up only to Daniel's and Freya's knees. The rocks were large and smooth, slowing them down with staggering slips, softened splashes, and swallowed grunts.

The stream wove gently in large curves, some of which took them much closer to the yfelgóp encampments than Daniel or Freya would have liked. Most often they heard sounds of squabbling and snatches of arguments, but around one fire the ugly creatures were engaged in chanting a song that the knights later told them was a rune rhyme—a series of blunt, coarse verses describing the yfel-gópes' alphabet and system of numbering. They beat the dirt with dull thuds and recited the words in a ragged chorus:

> *"Fýr is First, it burns, it thirsts;*
> *it feasts on flesh and fallen foes.*
>
> *"Urth is dirt, the Second house*
> *we dig the dead, decayed to dust.*
>
> *"Thorn is Third, it cuts, it carves;*
> *a cold and cruel crown for kings.*
>
> *"Ald is age it wastes, it wanes;*
> *want walks Forth; when time wreaks wreck.*
>
> *"Rech is smoke, the smog that smothers*
> *the Fifth sense, smell. It chokes, it chars.*
>
> *"Claw is Sixth, it snicks, it snatches;*
> *when sharp, it shivs, and dull, it catches."*

The verses went on, chilling Daniel's and Freya's hearts just as the icy water chilled their feet. After a time, Daniel's legs started to go numb. It was an unpleasant feeling. The water deepened until he was wading in it up to his waist. As he struggled to keep up, Daniel could make out the shape of Swiðgar striding confidently ahead of him. Then, startlingly, the knight bobbed swiftly downwards, the water now up to the large knight's torso.

Daniel braced himself for what was to come. He made his way cautiously to where Swiðgar had sunk farther in and put a twitching foot forward.

He suddenly felt himself sinking. Gasping as the water enveloped him, he sank farther and farther down. Panicking, he thrashed his arms. If mere exertion and prayer could have saved him from going farther under then he would have stopped right there, but he didn't. With a terrified *glub*, his head slipped under the surface of the water.

He strained his head upwards as his hands tore away at the ice water. After an age, dry warmth finally bathed his face and he sucked in a huge gasp of air.

"Quietly, quietly," cautioned Ecgbryt, his mouth pressed close to Daniel's ear. "Place your feet on the ground." Daniel stretched his legs underneath him as the knight lowered him back into the water. "I—I can't feel the bottom." His voice was an urgent whimper. "It's too deep."

"It is not. Be calm. Put your legs down straight. Unbend your back."

Daniel found this hard since the chill had started making him shiver uncontrollably. His feet kicked in vain for a time and then struck against something. He pointed his toes and found that solid ground was, in fact, beneath him. He put his feet down and found that the water only just covered his shoulders. "I—I—I can't . . . ," he stammered.

"Worry not," said the even voice of Ecgbryt. "I am here beside you."

Daniel gulped and started to move forward again. Swiðgar stood ahead a little distance, stopped, apparently waiting. Freya was swimming quietly and confidently a short distance off to his right.

It was slow, hard work for Daniel, who was finding trying to stay afloat in his clothes almost impossible. He paddled along as best as he could, but moved faster with his toes fumbling along the rocky bed.

Swiðgar, up ahead, motioned to them. He pointed to the spot where he was standing and ducked under the water. He didn't come up.

Daniel approached the area where Swiðgar had disappeared, Ecgbryt behind him. Freya was paddling around the area. She went down once and bobbed back up again, took a very deep breath, went back down, and didn't come up again.

Daniel could feel with his feet where the ground fell sharply away. He stopped, paralysed, trying to find enough breath and courage to move forward.

"It is well," said a voice behind him. "Swim as you can and push yourself along the rocks. It's not far."

Daniel swallowed and took a deep breath. He bobbed up and down in the water and then plunged his head under. He tried to pull himself forward and felt a strong hand on his back giving him a push that sent him surging forward faster than he liked. He put his hands out in front of him and felt them scrape hard on the floor of the underwater stream. The pain made his face clench. He wanted to let out a scream but didn't dare open his mouth. Suddenly, there wasn't enough air in his lungs. He made a mistake—this was wrong. He didn't have enough air. Should he go back, or was he already there? He tilted his body upwards, thinking or hoping he must be there, but banged his head against a rocky ceiling instead. He saw red and white lights before his closed eyes. Throwing his hands outwards, he tried to push, claw, or scrape himself along. He gained a little momentum but not a lot. He kicked his feet, but they felt heavy and slow in his water-filled shoes. His lungs burned. *This must be what dying is like*, he thought.

He felt a large hand grab his back and he was once again lifted out of the water. His breath exploded outwards. He sucked air deep into his lungs, marveling at its taste and warmth. He had survived.

"It is done, lad." It was Swiðgar this time. "You made it. Stand."

Daniel put his legs down. The water was shallower here but moved much faster. He stood coughing and sputtering in the absolute darkness. "Freya?" he said when he found his breath.

"Yes," came a reply in what, to him, seemed a very calm and collected voice, though shivering slightly with cold. "I'm here. Are you okay?"

"I think so," he said, grinning. "I wish I had tried harder in swimming class."

Ecgbryt surfaced behind them, his metal armour jangling as he struggled for a footing on the wet rocks. "It gets the blood flowing," he said, laughing, "does a good dip like that."

"I'll say," Daniel said.

"Let us press onwards," Swiðgar said. "Freya, hold on to my shoulder; Daniel, take Ecgbryt's. We will lead you."

With Daniel and Freya shivering uncontrollably, the four moved through the near-total darkness. Time had become abstract since entering the tunnels, and now didn't seem to touch them at all.

They had just begun to think they would wander around in the dark forever when a quivering outline could be made out on the surface of the water up ahead. "It is here," said Swiðgar. He stepped beneath a dim halo of light that fell from the well's shaft above them. A soft luminescence cascaded down his face and shoulders, throwing his high-browed features into sharp relief. It was the first clear image that Daniel and Freya had seen for some time, and it stung their eyes.

"There are rungs for climbing set into the stone," he explained. "I will lift you up as high as I may, then follow behind. A warm fire and dry dress will be waiting for you, think on that. Daniel, you come first this time."

Swiðgar knelt, allowing Daniel to put one foot on his squared upper leg. Reaching up, he found he could touch the bottom rung. Swiðgar made a cradle out of his hands and Daniel, putting his other foot inside it, found himself launched up into the round, rocky hole. With a cry of surprise, he threw his arms out, bracing himself along the sides of the well to keep from falling back down. Just above his right hand was a rung and he grabbed it. Below that was another, which he managed to get his foot on. "Alright," he called down.

"Start climbing," came the reply. "I'm sending up Freya behind you."

With water cascading off of his drenched clothes, Daniel started to haul himself up, relishing the idea of putting those dark and extremely wet caverns and creatures behind him and wondering what was ahead.

He kept his head up and eyes fixed on the little circle of light still far above him. He started climbing faster, even though his arms and legs were very tired and unbelievably heavy.

Eventually he came to the end of the rungs. He paused before putting his head through the opening. Then, placing his hands on the rim of the well, he pushed himself forward and tumbled up and out of the darkness. He slid off and onto a stone-paved floor, exhausted. He lifted his head, looked around slowly, and gaped at what he saw.

4

A huge tree towered above Daniel, stretching up into the darkness. It was unlike any tree that he'd ever seen before; it was carved out of a pale, almost golden stone and set tight against two trees exactly like it—and more after each of those, and on and on into the distance. Their branches interlaced with each other in the most elaborate and bewildering patterns. The leaves were painted green and traced with something metallic that glimmered like gold. Long garlands of ivy were chiseled into the trunks of the trees—all of them twirling around in the same direction. Daniel became completely lost in the design of the branches, which he now saw contained small sculptures of birds, animals, and insects. He walked slowly up to the tree, clothes still dripping, and reached out his hand to touch a leaf, half expecting it to be soft and thin. It was rigid and cold. "Wow," he said in awe.

He turned around to help Freya and took a moment to examine the well—the Western Well. It was carved out of the same stone as the wall but in a much different style. Swirling shapes rose up from the ground in a short pillar of water and continued seamlessly into a large iron frame, which rose above the well's rim and supported a pulley mechanism.

There was a wet slopping noise from inside the well, and Freya appeared from the darkness. He helped her up with an effort and she toppled onto the stone pavement behind him. He couldn't stop himself from grinning as she did a double take at the wall of stone trees.

"Can you believe this?" he asked her in amazement. "An underground city! I wasn't sure I believed it but it's here! Look at this wall, it just goes on and on! And these . . . just *look*!"

Buildings rose up on the other side of them, about ten storeys high, carved out of the stone, with strips of intricate tracery around

the doors, windows, and roof. In the spaces between, Daniel and
Freya could glimpse more buildings—some grander, some smaller,
but all of them displaying a wealth of fascinating details. More of
the silver lanterns could be seen being used as streetlamps and
houselights.

A hand tugged Daniel's elbow. Freya gripped his arm and
pointed a shaky finger.

Approaching them was a scowling man holding a long, glis-
tening sword. There was a scraping sound behind them and they
turned to find themselves surrounded by three more men drawing similar weapons. All four faces were pale and almost deathly
grey. Features like eyebrows, noses, and chins all blended into the
pallid skin, making the faces look oddly similar.

"What should we do?" Freya whispered.

"Just wait and see what they say. Don't worry, I won't let them
hurt you."

One of the men opened his mouth to speak, when the grunting and muttering of Ecgbryt was heard behind them. He climbed
out of the well and shook the water from his wet clothing. Swiðgar
came close after. The two knights glared at the circle of guards
around Daniel and Freya.

"We are Ecgbryt and Swiðgar of Oxenaforde with two lifiendes.
We seek Ealdstan the Wise. Is there one who will take us to the
Langtorr?"

One of the guards standing around Daniel and Freya acknowledged the knight's request with a nod. "Well met," he said in a soft
but gruff voice. "I am Breca; I will take you there." He turned and
led them away through an arched passageway between two buildings and out into a wide street.

Freya's and Daniel's heads swiveled in every direction as they
walked down the streets of the underground city, trying to take
in as many of the amazing details as possible. Ecgbryt watched

them and smiled. "Welcome to Niðergeard, young lifiendes," he said proudly. "Perhaps the greatest of the hidden wonders of the world! I have heard of far-off kings, who spoke in tongues now dead, living in sandy kingdoms who have built strange and enormous structures to their own memory. I have heard tell of Elfin palaces in twilight kingdoms whose citizens have harnessed the power of the moon just as the *Laedenware* have tamed the rivers to their towns' purposes. There are people on the far side of this strange world who live in rooms of parchment, wear gossamer robes, and kneel to eat. There are dark men who live in forests with trees so vast and large that the sky is never seen. But were all of these far-off brothers and sisters to arrive here, in this hallowed place, they would think their homes small and their birthplaces of little consequence to the might and glory of Niðergeard, the *Slaepera-Burgh*!

"See that building there?" Ecgbryt continued passionately. "Carved out of the solid rock; no stone-joiner ever found a day's work at that place! And see there, that tall walkway which stretches near across the city, the work of twice twenty years' worth of solid labor—a hundred men, every day!"

"Did you hear that, Freya?" Daniel said, leaning towards her but not taking his eyes off the spectacle of a thin stone bridge that arced clear across the city. "It's absolutely amazing!"

The structures were truly incredible, although they had apparently needed repairs over the centuries. New stone looked incongruous against that much older. The streets and stairways were bowed and worn away, drooping in the centre like warm butter. Here and there, in the doorways and windows, Freya could see people watching them—their faces pale and drab. Living underground for hundreds and hundreds of years, their skin had turned almost grey, and their clothing was faded and worn.

"Why does everyone look so tired and . . . sad?" Freya asked.

"Is that it? Is that the Langtorr?" Daniel exclaimed, the unfamiliar word clinging to his tongue. He pointed to a massive pillar that rose before them, carved out of one of the enormous natural supports to the underground plain. Only the lower part of the tower could be seen in the light of the city's flickering torches, but its top must have reached to the roof of the underground land. The light of flickering torches could be seen through chiseled windows rising above the city, hanging in the air like a giant column of rectangular stars.

"Yes," said Ecgbryt, "also called the Tall Tower. It is the heart of Niðergeard, designed firstly to hold the people of Niðergeard, should the town be invaded."

"Have they ever had to use it?" Freya asked.

"To my knowledge, no. The walls have always been sufficient to repel attackers."

"But why is all of this here? Why have an underground city?"

"Niðergeard exists to provide service to all the knights and warriors who sleep in these isles."

"What do you mean?"

"There are times when tunnels need to be strengthened or closed or better hidden, when armour and arms must be polished, horses shod, and so on. A myriad of responsibilities. Those in Niðergeard have dedicated their lives to these small acts. That is their sacrifice."

"How many sleeping knights are there?"

"Very many. I do not know the number, for many more would have been laid down since we went to sleep."

Daniel and Freya, the knights, and their escort walked a path into the middle of the city, gradually approaching the Tall Tower. After passing through a particularly narrow alley, they entered a large open plaza. Ahead of them they could see the base of the Langtorr, as well as the entrance across a plain, smooth floor paved mostly with white marble, paths of red and green marble tracing a complicated, seamless pattern that wove dizzyingly in and out of itself. Daniel tried to follow it but had to look up as he started to sway and lose his balance, staggering. He laughed and quickened his step to join the others.

Freya noticed one building near the Langtorr—a squat, circular building about twelve feet high. It was not ornately carved or adorned in any way; its rock was roughly hewn and reinforced with iron bracers. Atop it stood five stout, simple columns supporting a flat, stone roof.

"What is that?" Freya asked, squinting at a gleaming line of gold. "What's inside it?"

Caged in by the columns was one of the weirdest and most haunting objects that either Daniel or Freya had ever seen. Supported by a chain dangling from the roof and lit from underneath, it looked like some sort of ornate, golden horn. It started at about the width of an arm at the bottom, but the barrel gradually widened at the top where it ended in an odd animal-head shape. It had large, completely circular eyes and a blunt, sharp-toothed snout that opened up wide, as if the thing were shouting.

Swiðgar saw Daniel and Freya staring at the object and gave a small smile. "It is the Great Carnyx, æðelingas," he said. "The trumpet that will wake all the knights and summon them to battle. It is the most guarded and valued item in Niðergeard—perhaps in all of the isle."

They walked slowly past the Carnyx and came at last to the large, ornate doorway of the Langtorr. A huge stairway made of curved steps proceeded from the entrance. Every step was lit by a silver lantern that illumined the path to a thick archway containing many smaller arches, each one nestled inside the other, bearing wonderful designs. The farthest inside the arch bore an interlocking zigzag pattern, the next featured a row of stylised bird heads, the next a row of animals, then a row of warriors standing guard, and finally on the outside arch, a row of mythical beasts.

Two alcoves were tucked into the massive pillars on either side of the doorway. Here stood two guards with hair so white it almost glowed and pulled hard along their scalps to fall in long, thick braids, which were bound with gold circlets to their shoulders. Full beards jutted out from their chins and forked in the middle to reveal bands of twisted gold around their necks. They wore no armour, but their broad chests and massive arms had a heavy, immovable firmness. Here and there on the chest, arms, and legs, small, delicate whorled patterns were traced in faint blue dye. This, together with their blanched skin, made Freya believe, unquestioningly, that these guards were exquisite carvings—so she couldn't help gasping when they started to move.

5

The pale-faced escorts of the party marched wordlessly up to the two ghastly guards. Low, unfamiliar words were uttered and the stony guards silently moved to one side, allowing the company to pass. Daniel and Freya mounted the steps behind the knights, feeling very insignificant amongst all the ancient grandeur. Passing under the magnificent archway, Daniel stared awestruck at the huge metal doors that stood open against the walls of the inner forecourt; they seemed to be made of large plates of sheet metal, decorated with climbing wrought-iron swirls and whorls, all layered on top of each other, giving the effect of a massive wall of fire, frozen in metal.

Beyond the doors was a narrow greeting chamber. There was a red woven rug on the floor, a gleaming chandelier made from the silver lanterns, and several tall, dark tapestries on the walls. Though they were dark with age, Freya could just make out the positions of a few of the larger figures, one of them climbing a rock face, one of them in a boat pitched at a dramatic angle.

The party passed through this room and strode towards a stairway that flung two flights of stairs out and up around the circumference of the inner wall. Daniel and Freya craned their necks to try to see the ceiling, but the hollow core of Langtorr ran straight up through the centre; the stairs rose with it, spiraling up and up like two paper ribbons in a tornado.

As they marveled at the ever-ascending steps, they became aware of someone walking down them. A tall, slender, willowy woman so graceful she seemed to drift on a cushion of air. She wore a long bright-green dress under a heavier dark-green robe edged with silver thread. The colours of her clothes reminded Freya of a tree budding in the spring. She looked neither old nor young. Her hair was auburn with dark streaks of rich brown and was swept back, secured at the back of her head with pins of gold, then left to fall about her neck and shoulders. Silver gleamed at her neck and waist. She wore a belt of finely polished silver discs and a weblike necklace made from many twining strands of the same metal.

Her face was pale, but her lips were a deep red, which seemed darker against the alabaster whiteness of her skin. Her eyes were large and sad looking, as if remembering a sorrow from a distant time. She paused a few steps from the bottom of the staircase and crossed her arms, tucking her hands into her sleeves. Swiðgar and Ecgbryt knelt in front of her. Daniel and Freya, unsure what to do, stood behind the knights, their hearts pounding in anticipation, overwhelmed with awe. Daniel thought her face the most beautiful he had ever seen—it filled his mind and made him forget, for a few seconds, all the things he had gone through to get here. Freya's awe was sharp and felt like a cold wind blowing through her; for some reason the woman's grandeur and self-possession made her afraid.

"Greetings, Modwyn, Richéweard," said Swiðgar.

"Well betide you, *niðercwen*," said Ecgbryt humbly.

The stately lady in green curtsied. "You are welcome in Niðergeard, Swiðgar and Ecgbryt, noble knights both. Rise." A servant woman in a velvet dress appeared from a doorway beneath one of the stairs, approached her mistress, and handed her a silver pitcher and a small cupped dish. Stepping forward, Modwyn poured some golden liquid into the bowl and handed it to Swiðgar. He raised it to his lips and drained it while looking Modwyn in the eye. Taking the bowl from him, she refilled it and gave it to Ecgbryt. He likewise emptied it and handed it back.

Modwyn's eyes then flitted to Daniel and Freya as the two knights rose to their feet. Her expression remained stern and serious, but her eyes seemed to grow more intense and lively.

"My lady, I bring before you Daniel Tully and Freya Reynolds, two lifiendes who have awoken us. We have escorted them here to beg your protection and petition your counsel."

"I accept their charge," Modwyn said in a low, emotionless voice. "Daniel and Freya," she continued, turning her eyes to them, "do you accept my hospitality?"

Daniel and Freya did not speak. For some reason everything felt as if it was happening a long way away, and to someone else. They looked to the knights.

"Children, this is Modwyn, the ward and protectress of Niðergeard. It is her constant and capable hand that ensures the safe and easy governance of this land. She is asking if you wish to have her protection."

Daniel looked back to Modwyn and managed to force out, "Yes, please."

Freya looked to Modwyn and blurted, desperately, "We need to go home now, please!"

Modwyn regarded Freya. "In time," she said so softly that they were not sure she had said it at all.

"I welcome you," Modwyn said, stepping past the two knights to stand before them. "Our doors are open and our fires high. Find rest and safety here." She poured another bowl of drink and offered it to Daniel. He took it uncertainly and sniffed it. He was met with a sweet smell and tingling sensation in his nose.

"It is well," Swiðgar assured him. "Drink."

It was sweet like honey, slightly fizzy, and had a spicy flavor, which pricked at his throat and excited his stomach. There was also something in it that warmed Daniel and made him shiver slightly.

He returned the bowl to Modwyn and she filled it again and gave it to Freya. Looking into the bowl, Freya saw the shimmering dance of refracted golden light, which showed a deep golden hue. The scent made Freya's nose tingle and warmed her face. She stifled a sneeze.

"You are both wet and chilled," Modwyn said, reclaiming the bowl. "Please dry yourselves and take some rest. We will talk when you have taken some sleep."

At the mention of the word "sleep," Freya felt herself becoming very drowsy. "If you please, miss," she said hesitantly, "we would like to go home."

"I understand," Modwyn said, smiling a thin smile that failed to light her dark eyes. "But you have come very far and will have farther to return. That will be for Ealdstan to decide. For now, it would give me great pleasure to provide some food, dry clothes, and a bed for you both. Will you accept these offerings?"

Freya did not answer, only nodded.

"Okay . . . ," Daniel said, his head starting to swim and his eyelids becoming extremely heavy.

Modwyn inclined her head. "I am glad."

Two servants appeared from behind Daniel and Freya, entering so quietly that they were unnoticed. They were dressed almost to the knees in dark-green shirts, bound around the waist with bronze belts that also held up loose light-green leggings. Both had light-brown hair and broad faces. "This is Cnafa and Cnapa," Modwyn said. "They will fetch and provide you with everything you might require. Now they will show you to your rooms."

"Will Swiðgar and Ecgbryt be here when we wake up?" Daniel asked.

"Yes, assuredly," answered Modwyn.

"What about Ealdstan?" Freya asked. "Will we see him?"

The two knights smiled encouragingly. "Go take your rest," said Swiðgar. "We will meet again once you have been refreshed."

Daniel and Freya followed Cnafa and Cnapa very sleepily up one of the spiral staircases. Below them they watched Modwyn gesture to Swiðgar and Ecgbryt and lead them off through a towering doorway beneath the opposite set of stairs.

They were led up to the second level and down a hallway that ran along the tower wall. The high windows gave them a view of the tower's courtyard, and the city of Niðergeard.

"This will be your room, young master," either Cnafa or Cnapa said to Daniel, opening a large wooden door to a spacious bedroom.

"And this," said the other servant, walking one door farther down the hallway, "will be your room, young mistress."

"You will find dry clothes and linens on the table, as well as clean water in the jug," Daniel's servant informed him. "May your sleep be guided, your body rested, your mind restored, and your soul renewed."

Daniel and Freya said their thanks and, before stepping into their rooms, glanced at each other from down the hall.

"*Scared,*" mouthed Freya.

"Me too," Daniel replied, as the two servants pushed them each into their rooms.

CHAPTER FIVE

A Leaf from Another Forest

---- 1 ----

Now ...

Freya trudged through the wet streets, walking so fast that her shins hurt. As she approached St. Michael and All Angels, she saw Daniel, looking agitated, leave the church and run down the path. He looked up, recognised her, and raised his arm—in warning?

He opened his mouth, as if to shout, and at the same time put a hand on the low wooden gate that led out into the street. He pushed it open and, with his foot raised to take a step forward, seemed to stumble, and disappeared into thin air.

Freya yelped and jumped backwards. *Danger* was the only thought in her mind. She wanted to run, but didn't know where. Daniel had been taken from the open air, underneath the rickety wooden arch of the lych-gate—she didn't think that was possible. What was to say that she wouldn't be as well? She became paralysed. Any step in any direction could be a step across a threshold that might send her into peril. In full panic, Freya's mind closed up and terror filled her. She fell into a crouch and buried her head in her arms.

She was aware of a sound growing around her, which built and trickled down her spine. It was laughter. Raising her head, she found herself looking up at the vicious figures of two yfelgópes, their lips curled in a sneer around their needle-like teeth. Freya, now more terrified than ever, flinched instinctively away from them, sprawling on the pavement. She closed her eyes and covered her face.

"Back!" she heard someone shout. "Back, you devils!" There were the sounds of a scuffle, a roar of pain, and then nothing. Freya felt a hand on her shoulder and her heart chilled.

"Freya? Is that you?"

She fought to control her breathing and opened her eyes. It was Professor Stowe.

"Freya, good heavens! Are you mixed up in this?"

She opened her mouth and tried to speak.

"You're in bad shape," Professor Stowe said. "Come with me. Stand close."

She realised it was raining. Stowe shook out an umbrella and held it above her. Clinging to his arm, she huddled close and they walked away from the church.

He led her back down Banbury Road to his rooms in Norham Gardens. "We're not staying here," he said. "I just need to check on something first. Here, take this and dry yourself off."

He handed Freya a towel and left the hallway. Freya pushed the towel through her hair—when had it become wet?—and looked around the small hallway. There was an engraving on the wall behind the door of a large tree, intricately detailed, its smallest leaves described. It spread its branches into the heavens, as if it were holding the sky in place or pushing it away from the ground.

Professor Stowe came back and led her out of the room and down the staircase. But instead of leaving through the front door, they descended another short set of stairs and exited through a back door. This placed them in a narrow, overgrown garden.

"Where are we going?" Freya asked.

"To a special place—the Old Observatory. I stay in this house by design, not chance. This house contains one of only a few routes into a forgotten building, which is now an important meeting place for an important group of individuals."

"I—I just want to go back home," Freya said, and meant it. She wanted nothing more than to crawl into her own bed and not to come out again, ever.

"I'm afraid it's not as simple as that."

"Why?"

"Like your friend Daniel, you are just on the cusp of falling out of this world. I tried to reach him, but I was too late. There are forces that want to push you out of this world. Have you ever . . . experienced . . . anything like that before?" He shot her a sideways look.

Freya kept her eyes on the pavement in front of her.

"Freya? I'm talking about the feeling that you may have fallen through into another world?"

She wanted to tell him—had wanted to tell someone for so long, but all this time she'd stayed silent . . . she couldn't.

"I suspected as much. Please do come with me. We can help you."

Freya swallowed and ducked through the wild foliage that grew in their path. They came to a thin wooden door, warped with age, which hung in a narrow gap between two crumbling brick walls. Stowe took a key from his pocket and unlocked a padlock that hung from a shiny latch. Then he went through.

Freya paused instinctively, took a breath, and moved through the doorway—then back out again, and in and out several more times after that. This didn't make her feel much more comfortable in the circumstances, but it didn't make her feel worse.

She found herself in a small courtyard where tall hedges blocked nearly everything out of sight except for a small swatch of the sky above them. Professor Stowe had disappeared.

"Here we—Freya?" his voice called. His stepped back into view from between two of the hedges. "It's just over here."

She followed him down a red-bricked path that was almost completely grown over with moss and ivy and then was confronted by a squat door, stained black, set into a low arch. Professor Stowe searched his pockets for a dead bolt key and unlocked it. He stepped through and waited for Freya.

Freya stood rooted to the spot. She fought to keep the flood of panic from overwhelming her again.

"Freya? It's okay," Professor Stowe said, holding out his hand. "Come on through."

With a visible effort, Freya lifted her leaden feet and stepped through the doorway. Stowe was just about to close the door behind her when she hissed, "Wait!" and tugged at his sleeve. This was too important, she felt, to be embarrassed about.

She ducked out of the doorway, looked up at the sky, and crossed back in. She repeated this three more times and stood uncertainly inside the doorway.

"Okay," she said.

"Are you alright?" Stowe asked her, less concerned than amused.

"Yes," Freya replied, feeling calmer.

"Good. Come on upstairs, then."

They walked down a short hallway with a claustrophobically low ceiling and came to a cold, square room that contained an iron spiral staircase. Freya felt a chill and looked up—the room rose several stories and finished in darkness. There were narrow, dirty windows in the walls that let in the last light of the evening.

"Not far now," Professor Stowe said, mounting the staircase with Freya behind him.

"This is the Old Observatory?"

"Yes. This is a private place. That is, the university owns it, but I'd think the administrators have completely forgotten about its existence. It was appropriated many years ago by people of . . . our *cause* as a secret meeting room where we could discuss action against those who wish to invade this sphere."

Freya's hand tightened on the rail and she stopped. "I can't do this," she said. "I won't be of any help. I'm sorry. You don't want me."

Professor Stowe turned and said in a low, comforting voice, "Don't worry—it's unlikely that you will be asked to join our group. I only asked you here so that you can further help us with what we know—perhaps fill in some blanks—and most of all to keep you safe. We *can* keep you safe."

Freya started up the stairs again, reluctantly. They rose three storeys to a door that stood open, letting out a warm, electric-yellow glow.

Stepping through the doorway, Freya was met with a warm blast of air and the rich, heady aroma of something burning in a fireplace. From the front hall, she could hear a soft susurrus of people talking in the front room.

"There is a meeting already in progress, so come through here," Stowe said, and led Freya into the kitchen. "Put the kettle on while I tell them who you are. I shall return shortly," Stowe said, leaving.

Freya filled the kettle at the sink and then replaced it in its holder and turned it on. The front room, adjoining the kitchen, was silent. From where she stood, she couldn't see into it and didn't want to. She was already feeling very self-conscious.

When the kettle boiled, she filled the mug and stirred it with a teaspoon from the dish drainer. There was a small refrigerator below the counter and she opened it to find that it contained a single bottle of milk in an old-fashioned glass bottle. She sniffed it—it seemed fine—and poured a little into her tea.

Professor Stowe returned. "Are you ready to meet the Society?"

"You're a society?"

"Yes—the Society of Concerned Individuals. It's a deliberately vague and eccentric title. This way, if you will . . ."

Steeling herself, Freya followed Stowe and stepped into a large octagonal drawing room. It was fairly well furnished—a large Turkish rug lay on the floor and thick drapes hung on the windows. Where there weren't windows on the walls, there were framed prints. On one side of the room there was a wide, shallow fireplace that was cheerfully burning coal and warming the room nicely. There was a circle of mismatched armchairs clustered around a low coffee table. Four of the chairs were occupied by three men and one woman who stared intently at Freya as she entered. She smiled sheepishly.

"Please, take a seat," Professor Stowe said, indicating the one closest to Freya. She lowered herself into it and huddled over her mug of tea.

"Let me make introductions, first of all," said Stowe, settling into his own chair. "The gentleman on my right," he said, indicating an elderly gent in his seventies who wore a full head of white hair and a tweed suit, "is First Lieutenant Gerrard Cross, retired, a former lecturer in British Mythology—and a specialist in Scottish ballads.

"Sitting next to him is Ms. Leigh Sinton." A thin, dark-haired woman in her forties wearing a dark-green jumper gave a small wave and then very primly and unnecessarily straightened her tan skirt. "She's something of an all-rounder with an enthusiasm for archaeology and is a tireless mountain trekker.

"Next is Mr. Wood, though I'm sure that he'll insist that you call him Brent."

"S'right," grunted a well-built, heavy-set man in a dark jacket and grey waistcoat. His face was stern and his lips gave the impression of being buttoned in the centre, but his cheeks glowed attractively.

"There's nobody who knows the university like him. He's currently a porter at Jesus College. And finally, there is the Reverend Borough. He is fully ordained, but attached to the college—not the church."

A man in his late thirties, nearly bald with traces of red hair above his ears, gave an awkward bow to Freya. "Peter, please."

"And finally, there's me, your good professor." He gave her a warm smile. "Although while you are here, you may address me as Felix."

Everyone was looking at her expectantly so Freya gave a small wave and introduced herself. "Freya Reynolds, hi."

"Freya is a childhood friend of Daniel Tully, the boy I was following and who, I regret to inform you now, has been taken."

The room reacted to this news in dismay. The elderly Mr. Cross pursed his lips and clucked his tongue; Ms. Sinton wrung her hands and exclaimed, "Oh dear!" Brent Wood slowly shook his head side to side, and the reverend closed his eyes and soundlessly moved his lips.

"In fact, she was with him when it happened," continued Stowe. "I say she was *with* him, though it would be more accurate to say that she was *near* him. He was coming to see her when he stepped across a lych-gate and just . . . vanished. Do I have that right?"

This last sentence was directed at Freya. She nodded in agreement.

Ms. Sinton leaned forward. "This is no doubt cause for concern—and Felix will give us specific details later—but he told us just now that he believed you had been, for want of a better word, 'taken' when you were younger. Is this true?"

Freya's eyes dropped to her tea and looked into the steam

swirling up from it. Then she started to retell, in a halting voice, the lies and half-truths that she had told the police and all the psychiatrists over the years. She made sure to include all of the rehearsed halts, pauses, and stutters she had tailored into it.

"When we were younger," she said, "Daniel and I, we found a tunnel that we explored. When we tried to leave, we couldn't find our way out again. We were missing for almost a month. We wandered through tunnels underground, we licked water that dripped from rocks, we ate insects sometimes, and then we were found—up north somewhere. I don't remember where."

The group looked at her with blank faces.

"And that's it," Freya said.

"You'll forgive me, my dear," said the stout porter, Wood, "but I believe that is far from 'it,' as you say!"

Freya was shocked by this outright attack. She automatically started replaying another side of the story she usually held in reserve to make people think that they had earned her trust. "There were people, I think, and they helped us, maybe, but—but I don't remember much about them."

"And I say it was nothing of the sort!"

"Please, Brent," said Rev. Borough. "Don't antagonize the girl. I'm sure I would not wish to open up to a group of strangers about events that most would think me mad for relating. She simply doesn't know to trust us yet. Perhaps we should let her rest and she can explain more when she's recovered."

"Thank you," Freya said, spying an out. "I'm just—there's a lot that's happened recently, with Daniel, and I don't think I can talk about it yet. Please, tell me, what do you—I mean, the Society—do?"

"Lt. Cross," said Professor Stowe, rising, "perhaps you'd like to give our guest a short—very short, mind—account of our history. I have a matter I must attend to. Excuse me." He left the room.

"Well," Lt. Cross began, "the Society was formed in April of

1917, when Elsie Wright and Frances Mitchell began meeting regularly with Sir Wilfred Rewlbury, the head of the Royal Society of Biology, and, in May of that year, Nils Ogred, a Swiss botanist. Initially they met in a small tearoom in Bradford, which was convenient for charting incidents in the area. They were, over time, joined by Robert Trebor, the historian and lecturer, and Arthur Rutherford, Lord Sansweete. In August of 1919, Nils Ogred moved to Holland, and the group relocated, meeting in the chapter house of Westbury Cathedral. They were joined by Rodney Woodrue and Nassar Rassan in October 1921, after Lord Sansweete left in June of 1920. In September 1926, the group was on hiatus following Sir Rewlbury's son's disappearance. Once that situation was resolved they started meeting again, but this time in the Bury St. Edmunds Town Hall. They were joined by gentleman scientist Rian Buford, Clark Sassoon, and Lady Gail Nyman. It was at this time that rifts began to form, and in July 1928, the group first split, with Wright, Woodrue, Rassan, and Sassoon meeting on Thursdays of alternating weeks, and the rest meeting, from November of that year, on the first and third Mondays of every week at the private library of Joseph—"

Freya wasn't following any of this. She was so desperately tired that for a few moments she couldn't decide if it was more polite to excuse herself or just fall quietly asleep. "I'm sorry, I'm not really—I think it would be best if I left," she blurted, but made no effort to move, or even lift her head.

"—Wimbourne, twenty-eighth Earl of Winton. The following year, February to be specific, was when Mitchell's faction began their private royal presentations, at that time before George V. He allowed Mitchell's group use of the Royal Gallery's Eastern Rooms, which, in March of 1931, was abandoned for the Gallery Room of the Royal Gardens' Eastern Offices. Meanwhile, the Wright Society—"

Freya thought that she protested once more at this point, but she didn't have time to recall what she'd said because the next instant she was asleep.

2

The trip up to Dunbeath, the largest village next to Morven, took just a couple hours and was a scenic, costal drive. As he came closer to Morven, the sky became overcast, threatening rain. The clouds were so dark and deep—almost purple, in fact—that one could almost think it was starting to be evening. Alex looked at the dashboard clock; it read 9:47 a.m.

Instead of finding a place in the village to park, he turned inland and looked for the farm. Farmers were more tied into the area, not just in terms of community but of the land as well. He came across a group of small buildings near a sign that read Bainabruich. He pulled the Land Rover up a dirt driveway, killed the ignition, and let himself in through a cattle gate. After knocking and receiving no reply at the front door, he circled around the house to the large open barn.

Through the doors in the back he could see a tractor moving across one of the fields. He spotted the path to the field and started along it. When the man in the tractor saw him, he turned off his engine and climbed out of the cab.

"Hello," Alex said, reaching into his pocket and pulling out a wallet that he had stuffed his police badge into. "My name is Alex Simpson. I'm with the Northern Constabulary," the truth; "I work in the Special Crimes Unit," the lie.

"Oh, aye," the farmer said cautiously, reaching into his jacket pocket for a tobacco pouch and a packet of Rizlas.

"Can I ask your name, sir?"

"Rab Duthie." He stuck out his hand.

Alex shook it. "My department deals with crime patterns by

location and sociological region. I wonder if you wouldn't mind answering a question or two about the area."

The farmer licked his cigarette paper and nodded.

"Grand," Alex said, pulling out his notebook, more to stall for time than anything else. All that nonsense about worming your way into the affections of the local folk by handing out cigarettes and making sly comments was pure fantasy—something just to keep the mystery serials on TV moving along. The farmers he'd grown up around weren't that gormless. He was going to have to blag his way through and hope that his officiousness carried him to where he needed to be.

"There have been reports of animals missing in the area. Anything of your own gone walkabouts?"

Duthie lit his roll-up and took a puff, squinting as he thought. "Nothing missing, as such. But there have been some . . . breakages. Vandalism, ye ken."

Alex scribbled in his notebook. "Where did this occur?"

"East Fold," he said, gesturing. "Hedge been flattened."

"The hedge?"

"Aye. Flattened right down to the ground. Torn up places, but mostly"—he made a squashing motion with his palms—"had to put up some planks to stop the sheep all from wandering awa'."

"That's odd. Could we go an' have a look?" Alex asked, looking out across the field.

"Sure, nae problem. Hop on." Rab Duthie started up the tractor and they rolled off, Alex perched on the footstep, holding on to the cab

After some maneuvering around dirt tracks and muddy paths, they came to a long thick hedge that must have been, Alex judged, at least a hundred years old. It was only about five feet high, but over four feet wide. The tractor shuddered to a stop and Alex hopped down.

"Ye can see it there," said Duthie, climbing down and discarding his cigarette and pointing to a gap in the hedge. "I no ken how it happened. Too narrow for any car or tractor—and I've seen both get stuck trying to travel through thinner—in addition to there bein' no tracks. No animal I know of would have the power tae do it. Except an elephant, mebbe."

Alex poked around a little but found nothing peculiar. "You really have no idea what did this?"

The farmer looked at him for a second and then shrugged and shook his head. He stuck his hands in his pockets.

Which meant that he did have some idea, but that he wasn't willing to share it.

"Anything else odd in the area?"

"Weel, there's been carjackings. Joyriding and the like. It's been awhile since we've had that up here," Rab Duthie said, looking off into the distance, his voice getting high, stressed. "It's like a wee crime wave up here. Been thievings, fights most nights down at the pubs, even the quiet ones. People are fashed—right desperate, ye ken? Spirits are low. We've had a bad season—nae enough rain or sunlight. Everything ye put in the ground comes up weak and yellow, if at all, and that gets ye doon, natural, but folks took it hard this year. Some farmers hae kilt themselves and done tried kilt themselves. Children. Children done kilt themselves. Teenagers with their lives ahead of them—" Duthie paused and spat on the ground, twice. His voice was getting low and raw now. Alex said nothing.

"Their lives ahead of them and they can no see a way for'ard. More afeared of life than they are of death. Every one of them is a blow, even the ones that pull through. It gets to you. It mounts up in your soul and you find yourself looking at a bottle of pills or a rafter in the barn, and you think, weel . . . weel mebbe . . ."

Duthie cleared his throat noisily and spat again. He didn't look like he felt like saying any more after that.

"Well," Alex said eventually. "It seems to me as if you have more problems than just a gap in your hedge."

Duthie forced a laugh.

"What do you think is causing it?" Alex asked.

The farmer turned his head.

"Crime, suicide, depression, violence, drunkenness, vandalism . . . and this gap in your hedge. To you, they all seem connected. What's causing these things?"

Duthie turned to stare Alex straight in the eyes. His sturdy, weathered frame swayed slightly in the brisk morning air. "Aye, I have a ken of what's causin' this—this atmosphere of hate and fear."

"And?"

"You would nae believe me!" Duthie shouted, almost angry in his desperation.

"Try me."

"The De'il!"

Duthie seemed shocked to hear himself say the words out loud. He stood, trembling. The Devil.

"Aye, now we're getting somewhere," Alex said, grinning.

Duthie turned to look at Alex out of the corner of his eye. "You don't think I'm crazy?"

"Not at all," Alex said. "I think you're clever and brave to say that."

Duthie nearly broke down completely. His eyes became watery and he had to look away. "My wife—she dusnae get up most days. Says she can feel the presence of evil here—like a giant hand that's pushing everyone doon."

"Who hereabouts—or in the village perhaps—would I go to find out more about this?" Alex asked. "A town official? Mayor? Priest? Wise old woman?"

Duthie pushed at his cheekbones with his palms. "Rector," he said, clearing his throat. "Rector Maccanish. He's your man."

"Where will I find him?" Alex asked.

"Down the kirk. I'll tak' ye to him," Duthie said, climbing into the tractor once more.

"If it is the De'il," he said before he started the engine, "is there anythin' a man can do about it?"

"Of course there is," Alex answered. "That's why I'm here."

3

"Oh no, not again."

Sitting upright, Daniel looked around. Everything was different. He was now in a meadow covered with lush green grass that stretched out, vast, flat, and empty, in all directions. Ahead of him, just visible on the flat horizon, was a thick green line between the sky and the plain. A forest?

He twisted around. Behind him, the ground seemed to slope up slowly, over the miles, and far, far into the distance rose an enormous mountain. It was so far away that it was actually rather hard to see—it blended in almost perfectly with the sky, so that only the edges and top could be traced. It rose to a single peak and its sides flowed down smooth and straight. It was as if someone had poured an enormous pile of sugar out onto the landscape.

But that was it—there was nothing else around him, not a hill, not a bush, not a tree stump. The sun in the sky above him seemed massive and that, along with the mountain, gave him the feeling that he was now inside of a larger world than the one he had been in just a few moments ago. This thought—that he was in a different world—a different planet—made his stomach lurch. He stood and scanned the horizon, looking for any detail at all, but there were just those few elements: the plain, the forest, the mountain, the sky, and the sun. And each of these was so absurdly simple, so . . . iconic, as if a child had drawn them.

He stopped turning and listened. There was the sound of a gentle wind blowing past his ears, but nothing more.

"Hello?" he asked out loud.

There was only silence.

Well, there was no point in staying in one place. He had two options now—the mountain or the forest. He chose the forest. At the very least there would be some sort of basic shelter against the sky, and perhaps food.

He started walking.

After more than an hour of walking, the forest didn't seem any closer, nor the mountain any farther. Looking to the sky he saw that the sun had moved, but not by much, not as much as should have. Living on the street had given him a well-tuned sense of time of day. This was undoubtedly a different world. He had suspected this from the start, from a dozen almost indefinable differences in the air, horizon, gravity, the distance he was able to see—all these things, differences in constants he had known from birth, added up to a general feeling of unfamiliarity with what was around him.

Where *was* he?

And why was he alone?

Oddly, he didn't feel hungry or tired—well, no more hungry or tired than he did when he came here. It was something in the air that felt nourishing—or maybe sustaining was the correct word. There was a fairly stiff wind, but he felt warm. He had taken off his heavy jacket for the first time in months. Then he unslung his sword from his shoulder and fitted it around his waist. He didn't feel the need to hide it now. In fact, it was probably better that anyone he came across *did* see it.

Perhaps it was only *his* sense of time that was distorted, and not the world's. He counted silently in his head and then out loud. He measured that against the steps he was taking and the progress that he didn't seem to be making. Everything he was doing seemed to be normal and easiest explained by the fact that he was somewhere very vast.

And where was that? Another planet? Another dimension? Could he be in his own mind—a hallucination? Perhaps he had been hit by a car and was lying in a coma somewhere. Maybe what he was experiencing was only a representation in his mind of what was really going on.

The steady regularity of his footfalls started to entrance him and his mind started to idle, not really thinking much of anything. After a time, he was aware that he was holding something—the slip of paper he'd been given in the church. It fluttered in his hand, spinning gently in the wind. It seemed an ordinary slip of paper, but . . . what was written on it? Was there anything on it? If there was, then he felt he should be able to read it, but he couldn't. Perhaps it was blank.

He twirled it between his fingertips. It was comforting to him.

Hour after hour passed and he was gratified to see that he was definitely getting closer now. Not only had the green brushstroke along the horizon grown thicker, it now nearly encompassed his whole field of vision. This was encouraging to him, even though he doubted that he had traveled much more than half of the distance necessary. The sun, he could see now, was descending directly behind him, gently warming his neck and shoulders. He judged it would hit the mountain around the time that he reached the forest.

Evening, in other words, just as he met the border of two different places. The phrase *like a pillar of smoke through a field of fog* went through his head. He began to feel strongly—though acknowledging he had no reason to—that he would meet someone once he reached the forest. There would be a *coincidence*.

He started to pepper his pace with bursts of jogging, eager to get the meeting under way, if it was to happen, or just to reach shelter if it wasn't.

The bottommost edge of the sun touched the very tip of the mountain, which was now very clear against the sky, being a dark purple. Daniel felt he would be able to say to himself that he was "almost there." He could now pick out individual trees from among the leafy mass, but they seemed huge, like the redwoods he'd seen in pictures.

A couple more hours—the timescale was making him feel anxious now—and he was about throwing distance from the first trees of the forest, which looked to be fairly tightly packed. The sun was low enough that the mountain seemed to be wearing it as a halo. It threw a long shadow across the plain, overtaking him and making him cold once more. He put his coat back on.

Daniel approached the forest cautiously, on the lookout for any sign of someone besides himself. His eyes searched the landscape for anything else in this place that wasn't grass or trees, and he found it in a speck of white that moved along the base of the tree line, far to the left of his vision. It was a cloud of dust rising from the ground and speeding towards him. Ahead of the cloud was a frantically moving speck of light grey that occasionally flashed white.

There was a moist, nostalgic smell of decaying leaves coming from the forest. The setting sun, now bisected and peering out from both sides of the mountain, displayed two orange sections that bathed the trees in a reddish light, making the treescape eerily beautiful. It reminded Daniel of another wall of incredibly beautiful trees . . .

A feeling of nervous anticipation grew inside of Daniel as the white fluttering shape grew nearer—it was a person on horseback. Daniel stopped near one of the trees and waited for the rider to catch up to him. He wondered if he should draw his sword.

In this new vast and slow place, he was able to watch the small image grow larger and larger until it slowed and stopped before him. The rider was a man, a young man, on a brilliant white horse.

"Hail," the rider said, halting his magnificent animal.

"Hail," responded Daniel. The two took a moment to study each other.

The rider's face was fair and unwrinkled and was wearing a wry grin. He had loose blond hair that was cropped short around the ears and neck and fell forward over his long brow. He was dressed in a loose white shirt that billowed around the chest and shoulders but was gathered up and bound down the forearms to the wrists with ornate bands of cloth that appeared to be woven with gold. He wore dun-coloured leather trousers that stopped just below his knees, and his feet were bare. He sat atop the horse on a blanket that was bordered with intricate patterns. The horse was of a medium size—Daniel had seen bigger—but it had a narrow muzzle and long sinewy legs that made it very fast.

"Thanks be to the king," said the rider. "I truly believe you are he."

Daniel didn't know what to say, so he asked the question most pressing on his mind. "Where am I?"

"You are in Elfland—the Faerie realms, to be specific. And because of that, I cannot speak long. It is important that you mark all that I say. When the sun's last rays vanish, then I will be found, and at that time, we must already be parted."

Elfland? This was probably worse than he imagined. "What's your name?" Daniel asked.

"My name is Kay Marrey. But first, before any more is said—" The rider quickly and effortlessly dismounted. Daniel now saw that he was quite tall, around six and a half feet. He looked back to the horse, reestimating its height. Elfland was taking some getting used to.

Kay took a long stride towards Daniel and snatched his coat from his hands. He started going through the pockets.

"What are you—?"

"I can feel it . . . like a buzzing insect. Ah, here."

Kay reached into the front pocket and pulled out the slip of paper that Daniel had been given. Except now, when Kay held it, Daniel saw it was a leaf. A large yellow oak leaf.

"Where did that come from?" Daniel asked.

Kay Marrey held it upright by the stem, between his thumb and forefinger. "You were given this, yes? In your world. Did you know what it was?"

"At first I thought it was money."

Kay nodded. "It is a leaf of a different wood. It was taken to your world as a way to mark and snare you." Still holding the leaf, he rounded the horse and opened a satchel that was attached to his riding blanket. He drew out a suede leather cloak that was a very light-grey trimmed with white. "I am allowed to give you three gifts for you to keep for as long as you are in this land," Kay announced, unfastening his cloak. "And this is the first," he said, whipping it off his shoulders.

"Thanks," Daniel said, reaching out his hand.

"Wait," Kay said, pulling it back. "Give me your coat first. Take what you need from the pockets."

Daniel did this and then handed his coat over. Kay told him how to fasten the cloak around his neck and then helped him on with his backpack. "How do I look?" Kay asked, pulling on Daniel's coat and holding his arms out for an appraisal.

"Very . . . odd," Daniel replied.

Kay laughed and stuck the leaf Daniel had been given in the pocket of the coat he was now wearing. "Now, listen—this is what you need to know . . ."

Kay put his hands on Daniel's shoulders and looked him in the eyes.

"This place is not like yours—it obeys different rules. The most important of these, for now, is that objects have *ownership*. It is essential that you don't *take* anything that isn't *given* to you—for if you steal something, then that thing will own *you* and not the other way around. For instance, I gave you my cloak. If you had taken it, you would have been beholden to it. Do you understand?"

Daniel nodded slowly.

"Now I may give you your second gift." He held out a sewn-up skin covered in soft fur and laced with intricately woven straps. It was evidently a water container of some sort. "Carry it with you and take just a few sips at a time. It holds more than it appears to."

Daniel removed the stopper and took a gulp from it. He was parched.

"You are about to enter one of the enchanted forests," Kay continued. "If you take anything—a seed, a leaf, a pinecone—and put it into your pocket, you will not be able to return home. If you eat anything—a berry, a fruit, or an animal—then this land will own you, and you won't be able to return home. Do you understand?"

Daniel nodded again, his head starting to spin. What had he fallen into now?

"However, this wood is a friend of my people. One moment, I will introduce you to it."

Saying that, he turned to face the line of trees and started to sing in a different language. When he had finished, the forest seemed less intimidating somehow.

"That's done," said Kay as he turned back to Daniel. "So all you must do, if you need anything, is to ask for it and wait for it to be presented to you. But to do this, you must ask in a respectful way—you must ask in verse."

"In verse?"

"Tunefully. Or, if it's easier for you, in poem. Nothing fancy. Couplets work well. Just so the forest knows that you honour it. But don't ask for anything frivolous, as you may anger it. This applies to everything, even the water with which you are to fill the skin. Everything must be asked for and never just taken."

Daniel's head took another spin. Couplets?

"Fauna: smaller birds can be trusted. Anything larger than a kestrel cannot—and that includes kestrels. Burrowers are honest, but they're stupid, except for foxes, of course—don't talk to the foxes. If you see a fox, ignore it. Bears . . . stay away from bears. Wolves shouldn't be a problem, so long as you stick to the path."

"The path?"

"Ah, the path—thank you for reminding me. When I have left, you must enter the forest and travel until you reach a clearing—any clearing will do. Then ask the forest for whatever you need in the night—food, bedding, a fire. Don't ask for anything until night—you may be seen otherwise. When you are able to see the sun through the trees once more, ask the forest to show you the path to the wood-burner's hut. Follow that path until you get to the wood-burner's hut."

"The wood-burner's hut. Then what?"

"I cannot tell you."

"Why not?"

"Because I do not know."

"Will the wood-burner get me out of this place?"

"I don't know that either."

"So what do you know?"

"Only this—what I am doing now, that which I was told to do, which is far more than those who sent you here will suspect. They sent you here thinking that this world would claim you—these measures will prevent that, so that you may, one day soon, return."

"How do I know that I can trust you?"

"Because I came here at great cost." Kay Marrey looked over his shoulder to the setting sun. Just the tiniest slivers were still visible on either side of the mountain. "A cost that grows greater the longer I stop here."

He reached into a pouch at his belt. "This is my final gift," he said, unfastening a pouch at his belt and handing it to Daniel. Daniel opened it and shook a flat stone about the size of a two-pound coin into his palm. It was a reddish-brown colour and rough. "Keep this in your mouth when you stop to rest or are idle," Kay instructed him. "It bears no enchantment, but those of your kind need such as this if they are to sojourn long in this land. That is all I have to explain or give. Do you have any more questions?"

Daniel turned the stone over in his hand. Questions? Where to begin? "Where are you from, and who sent you here?"

Kay turned and went back to his horse. He brushed its head and nuzzled it affectionately. "I was sent here by the Doubted King of this world who will one day return to rule righteously."

"Is he a good king?"

"Yes, but that doesn't mean he'll be good to you. He does what is right for his kingdom, even if that means that he's hard on his subjects."

"Am I one of his subjects?"

Kay rubbed his cheek against his horse's muzzle and patted its head. "I don't know, are you?"

"If I'm not, why should I do what he wants?"

Kay whispered into his horse's ear and gave it a smack on the rump; it turned and cantered off the way it had come. "Because he's right. No time for more questions," he said, turning and scanning the sky. "Enter the woods quickly now, for I am being pursued by our enemies. Don't exit the woods, no matter in what trouble you see me. Hurry now, your life depends on it. Don't forget—take nothing that is not given!" he called out. "Oh," he added, "and don't talk to dead people!"

Daniel started jogging towards the woods and then remembered that he hadn't heard the answer to one of his questions. "You never told me where you were from!" Daniel shouted.

Kay told him just as he started off at a run along the tree line.

Daniel reached the trunk of a large pine and crouched behind it. He watched Kay speed away from him, running easily. The sun finally set, leaving the sky a dusky pink. Just as Daniel was about to stand, he heard a screech from the sky, which was followed by several more. His eyes flicked upwards and he saw eight large birds, black against the sky, flapping and diving furiously at the small, dark figure.

The black birds—crows, maybe—descended upon Kay, hurling themselves at his back and shoulders. They were like guided missiles with sharpened beaks and talons that clawed at him. Then, opening their wings, they took to the sky, only to swoop down upon their target again. Even at this distance, Daniel could see that his thick coat, which had helped him tough out the cold streets of Oxford, was very quickly and easily ripped into shreds. Kay ducked into the forest, and the birds gave a long piercing cry and followed him in. Then it was silent and still.

Daniel took a breath and stood up. It was getting colder now that the sun was gone, although the sky was still bright. If there was anyone after him, he needed to make some headway into the forest before it got really dark.

And all the time, the words of Kay the Rider echoed in his ears: "I come from the Elves in Exile, who will one day return."

CHAPTER SIX

Lights in the Dark

1

With a start that jerked him nearly upright, Daniel awoke. In less than a second, the details of his dream flew from his memory and he was left with just a vague impression of fear and of falling. He lay in the large bed a moment under the heavy covers. The mattress was hard but not uncomfortable, and the pillows soft and deep.

He rolled onto his back and looked up at the stone ceiling. It was carved in what was becoming his favorite style—with leaves and vines, branches and twigs, insects and small animals. *In an underground world, the only thing available is a lot of stone, and in hundreds of years, with little else except for that around them, they've become very good at using it,* he thought.

His gaze floated around the unfamiliar room and picked out odd features. His eyes became lost for long seconds as they wandered around the spiral pattern of the hanging carpets, before moving on to a stone alcove lined with sitting cushions, a brass stand holding a funny sort of clay lamp, a stone-topped metal table with a bronze basin and clay pitcher on it, and finally the wide fireplace with a long, hanging wrought-iron frame that held his drying school clothes. He felt slightly dizzy. He'd never slept in a room this big or nice before, so he made himself smile. He figured he was allowed to smile just to mark the occasion. He was wearing a white linen sleeping gown, which he had found folded on the table. It was loose and comfortable and warm. Too warm. His face was slick and clammy; he had been sweating in his sleep, either because of the thick bedding or the disturbing dream, or both. He pushed the sheets aside and stood up. A thin sheen of sweat made his skin cold as he padded over to the dressing table. He poured some water from the pitcher into the wide bowl and splashed a handful across his face. The freshness was bracing, and after drying himself with a thick linen cloth, he felt like he was wearing a new layer of skin.

Now feeling rather cold, he shuffled over to the fireplace and stretched out his hands expectantly, but after a moment or two he found that they were not warming as they ought. The fire was large and crackling, but squinting into it, he saw that it was not really burning. The flames that danced energetically around the logs and up the chimney were not healthy orange and red flames, but were pale and yellow, almost green in places, and appeared very thin. No smoke was given off, and he almost had to climb into the fireplace just to warm his palms. *Enchanted fire*, he thought with a frown.

He moved back to the table. Next to the bowl, where he had found the bedgown, some new clothes had been placed while he was asleep—his mind went back to his own house and the presents he never received. He shook out the first item and held up a dark-blue shirt, the type that the servants Cnafa and Cnapa wore.

He smiled. New clothes. He quickly shook out the other items, wondering how to put them on.

The thick shirt made Daniel think of a sewn-up bathrobe and was probably meant to be worn on top. It was made of a heavy, finely woven cloth—wool, maybe. It was rough on the outside, but lined with very smooth linen on the inside. It had large sleeves and was embroidered with blue on a darker blue floral design. Beneath the shirt were some pale-blue leggings, a thin shirt, some leather slippers with laces, and a broad belt.

He pulled the thin undershirt over his head and then started hitching up the leggings—which he found had no opening in the feet, meaning that he needed no socks. He was able to fasten them with a thin drawstring that cinched just below his belly. He shrugged on the thick blue overshirt, which reached halfway down his thighs, and fastened the leather belt around his waist. Then he sat down on the edge of his bed to try to put on his shoes, which were more a kind of slipper. The soles were thin but tough. There was a single, long leather lace that crisscrossed the top of the shoe, and once he tied them tightly around his feet they became, with the stockings, rather comfortable and snug.

He smoothed his new clothes down and straightened himself out as well as he could, not having a mirror. He walked around the room a couple times, wriggling his arms around, enjoying movement in this strange outfit—its crisp cleanness and smell. He liked how the clothes felt—tough, yet comfortable. He started running and then jumped up and down several times, laughing. He hoped he'd be allowed to keep them.

He wondered if Freya was awake and what her clothes were like. He pulled open the heavy door and stepped out into the hallway. Going towards her room, he ran into her halfway down the hallway, sitting in an alcove and staring out of one of the tall, thin windows. She was in her school clothes, which were dry but very wrinkled and dirty. She had one arm wrapped around her legs and one close to her chest. She was fingering the little pendant on her silver birthday necklace.

As Daniel approached she turned her head away from the window and looked him up and down.

"What are you wearing?" she asked, frowning.

"They laid these out for me. Didn't you get any?"

Freya's eyebrows pinched together as she studied Daniel. "Don't you want to go home?"

"Of course. What's that got to do with anything?"

"And you're going to go back dressed like that?"

"Why not?" He smoothed down the front of his shirt with his palm. "They're very warm, comfortable . . ."

Looking at Freya's expression, Daniel felt as if he were a bad essay that she was marking. "What?"

"Don't you miss your family?"

Daniel looked at the floor. His joy was slipping away, as if draining out of his feet.

"I mean," pursued Freya, "we don't even know how long it will take us to get back."

Daniel shrugged.

"Or even if we can get back," exclaimed Freya, becoming agitated.

"So what if we never go back?" Daniel murmured. "What's so good about normal life anyway?" he said angrily. "This is a real adventure! It's better than ordinary life any day."

"Better? Have you looked out there?" Freya said, jerking her head towards the window.

Daniel raised himself up on his toes. Outside the window, past his own reflection, he could see the streets and houses of Niðergeard, illuminated in the torchlight. Beyond the tree-carved wall lay the dirty campfires of the yfelgópes, stretching off into the distance like a flickering ocean of stars.

"There must be thousands of them out there," Freya said quietly. "I've been watching for a long time. I can't see any of those . . . things, but if each one of those dots of light has even just three or four around it . . ." Her voice trailed off. "What if they all decide to attack us?"

Daniel sniffed. "Then we'll kill them. Just like we did in the tunnels."

"We?" Freya echoed.

Daniel sucked at his top lip. "Anyway, we're safe here, with the walls and guards and everything," he said defiantly.

"We don't know that," Freya said. "We only think we're safe. How do we know what those knights want to do with us? If they wanted us to be safe, why didn't they take us home? Why didn't we wait in the church until the doorway opened again? Who is this Modwyn? When do we meet Ealdstan? What's going on?"

Daniel said nothing.

Freya turned back to the window. "Look at those people wandering around below. Look at those buildings," she continued, her voice rising. "How could something like this exist and nobody know about it? How could we not hear about it in school or on TV?"

"Well," said Daniel after the shortest of pauses, "grown-ups don't know everything. They always pretend that they do, but haven't you ever gotten the feeling that . . . I don't know . . . that they don't really believe a lot of the explanations they have—that they're saying them as much to themselves as they are to us, to make them feel better? This place explains so much! Didn't you ever think that there must be another world underneath the real one?"

"No. Daniel, this is insane! This shouldn't be happening at all. Ancient knights and enchantments? That doesn't happen anymore, if it ever did happen! No one believes in it."

"It's happening now, whether you want it to or—"

"So you're saying you believe in all of this?"

"What are you talking about? I can't choose what I believe, like you apparently can. Especially when it's actually happening to me."

Freya frowned grimly and shook her head. "It's like a bad dream."

"Yeah, but you can't stop a dream. You have to go along with it until you wake up."

"What if you don't wake up?"

"Then you try to change it."

Freya turned to look back out the window. "I just want to go back home where I know I'm safe," she said. "I feel as though—it's like in *The Wizard of Oz*, you know? I feel like I've been ripped up by a tornado and I'm just spinning and spinning and still haven't really come down yet."

Daniel picked at the hem of his shirt. "Anyway," he said after a time, "let's go find Swiðgar and Ecgbryt, and then maybe this mysterious wizard Ealdstan. I can get a brain, you can get some courage, and then we can click our ruby slippers together and go home."

Freya gave a broken laugh and sniffed. "Okay," she said, sliding out of the alcove. They started to walk off down the corridor.

"So what did you get? Was it a dress or something?"

"Yes. A dark-red one."

"Go put it on. I'll wait."

"No."

"Sure?"

"Yes."

"Go on, I bet you'd look nice."

"Be quiet."

2

As Freya and Daniel started down the twisting staircase, a loud and lively clamor drifted up from below them.

"I hope they have food," said Freya. "I'm starving."

"I think they do. Do you smell that? Smells smoky. But nice."

They reached the ground floor and looked around. The noise, a pleasant rise and fall of happy voices, was coming from a wide doorway under the opposite staircase. They walked through it and found stone tables and benches ranked down a long hall. The benches closest to the door were empty, but there was a cluster of people at the other end making a respectable racket. Ecgbryt was one of these and was the first to notice them. Standing, he raised a horn-shaped object above his head and hallooed them in a bellowing voice. "*Wes ðu hale*, young Daniel and fair Freya!" he called out.

Cnafa approached Daniel and Freya and motioned them to follow. He led them to the table at the end of the hall. On one side of the table sat Swiðgar and Ecgbryt, and on the other, two broad, grizzled men, with the pale, dry faces shared by all who lived in Niðergeard. The table was empty save for a large clay jug and oddly shaped cups in front of each person. Ecgbryt and one of the gentlemen had clay pipes in their mouths and were smoking a rich tobacco.

They slid onto the bench with the knights. "Did you sleep well?" Swiðgar asked.

Daniel and Freya nodded wordlessly. From a door in the corner two servants entered carrying several platters. They silently approached the table and laid the strange dishes before the new arrivals. One held a dried meat sausage as big as Daniel's arm; the next contained a pile of thin, crispy bread; the last was a plate of orange and lime slices. Shallow clay bowls were placed in front of them, along with two very sharp knives.

Freya broke off a piece of bread. "How long were we asleep?" she asked, popping it in her mouth as Daniel picked up his knife and started to saw into the meat.

"Oh, not very long," answered Ecgbryt as he drew on his pipe. "Only five or six years."

Daniel's eyebrows shot up.

Freya nearly choked on the bread she was chewing. "What?" she gasped.

"As I said, not long, not long at all—" A smile broke Ecgbryt's solemn face and he broke into laughter. The other men at the table did as well. Daniel grinned sheepishly and Freya muttered something under a frown.

"The boy's eyes nearly fell into his plate," hooted one of the other men.

"No," said Ecgbryt, bringing his laughter under control with an effort. "Hours only. Hours, not years. Forgive me, but—but this is excellent ale." He held his silver-rimmed horn aloft and clanked it against his neighbor's cup. They both drank.

"Glad to see you awake," said Swiðgar to Daniel and Freya. "You will not have met these men. I will let them introduce themselves."

"Greetings," said the man across from Ecgbryt, wiping his mouth. He had a squarish build and a large mane of dark, shaggy hair that stuck out at every angle. His face was blunt and puckered here and there with scars. To Freya it looked as if he'd been chewed up by some giant beast and spat out. For all she knew, she reflected, he had been. "My name is Godmund," he said, slapping his chest with a fist. The fishscale armour that encased him clanked and rattled. "It means 'good-hand,' and was given to me by Ealdstan himself. I am Niðergeard's Shield Thane—its protector."

"My name," said the man next to him, a bald and thin man with a pinched face, long moustache, and wiry arms, "is Frithfroth. I oversee the order of this magnificent keep. I am the Torr Thane. If ever you have need of anything on this side of the Tall Tower's door, but mention it in my presence and it will be brought to you with all possible speed. I give especial welcome."

"Hi. I'm Freya Reynolds."

The heads at the table turned to Daniel, who smiled and announced grandly, "My name is Daniel Tully. I am a student of the Isis C of E Secondary School in the town of Oxford. My mother gave me my name, though I don't know what it means. I greet you!" He raised up the horn in front of him in a salute to the delight of the table. He put the cup to his lips and lifted the bottom up, up, and up until it was upside down over his face. Nothing came out, to the laughter of everyone in the hall. Even Freya muffled a small snort behind her hand.

Swiðgar reached across and took Daniel's cup from him. He poured a small amount of pale liquid from one pitcher and some water from another. He handed it back to Daniel, who completed his toast to a cheer.

Those around the table gazed gleefully at Daniel and Freya as they ate. Suddenly, Godmund's pipe jumped from his lips. "I have it!" he cried. "It is an onion!"

"And not before time," Frithfroth said, smirking. "Take your turn."

"Very well," said Godmund, laying his pipe carefully on the table and interlocking his fingers. Clearing his throat, he spoke slowly and deliberately:

"A deadly destroyer, divinely descended,
awakes only when warring,
stirring when silent objects are struck.
He is highly borne to battle by foe
to fight against foe. Though incredibly fierce,
and madly wild, a woman will wrangle him.
Though satisfying they who serve and tend him,
the more you feed him, the hungrier you make him.
He who builds this battler up

is doubly delighted, but death follows he
who carelessly lets this warrior loose."

"Samson," Ecgbryt answered immediately. Godmund shook his head.

"Anger," answered Swiðgar. Godmund smiled and shook his fuzzy head once again.

The hall was silent as the puzzler looked smugly around the table. Each in their own manner either scratched his head, silently repeated lines of the riddle, or stared into nothing. Daniel and Freya looked on with interest as they continued placing meat and bread into their mouths.

Godmund smiled and tapped out a layer of ash from his pipe. Picking up a splint of wood about the thickness of a match, he held it to the candle in front of him and then brought it up to his cold pipe bowl. He puffed a few times and then held it away. His face appeared thoughtful, gazing at the flame as it traveled up the splint towards his fingers.

Ecgbryt, his eyes flickering idly across the table, saw him gently blowing on the flame rather playfully. He thought a moment and then his eyes grew wide. "Fire!" he exclaimed. "The answer is fire!"

Godmund blew out the flame and nodded as the table applauded the guesser.

It was now Ecgbryt's turn. "At last," he said, stroking his long moustache. "And I have a most excellent riddle for you all—a rare and wise riddle it is as well, for King Ælfred the Great himself did teach me this riddle from his own lips." He cleared his throat.

> *"A river twice wet me*
> *After woodframe had stretched me,*
> *Once sharp knife had scraped me,*
> *And a young man first cut me.*

"Then the sun, it did dry me,
Now my hair had all left me,
And some cinders then rubbed me,
Before fingers had folded me.

"A feather has dyed me,
A reed also stained me,
Now two boards press on me,
And gold bands gird 'round me.

"What am I?"

Ecgbryt sat back, finished and very pleased with himself for a full three seconds until Swiðgar said, "I have it."

"Hold, knight," said Frithfroth. "You've answered your share—rather, you've answered your share and three others'. Let the rest of us try."

With a twinkling eye, Ecgbryt poured himself a horn.

"Kippered herring," Frithfroth answered, somewhat hastily.

"No, but a near guess."

The table dropped into thoughtful silence a moment more. "A fishing bark," answered Godmund, "with oars and, hmm, feathers . . ."

"No."

There was a further silence until: "Kippers," Frithfroth insisted. "Kippers or cod!"

Ecgbryt laughed and shook his head.

"If there are no more guesses beyond 'kippers,'" Swiðgar drawled, "then perhaps I might be allowed . . . ?" The table assented. "A book," he said simply.

Ecgbryt reluctantly clapped his hands as the rest of the table nodded to themselves.

Swiðgar began his riddle:

"There is a strong, savagely bold house-guest
Who is the lord of my heart's dwelling-place.
Hunger does not hurt my ferocious friend—
He thirsts, ages, but is not diminished.
Treat him honourably, and with respect,
And you will receive good fortune when you
Travel with him all the days of your life.
And at the end of the highway you are
Ensured a warm welcome into his vast family;
But misery rewards the servant who
Mistreats this most holy of visitors.
With him ahead of me, I will not fear
When this friend, kinsman, guest, travels onward
While I am forced to stay by the roadside,
Ever willing to part, as once we must,
Never again being able to meet.
Friends, if you please, speak the name or title
Of either this royal household-dweller,
Or my own name, both whom I have described."

There was a groan from Frithfroth as he placed his head in his hands. "By the devil's nose hairs, you're a hard riddler."

"It sounds like fire again," Godmund grumbled.

"There are," allowed Swiðgar with an agreeable nod, "similarities between the two, yes."

The table was stumped. Ecgbryt scratched his head, Godmund kicked the table, and Frithfroth muttered oaths not heard in the British Isles for centuries. Eventually, Swiðgar was convinced to give them the answer. "The soul. The body is the host, the soul the guest."

Frithfroth and Godmund insisted on a second reciting of the riddle and then sat in silence, rather morosely.

"'Forced to stay by the roadside,'" muttered Godmund, and blinked his grey eyes slowly. A heaviness fell upon the hall.

Daniel and Freya, being adequately fed by their dry meal, sat in silence, amused and bewildered by the game.

"I have one," Daniel piped into the melancholy. "What's brown and sticky?"

Nobody at the table guessed; they just shook their heads.

"A stick," Daniel said.

Everyone burst into laughter, as much in relief as in actual humor. Daniel himself laughed as hard as anyone.

"Here's another," he said. "Which room has no door, no windows, no floor, and no roof? No guesses? A mushroom! Now, what is—?"

"Enough, Daniel, enough. Give another a turn, or at least a chance to breathe," Godmund said, his pallid face sweaty and bright with laughing.

"One more, one more—what's red and sticky?"

"Beeswax."

"Strawberries."

"Earwax."

"Honey."

"Nope, all wrong. Give up?" Everyone nodded enthusiastically. "It's that bloody stick again!"

This brought the loudest roar yet, and even tears to some eyes.

Which was why no one noticed that Modwyn had entered. Stiff-faced, she waited patiently for the laughter to die down. Everyone sobered when they caught sight of her, and the bellows gave way to chuckles that died silently.

"Ealdstan will see you," she announced.

3

The grandly dressed Modwyn led Daniel and Freya, followed by Swiðgar and Ecgbryt, up staircase after staircase. They followed her with an increasing sense of cautious curiosity as they crept farther and farther up into the dark centre of the tower.

Daniel, walking behind Modwyn, broke the silence of their ascent. "Is Ealdstan really seventeen hundred years old?"

"As near as can be counted," the *niðercwen* replied. "Time was measured differently when he was young. Days of birth were not recorded as they are now."

"Is he a wizard?"

"Yes," she began thoughtfully, "he could be considered one. The word *wizard* simply means 'wise one.' And Ealdstan is unquestionably the wisest of men."

"Is he like the wizards in the books and fairy tales? Like Merlin or someone?"

"He may be," Modwyn allowed. "It is possible that you have read about him already but do not know it. He has been called by many names throughout his life—cast his shadow upon the ages." She thought for a few moments, then said, "What evidence there is in history, and what truth there is in myth, of the wise old men in your books and fairy tales has undoubtedly been Ealdstan. He has counseled kings, bishops, and emperors—but it is long since anyone sought his advice."

"How long?"

"Over two hundred years."

"Does he still go up to the real world?"

"No."

"What does he do?"

"He studies now. There are his books, his own writings, the writings of others, the myths and wise tales of days long ago."

"It sounds lonely," Daniel said.

Stair after stair fell behind them. The carvings on the walls became less and less elaborate the higher they went until what was a beautiful embossed frieze depicting ocean life devolved, gradually, into a primitive running spiral. The bannister turned from an ornately wrought metal lattice of eels and seaweed into a simple twisted band. "That is the price he pays," she said, and it took Daniel a few seconds to realise that she was still following the conversation.

"The price he pays for what?" Daniel asked.

"The price he pays for his wisdom. Wisdom, which is experience and reflection over time."

"So the older he gets, the wiser he gets?"

"As do we all—almost all. There are some people and creatures who are proud, and who have exchanged wisdom for vanity."

Daniel considered this. "But how wise is he, anyway?"

"How can I tell, unless I am as wise as he? Only wisdom can recognise itself."

"Well, you're old, so you must be wise too—unless you're proud."

Modwyn's lips thinned in a small, brief smile. "The only thing I have learned in my long years is that I have not learned enough. I have always been wise enough to know that I am not as wise as I would like to be."

Daniel frowned and Modwyn continued.

"But as for Ealdstan—he is the most intelligent of all earthly beings. He has meditated lifetimes on single ideas. He has pursued trains of thought for hundreds of years and his interests are unlimited. He has sowed patience and reaped knowledge, has sifted it and nourished himself on the grain. I do not think that any created being knows as much about the workings of the world as he—it would be impossible for anyone to conceive of learning it. There is more than he could pass on in a lifetime."

They turned off the staircase and into a cold hallway, past dark, crudely carved rooms, which contained books and loose papers crammed into bookcases. Up ahead they saw a fluttering light. They approached it and filed into what turned out to be a narrow room that contained many barred windows that opened out into Niðergeard.

It was from behind, as he gazed out one of these windows, that Daniel and Freya first saw the bent form of Ealdstan. He was wearing a robe made of bright red and yellow, patterned with bands that wove in and out of each other in alternating rows of red and purple. He did not turn immediately as they entered, but slowly pulled his gaze away from the window and let it drift around the room.

Ealdstan's age showed in his manner, if nowhere else. His ancient face, although weathered, was not decrepit. A yellowing beard stretched down past his waist, but it was bushy and full. His head was high domed, but not bald; lustrous hair fell down behind his shoulders. His arm, seen when his sleeve was drawn, was not withered; it was smooth and well muscled, with quick, dexterous hands and fingers at the end of them.

But his eyes were pale grey, watery, and very, very weary. At first, Daniel thought Ealdstan was blind, his pupils were so drab and unresponsive—lying listless in their hooded sockets. It took a long time for his face to show any acknowledgment of their presence, and when he raised his voice to welcome his visitors, it was the two smaller figures he greeted first.

"I don't believe," he breathed in a thin voice, "that I've had the pleasure."

There was an expectant pause.

"I—I am Daniel Tully, sir."

"I'm Freya—Freya Reynolds."

"Really . . . ," Ealdstan trailed, his voice not much above a whisper. "Are you really . . . ?"

"Are you Ealdstan?" asked Freya.

"Yes, I am . . . or as much of Ealdstan as is left . . ."

"We have heard that you are very wise."

"Am I? I suppose . . . speaking . . . comparatively, of course . . ."

All of Ealdstan's sentences trailed off, making conversation awkward. It was hard to tell if he was at the end of a breath or a reply. "Shall we sit?"

At the other end of the room were a long stone table and many short stone stumps that were used as stools. Ealdstan placed himself at the head of the table on the far side of the room. Daniel and Freya sat at the opposite end and the others found places in between. The table was covered with bits of paper of many different types, shapes, and sizes. Some were thick and brown and were written on in faded ink in blocky, raggedy-edged letters filling sheet after sheet, each word looking indecipherably similar to the last. Other pages were newer, thinner, almost translucent, with rough fibers here and there showing through the paper. They were mostly scrawled on with an elaborate, spidery script. There were some oddly bound books, both large and small, of the type that Freya had seen only in museums, which gave glimpses of illuminated letters and detailed pictures.

"So . . . ," Ealdstan breathed, apparently to himself. "Swiðgar and Ecgbryt have come back, have they? And why is that? Swiðgar . . . ," he repeated, as if trying to remember who went with the name. "Ecgbryt . . ."

He was silent long enough for Swiðgar to jump in. "It was because of the lifiendes, Ealdstan *dryhtwisa*."

"The mortal children? Yes? And why did you not chase them off or put them to the sword?"

Daniel blinked. Freya gasped and opened her mouth soundlessly for a few seconds before she managed to stutter, "You—you couldn't have just—"

"We can and do . . . ," Ealdstan interrupted. "Do you children think that you are the first to happen upon one of the chambers of the sleeping knights?"

"And you killed them for finding you?" Freya turned from Ealdstan to Swiðgar.

"Hmm. I have never killed an innocent," Swiðgar said. "The enchantment is strong. It stops all from entering. Nearly all."

"*Swa swa*, Swiðgar," Ecgbryt said, his face suddenly bright. "Do you remember that curate who stumbled upon us? When you grabbed his sleeve he leapt so far back that his cassock—"

"Shush, broðor, this is not the time," said Swiðgar peevishly.

"We are fighting a hidden war," Ealdstan said. "The position of our troops is of the foremost importance. Even a guileless fool can let slip vital information that would allow the enemy to strike a severe blow. We battle for the souls of millions, and the lives of a few are light in the balance . . ."

There was a short silence following Ealdstan's words, which was broken by Swiðgar. "Ealdstan," he said, "we have observed the situation outside the wall."

The old man turned tired eyes on the knight.

"How long has the siege lasted?"

Ealdstan did not answer, only just gazed at him.

"Some months," Modwyn eventually replied.

"What has been done?" asked Ecgbryt roughly.

Modwyn looked to Ealdstan, who still gave no reply. "Very little," she responded. "We still have many supplies and are able to travel rather freely—the yfelgóp have not discovered all routes in and out of the *geard*."

"But something must be done," insisted Ecgbryt. "What are their numbers?"

"We cannot tell," Modwyn spoke slowly. "Or even estimate. All we can do is count the campfires."

"How many are they?" Ecgbryt pursued, stern in his questioning.

"Of hundreds, nearly nine."

"How many to a fire? Can you assay that?"

"We do not know, perhaps as many as eight."

"You have made no sallies?"

"None. There are times when a handful of them will climb the walls, but they never get past the parapets, and we never capture them alive."

"Who leads them?" asked Swiðgar.

"Once we used the tunnels to listen to them," Modwyn continued slowly. "There are two leaders, a master and a general, though they would mention only the general by name. He is called Kelm Kafhand."

"Do you know anything of the master?" asked Swiðgar.

"Only that he is powerful, cruel, and commands much fear to rule the yfelgóp."

"It is Gád," Ealdstan said and sneered, startling the others. "Gád Grístgrenner, the *gástbona*," he spat, as if each word were a mouthful of bile. "It is him. He was . . . the worst of all the old enemies."

"Yet I've not heard of him," said Swiðgar.

"Nor I," said Ecgbryt.

"He is cunning. It has been many years since he has trod the earth, but now his power grows and he has become bold."

"I do not wonder—with so little to challenge him," Ecgbryt remarked darkly.

"What would you have us do?" Ealdstan replied. "Run out of the gates and smite down the enemy? Our numbers are few, Ecgbryt Hard-Axe."

"There are over one hundred sleeping knights underneath this very tower—the finest warriors that have ever existed! What have numbers ever meant to Ealdstan the Ancient?"

"Do not goad me. Of might and wisdom," Ealdstan hissed,

"we have ever exercised the rarer and more precious of those virtues in Niðergeard."

"Might is no virtue," Ecgbryt knocked back, "but determination is!"

"Remember your place," Ealdstan rasped, his face contracting, spittle flying from his lips. "Remember it, or I shall name you Hardhead to go with your virtues! Hardhead the Hack-Hand!"

"When Ælfred fought off the Danes at Æthelney, he would—"

"Your precious Ælfred is dead!" Ealdstan spat. "I buried him myself! So you will have to continue along as best you can with who he has left behind!"

Ecgbryt smoldered under this reprimand. Ealdstan was now incensed. He bent forward in his chair, breathing quickly, eyes flashing in their deep sockets. He calmed, gradually, and leaned back again, pinching out a long sigh.

"Compared to the battle that is to come," Ealdstan grumbled, his voice suddenly as sharp as the sound of stone scraping against stone, "this is not even a scuffle. Armies greater and more frightsome than we can comprehend are gathering in the dark corners of this rock—armies that may crush us into powder. That is the conflict we must cast our minds to—not this insignificant tussle. The grand cataclysm is approaching."

"Very well," said Swiðgar. "Then what must we do to prepare?"

Ealdstan cleared his throat and suddenly his voice was weak again and faltering. "I have been reading . . . studying the manuscripts." His hands started to move and he shifted some of the papers around the table uncertainly. "It is hard to know where . . . current events fall . . . the prophecies seem . . . shuffled now . . . accuracy is not—accuracy has been . . . lost."

"To hell with the prophecies," said Swiðgar. "You know of the coming conflict—the cataclysm. What is to be done?"

"This age," moaned Ealdstan. "This age is so cold . . . hearts are bitter and guts are bilious. There are no more heroes. There are none to help us from this era—none with strength in their soul to do what needs be done.

"What is to be done?" Ealdstan repeated, turning his grey eyes to Swiðgar. "Only this: pray that we have done enough in the past to be ready for the future. There is nothing further to prepare. The people of this time have forsaken us."

"Are you certain that it is not you who have forsaken them?" Swiðgar replied.

Ealdstan's lips clenched together tightly as he ground his teeth. Daniel's and Freya's pale faces looked around the room. Ecgbryt glowered at the centre of the table, fuming. Swiðgar sat with his chin stuck out and his fists clenched in front of him. Modwyn's eyes met theirs, and for the first time, they saw living emotion in them—emotions of sorrow and dismay.

It was Ecgbryt who spoke next. "Niðergeard under siege is not a scuffle. When was the beacon extinguished? I've seen men fight without an arm, but never without a head. In the war we wage, all battles are vital, and action *must* be taken. If the yfelgóp opposition is truly inconsequential, then let us rid ourselves of them and press our advantage. I propose we make a foray to test their strength and numbers. Information may be gleaned that could shed more light on events."

"*If! May! Could!*" Ealdstan spat testily. "You have *no conception* of Gád's powers! He'd swat you away like a child fanning a fly." He leaned forward and made brusque sweeping motions with his hand, then settled back peevishly. "Very well. Make your attack. In the event that something is found of which I have no current knowledge, please . . . feel free to share."

"We have your permission, then?"

"Permission? Why should you want that when you will not accept my counsel? Permission? To do what? Risk death and capture, simply to smell the enemy's sweat? Yes, by all means. Go. Leave me in peace. Don't leave the doors unbarred too long."

Ealdstan stood, and the others rose with him.

"Thank you, *wys fæder*," said Swiðgar, bowing his head.

"Be gone."

The others muttered similar thanks as they started to file out of the room. Daniel and Freya hung back, the last to leave, standing in the doorway a little bewildered.

"Wait a second!" Freya blurted nervously, calling after the others. "Wait! We didn't come here for this, Mr. Ealdstan," she said, turning to him, "sir, Daniel and I—we came here because we want to go home, but we couldn't because the tunnel was sealed up and we didn't really have a choice. We don't belong here. We belong at home, with our parents. Can you please show us the way out of here?"

Ealdstan listened to her with his head bowed over a dusty parchment so old it was cracking. As Freya finished, he raised his head and blinked at her. "Out? You cannot leave this place . . . Weren't you listening? It's far too dangerous. You'd be killed or worse."

"Modwyn just said that they hadn't found all the exits yet, so there're tunnels—passages that those yfelgóp things haven't discovered yet. We came along the river. We slipped in, I know that we can slip out again. Maybe we could—"

"There is no safe passage. No escape." He bent his head back down to the table and finished by muttering, "If there is no escape for us, why should there be any for you?"

"But we're not a part of this—this world. None of this matters to us—we're not important. They might not bother even chasing us."

"No."

"But—"

"LEAVE!"

Freya was shocked—the blood drained from her face,

leaving her cold, frozen to the spot. She felt Daniel tugging at her arm and whispering her name, but she pulled her arm out of his hands—this was too important to back down from. "We want to leave!" she yelled at the top of her lungs. "But you won't let us! You have knights! You have magic! You have secret tunnels! Let us go!"

Ealdstan's face twisted into an ugly mask of spite. "Stupid little brown-skinned girl," he sneered through a clenched jaw. In several unexpectedly quick strides, he approached Freya. His ancient hand gripped her arm and with surprising strength he flung her out of the doorway and into the hall. She staggered a little and then ungracefully fell on her rear.

"Hey!" Daniel shouted. "Don't do that! *Don't* do that!"

Ealdstan ignored him and grabbed the edge of the large metal door and slammed it shut with a fluid motion. And because Daniel was still standing in the doorway, he took some of the force on his shoulder and one of the door's rivets punched into his arm. He closed his eyes as excruciating pain flooded his body. He grabbed his arm and swore with all the worst words he knew. He didn't think he'd ever been hit that hard. He kicked and pounded the door, which was so heavy and strong that it hardly made a noise.

"Oi, you!" Daniel shouted between pounds. "Ealdstan! Get out of here, you coward! Why not take me on, instead of pushing around a girl? Oi! Ealdstan! *Ealdstan!*"

Daniel pounded and kicked for another moment, until his hands and feet ached. Then he turned and saw that Modwyn and the knights were standing around Freya. Ecgbryt must have helped her up—his hand was still on her shoulder. Freya was looking at him with wide, watery eyes.

"Come, lifiendes," Swiðgar said. "We have matters to discuss." He then turned and they all started down the hall.

Grimacing, Daniel came alongside Freya. "Don't worry, Freya," he said. "We'll find a way to get home—soon."

4

They all started down the stairs in silence. Modwyn led them to a room on the fifth level that was nothing more than a completely square chamber with carved ledges in the wall that were used for seating. There was a low metal table in the middle of the room. Modwyn pulled a rope and a small bell tinkled in the distance.

"How long has Ealdstan been thus?" Swiðgar asked.

The door opened and Cnafa stepped into the room. "Bring a map of the Niðerland and send Godmund here," she instructed, and then turned to Swiðgar. "Ealdstan has been in such spirits for some time, even before the siege," she replied in a hushed voice. "Listless and melancholic. We do not see him for months on end, and when we do, he passes by without acknowledgment or sign, leaving us to wonder if we have, in truth, seen him at all."

"I am sorry that my temper overcame me, brother," Ecgbryt apologised. "You should not have let me hound the man."

"No, it was well that you did. I doubt many have challenged him of late. And I agree—why not simply wake a band of knights to come and break the siege?" Swiðgar asked gruffly. "Drive the nasty filth back into the deep tunnels. The solution is so simple that it's maddening."

"I would challenge him, were it my place," stated Modwyn.

"It would not have been right," agreed Swiðgar. "Ecgbryt and I can be excused our rudeness—"

The door reopened and Godmund entered with a long scroll, which he placed on the table. He unfurled it to show a map of the underground realm, a large oblong with little branches that represented tunnels leading off the sides. Niðergeard was marked in the middle, a small knot of structures and streets. They started talking about where the yfelgóp army was thickest, where they had come from, and many other details. Daniel watched with fascination as the small military strike was planned and tactics discussed.

"We have no idea where their main force is," Godmund said. "We suspect it may be here"—he placed a hand on a section of the map—"but who is to say that they do not move it, or that they are split equally in different areas?"

"What are their main routes into the plain?" Swiðgar asked.

"There is no way to know that either. Seeing that you encountered them, it is possible that they have infiltrated most of the upper tunnels—there would be little enough to prevent the beasts from overrunning them. But do they circulate randomly? Are most of them here? Are they gathered somewhere else? How can we know?"

"None of that matters right now," came an unexpected voice from among them. All eyes turned to Freya, who was standing near the table, looking down on the map.

"We won't learn everything in just one raid," Freya continued, her voice quavering slightly. "The important thing is to test their numbers, their strength, and their reaction after that—that will tell us a lot. Then we can judge the appropriate measures to take, once we have evaluated our resources. Then we can go home, you can find a way to break the siege, and so on."

Ecgbryt smiled grimly and placed a huge hand on Freya's shoulder. "The girl has a good head for these matters," he said.

"I just want to go home," Freya said, trying to avoid Daniel's gawking stare.

Swiðgar frowned. "Then it's decided," he said. "We will raid them, leaving through the main gates here." He brought his hand down on an area of the map. "Enough talking. That is what we will do next."

5

In addition to Swiðgar and Ecgbryt, the raiding party consisted of Godmund and three of his best men, his champions. To Daniel they looked like superheroes—stocky with a lot of weight in the chest and shoulders. One of them had a red bushy beard and long plaited hair; his armour was made of medium-sized brass rings, interlocked with one another. One man had black hair and skin that was still slightly olive colour, despite being very pale. The third was a man taller than any knight they had seen so far. He was so tall he looked slightly clumsy and uncomfortable. His whitish-blond hair was uncombed and matted, like a sheepdog's shaggy coat. He carried a spear in the same hand as his shield and casually gripped a massive war hammer in the other.

They were all big and strong, and although their dress varied, they all wore helmets made of iron with a sculpted figure of an ox on the crest. The three new knights moved sluggishly and creakily, slower than the others. Daniel and Freya wondered if they had just been woken—and if they could really stand up to the erratic frenzy of the yfelgópes, especially if there were as many out there as they all imagined.

And then, with no more preparations to be made, they were ready to depart. The six knights mounted their stallions and set off through the city at a gentle canter. The torchlight played on their armour, making it sparkle and shine; the gold tracing reflected the light brilliantly. It looked as if living fire were flowing through the metal.

Freya and Daniel followed, walking behind the six riders, and were soon joined by others. Niðergearders working in smithies, guards in their barracks, and masons in their workshops, seeing the knights pass by, dropped what they were doing, stood, and hurried to fall into step behind them. The silent procession had swelled to over fifty people when the knights reached the large city gate. They stood for a few moments making final preparations: adjusting the harnesses of their mounts, shifting weapons in their hands, and whispering short prayers.

Godmund, Shield Thane of Niðergeard and leader of the war host, motioned to two guardsmen on either side of the gate. The gigantic hinges started to creak. The large entrance opened a crack, and then—

A bell was heard in the distance—it was a deep, solid toll coming from the other end of the city. The crowd tensed and started to mutter in confusion.

"What's going on?" Freya asked. Daniel shook his head.

The effect of the bell on the knights was instantaneous and dramatic. Several of them jerked back hard on their horses' reigns, causing them to rear upwards and turn around. "Stop the gate!" yelled Godmund to the guard above him. "Shut it!"

The knights leaned forward in their saddles, scanning the buildings in front of them, ready to gallop back into the city. "Hold!" cried Swiðgar. "Hold! Wait for the horns!"

The gate shut behind the knights. Godmund turned to Ecgbryt. "Get everyone to the Tall Tower!" he shouted. Ecgbryt trotted through the crowd that opened a path for him.

"Everyone, this way!" Ecgbryt bellowed, leading them back into the city.

"What's going on?" Daniel shouted.

"Niðergeard is being attacked," someone answered behind him. "That bell tolls a breach at the south wall."

Just then, the sound of a high-pitched horn was heard from a far corner of the city. The other knights spurred their horses and galloped off along the smooth stone streets and were soon out of view.

"Hurry now," Ecgbryt said, shepherding the crowd. "Move

quickly. I do not know how they breached the wall without being seen, but I suspect devilry!"

6

Daniel and Freya tried their level best to stay with the crowd as they fled for the safety of the Langtorr. The streets, buildings, and city guards blurred past them as they struggled to keep up with Ecgbryt.

Horns sounded from other parts of the city. Freya and Daniel kept their eyes on the Tall Tower, remembering its thick iron doors. Freya grabbed Daniel's shoulder and pointed up at the tower. Following her finger, Daniel saw a flicker of bright red and yellow in one of the windows several stories up. It was Ealdstan, gripping the window frame, with one foot on its ledge. As they watched, he launched himself forward and fell, his robes billowing and flapping around him like flames on a burning arrow. He quickly dropped out of sight, below the roofline of the houses. Daniel tried to shout to Ecgbryt, but it was no use, he couldn't make his voice heard over the clamor.

They had just turned a corner and had their first glimpse of the Tall Tower's gates when the yfelgópes caught up with them. The creatures had scaled the buildings and were jumping from roof to roof towards the centre of the city, out of the reach of the guards.

Nine of the creatures dropped into the road ahead of the crowd. Ecgbryt halted his horse and ushered the fleeing towns-people down a side street. The yfelgópes, each of them sprouting sharp bits of metal from joints and fingers, ran towards them, snarling and barking.

From around the corner of a building, Daniel and Freya watched Ecgbryt charge forward, galloping into one end of the line of attackers. With his spear couched in his arm, he drove into the swarming knot of yfelgópes, skewering a creature on his left with his spear and batting another two away with the edge of his shield. Releasing his spear, he drew his axe and sliced cleanly through the neck of an yfelgóp that was slashing at his leg and stirrup. His horse reared underneath him as one of the twisted men raked at the horse's flank. Ecgbryt kept his saddle and brought his axe down into the attacker's head with a juicy *thok!*

The yfelgópes left standing became even more enraged and bestial. With quick, darting movements, they surrounded the lone knight. Ecgbryt reared his horse to make a break out of the ring when a shout rang out from a side street.

Five of the city guards, led by Breca, the guard at the Western Well, swept upon the invaders in a pale, gleaming fury. Their speed was controlled and effective—every blow that fell was either crippling or deadly. In a very short time the yfelgópes were dispatched.

"*Hwaet*, Breca," Ecgbryt said, addressing the guardsman. "What news?"

"The wall has been breached. Few have entered—very few. It is possible that this attack is a feint."

"Or that the force was not so great as we thought," Ecgbryt suggested.

"Perhaps," replied Breca, signaling to his men. "We go to join the forces already guarding the Carnyx. The rest have been ordered to sweep the city."

"*Swa swa*, I will join that number," Ecgbryt replied, tugging on his mount's reins, "when I have delivered the rest to safety."

"God by ye," Breca said, and turned to order his men.

Ecgbryt urged his horse forward and away after the fleeing citizens. Plucking his upright spear from the chest of its victim, he caught up with the crowd just as the first and fastest of them entered the gate of the Langtorr. Daniel, with Freya clinging to his arm, turned just as he started up the steps of the torr. He saw Ecgbryt halt his horse and dismount as people flooded in around him. He heard growls and screams as yfelgópes leapt from the rooftops, and two of the knights in the raiding party came into sight, being pursued by a swarm of the twisted creatures.

As they ran across the wide courtyard that separated the Langtorr from the rest of the city, Daniel paused to look at the squat building that protected the Great Carnyx. A body of guards, Breca amongst them, was encircling it on the outside as warriors on the inside ran to take up places around the structure's battlements.

Freya pulled Daniel's arm very hard and he allowed himself to be dragged forward. But in the pushing and jostling of the crowd she lost her grip on him. Springing up the steps, he tried to catch up with her.

Once inside the crowd scattered in confusion. Servants tried to herd the refugees into the banquet hall, but everyone was taking stock of themselves, looking for companions, and staggering in exhaustion. Daniel tried to see through the commotion but couldn't find Freya anywhere. He called out her name but had trouble hearing even his own voice over the din.

He was about to enter the hall with all the others when he saw a swift movement out of the corner of his eye. He looked up and saw that someone was running up one of the staircases: Freya. She must be headed to her room—but why? He leapt up the stairs after her and ran down the hallway to her door. It was closed but he flipped the latch and threw himself against it, expecting it to be locked or barred, but it swung open easily.

"Freya?" he hissed. There was no answer.

He tried again. "Freya? Where are you?"

A sound came from under the bed. "Shh!"

"Freya, what are you doing under there? Let's get with the others!"

There was no reply. He bent down and stuck his head underneath the bed frame. "Freya, it's safer in the hall."

"You don't know that."

"They have weapons to protect us."

"I don't care! There are too many of those—those—things. Find someplace to hide or go back to the others, but just get out of here!"

"I'm not going to leave you alo—"

At that instant the door flew open with a bang.

Daniel spun around and let out a shout of surprise. Then his heart froze.

In the doorway crouched a snarling yfelgóp. It wore loose bits of plate armour over its bare skin that was painted with an angry, black zigzag pattern. Its head was inhumanly white as if it had been bleached. The thing brandished a short, crooked, and fearsomely pointed spear in one hand, let out a curdling scream, and leapt.

Daniel dove out of the way and the creature skittered across the covers of the bed. Sinking its fingernails into the mattress, it spun itself around and crouched to leap at him again. Daniel lunged forward and pulled hard on the thick bed sheet, flipping the yfelgóp onto its back. He threw the cover on top of it as the thing spat and writhed.

Rushing to the fireplace, Daniel snatched up a poker, the only weapon he could see to hand, as the sound of ripping cloth came from behind him. He spun around and lofted the heavy, blunt length of iron. The yfelgóp crouched in the middle of a pile of shredded cloth, trying to free itself with a jagged knife—and jerking away the tough threads that were caught on its rough armour.

Daniel saw his opportunity. Yelling, he dashed forward, swinging the poker in a wide arc. The yfelgóp dipped sideways and deflected the blow with an armoured arm, but the blow clipped him on the temple. The momentum in the swing carried Daniel and he felt his feet slip from under him. He landed lengthways on the floor.

Grunting and snorting, the beast tumbled out of the bed and

landed on top of him—Daniel felt sharp knees dig into his sides as a claw-like hand gripped his throat. He saw the jagged knife silhouetted against the ceiling and desperately swung the poker against the ugly, snarling face but managed only enough force to bat the yfelgóp's head to the side.

Snarling, the yfelgóp slashed at Daniel with its talon-like fingers. Daniel cried out, his eyes squeezing shut in pain. When he opened them again, he saw the arm once again drawn back to strike. Daniel scrambled for the poker and felt his fingers close around it, but it was too late. The knife sailed through the air—and then clanked to the floor. The yfelgóp choked and glared hatefully at Daniel, its eyes angry and wild. It leant forward slowly and spat a gob of sticky blood against the side of his face and shoulder. Then it slumped heavily against him, letting out a ragged, gurgling sigh as its eyes rolled back in its head.

Daniel looked up and saw Freya standing over him and the body of his attacker. Her face was terrified and tear-streaked. She was holding the yfelgóp's black, crooked spear, still partially entangled in the bed sheet and now also planted between the creature's shoulder blades at the base of its boney neck. She gave the dark metal a sharp twist and the thing against Daniel twitched and lurched.

With a mighty heave, Freya tore the spear from the corpse and Daniel pushed the fetid body off of him. He stared up at Freya, who was huffing through clenched teeth, and he started to cry.

CHAPTER SEVEN

Useful Poetry

--------------------------------- 1 ---------------------------------

Now...

Freya awoke and tried to remember where she was. First she thought that she was back home, at her parents' house, but then she remembered that she was at university. She pulled the duvet tighter around her shoulders and burrowed into the mattress. It was quiet today. She couldn't hear any cars in the street below. Maybe it was early still.

She turned her head and opened her eyes to see how bright it was and froze. Then, with a sudden lurch, she convulsed upwards. She wasn't in her dorm or her parents' house. She didn't know where she was.

Morning sunlight shone through the window, falling on a bed that was definitely not hers. It smelled clean, but it wasn't the detergent that she usually used, which she found sickening.

It was a small but serviceable room, clean, and with no

ornamentation. Besides the nightstand, there was a little wooden chair, draped with her clothing, and a dresser. The ceiling sloped downwards at one end, where there was a dormer window with a scrolling shade.

And then there was a door. Shut. Leading to somewhere she didn't know.

She rose cautiously, ears keen for any sound at all. She grabbed her jeans and sweatshirt and dressed frantically, her eyes sweeping the room. There was a book on the nightstand—a hardback without a cover. Its spine was imprinted in gold and read HISTORIES VOL. VIII—PORT. There was a bookmark in it and she opened it up. She scanned the page but it didn't seem familiar—not the sort of book she would be reading. She closed it and placed it back on the table.

Trying not to think about the door, she went to the dresser and pulled out the top drawer. She peered into it and bit her lip.

Here were more of her clothes. Socks, underwear—enough changes for several days. All clean and tidy. The next drawer contained a couple more tops and another pair of jeans. In the bottom drawer was a small collapsible suitcase that she often used on short trips.

She ran a hand through her hair and tried to think—where was she, and why? What had she been doing last night?

She sat on the edge of the bed and thought. She looked at the door, afraid of going through it until she knew where she was. She felt like she'd grasp it, if she could just focus . . .

She had been sitting for a few minutes when she heard a knock at the door. She jumped.

"Freya?"

The voice was familiar. "Hello?" she replied.

"I heard you moving around. Breakfast is ready when you want it." It was Professor Stowe.

"Okay . . . thanks."

She heard footsteps moving away from the door and waited for a few moments. Something was coming back to her. She had been at the Old Observatory again—but doing what?

She went to the door and opened it. She now stood in a small triangular hallway. There were two other doors, both open, one of which led to the large sitting room that she now remembered from her first night here, and the other leading to the kitchen. There were pleasant smells and the faint sound of a radio coming from within. She edged around the doorway.

"Hello," said Professor Stowe at the cooker. He was stirring a pan of eggs with a spatula. "I don't have any appointments this morning, so I thought I'd come over and make breakfast. Are you feeling better?"

"I'm not sure."

"You push yourself quite hard. Maybe you should take today to clear your head—walk around a little. In any case, I hope you'll feel better after this. There's bacon already on the table. Have a seat and I'll get you some coffee."

Freya sat at a small table with stools arranged around it. Stowe placed a mug of coffee in front of her and she breathed a lungful of it into her. Maybe she *would* take today to relax. It'd been awhile since she'd walked around Oxford.

She gazed into the gently spiraling wisps of steam as they curled into the air, trying to remember exactly when she had last seen the city. She had walked around with her parents when she first arrived, but that seemed like a long time ago. She couldn't even remember what term it was now; either Hilary or Trinity, right?

"There you are, tuck in," Stowe said, placing a hot plate of scrambled eggs in front of her. "Toast?"

"Yes, please," she said, helping herself to bacon.

"What were you and the lieutenant going over last night?"

"Um . . . It was Dean's *Ancient Mechanisms*, I think."

"That's *Mechanisms Ancient*, I think you'll find. Cookham Dean has an interesting perspective—although reading through his prose can be something of a plough these days. Nonetheless, it does bear pearls."

"Yes," Freya said, things starting to fall into place now. "I also took some of Dudley Port's *Histories* to bed with me, but I didn't get very far."

"No, I don't imagine you would have." He chuckled and then moved forward and took her plate. "Here, I'll clear up, you go get some fresh air. Brent will pop in around noon. Feel free to send him away if you need the day off."

Freya looked down at her empty plate. She was still hungry. "Thanks," she said. She went to drain her coffee, but found that she'd already finished it.

She found her shoes by the door and went outside. She saw a black iron gate that led to a green expanse and she followed that.

Freya walked the circuit of University Parks. Maybe she *had* been overdoing it lately. She really should take the day off to relax—she'd work better after relaxing. Then tomorrow she could hit the studies hard again with a fresh mind. She sat down on a bench by the duck pond, put her head in her hands, and started massaging her scalp.

"Am I disturbing you?"

Freya looked up. Mr. Cross was standing in front of her.

"No," Freya said, sitting up straight and trying to put on a smile. "No, not at all."

"Felix told me you'd be here." His voice was abrupt and direct, with strong Northern inflections. "Would you not feel so ill if we had our session out in the open?"

"We could give it a try."

"Only it *is* important . . ." Mr. Cross sat beside Freya. "Look at those ducks," he said. "The silly buggers. Where did we leave off?"

"It was . . . I think—"

"Somewhere around Eniol, I believe." Cross cleared his throat and began.

"Eniol was still young at the time of Riniol's death, and so Isfatel was ruler until Eniol came of age, which was for thirteen years until he was fifty, and the ward of the crown was eighteen. But when he was forty-eight he became ill and had to share power with the Chancellor, Terenifil, who resigned his commission to become ward for the interim years, leaving Intafel, the Vice-Chancellor, in his position. This was Intafel who was Istafel's illegitimate son, by Tenil, the wife of Inhenial, who was also of the house Nerefon and whose other name was Berenon, and was the sister of Nonibere. They were the children of Intragon, whose name is not known, since this name means, simply, 'go-between.' It could be that this was Onterigon, who was the third son of Birenon's grandfather Grenithone, who was called the father of two houses, those being Gonteroc and Minetoc. Gonteroc was named for Gonithone, son of Grenithone, who had, of sons, five: Rentigon, Mentrigon, Fanigon, Vhanthigon, and Amonigon. Of daughters, there were seven: Gonterri who married Vascan, Gonshari who married Ritiol, Gonbruni who married Rasslon, Gonfortu who married Marthust, Gonpiriri who married Chirithust, Gonchuri who married Jhaltrot, and two more whose names have been lost to us . . ."

Freya, her attention already drifting, felt herself nodding off. She shook her head gently from side to side.

". . . but who married sons from the house Roniroc—Venron and Terron. That was house Gonteroc. House Minetoc was named for Minethone son of Grenithone. Of that house, there were sons four: Rommin, Treymin, Oromin, and Yummin. The names of their spouses are not known, but it is recorded that Retiniol, descendant of Oromin, was related to Entefiol by virtue of marriage to his sister. Daughters of the house of Minetoc were six: Minnah who married Tunnik of Artrinon, Mingrini who married Nintner of Grentner, Minotoo who married Dasten of Rocoone, Mindher who married Eleneth of Docrot, Minetee who married and survived Kaejey of Trownon to marry Lorlok of Kolor, and Minkanti, who had no husband. Those were the houses of the sons of Gonteroc and Minetoc, the patriarchs of which married the two sisters Erivah and Inilah, who had no official royal descent but claimed to be from the line of Britune, the mythical hero whose exploits are recorded in the Comeridion, the tales of people of Trisk, who at that time were ruled by Indinah, of the house Hanoc, and so Grenithone became beholden to Hanzhan by virtue of the marriage of his sons to his daughters. Onterigon, the third son of Grenithone, became a member of Gonithone's court and married Elewhine . . ."

Freya was now trying very hard to stay awake. She had abandoned trying to make sense of Cross's list of names and relations, and was fighting simply to keep her eyes open.

". . . If he was indeed the same man as Intragon, then that means that Berenon had strong ties to the house Thonetoc, through his father, and Nerefone, through his mother. It is uncommon that a male son would follow his mother to her family house while his father was still alive before reaching his age of manhood, and so it can be assumed that before Berenon was of age, Onterigon, or Intragon if it was he, was already dead. This presents problems but has no bearing whatsoever on Intefel, since it has been established that he was not of Inhenial, or Berenon, and therefore not related to the Thonetoc line.

"Now, to return to Eniol. He ruled for eight months, having previously married Riwlah, of the house of Riwetoc, who was the daughter of Eniriw . . ."

And she was asleep.

2

Daniel reached a clearing where several large stones protruded from the ground. The sky that was visible through the gaps between the leaves and branches of the trees was still light, but it had become very cold in the forest. The cloak was keeping him warm enough for now, but he would need more than that for the night.

He had poems to compose.

In fact, he'd already come up with a couple verses that weren't completely awful. With a mixture of anticipation and dread, he cleared his throat. *Here goes nothing,* he thought and spoke in a loud, clear voice:

> *"Forest great and forest good,*
> *May I have some firewood?"*

He waited and listened. There were no sounds apart from the breeze rattling the branches and rustling the leaves overhead. He looked around. No pile of firewood had miraculously appeared. Perhaps he had to search for it. Or maybe it wasn't a good enough poem. Or maybe Kay was pulling his leg.

He took off his new cloak and laid it on one of the rocks. Then, careful always to keep a couple of the large rocks in view, he started hunting among the underbrush for twigs and branches.

He didn't have to go far before he had collected an armload of wood, some of it small and relatively dry, some of it larger— about the width of his arm. He brought it back to the clearing and dumped it by one of the boulders. Then he went back out.

He brought back about a dozen more armfuls, making quite a sizeable pile. He had no idea how much he was going to need. He didn't know how much wood he'd need in his own world, let alone this one where the days and nights were twice as long. An armload might only mean about an hour's burning time. Better have too much than too little, he decided, and kept going back out for more, so long as more was to be had. He had made a couple dozen more trips, never leaving sight of the boulders, until he had gathered a pretty sizeable pile.

Daniel crouched and ran his hand over the ground, which was covered with a small amount of semi-decayed leaves that created a soft, surprisingly dry powdery substance. That was good. He knew from years of hard experience on the streets that lack of insulation against the ground could freeze you as quickly as the wind. Looking around, he figured he could easily scrape up enough of this dry matter to make workable bedding.

But now he had to actually *make* the fire. He sucked his breath in and let it out in a sigh. He hadn't felt that the success of the firewood poem had been conclusive. Asking the forest to give him some fire was really going to be the test.

He started fitting rhymes together in his head as he placed the wood into what he figured was a good pattern. Then he stood up and dusted off his hands. Here went nothing. Kay had told him to ask for fire, and this was it. He took another deep breath and recited:

> *"Thank you, forest, great and good,*
> *For giving me my firewood.*
> *But in order to survive the night,*
> *I need this pile of wood to light.*
> *Please give me what I require,*
> *To make myself a good campfire."*

Daniel held his breath and sucked on his lower lip. What was he going to do if this didn't work? Start rubbing sticks together, he supposed. He had just started to let his breath out in a sigh of defeat when there was a rustling above as of a bird flying through the branches and a whistle of something descending at speed.

He glanced up just as a stone tore through the leaves above and landed at his feet. It struck another rock and created a massive bouquet of sparks that leapt a foot into the air.

Daniel jumped back in alarm, looking about him at the tree cover. What was this now? Was the forest trying to kill him?

Blinking in surprise, he bent down and examined the object that had fallen. It was a wedge of metal, iron maybe, shaped like an axe head. When it fell, it had struck a fist-sized rock and broken a large chunk of it off. Looking at the rock closer, he found the broken edge glossy and hard—flint.

"You must be joking," he muttered.

He bent down and gave the metal and the flint a few experimental knocks together, generating more sparks. In a few short minutes he found a way to create a good number at once. He pulled out some dry, brown moss from the woodpile and started striking the rock and the metal above it. It took some time, but the moss started to curl and then smoke. After careful tending, a flame appeared, which he nursed and fed with more moss. He gently pushed it into the centre of the woodpile, then placed the piece of metal and stone into his rucksack.

He kept feeding and nurturing the fire until some of the thicker branches caught and then he sat back and let the fire take its course, watching the flames grow and lick against the larger branches.

He was tired now—incredibly tired. Whatever there was inside of him that had kept him going was almost completely exhausted. He had come a long way since waking up this morning on Magdalen Bridge. He was also hungry. Unbelievably hungry. He took a sip of water from the skin that Kay had given him and lay back to think of another poem. He looked at the stone that had also been given to him, sniffed it—it smelled of nothing—and slowly stuck it into his mouth.

It tasted faintly bitter—like just about any other rock, he imagined. He hadn't habitually tasted rocks since he was about four, but this one, even after all that time, failed to impress. It was making his gorge rise. He spat the stone into his palm and looked at it again, now glinting with saliva. Then he tipped his hand and let it fall to the ground. That was enough of that. He turned his attention back to the fire.

As he sat, his ears adjusted to the silence and eventually, over the sound of the hissing wood, he became aware of another noise. With a mighty effort he stood up, his muscles already starting to ache, and went to investigate.

The sound led him to a stream, nearly a river, which was as wide as he was tall. He stood for a moment, puzzled, since he hadn't seen or heard it when he was gathering firewood, but there was no doubt about it, here it was. The water trickled through a maze of rocks and pools at a fair speed. As he got closer, he noticed something shimmering within the water that flashed with a white, silvery brilliance even in the low light. Stooping over, he saw that it wasn't just one object, but many similar objects flashing by in the same direction—fish.

There were masses of them swimming past in clumps of dozens. He thought for a moment of going back and finding a stick long and pointed enough to make a spear out of, but the fish were so thickly packed at the spot he was standing, and so close to the surface that he thought he might be able to just reach down and pick them out of the water as easily as plucking apples from a tree—ripe for the taking.

He bent over and stretched his arm out, ready to dart it into the water and pull out a nice, lovely fish but suddenly pulled his arm back. *Ripe for the taking.* He had almost taken a fish from the stream, a fish he hadn't asked for from a stream he hadn't asked the forest to show him.

He drew himself back and sat on his feet. His heart was racing. He was almost gasping at his near miss, but then . . . how near of a miss had it actually been? The only reason he had to believe that there was any danger to him if he took things without asking was Kay's word; a man—an elf?—that he had never met before a short time ago. It could very easily be he was being lied to, if not ridiculed. That said, the piece of metal from the sky was a bit of a stretch to the notion of coincidence.

Daniel sighed and then thought for a moment. Then:

> *"Good forest, please, now I wish*
> *That you would give to me a fish."*

Even by his own standards, Daniel knew that it was a pretty lousy poem, but he was tired and hungry and more than a little confused.

There was a splashing sound, and a fish leapt out of the water, flipping end over end, and landed on the bank next to him, where it floundered half-heartedly. It was almost a foot long.

Daniel didn't know much about fishing, but he knew enough to grab the fish by its tail and smack its head against a rock to kill it. He did so, and sat for a moment holding it. He thought of another rhyme.

> *"Forest, I don't wish to be greedy,*
> *But I am hungry, cold, and needy.*
> *I'd like some fish, a couple more,*
> *Delivered to me like before."*

Daniel couldn't tell if his poetry was good or not. He'd have to try to come up with something better tomorrow for the path.

There was another splash and two more fish flopped out onto the ground beside him. Shaking his head, he killed them and then scooped up all three fish and walked back up to his camp where the fire needed tending. He did this, raking the new coals together, and got it all burning at a steady clip.

He spitted the fish, set them to cook lengthways against the fire, and started scraping up enough dead leaves for bedding. The birds in the branches above him started to twitter as if commentating and arguing about the scene below them.

Daniel's head swam with ideas and thoughts about the world he now found himself in. He was extremely tired, though, and before he fell asleep, he had been contemplating the serious and disturbing idea that the forest may be trying to deliberately trap him.

3

The kirk was a small stone building, rectangular and grey. There was no belfry or steeple, just an iron cross on the east end of the roof. Rab Duthie led Officer Alex Simpson through the large wooden door, beneath a carved wooden emblem of a burning bush and the Cross of St. Andrew.

Outside, the sky was grey and cold, but inside the church it was warm and bright. The lights and heater were on and candles had been placed on the altar, the windowsills, in freestanding holders—anywhere there was space for them.

There were about half a dozen people spread throughout the church, sitting in the pews, their heads bowed, some of them clutching their hands, some of them reading silently from Bibles. A man dressed in black walked towards them down the centre aisle. He had a head of well-combed iron-grey hair and a clean-shaven chin. When he spoke, his voice was soft with a very thin

Edinburgh accent. He greeted Rab first, shaking his hand in both of his, and then turned to Alex.

"Reverend, this is a man from the Constabulary—says he's looking into the—our troubles here."

"Is that so?" he said, turning a weary smile to Alex and offering a hand.

Alex took it and introduced himself.

"Rector John Maccanish," the reverend introduced himself. "How do you do? How can I assist you?"

"Well, Rab said it best," said Alex. "I've heard about the trials ye've been facing up here, and I've come to help."

"Of course, help with what, exactly?"

Alex gazed out into the church. "Ye've got a fair few in today— late-morning prayer meeting?"

"It's—" Maccanish seemed to wrestle with how much to say. "I've organized a few weeks of twenty-four-hour prayer. It's been— a hard time for the parishioners up here."

"Rab was telling me about that. There are the things that have been told to the police—the thieving, the vandalism, the suicides. And then there are the things you don't tell the police—the 'accidents,' the fighting, the drinking, the victimising, the bad crops, sickly animals, new mothers miscarrying. And then there are the things that you don't tell each other." Alex turned his eye to Maccanish. "The nightmares, the screams you think you hear in the night, the sleeplessness, the foul looks that you imagine people are giving you in the street, the curl of your own lip and the shortness of your temper to everyone you meet. Ill will. The sense that there's a thick, oppressive force covering the vale—as heavy and as dark as a wet, woolen blanket—smothering the very life from you, from the loved ones around you."

Maccanish stood staring at Alex, blinking his eyes. "And you're with the police?" he asked.

"Aye, the police." Alex gave another grin.

"Well, you're absolutely right about all of that—dreams, cries in the night, and the rest. Except for the part about no one telling each other—they tell *me*. All of them. Everybody feels it, and they come here. In their minds, the church is here to prevent all evil touching them—so they can just ignore it and get on with their lives, whether they step in the building or not. When that is found not to be the case—well, then it's the kirk's fault for letting it happen, isn't it? They come here angry, you understand, *livid*—demanding answers, explanations. I've got none for them. They don't prepare you for this type of thing in the seminary. I've been threatened, officer," Maccanish said, holding out his hands, "attacked! Not by men, by women—mothers in desperation. They want to know what to do. And what can I tell them? It'll be alright in the end? No. I say watch and pray, read your Scripture, search your hearts, and meditate on the Word. And they leave here angrier than they arrived—spitting, cursing, blaspheming all manner of obscenities. And where do I turn? I called the bishops, but they just fobbed me off. I wanted them to come up and see—*feel* what it's like to walk down these paths, and they agreed, but their secretaries refused to make appointments. We've been abandoned, all of us. We'd abandon each other, if we could." Maccanish ran his hands through his hair and composed himself. Then he continued.

"I had a sit-down with the wife, to work out what to do— we prayed long and hard, we listened for the Spirit to guide us, and you know what we heard Him say? Watch and pray. It was the hardest thing to hear at that time. But we set our shoulders to the task. 'John,' my wife said. 'John, go down to the kirk with this load of candles. Get down on your knees and I'll bring a pot of tea around directly.' I came down to open the kirk and I found three elderly ladies—parishioners—standing on the doorstep. I asked them what they were doing here and they said that they'd come to help me watch and pray. I nearly bawled like a bairn, I was so relieved. That was over a fortnight ago, and I've rarely left the building since. It's turned the church right upside down. Over two-thirds of my congregation has abandoned the building—won't even come in sight of the place. I go to visit them and their doors are barred. But there are those who previously wouldn't nod to me in the street, turning up every day, sitting and praying for hours on end. But praying for what? Watching for what?"

"For me," Alex said solemnly. "For me, Reverend Maccanish— you're in the middle of a spiritual battle. You've been invaded. And being taken off-guard and ill-prepared, the only thing you *could* do was dig in, keep your heads down, and wait for reinforcement."

"A spiritual battle," Maccanish repeated, his eyes shining. He began nodding his head. "Aye—aye. So what are you? Are you the reinforcement? Are you like—a spiritual general or something?" he asked eagerly.

"Me?" said Alex. "A general? No, I'm not a general."

He paused for dramatic effect—he couldn't help himself. "I'm Black Ops."

CHAPTER EIGHT

The Lifiendes

1

The yfelgóp laid perfectly still in a pool of its own blood.

As soon as Daniel and Freya felt able, they stood up, brushed themselves off, and then very cautiously opened the door and crept back downstairs. Modwyn was standing in the hall, talking to Frithfroth and two guards in an urgent and frantic manner. She looked up as Daniel and Freya descended and cried out, "There they are!" All eyes turned up to them.

They saw Freya holding the yfelgóp spear, saw the dark blood on Daniel's shirt and his own blood dripping from his hand to the stone floor, and gave a gasp of horror. Modwyn rushed forward, arms outstretched.

"Oh, my dear children! Where were you? What happened to you?"

Daniel and Freya felt hands on them, searching them for injuries. They heard questions that came so fast they could not answer them. They tried their best to give a short explanation of what had just happened.

"Frithfroth!" Modwyn called when they told her of the attack. "Tell the guard to sweep the tower! The lifiendes have been attacked." She turned back to them and examined the cuts on Daniel's face. Drawing herself up, she turned to Cnafa and Cnapa. "Lead these two to the kitchens," she instructed. "Then bring hot water, poultice, and bindings."

Daniel and Freya allowed themselves to be led through the silent hall. The kitchen was a cold room with a high ceiling. There were several large ovens that looked very dusty and long stone-topped metal tables that did not appear to have been used recently. Two metal stools were dragged before them, and they sat down gratefully. Cnapa placed a bowl of water and a cloth before him.

Modwyn entered and hurried over to them. Kneeling before Daniel and Freya, her green dresses flowing out around her, she cleaned Daniel's wounds as they explained what happened in more detail.

"My poor æðelingas," she said when they had finished. "I was so worried when I did not see you with the others." Daniel's wound had been cleaned of blood. "These are not deep. They will not scar."

Modwyn cleaned the cloth in the bowl and pushed it away. "The bell will sound again when the *geard* is cleared," she said. "Until then you must stay in the hall. I must go and find news of the battle. I will send Cnafa and Cnapa to bring you some food. I will return shortly."

With that and a sweep of her long gown, she left them.

Daniel and Freya went back into the main hallway and found a bench out of the way of the terrified Niðergearders. In a few moments Cnafa brought them a tea-like spiced drink, and Cnapa brought them some more of the flatbread and dried meat.

They sat, sipping at the drink from warm clay bowls and chewing very small mouthfuls of food, which they did not taste. As they ate, they noticed the townspeople watching them. They wouldn't say anything to each other, just stared and looked away whenever Daniel or Freya made eye contact.

After a time they heard the tolling of a bell. Modwyn entered the hall again.

"The attack is over," she announced. "The streets are clear. But be cautious in returning to your homes. Do not go alone."

She stepped aside to allow the people out of the hall and made her way to Daniel and Freya.

"Come with me," she said.

They left the Langtorr by the large double doors. Once outside she asked a guard at the gate whose arms and chest were covered with putrefying brown blood where the main force was gathered.

He had an odd look on his face—a kind of dazed, unbelieving look. He pointed with a wavering hand towards one end of the city. "Over—over there . . ."

"Is all well?" Modwyn asked the guard. "We were told that the city was clear."

"And so have I been told, *idesweard*. And so it seems," the guard replied. "But for my life I know not why."

"What mean you by that?"

The guard paused, seemed to choke slightly, and then continued weakly, "The wall has been breached."

"Yes, of course we know—"

"Nay, *niðercwen*. Not just the defenses, but the wall itself has been broken."

Modwyn's eyes widened. "Where?"

The guard could only gesture weakly. Her eyes blazing, Modwyn spun on her heel and started off in the direction he had pointed. "Come, lifiendes," she said. "Hurry."

They rushed through the streets of the underground city alongside Modwyn, passing people returning to their homes and assessing damages. Everywhere they looked—alongside walls and heaped in the middle of the streets—lay bodies of yfelgópes, nearly all of them headless. Daniel wondered why this was, but soon saw that groups of knights and guards were systematically gathering corpses together and chopping the heads from the dead enemies' bodies. He shuddered and looked away.

Rounding a corner, they saw the city wall with its massive carved trees rise up in front of them—but it wasn't as it had been. A large U-shaped section had crumbled away, creating an avalanche of stone that engulfed the nearby houses. Modwyn gave a startled cry when she saw the gap and ran towards it.

There were many guards standing in the breach, their shoulders tense and weapons ready. Swiðgar and Ecgbryt were there, perched on a pile of dusty stones, gazing out into the blackness, cautious and tense. The wall looked as if it had just fallen apart, like the wall of a sand castle.

They were still a fair distance away when they came to the first bits of rubble from the wall. Blocks of stone had fallen against some of the houses, piling like a grey drift of snow. As they started to climb the pile, they were surprised to find that the rocks crumbled to a fine powder underfoot—it was like walking up a snow bank. Daniel knelt down and picked up a large clump of painted ivy. He was able to lift it quite easily. It was brittle and he found he could flake pieces away with his thumb. The sensation was like holding a compressed brick of fine sand.

As they neared the peak of the dusty heap, they became aware of a rhythmic pounding sound: dull, soft, and strong, like the pounding of blood. Modwyn and Freya climbed up to stand behind Swiðgar and Ecgbryt.

"What is it?" asked Freya. "What's that sound?"

"It is the 'gópes," stated Swiðgar. "They are letting us know that they bide."

They all stood and listened to the pounding, pounding, pounding of thousands of hands against the dirt—a steady, synchronized, patient beat. "Why aren't they attacking?" Daniel asked.

Swiðgar pointed into the darkness.

Standing at the edge of the circle of light thrown by the city's lanterns was a dim, reddish figure pacing back and forth, just in front of the gap in the wall. "Who's that?" he asked.

"It is Ealdstan," said Ecgbryt.

"Ealdstan? But . . ." Freya remembered the figure falling out of the window as they raced to the Langtorr. She had forgotten about it until just now but remembered the fall replayed in her head, the swirling robes riffling like a falling flame. Ealdstan must have more power in him than he had given them reason to believe. The swaggering figure striding up and down the battle line in front of the haunting, pounding rhythm of the yfelgópes didn't act like the old man Daniel and Freya had met. He was strong and spry. Something about the way he held himself made him seem haughty—challenging.

Ealdstan turned and strode back the other way, his chest thrown forward, daring anyone to engage him. None did. Ealdstan made another pass and then spun on his heel and walked back towards the city.

Daniel and Freya shied away slightly as Ealdstan approached the group. Freya still had a bruise on her arm where Ealdstan had gripped her, and neither she nor Daniel had particularly wanted to see him again.

Ealdstan stood for a while, staring into the city, at the ruins of the wall and the bodies of the yfelgópes, lost in his own thoughts until Modwyn addressed him. "What is it that could accomplish this?" she said, raising a hand to indicate the wreckage.

"Gád did this. It is a spell of decay."

"A magic to corrupt solid rock?"

"He must have been weaving it for some time. He would have had to build an entropic force and then push it along an enchanted wind. The spell would have looked like a black cloud. It blew centuries away from the stone in seconds and then nested inside of it. It is in it now, slowly eating away at it . . . our first, greatest defense . . ."

At his words, a chunk of stone the size of a small shed tumbled down from the top of the wall and crumbled into a mound of dust.

"*Meotodes meahte!*" exclaimed Ecgbryt. "How can it be stopped?"

Ealdstan sighed like a professor answering an obvious question. "It cannot be stopped—not completely. I can slow it with my power, but it will not quit until Gád's life leaves him—at which time all spells that he has made will unravel.

"It cannot be doubted that he will strike again," he continued. "This is only one move in a game that he and I have begun to play. There is no question that he has more schemes in mind, some of which are this very moment being put into effect."

"He must be stopped and destroyed," said Swiðgar.

"The other knights must be roused," rumbled Godmund, tramping up the pile of rubble to join them. "They will arrive from all the corners of England and send the *yfelhost* into oblivion."

"No," moaned Ealdstan. "Not those sleeping, not yet. It is not their time."

"What then?" Modwyn exclaimed passionately. Daniel and Freya glanced up at her and saw a face as harsh as a thunderstorm. "A wall has been breached," she rasped, "that has never failed since it was made over twelve hundred years ago. Enemies have had their way with the city for the first time in a thousand. There were *yfelmen* in the torr, Ealdstan—one of them attacked the lifiendes! If you were to act, t'would best be done soon, and best be done well!"

Ealdstan stood motionless as the silence left by the end of

Modwyn's rebuke hung in the air. Eventually the old wizard said, "Gád will not be defeated easily. He will not die by spear-thrust, or axe-blow, for his life is no longer in his body. He has hidden his mortality somewhere else—somewhere safe, somewhere unknown to anyone. Only if that mortality can be found and destroyed will Gád will be vulnerable to attack."

The company took this in.

"What do you mean his mortality?" Daniel asked.

"His life," Ealdstan answered. "His heart's soul. It is an object of his—a hand or a finger, perhaps his very heart—into which he has placed his mortal life and then removed from himself. As long as it is safe and secret, none can touch it."

"How will it be guarded?" Ecgbryt asked.

"It will not be guarded," Ealdstan replied. "At least, not by any guard aware of his purpose. There may be obstacles, but Gád would rely more on secrecy than force. No, not guarded—hidden . . ."

"I do not understand," said Godmund. "How would he be terrified of his own weakness?"

"If he were to lose his power," Ealdstan explained, "he would still want to reclaim his life and use it. The hiding place would be near, but still forgotten . . ." As Ealdstan talked, his eyes and voice drifted off. "He would have placed it on the other side of the Wild Caves, on the other side of the *Slæpismere*."

"The Slayp-is-mere?" Daniel said under his breath.

"It means 'the sleeping ocean.' It is the name we give to the enormous lake of water that lies beneath this island."

"Then it is clear," said Swiðgar. "We gather a party and make a sally out to destroy this mortal heart. What could be more plain?"

"Even so," growled Godmund lowly, "even were the Grístgrenner killed, there would still be his general, Kelm, to settle with, and the only thing that can defeat the Kafhand is force of arms. Whence is that to come?"

There was silence. Ealdstan stood, muttering, "Not the sleepers . . . not now . . . not yet . . ."

"But with the enchanter," said Ecgbryt after a short silence, "surely there is no reason to dither. We must destroy Gád, come what may, and it would best be done as soon as possible."

"It is dangerous . . . ," breathed Ealdstan.

"I am the fiend of danger."

"No, you understand not. Gád's heart can only be destroyed . . . by a mortal . . . not by a sleeper, not by anyone who is now dwelling within Niðergeard. It must be destroyed by a lifiende."

Slowly, all eyes turned to settle on Daniel and Freya.

"I don't understand," Freya said. "What does that mean?"

"Dense children!" Ealdstan sneered. "It means that none in this city can destroy him—except one of you. You really want to leave this place? Then destroy Gád and break the siege. Either that, or grow old down here with the rest of us."

In the silence that followed, the wizard Ealdstan stalked away.

2

Modwyn led them into a room on the sixth floor of the Langtorr, high enough above the rooftops of the buildings for them to see the ruined section of wall and the work that was already being done to repair it.

Craftsmen from every corner of the city were coming to join the emergency workforce, working quickly, faces gaunt. Stone was hauled from storage by huge workhorses, rolled across the city on metal poles and lashed to the backs of the impressive animals. The old, crumbling rock was being chipped away, carved out so that the new stone would fill the gap precisely. It nearly broke Daniel's heart to see any of that beautiful, forest-like wall fall away, however necessary.

"Why aren't the yfelgópes attacking?" Daniel asked, staring down from the window onto the work. "Wouldn't they beat us all if they did?"

"I do not know," said Modwyn after a pause. "Their minds are so twisted that I cannot guess. They have always plagued us, but I have never known them to be organized thus. I fear their leader."

"Gád?"

"Yes, and also this Kelm. He is not an yfelgóp, I wist, but something more—something older and cleverer."

"I don't understand. Why hasn't this been dealt with ages ago, when you first saw the yfelgópes?" Daniel asked.

Modwyn sighed. "Ealdstan prevented it—he reasoned that Niðergeard is of little consequence in the face of the battle that is to come."

"What battle is that?" Daniel asked.

"Just one battle in the long war that has been raging across the universe since near time began. The war between Creation and Destruction. Ealdstan has cast his sight forward and seen great forces clashing upon this island. Although of great consequence to us, this land is just a small pebble in the vast arena, and this glorious city, no more than a grain of sand."

"But if Niðergeard is threatened," reasoned Daniel, "that means the knights are threatened, and that means that the country is in danger."

"Not necessarily."

Daniel and Freya gazed blankly at Modwyn.

"But," said Freya, "if protecting this city will help to win the battle—and then each battle afterwards—why not do it? Niðergeard may be a pebble, but if it falls, it could start an avalanche."

"There are many ways of winning a battle," Modwyn said quietly and unconvincingly. "What you must understand about Niðergeard," she continued after a moment's thought, "is that nothing changes here—it's not intended to. That is the enchant-ment's purpose. It is the price we pay when we give up our mortality; because our lives have no end, nothing we do can have an end. We must always look after the knights, we must always be opposed by the forces of destruction and decay, and we must always keep fighting against the opposition, whatever form it may take, though that fight has no end."

"That's—that's terrible," Freya said. "To keep doing the same things over and over again."

"Is that why everyone looks so worn out?" Daniel asked. "So tired? So . . . grey?"

Modwyn nodded. "It is our sacrifice. It is the nature of things. To gain a gift, we must relinquish a gift."

"What gift did you have to lose?"

"We had to lose the gift of death—the gift of completion. The door between life and death must always be open for us, but we may never walk through it nor cause others to pass through it. We cannot affect anything completely, neither start nor finish a sig-nificant act, such as to create life, share love, or . . . or even destroy an enemy. We must continue, unchanged and unchanging, until our purpose is finished."

"But you can kill the yfelgópes."

"They exist on a plane much like ours. Their curse, their sacrifice, is living a half-life, never fully alive. We can kill them individually, though not as a whole. Neither their source, nor their master, may be destroyed by us. We may operate within cycles and affect their course by degrees, but we cannot end or create them. We may alter the balance, but not overturn it—for our lives are thin."

"But what's the point of even being here if you can't change anything?"

"We do not exist to win the battle, you understand—that task has been given to others. We exist to support those who fight."

"You mean the sleeping knights?"

Modwyn nodded.

"So what are the knights waiting for?" Daniel asked after a time. "Why are they asleep?"

Modwyn drew a deep breath. "They await one of two things. Either for this island's enemies to invade it, at which time the knights will wake and drive the attackers into the sea. Or they wait for the battle at the end of time, when they will rise up with all sleepers everywhere and fight for Creation."

"How long until then?"

Modwyn's clasped hands started to fidget. She looked away from them and smiled coldly to herself. "To speak truly, we did not dream the wait would be this long. When the first knights were laid down, it was thought a hundred years, perhaps longer. But never more than a thousand."

They sat in silence. Daniel broke it by slowly saying, "But Britain has been under attack lots of times. Have you ever risen up and helped anyone then?"

Modwyn looked up at him and her smile seemed to warm. "Britain has warred many times, occasionally with itself and often with its neighbors, but its people have not yet been in the direst of danger, in peril of the death of their souls. Rulers come and rulers go—the Normans, the Saxons and Jutes, the Angles, the Romans, the Celts, the Picts, and the hidden races before them—and rule of the island is passed from one set of hands to another, but the spirit of the isle remains strong, and soon it is the island that conquers the conquerors. Its ways become their ways, its loves become their loves. In time, they fight for it and its people as fervently as those whom they replaced."

"So England hasn't been in enough danger yet?" asked Freya. "Is that what you're saying?"

"There have been times—as in the period now referred to as

the Dark Ages—in which evil spirits began to manifest them-selves physically, taking on twisted forms to enslave and destroy the people of this isle—flying creatures ravaged the skies, chilling the hearts of the people, and any manner of striding beasts stalked the forests. It was thought that the time of the greatest threat was near, and so many knights were awakened to join the living heroes who rose at that time to fight them off."

"You mean—dragons?" Daniel asked, amazed.

"Yes. It was the hardest task of all to rid the island of its dragons. There were some that had gained a firm hold. They are devious creatures—more cunning than men, with souls as cold and powerful as glaciers. They feed on fear and terror and are never wholly out of the hearts of men. But they were not the only foes."

"There were others? More monsters?"

Modwyn drew in a breath. "Yes, of many various kinds: those of the mischievous variety—wisps, brownies, kobolds, hobgoblins, and ghouls—as well as the larger types—ogres, trolls, and change-lings. All of these have been exiled to the lower parts of the world, where it is hot and watch is kept on their doorways. For if once a foothold is gained by that world in this, then the two start mixing. Babies are stolen to become elf princes; those who would be witches and warlocks sell their souls for power; men are knitted into were-creatures, and it is harder to separate the undead darkness from the world. That was how the elves—the hidden people—became corrupted. It was very hard to force them out of the land."

"And you said that the knights woke up to help the heroes of that time, right?" said Freya as she started to make sense of this fantastic information.

"Yes," said Modwyn.

"So you always needed living heroes because mortal people are the only ones who can destroy evil and put an end to the cycles," said Freya.

"Well said," Modwyn nodded. "It is just so."

"And right now," asked Daniel, "are we the heroes?"

"*They* can't destroy Gád or the yfelgópes," said Freya, gazing levelly at Modwyn, "but we can, because we're mortal."

Modwyn nodded again.

"Because we can die," Daniel added.

"That is right," said Modwyn softly.

"If Gád is getting more and more powerful," Daniel continued after another thoughtful pause, "and the yfelgópes are getting to be more and more, then doesn't that mean . . . eventually . . . that all the monsters will come back?"

"It will mean that," said Modwyn, "if we don't find a way of stopping him. The tides of darkness continually wax and wane, and we are in the middle of a strong flow at the moment. For years, evil has been building and gathering on these shores. But that question doesn't rest on us below, it rests on the state of the souls of those above. If things get worse—if events occur as Ealdstan predicts— then we may yet see monsters again on the Island of the Mighty. We wait and watch. It is what we do. It is what we have always done.

"But don't look so sad, children," Modwyn said with a genuine smile. "The battle against darkness is not our battle alone. Whether that darkness be within him or without, it is a war that man has fought since first he awoke. It is the most sublime battle in the universe, and it brings freedom to whoever fights in it, to whatever effect. Although our suffering may be greater than another's, so also is our blow against the opposer, and our victory and reward the sweeter. For this reason we were placed in this life to fight, and we are fighting as best we can. It may be dark now, and it may be darker henceforth. Our strength may leave us, but what we achieve will not be insignificant, and it will not be unnoticed. The greater the toil in our agony, the greater our glory at the last."

Daniel and Freya sat still, hardly breathing. They knew that something was expected of them—some sort of commitment or response—but it meant that they would be in danger of pain and death and everything in between. Neither of them could bring themselves to speak. Modwyn herself seemed to be pressing them to say what they knew they had to say.

But still, they said nothing, terrified.

"Come with me," she said, rising with stately grace. "There is something else you should see."

3

They ascended the stairs again and went higher up the tower than they had yet gone. She made several halting pauses as if she didn't completely remember where she was going.

Finally the three came to a metal door that Modwyn opened by turning a large wheel in its centre like a submarine hatch. Freya thought this rather odd and out of place, but had only a couple of seconds to wonder at it before she saw what was on the other side of the door.

They gasped. The room, which was as big as Freya's bedroom, was filled with modern machinery. At least, it seemed modern in comparison to everything else in Niðergeard. It was more like the sort of technology in old science fiction TV shows—large metal banks and cabinets with dials and switches on them—dials and switches like those in World War II bombers. There was an ornate wrought-iron chair of typical Niðergeard design at a small desk that held a pair of massive headphones that were connected to the bank by a dangling, decaying, coiled cord.

"What is it?" Freya asked Modwyn.

"Our radio," Modwyn replied frankly. "Ealdstan brought a man in to make it almost a hundred years ago. Our blacksmiths and craftsmen made each piece that he needed to his specifications. Ealdstan said that it would be very useful, and it has been in the past, but it's been some time since we've had any need to come in here."

She walked over to a large wheel that jutted out from the wall opposite the headphones. It was solid metal, about two feet wide and two inches thick. Modwyn gripped it by its edges and put her whole weight and strength into turning it. It moved slowly and continued turning when she let go. A red lightbulb above it glowed on.

"Do you still use radios where you live?" Modwyn asked.

They both nodded.

Modwyn flipped a large switch that fell into place with a *thunk*. There was a popping sound, and then a hum filled the room.

"As long as the wheel is turning, the radio will work. If the wheel stops, then give it another turn." She disconnected the headphones from the machine and a static susurrus filled the air. She went over to a large dial that had many numbers and radial lines on it.

"Turn this to hear different reports and sounds." With more difficulty than Freya or Daniel would have had, she found a station broadcasting an interview show.

"You may listen as long as you like. If you need something, come and see me or Frithfroth or Cnafa and Cnapa." She went to the door and turned to them before she left and said, "Destruction and evil is spreading in this world. Listen for yourself."

They sat for some time, listening to the soothing voices on the radio spar snidely about the current conflict in Palestine, as it related to a book that one of them had written. Shortly after that came the BBC Radio 4 call signal and a political debate show that discussed the proper response towards a certain African despot. Daniel stood up just as the discussion opened to include a South American dictator and turned the large dial to a music station. Then he gave the large flywheel a little more momentum and sat back down next to Freya.

They listened to songs number nine to five on a station's pop music countdown and then the playlist broke for a news roundup. There were four items: there was the African dictator again, a young boy who had been stabbed in London the previous night, a body count of people who had been crushed to death in a religious ceremony in India, and a car bomb that had gone off in a British embassy in a country they knew of but couldn't place. The three-and-a-half-minute segment ended with the prime minister announcing that the army, which was occupying that country, already had suspects in hand and "a very hard line would be taken with them, and those in the area, to ensure that such events do not happen again." Then there were some commercials.

They finished out listening to the top pop songs countdown, and Freya got up to turn the dial just as the news program started to repeat.

They didn't know how many hours they sat listening. Perhaps it was a full day. It was both comforting and disturbing to listen to the radio. Comforting because it was familiar and reminded them of home, but disturbing because they couldn't deny what Modwyn had said: a lot of bad things were happening in the world. Some of them seemed small—the shootings, kidnappings, and murders—compared to the larger events like wars, riots, and racial killings on a national scale.

"Do you think it was always that way?" Freya asked.

"I don't know, but it's that way now."

"It seems like a lot of these things are really big problems. Were there always rulers who killed lots of people? And wars?"

"Must have been," Daniel said. "But that doesn't mean that what Modwyn says is wrong."

"But it doesn't make it true either. She could have planned all this."

"Planned what? News reports on the BBC? Even if she could,

why? Why would she, or they, need to trick us? Why would they want us to do this quest?"

"Who knows?"

Daniel thought some more as classical music played on the radio. "Well, even assuming the worst, I don't see how we're going to get out of it. Either we go on this quest to destroy Gád's heart, or what? We stay here forever?"

"You'd like that, wouldn't you?"

Daniel thought for a moment. "I feel like I fit in here," he said eventually, in a low voice, almost surprised at his own honesty.

"You 'fit in here'? More than the place you grew up in—where you were born? Is school really that bad?"

"You have no idea how much I hate school. And it's not just that, it's . . . everywhere. Even in my own home I'm ignored, or in the way. At least here people pay attention to me, you know? Swiðgar and Ecgbryt and Modwyn—even Ealdstan—it's like we matter here. If we did this, we'd really make a difference."

"You don't think you matter in the real world?"

"Do *you*?" he shot back. "Sorry, of course you do," he continued sarcastically. "You come from a well-off family in a nice area who has a lot of stuff and parents who like you and give you hugs and presents and cake—"

"Shut up," Freya said angrily. Daniel didn't dare look at her but knew that she was glaring at him fiercely. He played with the straps on his shoes instead. "What if I do have all those things? I don't, but so what if I did? It's not my fault, is it? I didn't choose my family or where I got born, so I'm not going to apologise, am I? Anyway, I'm not making you poor, or lonely, or messing up your relationship with your parents."

"What parents?" Daniel murmured, an uncomfortable lump in his throat. "We've known each other since before primary school. I've been around your place, but why do you think I never invited you around mine? The last memory I have of my dad is him shouting at my nan. He left me with a mum who sleeps all day, goes clubbing every night, and is always rat-arsed wherever she is."

There was a pause.

"Rat-arsed?" Freya asked. For some reason, this struck her as funny. She couldn't stop a giggling snort from escaping her.

"What?" asked Daniel peevishly, but he was smiling too.

"I'm sorry." Freya gave another little laugh.

Daniel grinned a little wider. "It's not funny," he said, still trying to be mad but failing. "It's really not."

"No, I know, it's just . . ." She laughed again and Daniel joined her.

"What are we going to do?" Freya asked once they had stopped laughing.

"I don't see what option we have."

"Destroy the evil wizard?"

"Let's do it."

"This sounds important. It's an adventure," Freya said, smiling. "A once-in-a-lifetime experience."

"At least I hope it is." Daniel gave Freya a smile back and they rose together to find Modwyn.

"We want to help," Freya announced when they found her. "We're going to help you destroy Gád."

"And we want weapons," Daniel added.

4

Ecgbryt passed his torch to Freya before throwing his weight on a huge iron latch set into a tall stone door. He rattled some other levers, then leaned back on an iron ring, slowly setting the door in motion. Daniel and Freya took several steps back as it ponderously swung towards them. This was the armoury, and it was meant to be hard to get into.

A tide of musty air swept over them, making the torch flicker as Ecgbryt took hold of it again. He led them inside, and Daniel and Freya marveled as the torchlight was reflected and refracted from thousands of shining surfaces. The deep room was filled with shelves, racks, and stands containing swords, shields, spears, helmets, and various parts and types of armour.

"To be on a warrior's quest," explained Ecgbryt cheerily as he led them through the weapon hall, "means to be, in part, a warrior. And to be a warrior means, in part, to carry a weapon. For that purpose we are here."

They walked past shelves of helmets that ranged from simple half spheres of metal to those with noseguards and neck protectors, to those with face deflectors, to those with moveable visors. On the other side of the aisle were racks of axes, some of them like Ecgbryt's, with straight edges, some of them with curved single edges, some of them with two curved edges, some of them small—as long as his own arm—and some on thick poles much taller than he was. It was like being in a museum, but the artifacts were not behind glass, nor were they old and rusted. All of them looked well polished, well oiled, very strong, and often very, very sharp.

"Are any of them magical?" Daniel asked. "Or enchanted?"

"Enchanted? Nay," said Ecgbryt with an emphatic shake of his head. "At least," he said and paused, a disturbed expression flicking across his face, "I hope they aren't. No, no one would dare . . ."

"But—but wouldn't that be best? At least, for us?" Freya asked.

Ecgbryt frowned and shrugged. "I don't believe so. There's nothing better than a solid piece of steel strongly wrought and well crafted. That's as strong an enchantment as you will ever want in any battlefield—more reliable as well. Most hero feats were completed with a decent slice of metal and a bold heart. It is unwise to trust enchantments—they often let you down when you need them most."

Ecgbryt stopped at a rack and ran his finger along a row of sheathed knives and daggers. "Ah, these will do," he said, picking out two of them. "Here," he said, passing them along. "Take one each. A good knife is essential on any journey." They were small blades, comparatively speaking, only about the length of a hand, with snug leather sheaths, bone handles, and stout metal hand guards.

"I will not deny," said Ecgbryt as he continued down the hall, "that one may hear of an enchanted blade lending strength to an already strong warrior from time to time. But that warrior still must move it. Some blades of renown are even named and are famous for their names. Even so, can you name any blade more famous than the warrior who lofted it? For what is the use of any object, hallowed though it may be, without a strong hand to lift it? It would be like a horse with no rider—it serves nothing higher than its own purpose. Here we are."

They stopped in front of a line of spears bundled upright along the back wall. Ecgbryt pulled a couple apart, twice as high as either of his companions, and hefted them in his hand.

"I don't suppose either of you has started practicing combat yet?" the large knight asked.

"Of course not," said Freya.

"Pity. That will make it harder to choose the right form of weapon. However, you've killed an yfelgóp between you with very little at hand, and that's not a small thing. I have seen the body and recognised a masterly killing stroke." He gave Freya a sly glance. "Certain are you that you've never used a spear?" he asked again.

"No!" replied Freya, exasperated. "Well, I threw javelin at school a few times."

"She was good," Daniel said.

"Javelin, is it?" Ecgbryt grinned. "Then the choice is clear. I shall start you on your height and a quarter." He walked down the line a distance until he came to some irregular spears of different lengths. He sorted through them briefly and then uttered an exclamation. "Aha! The very thing."

He held before Freya a slim white piece of wood as tall as she was. It was lengthened by a metal shaft about a foot long and topped with a diamond-shaped tip.

"Not quite a javelin, but still it is of Roman design," Ecgbryt told her. "The Romans—or those we used to call the *Laedenware*—developed spearcraft to a brilliant form, and it will serve you well. The shaft is ash, naturally, the tip tempered iron. It has good balance, and this is how you can tell." He cradled the spear at both ends of the wooden shaft, between his thumb and forefinger. He then slowly brought his hands together. "The point at which the hands meet is the centre . . . right here." He circled his hand around the spot and then passed it to her. "Hold it. Heft it for yourself."

Freya reluctantly took the weapon from him. It was heavier than she expected. She found its centre for herself. "That is the point at which you would grip it," Ecgbryt said, "if you were to hurl it at an enemy. The Laedenes were keen on such tactics, but I would not advise anyone to throw away a weapon in the normal course of combat. It leaves one short armed and usually gives an opponent the advantage of, in this case, a well-balanced spear. Its tip is designed to pierce armour and yet come out again easily."

Freya regarded the spear she held in her hand with a doubtful expression. "No thanks," she said, handing the spear back to Ecgbryt.

Ecgbryt didn't take it.

"I don't—I wouldn't feel comfortable taking it. I don't know how to use it and—so, anyway, thanks." She pushed the spear at him again.

Ecgbryt took it but did not return it to the ranks. He held

it lightly, absentmindedly, between his fingers and thumb. He shrugged and turned to Daniel, raising his eyebrows.

"And now, young Daniel, we come to you. You defended yourself well with a poker, did you not? How did you find it?"

Daniel squirmed uneasily. "I don't know. It was . . . difficult."

Ecgbryt nodded patiently. "Aye."

"Also frustrating," Daniel added, "because I couldn't hurt him with it. I could only defend myself, and it was hard to move. Heavy."

Ecgbryt smoothed his beard braids. "Yes. A mace or warhammer would take much strength that would be difficult for you to muster—although you managed to wield it quite swiftly against a knife. Perhaps something to grow into." Turning, he said, "I have an idea which may be better."

"Wait, Ecgbryt," Freya blurted. "Wait a second." Ecgbryt turned to her. "All this fighting, all these weapons—are you sure this is the right thing to do?"

Ecgbryt's face appeared blank in the torchlight.

"I mean, isn't there a peaceful way to do this, without, you know, killing things? It might have been different in your time, but these days people like to talk about peaceful . . ."

Freya's voice trailed off as Ecgbryt crouched down in front of her, his eyes looking earnestly into hers. He knelt on one knee and squared an elbow on the other. "Bless you for saying that," he said in a low voice. "Bless you." His eyes lost focus, his gaze drifting behind her, beyond the walls of the room.

"In my time," he started and then stopped. He swallowed, looking down at the floor. His eyes came back up and they were steady and firm. "I grew up in the west lands of South Briton—the Kingdom of Sussex. Since before I was born, the Dane men had been making raids upon the northern kingdoms of the isle in their long boats. They would merrily leave their homes waving good-bye to their wives and children as if going on a hunting party. When they arrived, after working themselves into a battle-blindness upon the waves, they would kill another man's wife and another man's children for the gain of his pantry, sacking churches, monasteries, feast halls—

"As I grew they became bolder, going so far as to settle the land they were continually attacking in order to more efficiently ravage the south lands. There was no telling when they might strike or where. One summer the village next to ours was hit. Everyone was killed—everyone. Lads I had known since before memory were hewn in two like saplings and men gutted like pigs. The noble men and women were bound and taken away to be ransomed.

"It was then that Ælfred the Geatolic arose to defy the invaders. He was an honourable man. As bold as he was wise, as loving as he was fierce. And he was canny, oh so canny. But he was not jealous of his intelligence, for he built up men's minds and souls as he built his fleet, always strengthening and improving. In this way he was able to rally and unite the kingdoms of the realm and to continually press the Danes and harry them as never before.

"*Swa swa*," he continued with a sigh. "There was much fighting. Much blood. Terrible hardships. Their king, Guthrum, the Battle Wyrm, was wily and deceitful, and despite Ælfred's tenacity there looked to be times when we would not win through. But at Ethandun we did. It was a day lived in hell by every man there. We fought from dawn until dusk, bitter, hard, with watering eyes and grinding teeth, and we beat them back, all of them, to their burgh in Readinga. Come fortnight, they surrendered.

"And Ælfred, instead of killing the invading king as an example for all other would-be attackers, forgave him, schooled him in the way of The Cross, and stood father to him in the church as the heathen Dane had his soul washed. I was there and near wept like a babe.

"War is only barbaric when fought by barbarians—

dishonourable when fought by those with no honour. We did not fight for gain, ambition, our right, or even justice in those days. To revenge ourselves on the Dane would have forced us into atrocities as great as they raised against us and made our souls as dark. We fought for peace, for every man's peace—including those who opposed us. And our actions bear us out, for they were allowed to reside on the island from that day forth, so long as they lived in peace. Was there ever such fruit of war as that? Perhaps you have seen such. I pray you have, for I would pity you if you have not.

"That is why I fight now. For peace. And I will fight until the end of time to win it." He tilted the spear, still in his hand at Freya, but she refused it again.

Ecgbryt turned to Daniel.

"I want a sword," Daniel said, smiling. "A long one, I think."

5

The blacksmith staggered into his workshop, exhausted from hewing stones. He felt the uncommon chill of the room caused by the forge having grown cold while he had been helping to repair the wall. Moving to the fire pit, he stirred the embers with an unfinished sword shaft and shoveled in a couple scoops of coal. This was no enchanted fire but one that needed constant attention. Right now he needed it to be hot—a working flame. In a small handcart by the door he had chisels and picks that needed to be sharpened and tempered for work on the repairs.

As he watched the new coal catch, he became aware of a shuffling behind him. He expected his assistant, and was about to berate him for letting the fire burn so low, when he saw the shape in the doorway. Turning fully, he saw one of the lifiendes—the boy—clutching a sword in his hands. Clearing his throat, he gruffly asked the lad his business.

The boy held up his weapon and mumbled something. He asked the boy to speak up.

"I—I've seen some of the knights' swords have got writing on them," he stammered. "Could you do that for me?"

The blacksmith said that he could.

"I'd like to have my name on this sword, in the same writing as theirs."

The blacksmith huffed and stepped towards him, taking the sword from his hands. He turned it over and recognised the work and style. He tapped the steel with a hammer and listened for its hardness. It was a soft blade and he told the boy so. He saw the young one's face fall and hastened to explain that this blade's edge was as sharp as any hard blade's edge but had less chance of shattering than a hard one. It would serve him well, provided he didn't use it to fence with rocks. As to the name, he replied that it could be easily done, but why should it be done?

The boy said softly, "Because I'm going on a dangerous mission and I might not come back. And if someone finds my sword . . . I want them to know that it was mine, and that I tried."

The blacksmith smoothed his beard and nodded as he turned his broad back. He rooted around on a high shelf and found a scrap of parchment. He laid it in front of the boy and gave him a stick of charcoal, instructing him to write his name in plain letters, as he wanted it to appear on the blade. As he waited he noticed the child's thin legs, weak arms, and small chest. His mind went back to a time when children were not an unfamiliar sight, even in his own house. He thought how unsuited this child was to a sword of any type. Was he raised with an illness, or just born small and thin? Perhaps all children looked this way now. Or perhaps they always had and he'd forgotten.

The boy finished and straightened himself, placing the charcoal flat on the table. He scratched away for a few moments and then looked up. "I'd like a name for it. What are some good sword names?"

The smith shrugged and gave him some—many famous, others not so. Gradually, they came to an agreement about what the sword's name should be and the blacksmith instructed the boy that the work would be sent to the Langtorr in due time. The boy thanked him and then left.

The blacksmith returned to his forge, heaped more coal into the fire pit, and started working the bellows.

6

Preparations for the departure were almost finished. The group would be Swiðgar, Ecgbryt, Daniel, and Freya. For a time it looked as if Godmund would come with them—he would certainly have been appreciated—but it was decided that his skills would be needed defending Niðergeard if there was another assault.

So while supplies were being gathered, Ecgbryt took it upon himself to teach Daniel the principles of armed combat. Freya watched, and after a while decided to take part as well—she figured it would be easier to stay out of the way of someone else's weapon if she knew how they'd use it. The lessons involved far more talking and explanation than Daniel thought necessary, followed by an almost mindless repetition of motion—sword thrusts and jabs by him, and parries and blocks by Freya. This was done, Ecgbryt said, in order that the most basic strokes and motions of their weapons became as natural to their bodies as breathing.

They became tired very quickly. Daniel was sweating heavily and Freya's arms felt as if they were going to fall off. She found it hard to catch her breath. They went back to their rooms for a short rest and a wash in the shallow bowls on their tables. Daniel lay down on the bed and let himself drift off. When he woke up he knocked on Freya's door, but there was no answer. He wandered outside.

As he approached the stone bench—their stone bench—that gave the best, secluded view of the wall repairs, he found Freya already there. He smiled as soon as he saw her. She had her wooden practice spear resting next to her and was wearing a dress—one of the old-style gowns that had been provided for her. It was elaborately embroidered but of a simple design. The cloth and pattern were similar to his own shirt, but hers was a deep brick-red colour.

"I like it," he said.

Smoothing some of the folds of her skirt, she gave a self-conscious smile. "Thanks. My school clothes were getting really tatty. And with those traveling cloaks they made for us, I thought—why not?"

"It looks good—the dark red works on you. It's nice."

"Thanks."

Daniel nodded and took a seat next to her, his eyes on the reparations to the wall. The workers were starting to fill the gap with new cut stone and had moved large iron pulleys and winches onto the battlements to lift the heavy blocks.

"I really don't want to go on this . . . mission," Freya said.

"How did I guess?"

"We'll probably get killed if we go."

"We'll probably get killed if we stay."

"It's 'damned if you do, damned if you don't.' That's what my dad says sometimes."

Daniel smiled and picked up a few pebbles from the ground. "I think I'd rather die doing something than die doing nothing," he said, throwing one of his pebbles at a larger rock. "Especially something heroic. Something that no one else can do except for us. Something that will destroy something evil."

Freya sighed and picked up a handful of pebbles as well. She started throwing them at the same rock. "I honestly don't know what's going to happen. I don't think this is a happy story. The world is so much more complicated than that cheesy 'because they were children they were able to overcome the evil-but-stupid wizard' nonsense they feed to you in kids' movies. That stuff never really happens. It's just something grown-ups come up with to make children feel better—to make them think that they aren't small and insignificant."

Daniel threw another couple stones. "Maybe. Although we *have* come this far. We survived an yfelgóp attack. We even survived Ealdstan," he said with a grin. "Here," he said brightly, "look what I got." He lifted a bundle he'd been carrying that was wrapped in an oilcloth. Unwrapping it, he showed her the sword he'd picked out, pulling it partway out of the scabbard. The words that the blacksmith engraved were easy to pick out on the polished surface, but Freya couldn't read them.

"See this?" Daniel showed one side to her, which read *HAELEÞ-SCIEPPENDE IC EOM*. "It means 'Hero-Maker, I am.' That's the name of my sword, Hero-Maker. And on this side," he said, flipping the blade over, "it says *'Ic agenes a Daniel Tully'*, or 'I belong to Daniel Tully.'"

"Now if I stab anyone," he said, smiling, "at least they'll know my name."

Freya couldn't help laughing.

"Whatever happens," Daniel said, sliding his sword into its sheath, "I'll protect you. You know that, right?"

Freya turned to him, her eyes lively and a sardonic grin on her face. "Why would I need protecting from you? I was the one who saved *you* when that thing had you on the floor."

"Well, yeah, but—"

"He was going to eat your face," she teased.

"Gross! He was not."

Freya stood on the bench and grabbed her spear, brandishing it at him. "I completely saved you. You only want me to come along because I'm a better warrior than Swiðgar and Ecgbryt put together!"

Daniel started to duel with her using his sheathed sword. "Hey, you said their names right! You've been practicing, haven't you?"

"Maybe," Freya grunted, attacking him with the blunt end of the spear. "Admit it, you want me to come so that I can save your life again." He held on to her spear and she spun around and grabbed his arm, twisting it playfully around his back. "Admit it!"

"Ah! Okay, okay! You're right! Leggo!"

Freya released him and fell back, laughing. She seemed to come to herself again and her laughter stilled. "What is going to happen to us?"

"I don't know," Daniel said, a smile still on his face. "So let's find out."

7

The travelers gathered silently around the base of the Great Carnyx—Daniel, Freya, Swiðgar, and Ecgbryt. There were also those who had come to see them off—Modwyn, Godmund, Frithfroth, the servants Cnafa and Cnapa, and another man—one who stood a small distance apart, making it clear that he didn't want to talk to anyone; the blacksmith who had worked on Daniel's sword. Ecgbryt fiddled with his pack's straps as Swiðgar clamped his teeth on his empty clay pipe. Freya tugged at her dress and Daniel fidgeted with the hilt of his sword.

"Remember," Godmund said, reiterating the plan for the umpteenth time, "there are many paths through the Wild Caves that will take you to the Slæpismere—and all of them bend downwards. Once across the Slæpismere, look for any sign that might lead you, but remember that which you are pitched against is devious and diabolical."

They were waiting for Ealdstan, and he was not soon in coming. From time to time Daniel glanced up at the large metal horn—the Carnyx—suspended in its small, blunt fortress. The great horn possessed an oddly attractive power. It was captivating, hypnotic. They would tear their eyes away, only to be unwittingly drawn back to it again.

Daniel wondered how many knights would wake up and where they'd be if ever the horn was blown. How would they know what to do?

Freya, however, was wondering what sort of enchantment empowered it and how it worked. Perhaps there was a rational, scientific explanation. Perhaps it was a vibrational thing.

A bell tolled from across the city, signaling the change of the watch, and Godmund made his good-bye. He embraced Swiðgar and Ecgbryt and wished the "fair lifiendes every good fortune and preservation on the journey," which he hoped would be swift. He shook hands with them awkwardly and left.

Frithfroth puffed out his cheeks impatiently and scuffed his feet against the close-set green and red marble flagstones.

Removing his pipe and placing it in a small leather pouch, Swiðgar cleared his throat. "Time marches on," he said firmly, "and so must we."

"Hold," said Modwyn. "He approaches."

They turned to see Ealdstan striding across the square, a scowl on his face. He met them and turned his weary eyes to Daniel. "Destroy it, boy," he commanded. "Destroy whatever houses Gád's mortality—whatever the soul box contains—and all his spells and sorceries will unravel."

Freya didn't appreciate being ignored in this exchange but was glad she didn't have to talk to the mean-spirited wizard. Daniel returned Ealdstan's gaze with a fixed face and gave a solemn nod.

"I won't let you down."

Then, with a mournful look, Ealdstan sighed. "I truly wish it was not necessary for you to become involved." He raised his hands and uttered in a steady voice:

> *"May the Hand that Makes guide your hearts,*
> *May the Light that Illumines shine on your path,*
> *And the One that Goes Between aid your steps."*

He dropped his hands unceremoniously.

Then he offered one final piece of advice. "Follow the water," he said, and turned away. Modwyn frowned after him and turned to Freya. As she opened her mouth to speak, the alarm bell tolled violently. She stiffened, startled.

"Another attack!" Frithfroth exclaimed, his eyes wide with fear. He bowed quickly to Daniel and Freya. "Good-bye, children, may you return swiftly and whole, your task complete." He rushed away with the two servants behind him.

"You must hurry," Modwyn said, pushing Freya and Daniel towards the Carnyx building. "The entrance to the Wild Caves is within." They dashed into it, closely followed by the knights, passing under a low archway, next to which stood several anxious guards. Once through the arch, large metal doors were swung shut and locked behind them.

The inside of the building was like a small maze. The walls and paths twisted and branched, making, supposedly, the centre easier to defend. The knights very quickly led them through the narrow passages. Looking up, Freya saw that it was the central chamber that housed the Carnyx suspended above their heads. Set into the wall was another pair of stone doors a foot wide, tilted back at an angle, like the doors to a bunker or storm cellar. Ecgbryt and Swiðgar flung these open, revealing a tunnel that sloped downwards.

Grabbing two silver lanterns and passing one to Ecgbryt, Swiðgar hurried them inside. With tremendous effort, he pulled both the stone doors closed. They met with an earth-shaking *thud* and sealed so that they were neat and flush with the other stones in the wall—as if there had never been a doorway there at all.

CHAPTER NINE

Trolls in Morven

——————————— 1 ———————————

Now...

Alex moved carefully among the loose rocks and stones that formed the base of Morven's northern slope. Its name could be translated from Gaelic as either Big Mountain or Big Hill. Its technical classification was a "graham," but its name fit either way. At over seven hundred meters in height, it was certainly a big hill, though on the small side for a mountain. However, in contrast to the otherwise level plain of Caithness, it seemed enormous, being the only feature in an otherwise completely flat landscape.

The ascent was relatively gentle. Alex walked beside Reverend Maccanish, who had insisted on accompanying him and being his guide to the area once Alex had more fully explained what he expected to find, and what he would have to do once he found it. It took the reverend little time to change into hiking clothes and rubber boots. Alex changed into some heavier gear—motorcycle gear, actually. Tough, padded leather trousers and a padded leather jacket, reinforced in the forearms, upper arms, chest, and back with metal plates. He also grabbed a rucksack with different sorts of emergency provisions and a long black object, which he slung on his back. He finished by lacing up a pair of army-issue, steel-toe boots. And they set off.

They had walked only about forty-five minutes and had made it about halfway around the graham. It was a little after noon, so they stopped for a break.

"Are you sure it's a cave you're looking for here? I know of none around here."

"There will be . . . something," Alex answered. "But incidentally, do you know of any caves or other rock formations in the area?"

"No, nothing like that. Why, do you think it more likely we'll find the . . . creature there?"

"No, it's probably here," Alex said, offering another oatcake to Maccanish. "We just have to keep our eyes open. And our ears. Even our—" Alex paused. Even as he was about to say it, he caught a whiff of something rotten on the wind.

"What is it?" Maccanish asked, slightly alarmed, twisting around. "Do you see—?"

"No, it's alright," Alex assured him. "Finish up," he said, taking a long drink from his bottle of water. He packed his things together and brushed his hand over the long rectangular object wrapped in black that lay in his lap.

"Do you mind if I see it?" Maccanish asked, gesturing.

Alex thought for a moment and raised the black object— almost four feet long—and handed it to him.

Maccanish fumbled with it for a few moments and then found its rubberized handle and withdrew it from its scabbard.

"It's like no sword I've ever seen," Maccanish said, holding it upwards. It had just one cutting edge, which sloped and tapered at the top so that the blunt end was completely straight to the tip. It had a grey, brushed finish, which meant it didn't shine or glimmer, except along the sharpened side. It was nearly five inches thick at its widest point and would have been heavy because of this, except that it had three irregularly spaced oblong holes to cut down on mass. A rivulet ran parallel to the cutting edge.

"It's the latest modern design," Alex said with an ironic air. "I had it custom-made and designed, as well as stress-tested. I told them I was being commissioned by a Hollywood movie studio. I said I was making a vampire movie. It's high-strength, low-alloy steel that's been subzero treated and coated with a synthetic fluoropolymer. It cost a bloody fortune."

"I can imagine," Maccanish said, sheathing the sword once more. "And you've actually used this thing?"

"Just a couple times. When circumstance warranted it."

"Would not a rifle or machine gun do better?"

Alex shook his head. "Not for what we're hunting."

"My uncle has my great-grandfather's old Claymore, but I wouldn't put that up against this," Maccanish said, handing it back to Alex.

"Ready?" Alex asked, standing up.

The reverend gathered his things together and stood. "Ready. Lead on."

They set off again along the side of the mountain where the ground became firmer and covered with heather and ferns. The stench that Alex had smelt was still in the air and getting thicker.

"Do you know what that is?" he asked Maccanish. It was obvious what he was referring to.

"Something died. Maybe several things. Is it what we're looking for?"

"Could be. What's this crevice up here?"

It seemed as if there were a fold in the mountain, running

from the peak to the foot. It showed bare rock where rainwater washed the plants away.

"It's just a burn. It fills to no more than a trickle when it rains. There couldn't be anything there."

"Listen, do you hear that?"

Maccanish tilted his head. "It's a sort of . . . buzzing. What does it mean?"

"It means it's worth a look."

They started down the smooth, embedded rocks. The smell was almost overpowering now, the sick, sweet stench of rotting flesh—it felt like it was sitting in their throats. Bones, still yellow with brown decaying flesh on them were wedged in between the rocks, which a mass of flies were feeding and breeding off of.

"Disgusting," Maccanish said.

Alex unslung his rucksack and flung it to the side. He kept his sword hitched up on his back. He was getting close, he could feel it. He tried to focus his mind as he descended farther; he tried to clear away any unnecessary thoughts from his consciousness.

It was the body of a cow that indicated the cave. It was sticking out, head and forelegs, from a clump of ferns, still mostly covered in skin but with bits of bone showing around the crown of the skull and the joints. On closer, and more gruesome, inspection, it was revealed not to be just half of a carcass but a whole one that was sticking out of a cave mouth, about four-by-five-feet wide and tall.

"You should stay here," Alex told Maccanish, "if you're uncomfortable."

The reverend didn't say anything; he came and stood closer to Alex.

"Well, in any case," Alex said, drawing his sword and tossing the scabbard to the side, "stand a little farther off."

Maccanish nodded and hung back as Alex advanced. It was good the reverend was here to see this. Someone in the village should see this being done, even if no one would believe his account—that is, if he even told anyone. Someone needed to bear witness.

Alex pulled a glow-stick from his pocket, snapped it, and hung it from his coat's lapel. The green, iridescent glow was eaten by the walls and reflected on a floor covered with skeletal remains and desiccated corpses of animals. The bones bore regular gashes along them, clustering on the knobby ends. "See that?" Alex said, indicating them. "Tooth marks."

"Teeth of what?"

"At a guess? I'd say troll."

"You're kidding. What, billy goat's gruff an' that?"

"Close enough to."

"Are they . . . big?"

"Like you wouldn't imagine. Massive arms and hands. But slow at least. Stay out of reach and you'll do fine." Alex shifted his weight on the uneven ground and kept his sword in front of him. He was sweating. He willed his heart to slow its humming pace. The cave continued and bore to the right. As Alex banked to the left to see down as far as possible, he noticed something was slumped up against the bend that he had mistaken for an outcropping.

"Wait," he said, motioning. He stepped closer to it. It was as still as a stone, and as cold. Its bullet head was slumped forward onto its barrel-like chest. Arms the size of tree trunks were splayed outwards, palms up, fingers curled inwards. It had laughably small bowed legs and large flipper feet. But where its potbelly should have been was a gaping, sticky void. Dried entrails hung out of it, torn out and torn apart, gutted. Something had made a meal of it.

"It's dead," Alex said, straightening. "Go on, take a look."

"I wouldnae ha'e believed it," Maccanish said, a thicker accent creeping into his voice. "How long has it been here? It couldnae have been here the whole time. Where did it come from?"

"It's odd, but I honestly don't know. There's some as say they grow from the rocks or that the peaty bogs birth them from the skulls of thieves and murderers. It's possible that they burrow up here, but from where, I have no idea. They like solid rock, though, that's true enough. They're related to the giants, you know."

"Incredible. So is that it? It's dead—are we finished?"

"Unfortunately not. See, it's been killed, probably by something bigger. They usually go in pairs so it's poss— Oh, wait. Here we are."

Alex had stood and was creeping farther into the tunnel. Around the corner and slumped on the opposite end of the tunnel was the body of another troll. Not bigger this time, but smaller. It was likewise eviscerated, but its massive trunk-like neck was also torn up, nearly cut through completely.

"Another one?" Maccanish asked, moving around.

"This doesn't make sense . . . They look as if they been here for, oh, over a week. I don't . . ."

Alex peered deeper into the tunnel. His ears strained for a sound, his eyes for a movement. He caught a glimmer of something shiny piled a few feet beyond the second troll. He moved forward slowly, his feet crunching bone beneath him.

The shiny object was completely circular and reflective.

"What is it? What do you see?" asked Maccanish.

"It's CDs—dozens of them. All chucked together, just the discs." Alex turned his body, shifting the light he wore. "And the boxes are over here—DVD cases, album cases . . . discarded like spent nutshells. They just wanted the discs. I wonder . . ." He bent and prodded around in the pile and found other objects—necklaces, rings, metallic crisp wrappers, a few silver forks. Some of it was valuable, some of it was rubbish, but all of it was shiny.

"Oh no," Alex said, horror descending on him.

"What?"

"I've made a mistake." He sprang up and stared into the black emptiness of the tunnel before him. "Get out of here, quickly!" he hissed.

"What is it?"

"I'm not prepared for this," he said, gripping his sword with both hands. He turned to Maccanish. "Did you not hear me? I said run!" he yelled, and turned just as the dragon came swooping towards him, screeching out of the darkness.

In the dim light, Alex caught only a brief flash of long, sharp, reptilian muzzle and an angry flash of red eyes before he was on the ground, winded and pinned beneath a dragon almost six feet in length.

As he fell, he instinctively brought his sword up in front of him. It hit between the beast's shoulder and arm but did not bite— merely glided along the tough, slick scales. As they both fell, the sword twisted out of his hand and clattered to the ground. Luckily, his left arm had been in front of him and was now between him and the creature. He pushed it upwards just in time to fend off the sharp beak that was coming down to meet his head. It struck the ground just beside Alex's right ear. It had been a weak effort on the dragon's part; otherwise he wouldn't have been so lucky.

The close quarters were proving difficult for the dragon, as it was not able to maneuver its long, bat-winged arms to either gouge at his sides or even take flight. Its legs, however, it could use, and he felt one massive, clawed foot gripping the inside of his thigh, the other trying unsuccessfully to gain purchase just above his hip, but succeeding very ably in tearing away layers of clothing, and then skin.

As the dragon brought its head back up, Alex found he had some breathing space. Almost quicker than he could think it, he brought both hands up and clutched at the monster's throat. His hands couldn't meet around it. His thumbs embedded themselves in the soft, leathery gullet and his fingers fought for purchase on cold scales, no bigger than robin's eggs, but slick and hard as marble.

Its arms still not being able to gain purchase in the cave, the dragon was unable to leverage itself in order to attack with its mouth. It was a small advantage for Alex, but not one that afforded him escape or a clear way to defeat his attacker. Instead, he looked into the cold, red eyes in fear and horror as thin wisps of white smoke flowed from the dragon's mouth between its dagger-like teeth.

Alex felt his hands around the thing's neck grow warm, then hot. The white smoke was tinged with grey and black now. Frantically, Alex kicked and writhed beneath the animal, which was easily twice his own weight. Strange, choking sounds came from the dragon's gullet, and Alex closed his eyes for what was going to happen next.

"Alex, lower your hands, now!" came a quick command.

Alex let go of the thing's throat and covered his head. Between his arms, he saw his sword whiz past him in an upward stroke and sink into the dragon's head, entering just below the jaw. The sword's tip looked to be lodged in the base of the brain, or in its spine.

The dragon did a back flip off of Alex and started thrashing against the walls like a floundering fish, first against one wall and then the other. Alex tried to raise himself and was knocked away from the dying creature by its powerful tail. He landed in the arms of Maccanish, who pulled him farther away.

The dragon flailed awhile longer and then calmed. It made motions as if it was trying to wretch, but its mouth was shut firm. Black blood and bile dripped from its wound and, with a final few spasms, it fell to the ground and lay dead.

Alex and Maccanish stood looking at it for a time.

"Dragons don't go in pairs, do they?" Maccanish asked eventually.

"No, never," Alex replied. "Thank God."

"Amen."

2

Daniel awoke several times in the night. He was accustomed to sleeping in hard and uncomfortable places, and allowed himself to wake up fully enough to feed the fire a couple times, then settled back onto his leaf bed, pulled the cloak tighter, and went back to sleep.

But eventually his body had taken all the rest it had needed and he opened his eyes, wide awake.

And as far as he could tell, it was still the dead of night. What was it called when you crossed time zones and your body hadn't adjusted yet? Jet lag? What was this, then—world lag? How long would it take his body to adapt to forty-eight-hour days?

He tended to the fire again. There was a good pile of hot coals that he swept closer together. He fed more wood into it to get some flames going again and picked at some of the leftover fish he had cooked. He didn't eat too much since he wanted to save some for when he had to get going again, but there had been quite a lot.

Allowing himself to become mesmerised by the flames, he grew reflective. He dug around in his backpack for something that he always kept at the bottom of it, always wrapped in several plastic bags. He found it and unfolded it—a heavy, long piece of blue cloth that no longer fit him. He let his fingers caress the patterns. He lifted it to his nose, but it had lost its scent. But he didn't need to smell it to remember.

Very gradually, it became brighter and he felt that soon he would be able to make a move. He wrapped the uneaten fish in one of the plastic bags and stuck them in his backpack. Using his feet, he spread and stamped out the glowing embers of the fire, which he had allowed to die down. Then he turned to face the wood.

> *"Forest, for all that you gave me last night*
> *I thank you without exception—but,*
> *Now that it's morning and getting quite light*
> *Please show me the path to the wood-burner's hut."*

And then, uncertain what to do next, since no path instantly appeared at his feet, he left the clearing. He counted his footsteps and hadn't reached one hundred before he found himself on a small ledge above a beaten dirt path. Shaking his head and laughing in spite of himself, he set his shoulders and resolved himself to a long trek.

He kept his pace steady, but stopped and rested after a couple hours. There was a rock by the roadside and he settled himself onto it. The birds were flitting through the trees opposite him, pausing every once in a while on a thin branch. He didn't know much about birds. These were small, brown, and there seemed to be a lot of them. They would twist their heads and look at him, give a little peep of exclamation, and then flutter away to another branch to look at him from another angle.

He contemplated the strangeness of being in another place that was so different, and so similar to his own world.

He walked on, losing track of the hours, losing track of himself in the forest. When he grew hungry, he asked the forest for food and he would come across a bush full of berries or a clump of large white mushrooms. When he got thirsty and his water container was empty, he asked for water and would walk until a small spring or stream crossed his path. What he couldn't understand was whether the forest was creating these things for him on request or if they existed already and was just moving them into his path. Or if it was all just a coincidence.

The light was starting to get dimmer, and Daniel wondered if he would have to stop and make camp for another night when he noticed the sharp tang of burning wood in the air. As he continued along the path, it grew stronger, eventually getting to the point where his eyes stung slightly.

Anticipation grew within him as he noticed thick white smoke wafting through the trees up ahead. He must be getting close. Slowing his pace, he continued around a bend in the road, and then he was there.

Before him was a sight that was strange to his eyes—a large dirt mound, as wide as a house and about two stories in height. It was cylindrical but tapered towards the top where an open hole billowed smoke.

Standing near the large structure, leaning on a spade, was a tall, gnarled man who was nearly as knotted and twisted as the trees encircling the clearing. He had thick, corded forearms and large-knuckled hands. His hair was grey and his face was tanned and weathered. He wore a shirt and leggings of coarse green cloth and his shoes were carved out of wood.

Daniel edged nearer, stopping a good few yards off. "Hello," he said hoarsely.

The old man didn't turn right away, but when he did, it was only to cast a disinterested eye in his direction.

Daniel cleared his throat. "Are you the wood-burner?"

The other did not respond immediately. "You speak a strange tongue," the man said after a time.

"I'm not from here."

The elf's eyes flicked up and down him. "You are one of the heavy people," he stated.

Daniel looked down at himself apologetically. He didn't know how to reply to this.

"Make yourself useful," the man said abruptly. "Go and close the south flue. Take the pole over there." He gestured to a small rack of tools set into a tree.

Daniel went over and selected a stick about his height that had a crude bronze hook inserted into one end. Then he walked around the large structure—which was giving off a fair amount of heat—until he found a small metal door sticking out of the baked mud. Inside a vertical stack of logs could be seen burning with a bright yellow glow.

He used the pole to nudge the flue closed. There was a latch that he lifted and let fall with a *clack*. Then he walked back and replaced the hook on the rack. He returned to stand near the wood-burner and joined him in looking at the furnace in what he hoped was companionable silence.

"Kay Marrey sent me here," Daniel said after a suitable interval. He didn't get a reply or even as much as a twitch from the man. "He's one of the Elves in Exile."

"I know who Marrey is," the man said slowly, evenly. "Young, excitable. Always running hither and thither." He made a to-and-fro motion with one of his hands. "Where are you from?"

"I—don't know what to call it, but it's another world entirely. Can you help me get back?"

"In some weeks there is a market where many tradesmen and travelers congregate. No doubt someone will point you the right way. Travel between worlds used to be very common, after all."

"Is there any way I could find one sooner?"

The tall person shook his head. "It would take you longer to track one down. Best let them come here. Are you fit? Can you lift, chop, carry, climb?"

"I am as you see me," Daniel responded, holding his arms out slightly. "And I will lift, chop, and carry as much and for as long as I am able. Climb, I'm not so sure, but I'll give it a go."

"May be possible to get a second mound up, then, before the trade." The man straightened to what must have been eight feet in height. "We'll see. I use what the forest gives me, and it's given me you, so we'll put you to work, won't we?"

3

Freya came out of her sleep slowly, gradually becoming aware that she was slumped forward on a table. She hoisted herself upwards and looked around. She was in her office, sitting at her desk that was littered with page after page of complex numerical equations, all of them in her own handwriting. That was odd; she thought she was . . . somewhere else. It had become so easy for her to throw herself into her work, and she went so deep into it that sometimes she literally forgot where she was.

She sighed. When did she become a mathematician?

A large book lay open in front of her, propped against the windowsill. On the two facing pages were tables of letters and numbers listed in pairs, triplets, and quadruplets—in total about a hundred rows and a dozen columns. It was headed AKV STRINGS—NOMINATIVE.

There was a smaller but much older book also open in front of her that contained very small type. The right-hand page was in Greek and the left-hand page was in English. Her eyes went to the first paragraph and read:

Now, (the) wisdom belonging to afterthought, which is an aeon, thought a thought derived from herself, (from) the thinking of the invisible spirit, and (from) prior acquaintance. She wanted to show forth within herself an image without the spirit's [will];

and her consort did not consent. And (she wished to do so) without his pondering: for the person of her maleness did not join in the consent; for she had not discovered that being which was in harmony with her . . .

Freya rubbed her eyes and tried to remember what the text was referring to. She had gotten so involved in decoding and recoding all the nominations that she had lost perspective on the context of the words. Or maybe it was best to keep going through the text mechanically and focus on the meaning of the uncoded text.

"How's it coming?"

Freya jumped. The reverend was standing behind her, looking at her work.

"Oh, Peter—I'm so sorry, I didn't know you were there."

He smiled. "Perfectly alright. At least I know I'm not being a nuisance if you forget I'm even here. How is it coming?"

"Fine," said Freya. "I've just finished breaking down and gridding the third chapter. Now I just have to look for patterns—that is the easiest part for me—and then retranslate. I should have the whole book done by the end of the month."

"Good, good," the reverend said, smiling. She could never tell how much he took in; he was always so sweet-natured.

"Can I get you anything?" she asked.

"No, no. I was just thinking that I should leave. You carry on. I'll see myself out."

Freya went back to her work. She glanced over the different papers but found it difficult to see where she had left off. Why, exactly, was she doing this?

She looked at the clock. When was he getting back? It was starting to get dark. She knew she shouldn't worry, but she couldn't help it.

There was the sound of a key turning in the door. It opened and closed.

"Felix?"

"Hello, darling."

She got up from the desk and went into the hallway. "How was your day?" she asked.

"Not bad, all things considered. Yours?"

"I think I'm losing my mind. I was breaking down the Secret Book of John—"

"Beautiful book."

"Yes. Well, I was breaking it down and it all just suddenly became page upon page of meaningless numbers . . ."

"Those numbers aren't meaningless," Stowe stressed.

"I know. I just mean, it all became so abstract—like I lost perspective."

"Ah. Well, perhaps it's time to finish for the night. Why don't you have a seat and I'll cook something."

"No, don't," Freya said, putting her arms around Professor Stowe's middle. "You've had just as long a day as I've had."

"Perhaps, but my work is far less important than yours. Go into the lounge and I'll bring some wine in to you."

"Okay." Freya gave him a peck on the cheek and went into the sitting room. On the way, she passed her office and, without even looking into the room, snaked her hand through the doorway and flicked the light off. Then she settled into the sofa and closed her eyes, just for a moment . . .

"Sweetie?"

Freya opened her eyes. Felix was standing over her, gently patting her shoulder.

"Hello," he said, grinning.

She sat up and looked around her. "Where am—? Oh." She was on the sofa, coffee table in front of her, with several used plates, glasses, and an empty bottle of wine on it.

"You just drifted off, you silly goose."

"'M still hungry," she said sleepily.

"No, you're not—you're just exhausted. Here, lie still, I'll carry you to bed."

"What? Don't be ridiculous. I can—"

"No, I insist!"

"I'm far too heavy."

"Not yet, you aren't. There—see?"

Freya clung to his neck as he straightened up and then carried her through to the bedroom.

"My gallant knight," she said as he lowered her down and arranged the covers over her. "Are you going to join me?"

"My darling wife. I have an appointment with the lieutenant, remember?"

"Oh yes, of course."

"But I've got a few minutes. Shall I tell you a story? Something that happened to me today?"

Freya smiled and snuggled closer. "M'kay, that'd be nice."

"I was walking along the river when I ran into a friend of mine who I thought had seen me but proceeded to walk right past me. I turned around and caught up with him and asked if anything was wrong. He said no, he was fine, but he'd just been told the most puzzling and confusing story in his life. I asked him if it would help if he shared it with me, and he said it might. As we stood there in the street, this is what he said:

"I was with a group of friends in a pub when one of our lecturers wandered in and walked directly to the bar. We waved to him, but he seemed wrapped in his own thoughts, which was odd since he wasn't one of those absentminded academics, but a young and witty man who we all loved. He ordered a whiskey and stood staring at it, not even taking a sniff of it. I left my friends and went up to him to ask him what was the matter. This was what he said:

"I've just come from the hospital bed of a friend of mine. We've known each other since university, where he studied law. He was a very diligent soul who eventually became a high court judge, and was known for his clear-minded, evenhanded judgments. I had lost touch with him in the last ten years or so, but a week ago I heard from his wife, who informed me that he had fallen ill and that he had been troubled of late with a moral quandary that was doing him no favours due to his illness and would I mind paying him a visit to help thrash it out? I agreed, of course. When I saw my friend in his hospital bed, I knew that there was no real cause for alarm; he was still as strong and as vital as ever, but his mind seemed to be absent—he was not the sharp, incisive man I had known. At length, I managed to tease out of him the cause for his distraction. Clearing his throat and casting his eyes around the room, he replied:

"Three years ago I sat a case, which, at the time, was no more interesting than any other I'd heard during my career. The specifics of it are hazy to me, but the case itself isn't important. Suffice to say, my judgment effected a fine and eight months in prison for a young woman with no dependents. I thought no more about the matter. It was a year later that a letter—just one sheet of paper—was delivered to my office, written by the defendant. This is what it said, verbatim:

"Dear sir—you may remember me from a case twelve months ago. It was a charge of driving under the influence—my third offence—made more serious by a possession of class B drugs—my first offence. My impression was that you were lenient with me, dismissing the drugs charge, and instead sentenced me with the full weight of the driving charge. This struck me as generous, even kind, and that made me think that a man like you would be good in a difficult situation. I hope you won't mind, therefore, if I impose upon you to relate a story that I heard while I was detained 'at Her Majesty's pleasure' that was told to me by one of the guards. Usually alert and on the ball, I one day noticed her to be confused and somewhat distant. I asked her what was he matter and this was her answer:

"I have four children, two sons and two daughters, all healthy and happy, except for the last one, my son, and that only during the last ten days. He's a priest, by trade, in a Catholic church in a village in Norwich. We, that is, my husband and I, were visiting him last Thursday, and we were aware that he was totally distracted. It took us a solid hour of coaxing and cajoling for us to get the reason out of him. At length, he told us:

"Five days ago I was in the confessional and a person entered with the most queer story. I'm not breaking any vows or confidences—for he confessed no sins—to relate it. I will not tell you his name, all I will say is that he is a local businessman of great success. This is what he said:

"Every Thursday I volunteer at a shelter that serves meals to the homeless. We take turns at different tasks, and this day it was my turn to socialise with the guests. Just before we shut up—as we were clearing away and clearing out—an old man who was a regular there, grabbed my sleeve and pulled me into the seat next to him. He told me that he had something to tell me . . ."

Freya began to doze, slipping in and out of consciousness, trying as hard as she could to concentrate.

"I was sitting on a street corner," Felix was saying, "when I saw a man reading a book. He had the strangest expression on his face. I went over and asked him what he was reading, and he said it was the weirdest story he'd ever come across. I asked him what it was, and this is what he said . . ."

4

Daniel found the routine of charcoal-making satisfying and an easy style of living to fall into. It was a twenty-four-hour-a-day job—or however many hours there were in this new place, Daniel still wasn't sure. At first he found it hot and sweaty work, then he found it strenuous and exhausting work.

When he had met the collier—the name, Daniel found, for charcoal-makers—he had been entering the final stages of the process, intently studying the smoke issuing from the top of the mound, waiting for the right moment, when the smoke was thin and started to turn blue. As soon as this happened, he went around the mound and closed the ventilation holes. Then he climbed up the side of the mound and told Daniel to hand him some more thick sections of turf, which he piled onto the top. The air supply completely cut off, they waited for the furnace to cool.

He welcomed Daniel into his hut, which was spare but comfortable—no more than a wooden room dug partway into the ground with earth piled on top of it. But it was good shelter. It contained no bed or bedding material, only a ring of stones in the centre, creating a fire pit, and a hole in the ceiling to let the smoke out. There was a wooden box pantry of stores adjoined to a small stable that contained one massive horse that stood patiently, thoughtfully chewing oats.

The collier drew a pan of water from a small wooden cistern and washed, splashing water on his face and forearms, and then allowed Daniel to do the same. Then he opened the store cupboard. Peering around him, Daniel saw that it was filled with stoppered bottles and jars, all of different sizes. He pulled out a tall beaker-shaped jar and pulled out a wooden cork. He took a drink, paused, and then took another. He handed it to Daniel. "Drink," he instructed.

Daniel paused. "I was told not to take anything that I didn't ask to be given to me."

The collier gave him a nod. "Good advice. Though while you work for me, you won't need to ask, for you act under my authority."

"What authority is that?" he asked, curious.

"My own authority," the collier said simply.

Daniel took a sip from the flask and tasted a rich, spicy, cinnamony drink that was thick and sweet. "It is very good," he said.

"It is nourishing, that is all."

Daniel handed the drink back to the collier. "Do you have anything to eat?"

"Food?" the other returned. "Like animal flesh?"

"That, or bread or fruit or something."

The collier shook his head. "I am not used to entertaining those of the heavy races here."

"You don't eat?" Daniel asked.

"Not eat very often—only during festivals and feast days. Try to live on this—if it pains you, I will try to procure other fare."

Daniel nodded, as if that made sense. "What world is this, exactly?"

"This world is *our* world, we don't give it a name. But you stand on a continent that we call Elfland."

"And so you're an elf?"

"Yes, I am."

"And everyone who lives here is an elf?"

The collier nodded.

"I met an elf once, a long time ago. Do you have a king?"

"As you are here, you should learn to speak our language," replied the collier after a pause. "What was your question again?"

"Do you have a king?"

"Our word for 'king' is *reesh*. In our language, names come first, so you would ask me *reesh y'ka?*"

He looked at Daniel expectantly. *"Reesh y'ka?"* Daniel said to him.

"Filliu sa ennym oo reesh." The collier answered. "That means: *Filliu* is the name of our king."

Propped up against the side of the collier's hut as its owner sat on a stool, Daniel received his first lesson in the elf language.

Then they rose and went to the wood furnace. Under the collier's direction, Daniel helped to peel back the layers of baked dirt to reveal the rich, black charcoal underneath. Once done, they started to sift the charcoal, removing bits of wood that hadn't burned entirely and putting the rest of the black, sooty material into some of a dozen large barrels that the collier wheeled out one by one from behind his hut. The charcoal lumps were sorted, roughly according to size, by the collier himself.

"Filliu," the collier said abruptly, tossing a double handful of burnt coal into a barrel, "is our king in name only. His father was Ghrian, and he was the last good Elfin king of our land."

"What happened to him?"

"Ghrian died, and his younger brother, whose name was Aarnieu, took control of the throne in defiance of the king's son, Filliu, who was away at the time, hunting. The usurping king had nine sons, capricious men who reveled in submitting themselves to every perverted whim. They decreed the beginning of a new era, a new house of royalty. He and his sons styled themselves 'The Fær Folk of the Fated House.'"

The collier spat and then did not speak again. They worked in silence and by the time it grew quite dark, they had done a good deal of sorting, but still had over a third left to do.

"What happened to Filliu, the king's son?" Daniel asked during the evening meal. Their conversations were in the collier's native tongue, with halts and pauses for the explanation of words.

"Aarnieu held the funeral banquet for King Ghrian near the king's burial ground in a magnificent tent that he erected for the occasion. All of the nobles and warrior chiefs attended the feast, no less in love for the fact that honour commanded it. None were armed, except for the nine sons, and the banquet's servers, who were really Aarnieu's soldiers. They had knives concealed in their boots. At a certain moment in the evening, the command was given, and the servers drew their knives and plunged them into the throats of the Elfin lords Aarnieu knew to be loyal to young Prince Filliu."

There was another long pause as the collier continued with his meal. He finished his food, then took a swig of wine, wiping his lips on his sleeve.

"As it happened, there was a certain lord at the feast, by the name of Nock. He caught a gleam of a knife across the table, and this alerted him to Aarnieu's plan. He rose to defend Prince Filliu—whose assassin hesitated, perhaps due to conscience or the weight of the moment. This gave Nock the opportunity to defend the prince, and the blade intended for the boy returned to its master, sheathing itself in his bone and breaking. In a rage, Nock reached for a pole that was helping to prop up the tent wall and wrenched it from the ground. With this weapon, he was able to club off the other attackers who came at him only with knives. He broke many arms, legs, and skulls that night, dispatching many evildoers to their final judgment. In this way, he was able to save Prince Filliu. They were the only two of the old regime to escape."

"What happened to them?" Daniel asked.

"Aarnieu had not counted on any of the lords leaving the table, let alone the tent, and so was unprepared for pursuit, and the two were able to depart without much chase. The next day Aarnieu announced himself the first Faerie king and his sons regents to the throne who would, upon his death, jointly control the kingdom, now called Færieland."

For the only time Daniel knew him, the collier smiled. "That night, 'King' Aarnieu was found dead, stabbed nine times in the chest."

Daniel, fascinated though he was at this story, couldn't keep a yawn from escaping.

"You are weary. Do you need to . . . *sleep*?" This last word was in English.

Daniel nodded his head. "Yes, I'd better. Aren't you tired?"

"Elves do not sleep. Our bodies are light—not so leaden as yours. Your essences are always sinking, like earth and stone; ours mingle in the air. We tire and rest but do not close our eyes. Do what you may to make yourself comfortable and come and find me again when you"—he thought for a moment—"stop sleeping."

And so it was that the evening of Daniel's second day in Elfland found him in another pile of leaves and wrapped in his new cloak, but in the corner of the coal-maker's hut and not in the elements.

It was another very long night, punctuated by hours of silent thought where Daniel was able to meditate on his situation and the new language he was learning. Outside he could hear the collier still working, sorting through the charcoal and occasionally going into the forest. It was quite dark, even outside, but Daniel supposed that elfish eyes were better than human eyes. No doubt due to their "airy essences."

At length Daniel rose, before it was still quite light outside, to find that the collier had finished sorting the charcoal into barrels and was now sharpening two axes with a smooth stone.

He greeted him and handed him a drinking skin, which apparently held the day's breakfast. Living on the streets, Daniel was used to an irregular diet but wondered how long he could go with no solids.

"Come with me," the woodcollier instructed, handing Daniel one of the axes. "If you are a good worker, we may be able to start a second pit."

Daniel followed him eagerly into the wood, walking behind as he pointed out the trees that needed felling. These were usually trees that were damaged or diseased, or ones that posed a threat to other plants around them.

"This is why the forest allows me to take from it," the wood-collier explained. "I remove what is harmful to the forest—what is dead and decaying. The forest thanks me for this and allows me to stay."

"What would it do to you if it didn't want you to stay?" Daniel asked.

The woodcollier didn't answer. He was looking up instead at the treetops where a large limb of a tree had splintered away and was caught in the upper branches.

As easy as anything, the collier went over to a tree and started scaling it, as fast as walking, and with one hand still holding an axe.

"Are you coming?" the collier asked Daniel when he was already halfway up the tree.

"I don't think so," Daniel said. He tapped his chest. "Heavy, remember?"

He thought he heard the collier grunt and continue up to the branch. Daniel tried to see what he was doing. There were chopping noises and some creaks.

There was a call for him to look out, and then the sound of branches creaking and giving way. Daniel took several leaps back as the large tree limb landed before him with a loud *crunk*.

The collier descended and went to the branch, straddling it. "Watch what I do," he said, raising the tool above his head and bringing it down at the base of a large branch. He did this a few times, placing one cut over another, until the branch gave way completely.

"Now you," the collier said, dragging the branch away and gesturing to a branch of the same size on the other side of the tree.

Daniel moved into position and hefted his axe.

"Stop," the collier commanded. "Already wrong. Stand here. Cut upwards with the grain. Strike here." He pointed across the branch.

Daniel did as he was directed. The head of the axe lodged in the wood and sent a rough vibration up his arm.

"Good, but don't push the head into the wood—put some force into it and let the axe fall of its own. Use a strong, steady hand with a gentle touch. Continue."

Daniel made more strokes, some of which went embarrassingly wide of his mark, and finally, after about fifteen blows, managed to cut the branch away while the collier looked on.

"Good, keep going," he said, and then started working the other side of the tree, laying into a particularly large branch.

After a while Daniel asked, "Do the nine sons of Aarnieu rule Elfland now? Or Færieland, rather?"

"The Faerie Princelings, yes, they do. They used the death of their father and the disappearance of Filliu as an excuse to hunt down and kill the remaining supporters of the late King Ghrian. It was plain to anyone with half a brain what had happened, but the populace decided to play along with a comfortable lie rather than fight for a difficult truth. This has opened the royal court up to any number of flatterers and extorters. There is one I've had several run-ins with—Agrid Fiall, who is particularly devious."

Daniel had managed to remove two more branches and started on the third when the collier said, "Stop, you are weary. Never swing an axe in that state. Rest a moment."

In truth, Daniel's arms, particularly his shoulders, were nearly falling off. Daniel laid his axe on the ground and moved off to lean against a tree.

"Wait," the collier commanded. "Never leave any tool just lying around. That is dangerous, disrespectful of both the instrument and your craft, and speaks badly of the craftsman. Always keep it with you. If you must leave it anywhere, for any reason, leave it like this . . ." He raised his axe and struck the fallen tree with it where the trunk was thickest. The handle stuck out at a 45-degree angle.

Daniel crouched against a tree, out of the way. He rested there, sweating hard and studying the collier's form as he attacked the tree with a smooth and graceful confidence born out of experience.

"The Faerie rule is vast and now encompasses all the Elfin cities and villages. Only the farthest territories and hardest-to-reach places remain beyond their rule. At least, beyond their interest. Unfortunately, I cannot say that of this forest. The Faerie territories are ruled by the nine princes, who have all degenerated into frivolous perversities. Two hundred years ago, on a whim, each of them wed nine sisters who they pass around among them, with as little sense of proprietorship—not to say love—as dumb beasts."

When Daniel felt that he had cooled and rested enough, he rose and started working the tree again, at the woodsman's side. "What about the Elves in Exile?" he asked.

"We don't speak of them here," the collier said curtly. And that was the end of the conversation for another couple hours, until the tree was fully stripped and they made their way back to the hut.

"The Elves in Exile," the collier said, as they ate lunch in the shade of his hut, "is the name of the court of the true king of Elfland—they preserve the royal line, unbroken for over eight thousand years. They believe that one day, when the people most desire it, they will storm the Elfin palace and reclaim the throne."

By now Daniel was tired and exhausted. Daniel explained about his own time and the length of days, and the collier let him sleep some of the afternoon at the hut. He felt sure that he had been awake a full day, but the sun was still high in the sky.

When Daniel awoke he found another pile of branches, but no collier. He set about stripping them again. Then, as it was getting towards evening, the collier returned with the actual tree trunk itself, which had now been cut into three sections.

The collier taught Daniel how to saw and split the wood in the proper lengths, and he did this until it was too dark to work. They took dinner then and Daniel dozed off as they sat outside the hut together, in silence, under the stars. That was Daniel's third day in Elfland.

The days after that continued much the same way—long periods of work that involved going into the forest to fetch wood and then cutting it into lengths appropriate for the charring pit. Daniel steadily improved his skill at talking to the collier in his own language and was pleased at his growing fluency.

After two more days they had gathered enough wood to be able to build the pits. This was done by first scraping the current pit, then uncovering an old one in the same clearing but on the other side of the hut. Grass had grown over that one, which was to become useful later. The collier cut the turf into rectangular sections with a thin, flat shovel, and Daniel helped to lift these sections up and set them to one side. The bottom of it was then raked flat, and a thin base of the powdered charcoal was laid down on both sites. The two pits were carefully and cleverly piled with logs of various shapes and sizes, arranged in a circle, with a round gap or chimney at the centre. The collier took a thousand pains to ensure that the pits were built to a perfect standard, often giving logs just a minute turn so that the space between them was exactly so.

Then they set about covering the woodpiles with the cut turf, tightly packing it close together everywhere except the very top, which was for the chimney. Dry soil was spread over where the turf did not extend.

It was getting late in the evening when the collier was satisfied enough to light them both. He made a small fire with charcoal from the previous batch, and once that was burning nicely, he divided up the coals with his shovel and, with orange sparks dancing high into the night sky, tipped them into both of the bonfire's chimneys, where with a quiet crackle and a rich, musty smell, they started to kindle the rest of the wood. Then they sat back and watched.

It was vitally important that the piles burnt steadily, evenly, and not too hot. The collier took constant turns around the piles, laying his hands upon the turf walls, checking the vents, and gazing into the smoke that had started to billow from the two chimney holes. Daniel followed him around. There were a few energetic moments when fire broke through the turf wall and they had to hurry to repair the breach.

After these first few hours, the collier judged that the stacks were burning well enough that they could relax and take dinner— which was from a different bottle this time.

They drank and watched the piles. Daniel gazed up at the stars, which were strange and unfamiliar. None of the constellations he learned when he was young were there, which was disturbing but also exciting.

He had to get back to Freya.

Exhaustion overcame Daniel then, and he fell into a deep and well-earned sleep.

CHAPTER TEN

The Wild Caves

---- 1 ----

The Wild Caves were certainly wild, but it was hard for Daniel and Freya to think of them as just *caves*. At certain points they would open out into enormous expanses that seemed more like underground landscapes. It was hard to make out features in these areas, since the vast emptiness swallowed their feeble lamplight, but there would sometimes be a glittering seam that would throw their light back at them; or a pale green luminescence swathed against a rock face.

Then, without warning, they would enter another tunnel or turn a corner to find themselves in disturbingly small and claustrophobic passages that might wind on for miles without giving them a chance to stand up straight. The air hung around them, thick with cold and clammy moisture.

Generally Swiðgar led them along whichever path appeared to offer the quickest downward loop. The Slæpismere, they knew, was a long way down, so whenever possible they would follow water—anything from a small trickle to a river. Just about any stream of water would eventually lead to the huge underground lake, they reasoned. Sooner or later, however, each stream or trickle of water fell into a drain or slipped into a crack in the wall. This was frustrating, yet they always seemed to happen across another ribbon of water they could follow, refreshing themselves and refilling their waterskins.

When they had been walking downwards for what seemed like days, they came to a sharp ridge of slate where they paused. A draft rising from below sent warm waves of heat rolling over them, causing them to sweat. They stayed for a time, sitting on the ridge, opening up their clothing and taking off their shoes—exposing everything that they had to the warm air in order to dry them as much as possible. There was no way of telling where the air came from, but Daniel's mind pictured an open lake of lava beneath them, sending its heat up towards them through a series of vents.

But ever before and after that, the Wild Caves were invariably cold, wet, and miserably dark. The thick, oilcloth traveling cloaks and boots were snug enough, but not completely waterproof. Finding a place to camp was a constant difficulty. Since there was no way to mark the passage of time below the earth, and they had no watches, it was hard to estimate how long they had been walking or how long they should keep walking. Many times they would hunt around for a bit of dry ground and spend some time setting up camp, only to find sleep still a long way off.

The physical hardships would have been enough, but having no knowledge of how far they had gone or had left to go was what Daniel and Freya found most dispiriting. Only determination kept them from depression. Daniel's desire to get stronger and better at traveling helped him keep putting one foot in front of the other. Freya's thought of how many people depended on their mission kept her feet moving forward, long after they had started to cramp and ache.

Swiðgar was grim and serious. He seldom spoke, walking always in the lead, keeping his eyes open and ears alert for any clue of danger or trouble in the path ahead. Ecgbryt, on the other hand, exalted in the prospect of danger and adventure.

The knights were ideal traveling companions—they seemed to be walking libraries. Ecgbryt would go a ways in silence and then suddenly launch into a tale about a battle he had participated in, usually with King Ælfred against the Vikings. Daniel would always press him with questions about the details of his exploits, but would be forced into silence when his store of questions was exhausted.

Freya found Ecgbryt and Daniel exasperating at times, and preferred walking with Swiðgar up ahead. She was fond of his riddles, and he seemed to know hundreds of them. She only ever guessed a few of them correctly, but a good one would keep her mind turning for hours before she allowed Swiðgar to tell her the answer. She was never disappointed—even when she needed him to explain the answer. She even memorised a couple of her favorites.

Both Daniel and Freya enjoyed the knights' ballads. Both knew long ballads that sometimes took over an hour to recite; some of them were so complex, they had no idea how the warriors kept them all separate in their heads—although one of them would correct the other from time to time. Ecgbryt's songs and poems all seemed to be about battles and heroic deeds; Swiðgar's about journeys and strange experiences and observations.

They had been following the path of a small stream—barely a trickle of water that ran steadily downwards through a narrow, gutter-like tunnel—and this lead them into a larger, open space where the echoes of their movements grew further apart and softer, and a stiff wind blew across them. More significantly, they heard sounds that they did not cause.

"Whisht," hissed Swiðgar, motioning them to stop. They all held their breath, crouching to let their ears pick out sounds of

shuffling and scraping. The sounds were regular and continuous—not the sounds of people trying not to be heard.

"I think I see something," said Freya. "Just up ahead. It's a kind of swirling motion—things moving around a light—up there on that rock."

"*Swa swa*, so it also seems to me," said Swiðgar. "Let us approach cautiously. There may be danger in the shadows."

"Let it fall upon us," Ecgbryt huffed. "It will meet my axe coming up to greet it. The night before Ælfred harried the Viking chieftain Hastein at Appledore and Milton—"

"Hush, broðor," commanded Swiðgar.

"I am sorry, but my weapon is mighty tired from being carried around like an infant. It longs to stretch itself."

"I will stretch it across your head if you do not strap your tongue to your teeth," Swiðgar snapped testily. He halted in front of them but did not turn around. "God's wounds, you are a worse prattler than Asser."

"Aye, broðor," said Ecgbryt with a wink at Daniel, who grinned back at him. "Aye, calm yourself, it is well."

They crept forward, approaching the lit figure. Looking around, Daniel could see that they were entering what seemed to be a confluence of tunnels. The walls were honeycombed with black, twisting holes of various sizes—from tall, black, foreboding ruptures in the walls that spewed cold winds to holes small enough to perhaps only wriggle through, but that were so smooth they may have been sanded out of the stone. The atmosphere was a bewildering confusion of cross breezes and vortexes.

The wide, flat ground stretching before them was about the size and dimension of a football pitch and looked like some sort of abandoned mining site littered with old rickety frames and boards that were slowly rotting next to decaying bits of canvas and string. A dry and crumbling bucket lay beside an old well, and there was the occasional stone ring that encircled a fire-scorched spot of earth.

Freya could now make out the moving shapes more clearly; they were people, all milling slowly around a glowing violet light. She blinked her eyes and shook her head. For a moment she thought there was something wrong with her, but then she figured it out—it was definitely people that she saw, but as she came nearer, she found that they were very, very small.

At first she had assumed them to be far away, but now she saw that they were quite close. The tallest of them could be no more than two feet high. There seemed to be about thirty or forty of them, walking around a shiny, cylindrical object that was nearly as big as they were—a brass lamp that gave off a faint purple light.

Half of them were moving in one direction, and half of them in the other. The lines wove in and out but without any bumping, jostling, or confusion, like bees around a hive, Freya thought. Closer, she could see that the little people were wearing roughly woven clothes of dark and faded colours. Some wore curious felt hats, others had twine belts. Some had tattered shoes, but most were barefoot. The men had long beards, and the women wore long tresses. All were dumpy, with sagging faces, glumly circling the brass lamp, faces to the light, murmuring to each other in low tones.

All except one. On a smallish boulder that nonetheless placed him several heads' height above the others sat a fat figure, much better clothed than the rest, even if just as glum.

"Gnomes," groaned Swiðgar, shaking his head. "Cuthbert preserve us."

2

"Gnomes?" repeated Daniel. "Really? What do they do? I mean, what are they? Where are they from?"

"They are a long-lived people—perhaps the smallest of the underground races. They make their homes in the corners unused by the other earth-livers. They are generally happy folk and do not usually intend harm or mischief to any."

"Not that it would make much difference if they were to," Ecgbryt muttered.

"They mimic the actions of other races—of men, elves, dwarfs, and even goblins, I have heard tell. I would guess that the one on the rock is the king or chieftain."

Ecgbryt snorted. "The dwarfish races sometimes use them as cheap helpmates. They don't ask for money, content only to do what they see the dwarfs doing." He shrugged.

"Why do they copy others?" Freya asked.

"They are Healfmods," answered Ecgbryt, "that is, half-spirited, or half-minded—they do not think entirely for themselves. All of them share their thoughts, such as they are, with the rest. Apart, each of them is stupid. Together . . . in truth, together they are not much more."

The gnomes were still moving and muttering to themselves in low voices, just as they had before. The only sign that they had registered the presence of the four newcomers was a quick dart of the eyes towards and away from the strangers, although their faces still remained sad and mournful, not in the least surprised or interested.

The travelers stood and watched for a time. The steady, circling movement and purple light was oddly hypnotic and relaxing. Daniel feared that he might turn into one of those mindless gnomes if he didn't say or do something soon. Stepping forward, he drew a deep breath and called, "Hello!" in a loud voice.

The gnome on the rock jumped, his eyes comically wide. All of the gnomes stopped instantly as their heads spun around from every direction until they stopped at Daniel.

"Who said that?" said one with a bushy beard.

"Who's there?" said another, a woman with a hat.

"Who said what?" asked a third.

"Hello," answered a fourth.

"Who's there?" asked a fifth.

"What?" said a sixth.

This fit of responses took Daniel by surprise and he stood in silence with the others. The chief had looked at him expectantly, as if he had spoken, though he never said a word.

"Um," he began again, his eyes going from the chief to the crowd of gnomes and back again. "My name is Daniel and . . . uh, I'm—I mean we—are looking for a tunnel down to the Slæpismere. If any of you, that is, if all of you, er, know of a way down, then that'd be, you know, great. Uh . . . otherwise, if you don't, then that's okay—but if you do, do you think you could . . ."

Daniel could hear himself babbling stupidly but he couldn't stop. About sixty eyes were on him, staring steadily and expectantly. It wasn't until Ecgbryt put a hand on his shoulder that he broke off.

"Best go easy, æðeling," Ecgbryt said gently. Then he addressed the small crowd. "The Slæpismere. We seek it. Where is it?"

"They seek the Slæpismere!"

"Oh dear, where is it?"

"I say, what is it?"

"Alas! Who wants it?"

"Alack! Who is it?"

"Slæpismere. Oh my."

"The Slæpismere."

This time the chieftain closed his eyes and seemed to exert considerable effort before opening his mouth. "Hello," he managed eventually.

"Hi," said Freya. "What's your name?"

"Negan," the gnome answered after a shorter pause and a little less effort. "We are called Negan."

"Oh." Freya nodded. "Okay." The other gnomes were standing quietly, watching the travelers.

"We understand that you seek the Slæpismere . . ."

"Yes, that's right."

The gnome closed his eyes and nodded his head wisely. "Have you found it?" he asked, opening them again.

Freya faltered and Daniel picked up the conversation again. "No. Do you know where it is?"

This brought the gnome chorus back again.

"Where is it?"

"The Slæpismere, where's the Slæpismere?"

"The Slæpismere? Forsooth!"

"What's one of those?"

"Who had it last? Oh me."

"Where is it? Oh my."

The gnome chieftain closed his eyes and the murmuring stopped. "No," he said after a time. "We don't know where it is. It may be down one of these tunnels," he said, gesturing around him. "Not that we would know."

"Why not, haven't you been down them?" Freya asked.

"Didn't you make them?" Daniel asked.

"Down them? Ha!" began the chorus.

"Make them? Ho!"

"Been them? Hee!"

"Ah, what's the point?"

"Oh, what's the use?"

"Eh, so many tunnels."

"I wonder who did make them . . ."

The chorus stopped.

"No," the gnome chief replied simply. "We have not."

"They know nothing," said Ecgbryt.

"Perhaps they do," Swiðgar said. "How long has it been since you came here?" he asked the gnome chief.

"Long enough."

"Too long."

"Time flies."

"It's not so bad after a while."

"When weren't we here?"

"Ages."

"Long?" The gnome chief sighed. "Oh, we don't know. After a while all time is the same—a minute seems as long as an hour and the other way around. How long have you been here?"

"We just got here," Freya replied, growing frustrated.

"Oh. Well, you won't stay, though you're welcome to, I dare say. But if you do leave, I fancy you'll return, just like our cousin."

"Your cousin?"

"Yes, you're bound to see him if you wait long enough. His name is Gegan. He travels here and there. He'll be here in a minute or so . . . a couple hours at the most."

"Why aren't you all with him?" Freya asked with a cautious glance at the rest of the staring gnomes.

"Oh, there doesn't seem to be any point," said Negan.

"Why not?" asked Freya.

All of the gnomes answered at once. "What's the use?"

"What's the point?"

"Welladay!"

"Alack!"

"Alas!"

"I'm hungry."

"Woe!"

"Well, why *would* we go with him?" answered Negan peevishly.

"All roads lead one place—and you always end up where you happen to be. There's no getting away from it. Anyway, I'm already here, so why not stay put?"

3

"Ach," spat Ecgbryt, "there is nothing to be got from the wee men. I say we press on."

"But which way?" Swiðgar asked, stroking his beard.

Ecgbryt did not answer; he just trudged off.

Daniel looked around at the grim desolation of the gnomes' mining camp. "It's not very nice here, is it?" he said. "Wouldn't you like to go somewhere better?"

"Well, naturally," Negan the gnome chief replied petulantly. "But one could just as easily end up somewhere worse. Here at least, one has choices!"

"But it's only a choice if you choose it," Freya argued.

"Ah, yes, you see how futile it is," said the gnome with a nod of sympathy.

"No, I don't," said Daniel hotly. "It sounds like the stupidest thing I've heard. Just go somewhere, anywhere, and if you don't like it, then you can go somewhere else—somewhere better."

Negan shrugged. "I could be somewhere better than somewhere worse if I just stay here," he said.

"That's the stupidest thing I've ever heard!" Daniel shouted, throwing his arms above his head and stomping off. Freya and Swiðgar were left with the gnomes and nothing more to say. After a few moments, the tiny people began milling slowly around the brass lamp, wallowing in the purple light once more.

"Hey, look!" Daniel called from across the camp. "More lamps."

Freya turned and saw Daniel standing by a large metal rack

that held a long line of glinting glass and metal cylinders. He had taken one of them and was dusting it off. He held the base up to his ear and shook it. "It's got stuff in it. I think these might still work," he said. "Do you want one?"

Freya was about to answer but was stopped by a hearty shout of "Ho there!"

They turned to see another crowd approaching them, a second mass of gnomes with a character very like Negan leading them. He was so like the chief gnome that he was almost identical, except that his face beamed happiness and jollity. Behind him the flock of gnomes was clustered, four of whom carried a lamp raised up by two wooden poles. "Have you been talking to my cousin?" he bellowed brightly.

"Are you Gegan?" asked Daniel.

This provoked a chorus from the gnomes behind him. "Gegan!"

"Yes, Gegan the Great!"

"Gegan the far-traveled!"

"The thick-calved!"

"Sing praise for Gegan!"

"Hip-hippity ho!"

"Hooray!"

"Yes, I am Gegan," the second gnome king answered proudly. "Have you been here long? No? That's good. It means you couldn't have been talking to *him* long. We're sorry you had to talk to him at all; it must have been very depressing for you—it always depresses us."

There was a babble of voices from the Negan gnomes behind them.

"Gegan is back."

"Oh no, not Gegan."

"Back from where, this time, I wonder?"

"I don't like Gegan."

"Here we go again."

Negan, the glum king, gazed placidly into his own lantern. "Back again so soon, brother?" he called out drearily.

"Well, yes," said Gegan, "as a matter of fact, we are."

"Back from where?" asked Daniel, bracing himself.

"Here!"

"There!"

"Hither and yon!"

"Afar and beyond!"

"I can't remember!"

"Back," exclaimed the gnome king expansively, "from my travels!"

"Have you explored these tunnels?" Swiðgar asked, joining them. "Do you know where they lead?"

"Explored them?"

"Most of them."

"All of them!"

"How many are there?"

"How many are we?"

"Nearly all of them," Gegan said. "Many of them several times! Aren't they magnificent? Why, I never tire of them, even after all these years!"

"Really?" asked Daniel. "We were just deciding where we should go."

"Go?" repeated Gegan.

"Aye, our toes twitch and feet itch," said Ecgbryt.

"We are trying to reach the lower levels," Swiðgar said, dwarfing the gnome king like a tree. "To the Slæpismere. Which tunnel do we take for that?"

There was a murmur of confusion behind the gnome king. None of the gnomes actually said anything, just made doubtful noises. Gegan stroked his chin. "We can't rightly say, not having been to the end of any one of them—so we cannot say where they *lead*, as such . . ."

He trailed off, his hand moving up to rub his head. It was awhile before anyone spoke.

"But you just—you said"—Freya stammered—"that you've explored them all."

"Oh, we've been *in* them, true enough, but we never go too far before we turn back to try another one. We simply love to travel, you see, but once you take one road you can't take another. What if we were to choose a wrong one and ended up where we didn't want to be? Then what would we do? No, it's best to come back here and review my decision every once in a while. That's the only way I can be sure to find the right one." His cheeks propped up a hopeful smile.

Ecgbryt let out a bellowing laugh. "So, friend gnome, you are always walking and never arriving." Gegan's eyes shifted uncertainly and he frowned.

"You're just like *them*," Freya said, throwing a finger towards the miserable Negan.

"Ho!" Gegan laughed and shook his head. "There's a world of difference between us. He stays here because he hates to go anywhere, where as I . . . I . . . ," he faltered.

Daniel turned to the still-smiling Gegan and asked, "Which one of these tunnels goes the farthest downwards?"

Dozens of small arms and fingers pointed out in separate directions. Gegan thought for a moment and the arms and fingers swiveled one by one to indicate one of the larger exits from the cavern. "This one, probably," he said.

"Well, it's more than we knew before," said Daniel as Ecgbryt came to stand behind him. "It's worth a try. Freya?" Freya nodded reluctantly. "Swiðgar?"

"Yes, I suppose it will do."

"Wonderful. Let's go, Gegan," Daniel said.

After watching them pass with a thoughtful eye, Gegan ran up alongside them, his sandals clicking merrily and his clan padding eagerly behind him. "Yes, and we will come with you," he chirped excitedly. "If we cannot assure you by our words, then we will convince you by our feet that we really do love to travel!"

"Hold on a second," Daniel said, pausing at the rack of lanterns. "Freya, do you want one?" They picked out a couple they could use for as long as the fuel lasted. With little trouble they were able to light them. The lamps were heavy but gave off a good, steady light—even with the wicks kept quite low. The light seemed to go farther than their own lamps, but it wasn't easy to say if the purple light was brighter. They burned with a rich, sweet aroma, as if incense was mixed in with the oil.

Ready to depart, the clan Gegan dutifully took their place up ahead and the rest followed behind. For a good time the gnomes walked merrily along, singing strange songs with complex choruses that they sometimes muddled up. But gradually, the singing became weaker and the clan appeared to grow oddly agitated. Gegan himself began to twitch and rub his neck. Then he started to cast longing looks behind him, a strained smile on his face.

"You want to go back," stated Freya, "don't you?"

"Yes, well . . . no, it's not that, it's just . . . we have never been this far before."

"I thought that was the exciting part," Daniel said sarcastically.

There were groans and a cry of "wey-la-day!" before Gegan said, "Well, not exactly. The fun part is traveling, but we were just thinking—what if one of the other tunnels was better . . . what if it led more in the direction that you want to go? We thought this one a good choice, but now that one comes to it . . . what if . . . ?"

"We've only just started," said Daniel.

"The gnome speaks true," Swiðgar said, stopping behind

them. He and Ecgbryt needed to stoop down slightly to walk this tunnel. "The way was fairly steep downwards at the start, but since that time the tunnel has risen back to the level of the cavern, and more, I judge."

"Let us go a little farther yet," suggested Ecgbryt. "It may descend yet again. There is nothing lost if we be wrong."

"Nothing but time," said Swiðgar. "And that is something in limited supply. It may go farther down yet, but another path may be better. I think we should return to the cavern."

"And do what? Try another tunnel?" Ecgbryt responded, his voice rising. "Which of those was more promising than this?"

"Perhaps," said Swiðgar uncomfortably, "we could go a small way into each one—a short distance and follow the one most likely."

"But time presses, Swiðgar," Ecgbryt said in a mocking tone. "We will get nowhere by traveling short distances. Who's to know that the tunnels don't all meet up farther on down? Let us press on."

Swiðgar didn't move; he just glowered at Ecgbryt. "Wisdom dictates that we stop and consider before—"

"Oh yes, wise Swiðgar and his dictates!"

"You speak out of turn, broðor!"

"Then kindly inform each of us when our turn arrives, so we may speak then!"

Daniel and Freya stood along one wall, gripping their lanterns and watching the knights argue with wide eyes. Daniel looked at the gnomes and would have laughed if he weren't so afraid. Almost a hundred wide and fearful eyes were looking at the knights like frightened islanders would look at a hurricane.

Swiðgar's jaw clenched. "Have your say," he growled.

"We have barely even started down this route," Ecgbryt said, his voice steady. "The lad is right, let us just follow it a little farther."

There was a heavy silence as the knights glared at each other. "I agree with Swiðgar," Freya announced. "I think we should—"

She stopped abruptly when Ecgbryt turned his face on her, his eyes blazing angrily.

"I do too," said Daniel, stepping forward to stand beside Freya. "But I agree more with Ecgbryt," he said, turning to Swiðgar. "Anyhow, I don't see why we have to have it just one way. Let's just go a little farther and if it still doesn't look good, then we can turn back. That way we're all satisfied, yeah?"

Ecgbryt dipped his eyes and looked away. Swiðgar stroked his beard, and Freya moved a trembling hand across her hot face.

"We can still have it both ways, it's just that we can't know if this tunnel is right if we turn back now."

Swiðgar gave a curt nod. "Very well," he conceded, turning to the gnomes. "You are welcome to join us, but you are not bound."

All of the tiny eyes stared, blinking. "Ah, yes," said the chief nervously. "We would gladly join you, but if it's all the same . . . we won't. Still," he said, trying to sound hearty. Raising his hands, he declared, "May your legs move merrily along your . . . what-you-may-call-it, and may your feet never want for . . . thingy. And all that. Right. Okay," he said, turning. "Come along, lads."

The gnomes turned quickly and bustled off back up the tunnel, carrying their lantern with them.

4

As the travelers resumed their journey in sullen silence, they soon noticed the texture of the walls change from a crumbly black surface to a soft, lumpy white one.

"It looks like chalk," said Freya.

"Aye, so it is," answered Swiðgar. This was the first exchange in some time, and it died in silence.

"What's happening up there?" Daniel asked. "Does the tunnel just end?"

"It might just be a turn or something," Freya said.

Because of the white walls, the light cast by the lamps was brighter and went farther, but it still was only a few more steps until they saw that the tunnel did, in fact, come to a dead end.

"Well, that's that," said Daniel under his breath. "Now we know." He turned and tried to avoid Swiðgar's eye.

"Wait, look," said Freya. "That edge up there. Look, there's something on the other side."

"The girl's right," Ecgbryt said, stepping towards what looked like a depression in the wall. Once his torch shone across it, however, it was revealed to be a hole large enough for him to put first his torch and then his head through it. Standing on his toes and pulling himself up with his free hand, he examined the opening for a moment before pulling himself out.

"It appears to lead to the floor of another chamber," he reported. "I see a lot of walls and entrances. I think we should investigate it."

Swiðgar said nothing but stood pulling at his beard doubtfully.

"Take a look for yourself at least," Ecgbryt suggested.

Swiðgar stepped forward and examined the hole in the same way. "Very well," he agreed reluctantly, "let one of us go first, and then the æðelingas."

Ecgbryt was lofting his gear and weaponry through the hole before Swiðgar had even finished talking. With difficulty, and some widening of the chalk hole, Ecgbryt pushed through and was able to reach down to pull Daniel and Freya up as well.

Looking around, they saw that they were in the corner of what looked to be a grid-like construction of tunnels—or rather, one wide-open space that was supported by many thick columns of white rock.

"I believe this may be a mine. Much of the island is rich in good quality chalk such as this."

Daniel considered. "A mine? But I thought that we were going through the Wild Caves—not anything made by men."

Swiðgar nodded. "And so we have been until now. These caves were not made by Britons, though, but by the men of Rome, and possibly the Celts before them."

"Still," said Freya, "we can't be that far from the surface, can we?"

"We will have to see. But my fear is that we are straying from our true course."

"So little faith have you, Swiðgar?" said Ecgbryt. "You must trust more to fortune—it has been on our side yet."

Swiðgar's face went slightly dark and then cleared again. "Nevertheless," he said, "if you don't think it mocking fate, I would like to mark our exit."

Ecgbryt shrugged and hoisted his pack. Using the butt of his spear to scrape into the soft stone, Swiðgar made large Xs on the walls above the hole. They gathered their things and started exploring the new tunnels.

They walked for some time but arrived nowhere. Each section of the tunnel was the same as the last, a short corridor leading to a perpendicular crossroads, always carved out of white, powdery rock. Eventually their path ended in a wall so they turned and walked along that for a while. When that ended after a short distance, so they went in another direction. Freya's eyes were starting to water from the dust clouding up from their steps and from the endless repetition.

Eventually they decided to stop at a crossroads and rest. The light from the torches did not reflect off any wall down either end, as far as they could see. Frustrated, they sat together, not saying a word or even looking at each other. Daniel finished massaging his feet and very carefully put his socks back on. He drank some water and lay back on the cold floor, willing his muscles to relax.

It was as he closed his eyes and let his mind drift that he felt something on the back of his head—a dull vibration that came from the ground: a kind of pounding and scraping.

He opened his eyes. None of the others were doing anything to create the strange sensation he was feeling. He strained his ears to listen, trying to separate sounds away from each other, then realised that he wasn't listening to one sound but to lots of the same sound. The feeling of dread swept over him.

"Everyone, quiet," he whispered. "I think it's yfelgópes!"

All held their breath. Swiðgar and Ecgbryt stood, quietly drawing their weapons.

Soon they heard the sound of footsteps—many footsteps. A flickering light grew around them. Daniel stood up and took a few steps down the tunnel. He guessed what the source of the light was before he saw it—it was another lamp. In the deep blue glow they glimpsed a shape, which they quickly recognised.

More gnomes.

For a dizzy moment, Daniel thought that it might be the Gegan clan—whom they had somehow circled around to meet again. But the light of their own torches soon revealed a fatter, swarthier gnome with different clothes and hair. Daniel took a deep breath and stepped forward. "Hello," he said and introduced himself.

"Halloo!"

"Hail, and well met!"

"Welcome!"

"Pleased ta meetcha."

"Hello," said the rotund figure at the head. "Our name is Ergan."

"Greetings to you, friend gnome," Swiðgar said, coming to stand beside Daniel.

The gnome gaped up at the knight—many times taller than he—and blinked rapidly.

"Are you—do you have two cousins?" asked Freya.

The gnome turned his eyes to her and seemed to ponder the question. There was a confused muttering behind him. "Yes, we believe we do. Gegan and Negan are kinsmen of mine. Have you met them?"

Ecgbryt snorted and nodded his head. "For all the good it's done us."

"Yes," said Freya, "we have."

"They are silly folk," said Ergan. "One of them won't go anywhere and the other tries to go everywhere at once. So they end up nowhere!"

"Yes!" said Daniel. "Exactly!"

"When really," continued Ergan, obviously pleased at the reception he was getting, "it doesn't matter where you go, so long as you go *somewhere*."

"Right," said Daniel. "Exactly. Listen, we are searching for the entrance to the Slæpismere. Do you know where that is?"

"Oh . . . ," said Ergan slowly. "I think we do. That is, we must do—we have walked these tunnels long enough! Let us see . . . Let us see . . . We shall consult the maps. Bring the maps!"

There was a chorus of "bring the maps!" and after some bustling, several bundles of scrolled-up parchment were produced. The lamp was turned up to give enough light to read by, and the four travelers could see that they were now in the company of a much more sophisticated type of gnome. These seemed much more prepared than any of the others. Some of them were wearing metal helmets and had coils of rope across their shoulders. There was a call for more light and candles were produced.

"At last!" said Ecgbryt excitedly. "We can move onwards!"

"I thought that we *were* moving onwards, broðor," Swiðgar jibed.

Ecgbryt glowered. "For lack of a leader," he said, "we were simply moving—or drifting, rather. Rudderless, directionless."

"So, you disregard my advice and claim that you had no direction?" Swiðgar charged, his voice rising.

Ecgbryt batted the question away with a flip of his hand. "Bah, he is starting to sound like Ealdstan," he muttered to himself, bending over the maps that the gnomes were spreading out.

Swiðgar's teeth clenched. He folded his arms across his chest and turned away.

"Ah, here we are," announced Ergan. "We haven't come across the Slæpismere yet, but we know several places where it *could* be."

"Show us," said Ecgbryt, bending over.

"Show him," commanded Ergan with a signal. Instantly, four gnomes sprang forward and pointed fingers at different points on several of the scrolls that had been unrolled before them. "The lowest points of the tunnel we've found are here, here, and here," he explained. "Found on maps 27-12, 18-39, and 111-3e7. However, none of those tunnels diverge and at no point are any of the tunnels crossed by any streams or tributaries."

Ergan paused as Swiðgar and Freya joined them to look over the mapwork. "However," the gnome chief continued, "however— ah, do you know in which direction this Slæpismere lies?"

Swiðgar shook his head.

"Pity," said Ergan. "Because that would have helped us narrow it down. You see, there are, as yet, at least one hundred and thirty-four unexplored branches and divergences." All of the rest of the gnomes reached into their satchels, pulled out unrolled maps, and waved them in the air.

Swiðgar sighed and removed his helmet. Daniel and Freya watched him run a hand several times across his head.

"This is what you do?" Swiðgar asked. "You search through the tunnels and make maps of them?"

All of the gnomes' heads began nodding furiously. "Yes," said Ergan proudly. "That is what we do."

"How long have you been doing this?" asked Freya.

Every shoulder of every gnome shrugged once; Ergan shrugged too. "Years and years. Maybe a hundred. Since I was this high." He placed his hand at his waist, roughly twelve inches from the ground.

"And not once have you discovered the Slæpismere, or imagined where it might lie?"

Ergan shook his head. "No, we can't say that we have."

"What have you discovered?"

"Tunnels!" squealed Ergan delightedly. Several gnomes behind him echoed the word in a happy fashion. "Lots and lots of glorious tunnels! Every one of them a marvel. Don't you find them simply fantastic? How many people have wandered these tunnels over the years? Who made them? What stories do they have to tell? Why, when we think of how much there still is to do, it makes our hearts ache. So much to look forward to, and so much that we may not live to see. Still, at least future generations will be able to enjoy the benefits of our work and go wherever they want, whenever they want. You—do you not think that grand?"

Ergan faltered when he realised that the look on the companions' harrowed faces was anger dangerously mixed with a little fear.

"What?" squeaked Ergan. "Whatever is the matter?"

"I think I understand," said Ecgbryt calmly, drawing his axe. "Hold by, gnome. I am a master axeman and this will be done quickly . . ." He took a couple steps towards the small figure.

"What are you going to do?" asked Freya.

"Since we cannot coax the direction we need from them, I am going to peel the chief's skin back and see if it lies inside of him. And if not him, then I'll try the next. I'll unravel every last one of them, if I have to. Unpleasant work, certainly, but I am resolved to it."

The gnomes' faces blanched in terror, their eyes staring from their round heads. There were many confused cries and shouts.

A dozen hands were placed on Ergan and with a chorus of voices yelling, *"Save the chief!"* they fled back down the tunnel. The light from their lantern bobbed in the darkness when they could be seen no longer, and then it too disappeared.

Ecgbryt was laughing as he sheathed his sword.

"That was mean," said Freya.

"And pointless," said Swiðgar.

"But hilarious!" exploded Daniel.

"Aye, the boy has me," said Ecgbryt. "It was all for the look on their funny little faces."

"But now we are worse off than before," said Swiðgar gravely.

Ecgbryt shrugged. "Perhaps."

"No, we aren't worse off," said Daniel. "In fact, we're better. All those gnomes were just confusing us, and I think they were meant to. What if *this* is a trap of some kind? We're probably meant to wander around forever and become just as confused as those gnomes. We have to go back to the big cavern—I think there's something we've missed."

Swiðgar frowned. "What you say may be true, but then again, it may be that the path lies some farther distance up and we do not know it yet."

"Of course," said Daniel, "but I don't think so. Remember what Ealdstan said? Gád would want to make sure that he could get to his heart quickly if he needed to. So the hiding place wouldn't be too far away. Besides, those gnomes have been wandering everywhere and haven't found a thing. No, we went wrong at the start of this, somehow."

"A riddle!" Ecgbryt exclaimed gleefully, rubbing his hands together. "Now my blood is running and my feet shall go no slower. Come, æðelingas, I wist you will have a job to keep up."

Daniel and Ecgbryt virtually leapt back down the way they had come, with Freya and Swiðgar trailing behind them. But after a few steps, she hesitated and stopped, wanting to turn to Swiðgar, who she knew was still standing there unhappily. She decided not to in the end, thinking it might embarrass him. Instead, she spent an extra long time adjusting her pack.

Behind her, Swiðgar said something she didn't understand, and then there came a crash, a smash, and a rattling clatter as the lanterns bounced into the darkness. It startled her, but she hid this by hiking her pack up onto her shoulders. Then Swiðgar passed her with his enormous strides and she hurried to catch up to him.

5

They made their way back to the big cavern. The journey was uneventful and embarrassing, and bad feelings still hung in the air. Freya only hoped that they could solve the riddle quickly so that they could get on with their journey and put the unpleasantness behind them.

After a time they were able to see the purple glow of Gegan's lamp through the worming tunnel. They unslung their packs when they came to the mining camp and stood a fair ways off from the static gnome chief and his orbiting clansmen.

"So, what are we looking for, Freya?" Daniel asked. "We're underneath Britain, wedged between solid rock—it has to be a tunnel."

"We have plenty of tunnels, but we think that they're here to distract us. So maybe it's a tunnel that doesn't look like a tunnel."

"A hidden tunnel?"

Freya nodded. "Let's start looking."

The two of them, and after a short time the knights also, began hunting around the abandoned campsite. Daniel was searching the rack of lamps again to see if it concealed a hidden doorway, when, taking a step back, his calf bumped against a gnome. Startled, he flinched away and let out a surprised grunt. There were not one but four gnomes standing at his feet. "I nearly trod on you," Daniel said. "What are you doing here?"

The gnomes just stood, looking up at him. "Freya? Ecgbryt?" he called. They turned to him and bumped into gnomes of their own. Swiðgar almost squashed one completely, except that he shifted his foot at the last instant.

"What do you want?" Freya asked the gnomes. They just stood looking vacantly up at her. "Guys?" she asked nervously. "What's going on?"

Daniel and the two knights had begun to draw away from the corners they had been hunting in to stand closer together, and the gnomes followed their footsteps.

"Are you trying to help us?" Freya asked her gnomes, bending forward slightly as she slowly edged towards the others. "Are you trying to stop us?" The gnomes said nothing, just kept following.

Freya joined the others, who were trying to gently push the gnomes away with their feet. She looked up to the rest of the Gegan clan and saw that more gnomes were leaving the group and wandering towards them. Except for two.

Two of them were heading towards . . .

The well.

It all clicked into place for her at that moment. The Gegan gnomes' chief did know where the exit was, and while its main thought was to keep them away, it couldn't help also thinking about what it was keeping them away from—which was the well, another tunnel hidden, but in plain sight. Freya nudged Daniel and pointed. He looked at it for a moment before his eyes grew wide, and a smile flashed across his face. They silently communicated to the two knights, and they pushed through the growing circle of gnomes and collected their packs. They brushed aside the gnomes that were clinging to them or who had climbed on top of them.

They had just turned towards the well when they heard:

"Where are you going?"

"Where are you going?"

"Stay here."

"Stay away from there."

"Get ready, boys."

They paused instantly, and then Swiðgar said, "Let us be swift, æðelingas—the gnomes are starting to turn."

"Do they know?"

"They've twigged it."

"But do they know?"

"They've figured it out."

"Get them!"

As one, the gnomes leapt forward, gripping at their legs and climbing upwards.

"Run!" shouted Ecgbryt, booting a gnome halfway across the encampment. Daniel and Freya struggled forward, trying to shake the gnomes off of them. It was hard work, as their little pudgy hands gripped their clothes tenaciously.

"Slow them down!"

"Weigh them down!"

"Stab them!"

"Slit their throats!"

At these alarming cries, one of the gnomes that had swung onto Freya's sleeve produced a knife from its belt. Its blade was only two inches long, but it looked very, very sharp. Whipping her arm away, she sent it flying, just as she heard Daniel cry out. He reached down and clawed a gnome off of his shin and threw it away from him. More and more of the gnomes were producing knives. The well bristled with them now; the whole rest of the clan of gnomes was now lining its rim, waiting for them.

Daniel had an idea, though, and glanced across to the gnome

chieftain, still atop the rock near his the purple lantern. He was standing, hands clenched at his sides, glaring at them in anger, but there were no gnomes around him, and none between the two of them. Daniel saw his chance and jumped towards the chief, clearing the heads of several gnomes around him.

The gnomes were fast and energetic, but no match for a boy running at top speed. In any case, it was only a dozen steps before Daniel had reached him. During that time, he had shaken the gnomes from him and drawn his sword.

"No!"

"Stop him!"

"Help!"

"Don't!"

"Please!"

"Mercy!"

Biting down on his lip, Daniel brought his sword down and cleaved through Gegan, the chief gnome. The sword entered the gnome's shoulder and sunk to his belly. A second later the small, rotund little creature was dead.

The gnomes exploded into a frenzy. The ones that were on either the knights or Freya let go and fell to the ground. The gnomes lining the well ran all different directions, bumping into each other and falling in and off the well itself.

They scattered, screaming and wailing into the darkness. Soon they were gone from sight.

Wincing, and trying not to vomit, Daniel shook the dead body of the gnome off of his sword. It fell to the ground with a *plop*.

"That was fast thinking, Daniel," Ecgbryt said. "Well done."

"You gave me the idea for it," Daniel said, wiping his sword with a bit of his leather coat and sheathing it again.

"Let's move on," Swiðgar said. "Before the Ergan gnomes come back."

CHAPTER ELEVEN

The Faerie Fayre

————————————— 1 —————————————

Now . . .

Daniel awoke just as the sky—where he could see it between the billows of the smoking woodpiles—was just starting to lighten and the stars had begun to fade. Finally his body was adjusting to the incredibly long days.

During the night, the collier had extinguished the fires and was breaking open the first mound. He had paused in his task and was resting his hands on his shovel, his lips moving as if he were talking to someone. As Daniel watched him, rubbing the sleep out of his eyes, he thought he saw a shadow standing before the collier, which was roughly the size of a person.

The collier stood as if listening now, and then inclined his head and raised his arm in a farewell. The shadow evaporated and the collier turned back to his work.

Daniel sipped some water from a bowl taken from the cistern

and relieved himself behind the hut. After taking a sip from the breakfast bottle and ignoring the gnawing pit of hunger in his stomach, he picked up a shovel and went to join the collier.

They shared a "good morning" nod.

"My wife will be here, perhaps this afternoon," the collier announced. Daniel was surprised; he hadn't considered that the collier might be married.

"Is that who you were talking to?" Daniel asked. "Where is she now?"

"Not far off. I instructed her to bring food, and she says she has managed to find some."

"Oh, thank you so much. If she was closer, would she have been clearer?"

"You could not see her clearly? Discern her features?"

"No, she just looked like a shadow to me."

The collier grunted. "Little matter," he said after a time. "Are you ready now to help sort?"

"Ready and willing," Daniel said with a smile.

They worked in silence. During one of their breaks towards noon, the collier's wife arrived. She was leading a horse and cart and seemed, to Daniel, to be fairly old, with grey hair and a graciously wrinkled face. But her eyes and skin gleamed with a youthful sheen, her movements quick and graceful. She was willow-thin, and dressed in a bodice and skirt made up of many different layers of thin, coloured cloth. Her hair was braided around the crown in a crescent shape and cascaded down her back to her waist. As the sunlight filtered into the clearing, Daniel thought it almost glowed.

"Hello, husband," she said, dropping the horse's rein and dashing up to him. He gathered her in his long, knotty arms and held her close. "I've missed you."

The collier's wife's eyes then swept over Daniel. "Who is your new helper?" she asked.

"I do not know his name," the collier said, "but I have known him to be a good worker this past ten day. The young Marrey lad sent him."

"Tch!" the woman said in a chiding tone, still looking at Daniel. "Imagine not knowing a fellow worker's name in all that time. But that's my Kæyle."

Daniel shot the collier—Kæyle—an inquisitive look.

"And you haven't told him yours it seems. I'll never understand men, though I live to be a hundred thousand. My name is Pettyl," she said, giving a slight curtsey.

"I'm Daniel." He explained where he had come from and that he was trying to get back.

"So," Pettyl said when he had finished, "why don't you two work a spell longer, and I'll fix lunch."

Daniel and Kæyle returned to the first pile and continued sifting and sorting into the barrels. Lunch for Daniel was the food that Pettyl had brought with her—fresh fruits and nuts that Daniel had never seen before. He tried not to eat too much too quickly and stopped when he felt his stomach start to ache. The fruit he enjoyed most was purple and curved like a banana but wider and flatter with a thin skin that could be eaten and soft, juicy flesh, like a grapefruit. He thanked Pettyl profusely afterwards.

They toiled late into the evening and with Pettyl's help they managed to finish packing the charcoal. Kæyle announced that they would depart for the market at the break of the next day. Daniel ate a hearty supper of more fruits and nuts and fell asleep with the satisfaction of a hard job finished.

He awoke the next morning, aching as he always did since coming to Elfland, but still exhausted, unrefreshed by his sleep— which was odd, since he had slept the entire night through.

The horses had already been hitched to Pettyl's cart, which was larger than the one the collier used for moving wood around, and, Kæyle had loaded the barrels of charcoal, stacking them two high, lashing them to the sides of the cart with rope.

The sky was still not fully bright when they were ready to start off. Kæyle and Pettyl sat in the front of the cart on the driving seat; Daniel made a place next to the provisions box and atop the bundle of cloth that would become their trade tent. When everyone was settled, Kæyle announced, "I will ask the forest for a good road to the market."

Kæyle faced the forest and began to sing.

It was a song with no words, or at least none that Daniel understood. It started low in Kæyle's chest and grew into a reverberation that came from nowhere and everywhere. Then his call began to rise and fall in soaring major notes and falling minors, before eventually settling into a repetitious melody. The trees before Kæyle swayed and shifted, making way for the cart in a way that made Daniel's head spin—they seemed to be moving, but not moving, like they were shifting place into somewhere they had always been. Finally the tune began to break down, devolving into disparate notes and phrases that were common to the piece. And then it was over.

Dumb with awe, Daniel leaned back against a barrel as Kæyle took his seat and with a snap of the reins, the cart jerked off. It felt as if his insides were still quivering like chords on a harp that still held their notes. Daniel remained in this dream-like state for a long time into their journey before realising that the road that was stretching out behind him was very wide, level, and straight. It must have been a pretty good song.

2

Freya woke up with a queasy feeling in her stomach. Her body, evidently realising that she was awake, hit her with a full blast of nausea. Alarmed, she swung herself out of bed and lurched to the toilet, where she was immediately sick. She caressed her swollen belly as she spat into the bowl and wiped the corners of her mouth with a couple squares of toilet paper.

She couldn't help glancing as she flushed—why was there always so little? What was her body doing, throwing up what wasn't there to throw up?

She grabbed her dressing gown, leaving it undone, of course— she hadn't been able to draw it together for a couple weeks now—and padded into the kitchen.

"Hello, sweetie," Felix said. He was seated at the kitchen table, a mug of coffee in his hand, the morning paper spread in front of him. A welcome and comforting stereotype, she thought. She smiled at him and went to the refrigerator.

"Do we have bacon? I feel like bacon, toast—no, a bagel if we've got one—marmalade, and . . . mustard. Lots of mustard, with the bacon, obviously. Dijon, preferably."

Felix chuckled. "Okay, my little gastronome, have a seat. I'll whip you up something."

Freya lowered herself into one of their kitchen chairs, shifting her weight uncomfortably. "I heard you in there," Felix said as strips of bacon hissed in the frying pan. "How are you feeling today?"

"About average. This coffee's helping."

"I hope you're not drinking it—you'll get one of your headaches."

"No, I just like the smell." She spent a few moments in thought. "Do I have an appointment today?"

"Yes, you do. Leigh was kind enough to offer to take you, remember?"

"That's right . . ."

"In fact—" Felix glanced at the clock on the wall. "Oh dear," he said gravely. "You're running late. I let you oversleep. I'm sorry. Quick, go get changed and I'll have this ready for you when you're done."

Sighing, Freya hoisted herself up. As she passed the kitchen counter, she reached a hand out to take a scrap of bacon but received a slap on the wrist instead.

"Naughty," Felix said with a grin.

Stomach growling angrily, Freya went back into their bedroom and dressed, putting on the minimum of makeup. There was a knock on the door just as she was finishing her eyeliner. She heard Felix open it and the murmur of voices greeting each other.

"Freya . . . ?"

"Coming!" Freya shouted. She stood straight and looked at herself in the mirror. When did she become so old?

As she bustled down the hallway, a wave of dizziness hit her. She slowed as she reached the doorway and put a hand against the wall to steady herself.

"Are you okay?" Stowe asked.

"I'm fine, just stood up too fast, that's all. Hello, Leigh. You look lovely, as ever."

"Thank you. Well, we'd better get moving."

"I'll see you this evening, my love," Felix said, giving her a peck on the cheek as he helped her into her coat.

"Okay, bye."

It was only as Freya was getting into Leigh Sinton's car that she realised she hadn't had anything to eat.

"Don't worry, dear," the older woman said. "We can pick something up on the way back. It's been awhile since we had a good chat. How are you coming on Brize Norton's *Commentaries to the Names of the Guardians*, by the way?"

"I don't know . . . I'm a little hazy . . ."

"It is difficult, I agree. Do you want me to review with you?"

Freya was trying to remember who exactly Brize Norton was. The name rang a very faint bell, but she thought it was a place, not a person . . . Maybe one was named after another?

"These are the names of the guardians of knowledge: Hanamiem, Tusemptoulous, Alsanaz, Moem, Noetinous. These are the names of those who stand at rest before them: Teitauem, Aufaem—"

"Leigh," Freya said, deliberately interrupting. "Do you ever wonder why we're doing what we do?"

"We're doing very important work, Freya," Leigh said, turning the radio off. "We're retrieving information that's been lost for centuries."

"Why? For what purpose?"

"Why?" Ms. Sinton smiled, as if she just realised that she was being put on. "But you know why, dear. Listen, this is just the hormones. Relax, and you'll get through it. I remember when my sister had her first, it was months before—"

"How . . . how long have I been pregnant?"

"What?"

"How long, precisely?"

Leigh, still keeping her attention on the road, stole a couple sideways glances at Freya. "Well, I don't know how long *precisely*, but it's been about six months since your anniversary dinner when you announced it to us all—that was May third. You do remember *that*?"

Freya twisted her wedding ring around her finger.

"As I was saying, the names of those who stand at rest before the guardians are Teitauem, Aufaem, and Acsatalt standing at Hanamiem; Raeruoak, Zocuam, and Zyquruis standing at Tusemptoulous; Ribmisot, Ribmitet, and Fusout standing at Alsanaz; Tuiujiat, Viorinrhvut, and Fasynipiat standing at Moem; and Ingekaper, Atuhis, and Ingekipap standing at Noetinous. Proceeding from those standing before the guardians are those known as the myriads, who are Ekram, Zuler, and Kukilaor proceeding from Teitauem standing at Hanamiem; Umtip, Cenut, and Memeniat proceeding from Aufaem standing at Hanamiem; Jaekuq, Dojqubir, and Rylnshus proceeding from Acsatalt standing at Hanamiem; Iofunipiat, Eavashuapout, and Liomes proceeding from Raeruoak standing at Tusemptoulous; Tenclu, Teqiqiu, and Ujasu proceeding from Zocuam standing at Tusemptoulous; Rulaki, Ryngnge, and Shoqi proceeding from Zyquruis standing at Tusemptoulous; Cescimu, Guplacim, and Lukracem proceeding from Ribmisot standing at Alsanaz; Tumnot, Elsinuph, and Encutout proceeding from Ribmitet standing at Alsanaz; Raidi, Menc, and Cofiz proceeding from Fusout standing at Alsanaz; Jesnubim, Usuoeim, and Feaiovhe proceeding from Tuiujiat standing at Moem; Telme, Irjitoli, and Imimiv proceeding from Viorinrhvut standing at Moem; Guplivek, Ipieuak, and Cuoaega proceeding from Fasynipiat standing at Moem; Rujku, Angaragh, and Akakash proceeding from Ingekaper standing at Noetinous; Faquculur, Allugu, and Rasth proceeding from Atuhis standing at Noetinous; and Ullil, Akurri, and Ulamue proceeding from Ingekipap standing at Noetinous.

"Surrounding them are those who are known as the helpers of they who proceed from those who stand before the guardians and their names are Uzson, Lameffarrsiari, Ursapagla, and Thernilugfu surrounding Ekram proceeding from Teitauem standing at Hanamiem; Zerriol, Ujeiquaem, Ezegum, and Stamao surrounding Zuler proceeding from Teitauem standing at Hanamiem; Spugheom, Usgisi, Euzam, Leuleu, and Mazpesh surrounding Kukilaor proceeding from Teitauem standing at Hanamiem. Jimeolamemipem, Fareka, Ucuzul, and Replu surrounding Umtip proceeding from Aufaem standing at Hanamiem; Narpal, Eullauj, Ralungel, and Fareka, surrounding Cenut . . ."

Freya felt herself nodding again. She felt so tired these days. Something to ask the doctor about. Her head reclined back on the chair's headrest, and she closed her eyes and drifted away.

3

The journey through the forest took them three days. During the first night, when Daniel was curled up in the back of the cart, just on the edge of drifting off to sleep, he heard someone call his name so loudly and so clearly that he jerked around and sat up, staring into the darkness for some time, hardly daring to breathe.

"Daniel!"

He would have answered, but the voice was clearly, unmistakably Freya's. Kæyle and Pettyl were huddled close together on the seat up front. They had obviously not heard anything out of the ordinary. Daniel lay back down but didn't sleep. He was feeling tired—and more than tired, weak. He was obviously malnourished and kept thinking back to the stone that Kay Marrey had given him that he had foolishly let drop in the forest on the first night. Perhaps that contained minerals that he needed. Well, maybe he'd find something to replace it at the Fayre—or better yet, a way home.

They made good time, it would seem, since they traveled during the night. Daniel didn't know how they or the horses could still see the road, but he imagined that their elf senses were equal to the task. Kæyle and Pettyl took turns driving, allowing the other to sleep—stretching out in the back of the cart while Daniel rode up front. The only rest off the road they took was for the horses when they needed to be fed. Daniel enjoyed the journey. The movements of the cart, though not always gentle, were comforting, and the shifting green treescape was like a tonic for his soul. It was three long days of calm and peace, and the last of that for a long time afterwards.

He came to know Pettyl better. She was very talkative and told him stories of Elfland and histories of the forest, in particular tales of the birds that Daniel found especially compelling.

On the afternoon of the second day, Daniel heard Freya call his name again as they stopped to feed the horses.

"Daniel!"

He was drinking a hot tea-like drink that Pettyl had made and nearly spilled it all over himself when he leapt off of the stone that he sat on.

"Daniel," Pettyl said, "are you alright?"

"I'm fine. It's just a little hot," he said, holding out the tin cup. He sat back down and drank, trying to hide his anxiousness. It sounded like Freya needed him, and badly.

And so it was that they came to the lowlands and joined a road that Kæyle had not asked for. And so they left the forest, but not before Kæyle gave a song of thanks to the forest for what it had provided them.

This last leg of the trip was a short one, but fascinating, for they now traveled along a road that was intermittently cobbled and well worn. The landscape was open, and the strange distortion of distance meant that Daniel was able to see miles farther than he could in his own world, giving views of hilly farmlands where houses of bulbous design, constructed from white carved stone and wood, dotted the landscape.

"Who lives in those?" Daniel asked Pettyl.

"No one very much, I should think," answered Pettyl. "Many of these are now abandoned since the nine princes gained rule of the kingdom. Some of the farmers have been chased off, some killed, and some dead in the wars. The widows and daughters will have worked the farms for a short time and then dispersed to wherever their relatives were still living—or to become married elsewhere."

"That's too bad," Daniel said, gazing glumly at one of the odd structures.

Not long after, they passed through an entire elfin village—

similarly deserted. There were only a dozen or so buildings, but they were magnificent. They were carved out of the same white stone as the farm buildings, and the shapes—unlike Niðergeard's, which were all lines, ridges, and arches—were organic, as if they had grown like shells to house strange, enormous creatures. But they were old and decaying. Roofs and walls had collapsed and spilled out into the streets, allowing a view of the rooms inside, which looked like honeycombs, no less organic than the exterior.

"This place was beautiful once," Pettyl said. "We came here often, being the nearest settlement. The spires and edifices were decorated with flags and banners of every colour under the sun. Banquets and parties were common, for the elf-folk in these parts love a festival above all else and make it the chief aim of all their work. There are twenty-seven grand festivals in the rural elf's calendar, and any number of lesser local ones. The feast hall over there"—Pettyl pointed to a large amphitheater structure that had a wooden roof on it that had partially collapsed—"held most of the festivities when the weather was inclement. Other times, marquees would be raised and bonfires built. It was customary to visit other villages during local celebrations, so that elves from hundreds of miles around would come to know each other, enjoy each other, love each other . . ."

Pettyl's voice trailed off. The cart rattled on through the dead streets and soon the village was behind them.

"Where are we going?" Daniel asked. "Where is the market held? Is it in a city?"

"No, but it will seem like a village, if one made of tents and booths. It is a gathering place—a very old one. It is near a large standing stone which marks the confluence of several counties and has been a festival site for many generations. In times past it used to be a station on the King's Circuit—he would visit once a year and dispense justice to those who gathered there. Obviously, that doesn't happen anymore. The princes sometimes keep this custom, but if they do, it is only to revel."

"When was the last time you were here?"

"On market day last season."

Their path joined a wider road, and Daniel could see another cart, this one covered, some distance ahead of them and, after cresting a hill and looking down upon a shallow valley, more wagons ahead of that. The traders were coming to market.

A procession of riders on magnificent horses passed them. First came what Daniel assumed were guards—they were dressed in leathers stained stained forest green and wore armour made of silver; each carried a long spear that was tipped with a head of bronze. Then came a young noble and his lady. He was dressed in blue and purple garments—a large, flowing cloak, heavy waistcoat, and trousers that ended at his knees where long riding boots began. He wore a wide-brimmed hat with long feathers of purple and black. Behind him, riding sidesaddle in a dress made up of layers of green silk and velvet, was a beautiful young woman. She also wore a large hat with black and green feathers. Unlike the Elfin gentleman, there were little silver bells attached to her clothes, gloves, saddle, and bridle, which jingled softly, like wind chimes, when the horse pranced past.

The riders passed by without a word being said on either side and eventually disappeared into the road ahead. "Who were they?" Daniel asked.

"Just travelers. A lord and lady, by the look of it," Kæyle remarked tersely.

They were passed by another elf on horseback, this one dressed in clothing that was quite hard to make out, since it was completely covered with brightly coloured ribbons of varying lengths. His hat was squat and had streamers erupting from the top of it. All this was dazzling, but that was nothing compared to the elf's smile, which was like a blazing sunbeam when he flashed it in Daniel's direction.

"Good day to you, collier Kæyle," greeted the rider. There was a large instrument, rather like an oversized cello, lashed to his saddle, the neck of which was wide, fretted, and extended above his head.

"Good day, Awin Kaayn," responded the collier. "Where will you be performing this market?"

"In the usual place—the common court—except for this evening when I will be entertaining the Elfin Prince Lhiam-Lhiat in the feast hall."

"Is he one of the nine?" Daniel asked Pettyl in a low voice, but loud enough that the musician heard him.

"Aye, he is," the brightly costumed Faerie said. "The Second-eldest of the Nine Great Rulers. Do you want to meet him?" he asked with a sly grin.

"Would I be allowed?"

"All things can happen for a price."

"I don't have any money—"

Daniel stopped talking as the collier placed a hand on his knee. This act was not unnoticed by the minstrel, who merely continued to smile wryly.

"All of us are given great treasures at birth that may be negotiated and bartered with. Do you have an artist's eye? What good is it to you if you don't use it—you might enjoy having a musical ear instead, so why not trade it? Why hold on to your dancer's toe if you never exercise it? Better to have a hound's nose or the tongue of the birds. Nearly every virtue is saleable—as are all of the vices, except for one—do you know what that is?"

Daniel didn't respond, but Awin Kaayn seemed determined to wait for an answer, so he shook his head.

"Greed! You'll never find anyone willing to part with it!" He laughed merrily at his joke. Kæyle and Pettyl frowned and continued looking stonily at the road.

"Well," the minstrel said, evidently knowing when a crowd had turned sour. "I'll be off. Find me at the Fayre, young master," Kaayn said to Daniel, "and I'll play a song just for you."

And with a final flash of his smile, the minstrel spurred his horse and galloped on ahead, disappearing from sight a few minutes later around a bend in the road.

"It will go better," Kæyle said to Daniel after a time, "if you allow me to deal for you at the Fayre, or you will find return to your own world quite beyond your means."

Nothing more was said and no other travelers greeted, until the Fayre was finally visible. There were indeed tents and booths set up, into the hundreds, and some were well over two storeys and made of many different composite parts. The booths were generally cubic and regularly spaced. The tents above them were of variable heights and sometimes spanned multiple booths. All were festooned with bright flags and banners embroidered with symbols of their trade. Freestanding tents were often erected in complex star-shaped patterns layered on top of each other, sprouting other tents out of their sides and sometimes out of their tops. Daniel wondered if they actually had different floors in them— some of them seemed as big as hotels.

The people were no less strange and vibrant. All of them were dressed in such dazzling colours and fabrics that Daniel nearly became hypnotized by the ever-shifting crowd. More than a few nobles were swanning about in clothes decorated with glittering metals and stones.

Due to the size of Kæyle's wagon, they were made to circumnavigate the Fayre in order to reach the area where the collier would set up his stall. This was in a lower part of the site, which was already quite muddy and where elves dressed in less ostentatious outfits seemed to be engaged in bartering for livestock or food stock.

The collier hopped down from the cart and led the horses by their bridles to a large authoritarian figure whom the chaotic swarm of workmen seemed to orbit. They exchanged a few words, and Daniel saw the rotund elf point towards a bank of flimsy structures that some worker elves were attempting to erect. Kæyle led the cart to their designated booth, which was little more than three flimsy walls that reminded Daniel of the fencing around his garden when he was young. There was also a large central post that rose from a hole in the middle of the site, which leaned at a disconcerting angle.

As Daniel helped Pettyl unload some of the smaller barrels packed with charcoal, Kæyle went to borrow some tools from the workers. He returned with a mallet and some wooden pegs, which he hammered into the ground alongside the walls and central posts in order to more firmly anchor them. It was the work of a moment and made the thin panels sturdy and upright.

Then they set up their stall. Pettyl took the job of raising the tent as the other two unloaded the large barrels of charcoal. Daniel watched Pettyl scale the central pole, gripping a loop of string that she tied at the top and used to hoist the canopy, which was green and grey.

"Those are the colours of our trade," Pettyl explained when asked. "Red and yellow are the goldsmith's, white and grey the silversmith's, brown and black the bronzesmith's, white with black and red feathers is the fletcher's, yellow and orange the brewer's, and so on. You will soon learn them."

"What about the . . ."—he didn't know the word in Elfish, so he used the English—"*blacksmith's*?" He was interested in what elfish weapons were to be had. "What colour is that? Red and black?"

"What is a 'blacksmiths'?" she asked, unpacking and smoothing down the surface of a long banner.

"Someone who shapes, um . . . *steel*," Daniel replied. "An *iron-monger*." He drew his sword and tapped it.

Pettyl twitched, as if shocked. "Put that away! Let none see it!" she whispered harshly. "Hidden prince," she said as an oath, "if I had known that all this time, you—good elves have no need for such a thing!" she exclaimed.

"What do you use for swords and tools?"

"Bronze is good, as is brass or any number of mixed metals. Some swords are even made from stone, but those are expensive and rare—the art to wright those is being lost." She frowned. "Steel is a cold, hateful metal, and iron is downright heartless. It houses none of the passion that the warm metals keep. It despises our flesh and corrupts it. We have no dealings with it."

Daniel sheathed his sword again. This information sparked a train of thought. He now recalled, vaguely, that iron was tied up with elfish lore and myths somehow. There was iron in his blood, he knew. Maybe they didn't have any inside them. But did they get any of it in their diet? Had *he* been getting any of it in his diet? Maybe that was why he was feeling so fatigued.

What would happen if he never got it? Would he die?

"When will I be able to talk to someone who can send me back home?" Daniel asked the collier and his wife once the shop had been completely set up. Daniel was impressed. Various streamers and flags had been arranged to make a compelling pattern. Sawdust had been strewn all about the ground so that it was dry and clean, and a long banner with the colours of their trade and an elfish script describing their name had been fixed to a pole a little distance away from the tent, closer to the general flow of elves walking within the Fayre.

"That is best done soon," the collier said. "Pettyl will mind the stall now, you come with me."

The two followed a wide path that took them into the heart of the Fayre, where a group of more interesting and esoteric stalls stood. They passed cloth merchants selling clothes with fantastically woven patterns and pictures. Smaller vendors offered strange foods, calling out their names: Roc Eggs, Christian's Delight, Old Man's Temptation, something called snake's hoofs, suckling roasted carbuncles, spiced mandrake root, and more besides. There were drinks and potions also: Honeymooner's Mead, Red Absinthe, sweet milk, moly tea, and wines and cordial made of fruits and berries Daniel had never heard of before. Then they came to a part of the Fayre that sold charms and trinkets—table upon table of bright, dazzling pieces of metal- and stonework, as well as vials containing potions and elixirs.

"The rule for the forest goes the same here—perhaps more so. Lest you be trapped here permanently, touch nothing."

Daniel kept his hands in his pockets but took in all he could with his eyes. There was a banner outside one blue-and-black tent that caught Daniel's attention—he couldn't read what it said, but it bore shapes that apparently represented different realms, because one of them was shaped exactly like Great Britain.

4

Alex inspected the wound at his side. It wasn't much. It didn't look as if he would need stitches. He went towards the dead dragon and started to work his sword out of it. "That was a good upwards swing," he complimented Maccanish. "And well placed."

"Thank you. I'm a keen golfer. What do we do with the body?"

"Whatever you like. Although it's not going to be around for long. The natural chemicals it makes in order to spit fire are highly corrosive. It'll be a pile of sludge by nightfall unless you know the proper way of removing them. Look, see—the head is already decaying." Alex finally managed to pull his blade free. He inspected it. Apart from being covered in acidic dragon's blood, it seemed none the worse for wear. It needed a good cleaning. Luckily, he had an alkali solution wash in his Land Rover.

"Remarkable. What about the trolls?"

"Again, whatever you please. Leave them here or call the Royal Society of Anthropology. That'd give them a fright. I always wondered what would happen if someone did that. In any case, my work here is finished. You had bigger problems than I thought if you had a dragon move in here."

"So what does that mean?" Maccanish asked. They stepped outside and stood in the cave's mouth. "What does that mean for the valley? For our troubles?"

"Well, you'll be back to being able to sleep, for a start. People will be less inclined to evil deeds and the feeling of dread and oppression will be lifted. But people will still be hurt, and they'll still be frightened, as they won't understand, or allow themselves to understand, what has happened. It'll be your job to help them through that. You need to keep an eye out, though. If the people hereabouts slide back into despair, these things and more could come back. Keep an eye out. And I'll give you a number where I can be contacted. But you can give thanks now that you have been delivered from evil." Alex stuck out his hand. "And I can give thanks that you've kept such an excellent golfing form."

Maccanish smiled and shook Daniel's hand.

"What are you going to do now?" Maccanish asked.

"There's one more thing that I need to check on. You go on back. Thanks again for your help."

"Thank *you*."

Rector John Maccanish started off, back down Morven. As

Alex watched him go, he heard the man begin to sing a hymn as the clouds finally opened and released a gentle rain upon the mountain and its plain.

Alex went back into the cave. He broke another glow stick and clipped it next to the other, which was dimming. He hung his sword by its hilt onto a carabiner on his belt; it bumped comfortingly against him as he walked. There would be no more danger here—he was no longer on alert.

Instead, he tried to get himself in the right frame of mind—doing the mental exercises his father taught him—and walked farther into the tunnel. He stepped cautiously over the body of the dragon and then those of the trolls. He turned the corner and passed the dragon's pile of shiny loot—its bedding. Then he came to a chiseled stone wall made of square one-foot-by-one-foot blocks, and about as high and wide as a standard doorway.

Alex put his hands up against it and cleared his mind, thinking only of being *between*. He had no intents or aims in life; he was open to all options. He was standing at the crossing of all paths. He visualized this last thought as standing in a country road with signs pointing in all directions.

It took a few moments before he felt his hands sinking into the stone. It was harder now that he was older and had a purpose in life, but his heart and soul were still open to new callings. Once his arms were through the stone, it was easy. He visualized himself being between the stones now. He stepped forward and, with a sensation like moving through water, he was through and into the hidden chamber of Morven.

It was much like the others he had been in. A simple octagonal room with a ceiling, perhaps lower than others. Silver lamps lined the walls, throwing their ancient light on the stone plinths and the eight sleepers that lay on them.

Except that these warriors were no longer sleeping—they were dead. They had been dressed in full plaids and sporrans and had been armed with two-handed claymore swords and *sgian dubhs*, but now their corpses were mangled, eviscerated, picked-over. Flesh had been torn from bone, joints separated, and the pieces scattered.

It had been a one-sided slaughter. Looking at the centre of the chamber, he saw the fragments of the stone-coloured oblong egg that the dragon had hatched from. It had been easy to see what had happened as the infant dragon hatched and fed first on one body and then the next, probably over the course of a couple weeks, maybe more. The trolls, attracted to the area by its atmosphere of evil, had set up in the cave and it had killed them too. As lucky as he was to escape with his life, it was a marvelous stroke of fortune—for him and the entire country—that Alex had come across the dragon now while it was still an infant and not a fully grown adult.

But who placed the egg here? Across the chamber, the wall, which was supposed to be enchanted like the one he had passed through, had been torn down—or rather, knocked through. Its stones lay strewn across the floor.

A hand clamped around Alex's foot and he started. He swallowed and looked down in horror—one of the dead bodies' arms was gripping his boot. It was connected to a shoulder, a torso, a head, and nothing else. The mangled face of the highlander moved and Alex heard the words, in Gaelic, *"Fuasgail sinne."* Release us.

The spirits of the dead men were still in their bodies—they had not been released from their contract of immortality yet. They had lain here all this time, waiting for the battle, and for them the fight had never come, only a painful, prolonged death. With a lump in his throat, Alex pulled his foot gently out of the knight's hold and strode to the wall where the horn was hanging. He blew a strong note on it, and the air seemed to grow warmer; a wind moved through the tunnel with a sound like a sigh of relief.

For a moment there appeared before Alex's eyes the silvery outline of a man in old highland gear with a gleaming sword in his hand.

"*Buidheachas*," the figure said, looking Alex in the eye.

"*Slàinte agad-sa*," Alex replied. "*Slàn leat*."

The apparition smiled and then faded. The lamplight returned to its full brightness, and the chamber was still.

Alex set about rearranging the bodies on the stone slabs as best he could—there would be no more honourable burial place than this cavern, where the lights would burn for all time. It was gruesome work, but after a while he managed to place the bodies and weapons in respectful order.

He stood for a time looking at the torn-down wall and wondered who had made it and where they had come from. The largest part of him wanted to follow it and track down whoever had done this, but he knew that wasn't the prudent thing to do. Instead, he left back through the wall he had entered by, went through the cave, and stepped into the open, still-drizzling air.

As he walked down the mount and back to his Rover, he pulled his phone from his pocket and rang his associate.

After relaying what had occurred, omitting no detail, his associate said, "The bleed has started—but it is hard to tell the extent, even yet. We must go to Niðergeard—that is where we will find answers."

CHAPTER TWELVE

Quick Blood

1

"I don't understand," said Freya. "What *should* we be looking at?"

"A vast underground lake, nearly big enough to be called a sea—its surface completely smooth and still, for no creature stirs it, nor the slightest breeze moves across it. But not this—this dark emptiness!"

Swiðgar took several steps forward and descended down a sand-and-stone slope, which ended after several feet in a flat, black, dry, cracked mud floor. "It's gone. The Slæpismere is gone!" he exclaimed in a harsh whisper.

"What does that mean?" Freya asked.

"It means that the hidden world is already feeling the affect of evil spreading in this land," Swiðgar answered. "They have already started claiming victories—decay has set in. This is why our task is of such import."

"What's that?" asked Daniel, pointing along the dry bank. There was some sort of wall that extended into the empty lake. They walked over and investigated.

"It is a pier," said Ecgbryt as their torches revealed it more in detail. On the far end, several wide, flat-bottomed boats dangled lengthways from a chain that was still attached to a metal pillar. Swiðgar gave one of them a push and it gave a couple tragicomic swings before scraping to a halt.

"Well, let's get started," said Ecgbryt. "We must go on if we are to keep the pace."

Walking along the dry lake bed was much easier than picking their way along the rocky tunnels now above them. The ground was basically flat, sloping gently downwards.

"Did I ever tell you," said Ecgbryt, "of the fight we had with the Danes off the Isle of Wight? A glorious battle! I arrived in one of the nine new ships built in the Northman's fashion that Ælfred ordered built, along with many of the Frisian warriors that fought with us on that occasion. Have I ever told you about the fearsome Frisians? Are they still as famed in this day as they were in ours? I remember a ballad about them that starts thus . . ."

Ecgbryt recited his ballad and then continued his long monologue about his battle and almost every ballad he knew relating to it. It soothed them all to listen, and Ecgbryt to talk. When he stopped they took a break to rest, and that's when Daniel, moving away from the torchlight to relieve himself, noticed a light shining up ahead.

"Does anybody else see that?" he asked.

"I think that it's on top of something," Freya said. "I think that there's a hill up ahead."

They had been walking an upward slope after having journeyed quite a long way down into the dry lake bed. "No, not a hill," Ecgbryt said. "Not a hill exactly—it's an island!"

2

The weary travelers circled the dry island to find an easy way up that didn't involve scaling sharp rocks and boulders. The ground underfoot crunched and shifted as they came upon a stretch of land made up of loose stones and gravel. In their own torchlight, they could see that this created a kind of ramp-like path up towards the island. "It's a beach," Freya said, laughing slightly. "Or at least, it used to be."

They mounted the top of the ramp on an ascent of fine, powdery sand. The light was stronger and grew from a point just below a small rise.

"Shh!" hissed Daniel. "Listen!"

They all heard the singing now; many voices in chorus—melodic, but indistinct. It sounded strange to them, after all this time of walking in the silent dark, but there it was. They proceeded up the rise, alert, ready for nearly anything.

But they weren't prepared for the smell. It was a homely smell of warm food and wood smoke—some sort of stew, at a guess. The singing had given way to an amiable chatter. The travelers rounded the mound, drawing closer, and Freya immediately wondered if it might all be some sort of illusion meant to confuse them, for as they came around the base of the mound, they saw a group of people sitting around a large fire, their hands moving vigorously in industrious work.

Creeping closer, Freya counted eight women, all of them ancient, sitting in a circle around a modest campfire, working on a long piece of grey patterned cloth spread across their laps. At one end, two old ladies worked spinning machines—turning a large pile of thin, wispy material into spools of thread, which were placed onto a loom that was operated by two others. This loom spewed a fine fabric from its top that was gathered by another who stretched and pulled the cloth. The cloth then crossed the laps of two other women, who placed the woven fabric into large embroidery frames where they added borders of an elaborate swirling pattern. The finished cloth then entered a large stack of long rolls that were piled behind the group. Because of the darkness, Freya couldn't make out how many rolls of cloth there were, but she had the impression of quite a large number, as its production had apparently been going on for some time.

The last old lady flitted around the others to help—toting spools to the loom, fixing the frames in different places, and doing whatever else needed doing. She also paused occasionally to stir the large pot on the fire at the centre of the circle.

Freya and Daniel and the knights watched in silence for a few moments and then entered the circle of light cast by the fire. They stood between the weaving machine and the embroiderers. Freya felt a tingle of anticipation as she drew breath to speak.

"Hello," she said.

All of them continued, oblivious, except for the old woman at the large pot. She stopped stirring and turned towards them. "Well, hello there, sweet child," she replied. "Where did you spring from?"

"Um, we've been traveling. We saw the light and came here. We thought you might be able to help us."

"Who's 'us,' deary? Who is 'we'?"

"My friends and I. We—oh!"

The old woman tilted her face so that the light from the fire fell on it more directly. Her eye sockets were empty and puckered—blind. Glancing quickly at the others, she could see that all of the women were blind. Haltingly, nervously, Freya introduced herself and the rest of the group to the weaving women.

"Very pleased to meet you, I'm sure," said the old lady. "Now, I must ask you an important question. Think carefully before you answer: would you or would you not like to have some good, hot stew?"

Freya grinned. "Yes, please," she said.

"I can hear your smile," the old woman said. "I daresay you have answered correctly. Come then, all of you. Come get some eats!"

"Freya," Daniel whispered, "I'm not sure that we should." He looked cautiously around at the group of ladies. Although they had not stopped working, it was obvious that they were all paying attention to what was going on. "Not until we find out—you know—if they can be trusted or not."

"Young boy—Daniel, is it? What is there to worry about? Why not trust us? What reason is there for suspicion?"

"Well, for a start, you know my name. Who are you, and what are you doing here?" he asked.

"Weaving, my dear, weaving."

"Why?"

"There must always be weavers—and gatherers, and combers, and spinners as well. It is the way of humanity. The first thing that man understood when he knew things as God knew them was that there must be weaving. And so here we are. We weave."

"But—what is it?"

The old woman smiled, showing a full mouth of healthy white teeth. "All the known and unknown stories of the world may be told through our tapestry. We roll up the past, weave the present, and spin the strands of the future. It's all one to us."

"But you can't see," Daniel blurted.

The old woman waved a wrinkled hand. "Don't need to bother with that no more. Gets in the way more often than not. All we have to do is feel and then move our hands. Now, are you satisfied enough to chance a taste of my stew?"

"I would," said Ecgbryt, pushing his way into the circle.

"As would I," said Swiðgar behind him, "and thank you for your generosity."

Daniel said nothing but followed the knights and Freya and stood in front of the big pot. Smiling, the old lady gathered up some clay bowls and spoons that were lying on a low stone table nearby. "My, you're a strong thread, aren't you? You and the girl both. Such a shame though . . ."

"What?"

"Well, in tough times, when the fabric wears thin and weaker threads break, the stronger threads have to pick up the slack."

Daniel frowned as he was handed a bowl of steaming stew.

"So, can you predict the future?" Freya asked. "Because of your weaving?"

"Oh no," said the woman. "None see the future. But when you've lived as long as I, you get to know the pattern. All the threads follow their own paths, but each is affected by those around them. Each strand is small in itself, but all are great together. A very many threads seen together will give you a pattern or a shape, but even that will only be small in the larger work." She spooned up another bowl and passed it to Freya. "The threads go here and there and make all manner of twists and turns, but it is always to a purpose, though it may not seem that way to the thread. To the thread all that happens feels accidental, but those as sees more, knows better."

"So the threads can't decide where they go? Or choose what part of pattern they're in?"

"No, of course not," said the woman lightly. "How could they? They're only threads, not people." She handed the last bowls to Swiðgar and Ecgbryt.

None of the other weavers had stopped working during this exchange. Freya eyed the rolls of fabric. "How long have you been here?" she asked.

"Oh, year unknown upon year innumerable," came the reply.

"Have you ever tried to leave?"

"Where is there to go?"

"Where do you get the stuff to weave with?" asked Daniel.

"Worms. Little worms. We are provided for. We don't ask for much. Even the meat for the stew comes to us freely."

Luckily, Daniel and Freya had already eaten a couple mouthfuls of the chunky broth and it tasted good enough to keep them from imagining what they were eating. Whatever it was, it tasted so incredibly good that they didn't want to stop eating. The warmth of the food started in their stomachs and spread to their arms and legs.

"Yes, all manner of things that you wouldn't dream of managin' to fetch up here," the old woman continued. "You could hardly credit it. All sorts of unimaginable persons and beasts and creatures . . ." Her voice was starting to drone. Daniel's and Freya's hands felt hot and heavy and a couple of sizes too big. Daniel felt himself rocking backwards as Freya began tilting forwards. She wondered if she should stop herself falling asleep but couldn't think of a reason why. It would feel so nice to lie down on the floor and rest.

As Daniel quietly collapsed, he managed to loll his head around to look at Swiðgar and Ecgbryt. They were still awake, but obliviously spooning stew into their mouths. Daniel's eyes closed—or at least he thought that they did. He felt himself spinning downwards even though he knew he wasn't moving, and he slept.

3

Freya woke up with a start. The first thing she was aware of was an odd rhythmic pounding sensation that went through her skull. It took her a few seconds to discover that the pounding was coming from outside her head rather than from the inside. Then she was able to discern chanting above the pounding. The ladies were reciting a work-song. They punctuated its melodic style with stamps of their feet and scrapes and clacks of whatever machine or tool they were using.

> "A Brownie takes milk, takes milk,
>   Takes milk.
> A Brownie takes milk, takes milk.

> "Oh, a child will do for a Faerie or Elf,
> A Pixie, or Kobold, or Hob.
> They will bear it away, to their home in the hills,
> And replace it with a small changeling sprite.
> But they cannot bide iron, so make you a crib
> Out of oak—with nine strong four-inch nails.
> And hang up a horseshoe over window and door,
> And the imps will as like pass you by,
>   Wist I,
> That the imps will as like pass you by.

> "But a Brownie takes milk, will take milk.
>   Only milk.
> Yes, a Brownie takes milk; it takes milk.

> "A Troll will want teeth, but will settle for toenails
> By the bushel, the yard, or the pound.
> And a Giant wants bones he can grind into meal
> To make bread for his mother to eat.
> Though these beasts are enormous, you will find them
>   quite slow
> At a riddle, a sonnet, or verse.

"*They will tear out their hair and will scratch up their face,*
But an answer they will give you none,
    not one!
No, an answer they can give you none.

"*And a Brownie will only take milk.*
    Ever milk.
Yes, a Brownie will only take milk.

"*A Dragon wants gold it can put in a pile—*
Something to stack and to count.
It may take a maiden, a sheep, or a cow
To assuage it and soothe its fierce greed.
It will give you confusion and fire and doubt,
For its forked tongue spouts flame and deceit.
You can kill it with courage and with valor and steel
But its treasure will not bring you health,
    Or wealth.
No, its treasure will not bring you health.

"*But a Brownie will only take milk*
    From a mother;
From a mother the Brownie takes milk.

There are others like Ghouls and Zombies and Wights,
Who desire your flesh and your skin.
And the merfolk: the Nyads, the Kelpie, and such,
Are jealous of all mortal souls,

"*Much like Bog Sprites and Will o' the Wisps*
Who will lead you astray unto death.

They do not have reason or morals, just wit,
So ignore them, and let them pass by,
    Oh, aye,
Just ignore them and they'll pass you by.

"But a Brownie will only take milk
    From a mother
That she uses to suckle her child.

"For a Brownie is patient, and a Brownie is sly—
And no matter how the baby does wriggle or cry—
The Brownie will hide and will watch and drink milk,
And will wait for the poor bairn to die.
So place you some buttermilk fresh from the churn
In a dish by the back kitchen door.
Do this every morning and once Sunday evening
And the Brownie will not grieve you more,
    No more,
Leave some milk from the churn on the floor.

"For a Brownie takes milk, will take milk.
    Does take milk.
Yes, a Brownie takes milk; it takes milk."

The weaving ladies stopped singing at this last, haunting verse, but continued moving their tools and stomping in time.

"What was that?" Freya asked weakly, sitting up. She had been placed on a pile of animal skins and furs. Her head was swimming slightly and her stomach felt queasy.

"You're up, deary," said the woman at the pot. On second glance, she seemed different from the one who had given them the stew, but it was hard to tell.

"You have quick blood," said the lady as she hobbled blindly towards her. "Here, chew this." From the folds in her clothes she produced a kind of twisty, stick-like thing about the size of a toothbrush.

"What is it?"

"Birch bark steeped in ginger. It will still your head and stomach. Go on, take it. *Take* it. You are safe here. The rest did you good, just as it is doing good to your friends there."

Freya moved her head and saw Daniel and the two knights stretched out beside her, also on skins and furs. They looked peaceful enough. Daniel was curled up on his side and Ecgbryt was snoring. She turned back to the old lady and felt a wave of nausea at the movement. She reached out and took the stick of bark from the woman and stuck it between her teeth.

"Let me help you up," said the lady. "Try to move around. Take this." The woman draped a soft, silky shawl over Freya's shoulders and got her to stand. She directed her towards the fire.

"Quick blood," repeated the woman. "First down, but first up. Fast thoughts and quick judgments. The waters may appear still on top, but there are faster currents underneath, eh?"

"Are you talking about me?"

"Perhaps not so fast then. Allow me to say to you that it does our hearts good to see one of our sisters on a business such as this—does us all good. Wars are unavoidable—some of them are inevitable—but the real business of life is a woman's business."

Freya was still very groggy and her head felt muzzy. She wasn't taking in much of what the old woman was saying.

"But men always forget that, the dear sweet idiots. Love to fight, bless them, but they too often forget what they're fighting for. Need one of us to remind them of it, on occasion. One that will make them heed. One to make those who lead go someplace, and one to make those who won't be led to follow."

"Are you talking about me?" Freya asked again, starting to feel better. The odd stick was doing its work and settling her system.

"Ah, a little swifter now, eh? Let's walk. Take my arm."

They moved away from the camp, Freya guiding the older woman and supporting her by the arm. "So you think I can do this quest sort of thing?" Freya asked when they had crested a ridge and the light from the camp was a pale glow behind them.

"My sweet, you were made for it."

"Made for it? So do I have a choice?"

"It's who you are, my dear. You can reject it, but you can't change it."

The old lady was silent for a time, which allowed Freya to think about this.

"In your way," the woman eventually continued, "you are rarer than any of the others. There will always be fighters—lots of fighters. But not many will be able to do what you will be asked to do. The decisions you will face will affect many, many people."

"Huh. You know," Freya began thoughtfully, "back on the surface, where I live, it feels like a lot of people think women aren't as good as men—like we aren't equal."

"Of course we aren't equal, my dear one. We're much better than they are."

Freya laughed.

"That was not really in earnest, and also not true. Equal doesn't really enter into it—we will never be equal because there are too many differences. But we're the real doers—the real makers. Men work the fields, hunt the animals, and we make the food and cook the meat. They raise the flocks, and we make the clothes. They provide the house, and we make a home—the children, the family. All the fruits of man's labor on earth must pass through our hands."

Freya twirled the stick between her lips. "All the wars," the woman went on, "all the kickin' and thumpin' that's been done has all been on our account as to make a space for us to do our work. All the kingdoms and walls as has been made has been made to protect us—what's worth protectin'."

There was a pause and when the old woman spoke again, her voice was lower and colder. "An evil has been building on these shores for some hundreds of years. It's been growing all around and creeping in at the edges, slowly like, so that none would notice at once—and when they did notice, they would be used to it, like. There's many a true heart up there that should be burning hot and bright, but because of the darkness and decay, it is dim and hardly gives a light at all. Us blind weavers may not be able to see with our eyes, but we know how dark the tapestry we're weaving has become. A whole island . . . fallen asleep . . . not knowin' it's bein' sucked into the mire. The world has always carried sickness inside of it, but it is falling into a swoon . . ."

Freya removed the stick from her mouth. "You really think that we can do this—whatever needs to be done?"

"You're the right thread—the right length and the right luster—and you're in the right place. It remains to be proved whether you are strong enough to hold yet. Just remember that inside you bear the strength of hundreds of thousands of your sisters before you. It will guide you, but you must listen to it, and nothing else."

She left Freya, and the girl remained, staring into the darkness. After a while she sat down and wrapped her arms around her knees and didn't rise again until she heard the voices of the men behind her.

4

They set out from the weaver women's camp feeling more rested than at any time since leaving Niðergeard. They had been given some short strips of dried meat that were as tough as leather but also rather flavorful.

The travelers left the dry island by the same beach that they had arrived. The ground from there onwards continued sloping downwards and they found it getting damper. Then they started coming across large puddles—still, black pools of water. Swiðgar cautioned them to watch their step as there was no telling how deep these pools might be; the surfaces they could see could be just thin films of water on rock, or they could be the skin of a fathomless sinkhole, the currents of which could take them away faster than it was possible to fight.

Even stepping very near the edges of the puddles was a risk, Swiðgar said, as a rocky bank could crumble away. For this reason the travelers spread out and tied the rope to their belts to connect themselves to each other for safety. Swiðgar took the first position with Ecgbryt following directly behind him. Freya and Daniel were led along an unpredictable and erratic path. As the puddles grew wider, more frequent and irregularly shaped, they found themselves at a dead end and were forced to turn back and find a different path.

The air was growing colder, chilled by the dampness that Freya now associated with darkness so deep that it felt massive. Because of the meandering path they were forced to take, their journey over the lake bed plain, although tedious and uneventful, was far from boring. They found the tension and uncertainty exhausting. They took more breaks than they felt were probably necessary. Daniel and Freya would fall to the ground, their heads nearly spinning from all the turns and U-turns they had to make out of dead ends and cul-de-sacs.

In the light of their lamps, they saw a structure ahead of them and they made their way to it. It was another pier, a longer and bigger one, but just as dry and ruined as the last. They scaled the bank and found that the pier was an extension of a large ramp that went steeply upwards. They had no choice but to go up.

They walked many hours and took many breaks, never knowing how high this underground mountain—which is what they came to think of it as—rose ahead of them. The last time Freya could remember climbing so high was while hiking in the Lake District. But climbing so high and still being underground was a very different sensation. She was glad that she couldn't see how far up they were. It felt as if they were leaving the Wild Caves far behind—which she was glad of—but how much farther did they have to climb?

There was an indefinable change in the air, and the noise that their footsteps made allowed them to sense a narrowing of the walls around them. The ground became steeper and then curled around them, shunting them to the left, creating a wall to their right.

Cresting the mound of scree, they found themselves on a rock shelf that ran to their left, and no option but to follow it. They moved cautiously, each of them inwardly terrified that the ground would give way beneath them. But to their relief it broadened and continued on.

Then they discovered the carvings.

All of a sudden the wall was covered with them. Most of them looked like writing, but with odd letters that were made of straight lines only, no curves. Some of them were long horizontal lines with perpendicular and slanting lines stemming from and intersecting the baseline. Daniel ran his hands along them; they were set very deeply into the rock. Sometimes there was just a single running line a couple of inches high and a foot long, scrawled here and there like graffiti. At other points, there were large blocks of tightly packed letters with no spaces, several feet in length and height, well blocked out and bordered.

One set of carvings quite startled Daniel. He had to stop and pull back his torch to see the full extent of them. Lines of words snaked through each other like ribbons, randomly twisting and splitting and converging. Caught in the middle of this was a man with a bearded face, kneeling, with his arms raised, the words twisting around him and his limbs. His face, almost cartoon-like in its simplicity, nonetheless wore the look of someone in deep anxiety.

The others, seeing Daniel had stopped, returned to stand beside him. They spent a few silent moments contemplating the picture.

Freya shuddered.

"Swiðgar," Ecgbryt said in a low voice, "you are more familiar with the old script than I. Can you read it?"

"Hmm, not easily," Swiðgar answered. "I wish Ceolferþ were here; he was more the scholar than I. The letters I know, but not their arrangement. It is not our tongue." He stepped forward and reached a hand out to some crudely etched words only a sentence long.

"Apart from these," he said, "which forbid the passing of any person. It is a curse, written backwards. Perhaps all these words are written backwards," he said, casting his eyes across the wall.

Daniel felt a chill ripple across his shoulders. The words and banks of letters were no longer an interesting puzzle but a wall of angry and oppressive words, aware of them, warning them away, cursing them.

"I fear no curse from man or devil," declared Swiðgar. "My heart has been sealed against both by one stronger than any enchanted."

A short distance farther, they came across a cave mouth—an archway in the rock. It was obviously man-made and bordered with row upon row of angry-looking writing that none of them even wanted to read. There were columns or standing stones that had been placed in front of the tunnel entrance like two rows of guards, three on each side, each stone covered top to bottom in angry-looking letters.

Thankfully the writing did not continue inside the tunnel—the walls were unmarked in any way. As the travelers stood, wondering what might be in that tunnel and where it led, they heard a slow, rhythmic scraping sound start up that grated on their spines. They stood silently, listening to it and holding their lanterns up in front of them. After a minute it stopped, and with deep breaths they entered the tunnel. Its walls were not rounded but octagonal; whoever had constructed the passage must have been meticulous in its carving, for though it twisted and turned maddeningly, the walls and diagonals kept their shape, never moving farther away or closer together.

The meandering passage bends became corners, then hairpins, tightly packed together, turning first this way and then that, and then the other. The travelers picked their way along and were starting to feel quite dizzy and disoriented, with all the zigzagging—right and then right again, full left, right, left, right, right, left—when suddenly the floor fell from underneath them.

CHAPTER THIRTEEN

Reunion

1

She was at her desk again. It was more cluttered than before. There were large open binders before her packed tight with grids of letters and numbers. She was transliterating from Greek into Arabic numerals, she remembered, and had been writing a guide for herself in English. There was a sheet of paper in front of her that was filled with her handwriting. She started reading it:

> Jesnubim, once separate from her passions, from joy became pregnant with the contemplation of the lights that accompanied him, i.e. the angels with him; and—they teach—craving (?) them she produced fruits after their (?) image, a spiritual offspring generated after the likeness of the savior's bodyguards. Now, of these three (essences) that—they say—were extant, one derived from her passion, and this was the matter;

another derived from her turning back, and this was the animate; another was what she brought forth, and this was the spiritual . . .

And so on. There were more sheets beneath it, all still in her handwriting and all seemingly gibberish. There's no reason she would have written all that.

She heard a small cry that sent a shock through her—it was an infant's cry—her child's. She stood up and rushed to the next room where the cot was. Stooping over the cot, she gazed at the tiny red face that howled up at her.

Abruptly she straightened, alarmed.

This wasn't her child.

But, if not hers, whose? And where was hers?

No, that was ridiculous; she didn't have a child. She was too young.

But it *was* hers. And it was still screaming. Freya reached into the cot and pulled it out. Shouldering the infant, she started bouncing it up and down to calm it, but she held it awkwardly, unnaturally. Was it a boy or a girl? Its name was Daniel, she was sure of that much.

"Oh no! Daniel!" she exclaimed, her body tensing. She nearly lost her grip on the child as her mind flashed to a terrible image— someone she once knew running towards her, falling, and then disappearing into thin air.

"Daniel—I have to help Daniel!"

The infant at her shoulder began wailing again. She put it back in the cot and then went back to her desk. How could she have forgotten something as important as this? There was a large black marker in a pencil cup and she uncapped it and wrote on the first sheet of paper that she could find—the page with her meaningless drivel on it—in large block letters:

MUST SAVE DANIEL

Then she stood back and looked at the words. Who was Daniel? The baby was crying. Why was it so hard to remember things all of a sudden? Her head was so . . . *foggy* these days.

The sky grew darker. She was tired—still tired. How long had she been asleep? A headache was growing at the base of her skull. She was hungry. When was the last time she had eaten something?

The fog was growing, but she had to push through. Everything felt . . . dissociated. All that she was truly aware of were the words on the page and the growing dread that she couldn't remember more.

"Freya? Darling?" she heard a voice call from the doorway.

She sprang around to see Felix in the doorway. One hand went to her papers and gathered them together.

"Darling, Sophia was crying . . ." He held the infant, who was quiet, though still red-faced and teary. "What have you been doing?"

She didn't know how to reply. "I was just . . . writing . . ."

Felix looked into her eyes. "Are you feeling okay? Did you take your pills?"

Freya opened a drawer and pulled out a small plastic bottle. "These aren't my pills. I don't take these."

"What are you writing, dearest?"

Freya brushed her papers closer together. "Don't touch me, please."

"Sweetheart, please take your pills. You always feel much better after them. I'll start dinner. Why don't you review what you've written?"

Felix left the room with the baby—*Sophia? Not Daniel?*—and she sat a moment in thought. She stared down at the pages in front of her. None of it made any sense—these weren't words in front of her.

What was happening to her?

And why was she so . . . sleepy . . . ?

2

Daniel pointed out the familiar shape on the coloured banner. "Kæyle, that's Great Britain," he said.

"Then I have taken you to the right place. This is our destination."

They made their way through the crowds and into a tent that was covered, apparently not wanting to display its goods. They pushed through a series of veils and curtains that hung under an awning into a room that was dark, lit by oil lamps. There were plush carpets underfoot and a dozen cabinets displaying mostly ornamental objects. In the centre of this tableaux sat the proprietor, adrift in the middle of a pool of cushions, rotund, and upholstered rather like a cushion himself.

"Welcome!" He greeted them brightly, thrusting squat little arms at them. He had a fat, jolly face with extravagantly curled whiskers that supported a large, bulbous, purple hat on his head that looked something like a turban. "I am Reizger Lokkich. What can I offer you fine gentlemen this afternoon? I have all manner of objects from distant lands and ages gone by. From coins and keepsakes to sculptures and machines whose use and operation are unknown, even to me! How do I fix a price on such items, you may ask? I have no way of knowing! A potential bargain lurks on every table!" He laughed heartily at this, amused, it seemed, by his own ignorance and generosity.

The collier gave the tables only the most cursory of glances. "We are here for another purpose than trinket gathering," he said. "This one"—indicating Daniel—"is from another land. The land of . . ."

"England," Daniel supplied.

"The land of England, and he needs to return. You were once known as a traveler, upon a time. Know you of any way to return him to where he needs to be?"

While Kæyle was speaking, the merchant's bushy eyebrows

were traveling up his forehead, and his mouth was contracting more and more until it was just a small circle below a long moustache. When the collier paused, his features snapped back into place; he stood up and approached Daniel. His salesman's mannerisms evaporated and he ran his eyes up and down in a professional manner, touching him on the arm and turning his palms outwards in order to study them. "It has been a long time since those paths were used by our people. They may be difficult to travel now."

The merchant tilted Daniel's head and peered into his ears. Daniel felt like he was being appraised and that a price would be offered for him shortly.

"Yes, he looks in fair condition to travel. Allow me to consult my chart book."

He rose and adjusted one of the lamps so that it gave off a brighter gleam. Pulling a large, square book from a chest behind the bank of cushions, he settled himself and started thumbing the pages, which seemed to be filled with dozens of interlocking circles of varying size, annotated with small scribbles. Within these circles were landmarks like mountains, cairns, trees, caves, standing stones, churches, and so on. Bordering these were pictures of the sun and moon in different phases. The merchant settled on one page and ran his fingers along it, reading the scrawls under his breath.

A young elf, dressed in suede leathers, pushed his way through the gauze veils of the tent. "Excuse me, Kæyle, but you're needed back at your stall."

"I will be done here shortly," the collier replied.

"But it is Agrid Fiall—he demands your presence. He refuses to have dealings with your wife."

Kæyle growled, annoyed. "Very well." He sighed. "I leave him in your hands, Reizger Lokkich." The merchant's eye flicked up.

"See that you do right by him. He is not to pay you. Since he is currently my property, all payment will come from me, *after* he has returned home. See that he does nothing to jeopardise his return. Daniel, can you remember the way back to the tent?"

He replied that he could.

"Make sure you take nothing away with you, and that nothing is placed on your person." And with that final warning, he left with the messenger.

The merchant Lokkich returned to his book and traced a path along the page with a fingertip. Then he looked up at Daniel, beaming.

"You're in luck!" he exclaimed, tapping the page. "We are just at the start of a cycle and in the ideal place to cross over—up at the meeting rock. We could try tomorrow night, in fact. It will be a weak pull, but one in the right direction. If that doesn't work, the one five days later almost certainly will. Tell me, how urgently do you want to get back?"

"Fairly urgently—I think my friend is in danger."

"Ah, then it's important that you leave as soon as possible. There are things that I can do to help you . . . but . . ." Lokkich looked sad.

"What is it?" asked Daniel, sensing a hustle.

"I'm afraid that the cost would be far beyond the means of a poor wood-burner."

"You obviously have something in mind. Let's hear what it is without the whole drama."

The merchant smiled. "Ah, you see through me. I see I have misjudged your cleverness. Forgive me, I meant no insult, it is just that sometimes a softer touch is needed with clients. No matter. We will talk as equals and lay everything on the table before us. Yes, there are things I can do to help, but they are expensive. In short, it means loading you up with some of my wares, which I have appropriated from your own world. These will act as forces to draw you closer your destination—all things wish to return to their place of origin. However, you cannot buy them, as you have no money. Nor can I just give them to you, as that would make you beholden to me and increase your ties here. No, you will need to earn them."

"How?"

"By doing a job for me—working for me, in short, like you work for the collier. I do not wish to trap or ensnare you—remember, it's in my interest to see you safely home. But the type of work will be determined by the value of the objects you need."

"Alright, let's see these objects, then," Daniel said, not too happy to be dealing like this, but if it meant he could get home faster, it would be worth it.

"Of course. Please, take a seat," he said, rising and arranging a few cushions opposite his own pile. Daniel settled on these as the merchant waddled over to a display cabinet. "Think of yourself as a magnet—and the more things you possess from your own world, the greater your pull back to that world will be." He fiddled around behind the cabinet and took out a drawer, carrying it carefully—almost reverently—and laying it on the floor between them. "The objects that are most recent will have the strongest pull and will be more worth carrying. The oldest ones will be almost useless to you."

Daniel laughed when he saw what the drawer from the cabinet contained—it was just full of junk. There was a bundle of pencils of varying lengths and sharpness—some even bore teeth marks— all tied up in a silk ribbon. There was a gardening fork lying inside a glass case. A jar containing coins, bottle caps, ring pulls, paper clips, and brass tacks. There was a pair of binoculars, something that looked like an oven knob, a bottle of ink, and more besides.

"It is up to you to choose the most recent or valuable to you. Tell me, do you recognise any of these items?" the merchant asked.

"I recognise all of them. How did you find them?"

"I have my sources," the merchant said guardedly. "Tell me, this manuscript, what is its nature?" The merchant reverently handed him a bundle of decaying papers.

"This is a comic book."

"I have studied it closely but do not understand the writing. Is it a history of one of your heroes?"

"It's a story—none of this really happened." He handed it back. "It's not so old. It was printed about twenty years ago."

"What about this?"

"That's more recent—it's a video cassette tape."

"What is it used for?"

"Amusement. You stick it in a machine and it plays a story for you. We have lots of them where I come from. This one is *Doctor Who*."

The merchant looked at him blankly.

"It's a science fiction TV show. That would probably help me out, if I had it. As would this, I suppose." He picked up liner notes from a CD and flicked through it. "And that, definitely." He pointed to a cell phone charger.

"So, these three items, the . . . *vidosette tape*, the small booklet, the wire with the weight on it . . . and the manuscript as well?"

Daniel shrugged. "Sure, the comic book as well. Why not?"

"What about these? Can you tell what they are?" He handed Daniel a rectangular red box made out of thin cardboard. It had ".38 SPECIAL 130 GRAIN FULL METAL JACKET" printed on its side.

"These are bullets," he said, turning the box around in his hands so that they were the right way up. He opened the box—it was full. "They can be quite dangerous."

"Would you take those?"

"I'd rather not."

"So," the merchant said, businesslike again. "Four items from your world, and valuable ones at that."

"And if I have these, I can go back tomorrow night?"

"Very likely."

"Can you guarantee it?"

"Not absolutely, but with my experience as a traveler between worlds, I can offer you *near* certainty. As certain as anyone can be in these matters."

"Okay, what do I have to do?"

"That moneylender," the merchant said, nodding at the tent flap, "Agrid Fiall, is a vile and detestable creature who has the throat of this nation in his grasp. He is a disgusting leech who holds entire cities to debt and squeezes them as dry as if they were in a vice. Families starve because of him, and yet he blithely carries on, squeezing and squeezing every debtor as dry as a bone. Due to his power, he has risen to a high position in court and as a shameless flatterer to the princely brothers. He is here in attendance with Prince Lhiam-Lhiat at this Fayre."

"I've heard of him already. What do you want me to do?" Daniel asked, already having an inkling.

"Kill him."

Daniel considered. "Would that be hard?"

"I have already devised a plan that will put you at minimum risk—one blow, and an easy escape. I must protect my investment, after all."

Daniel thought a little longer and then said, "Very well, I'll do it. But I'll need those bullets after all. And also," he said, pointing to a black, metallic object in the centre of the tray, "I'll need *that* to put them in."

"Are you sure you are up to this?" Lokkich asked. "Can I really count on you to complete this task?"

"It's not the first time I've assassinated an evildoer."

3

She lay in bed, tired, weak, and confused. Her body felt . . . wrong. It was almost too much of an effort to move. So many things felt . . . wrong. It was hard to think. There was something important she had to do. She had to rescue someone? Who? Herself?

Professor Stowe—Felix—was sleeping next to her. She could see his back and arm—pale, flabby, and it disgusted her. Repulsed, but still with a tremendous effort of will, she pushed herself up and swung her feet out of bed—dizzy, and she wasn't even standing up yet.

She pulled the covers off and hoisted herself to her feet. Gripping the side of the bed to steady herself, she made her way to the door. Catching sight of her reflection in a full-length mirror, she halted. She looked old. Much older than she used to look. Her face was gaunt and eyes sunken. Her lips were thinner—even her hair looked tired. It no longer displayed the black sheen that she was secretly proud of. She shut her eyes. This wasn't her. She was someone else.

A soft squeal from the corner of the room made her jump. The baby. She needed to escape. Should she take that with her? It didn't seem right to leave the child, and anyway, the crying might wake the professor.

Gathering strength from she didn't know where, she crossed the room and took the baby from a small white cot. Holding it against herself, she rocked it gently and staggered out of the room.

She was in the hallway. The air was cold and through the window, she could see it was snowing. Should she make her escape now? In this weather?

She was so hungry. Instead of going out of the flat front door, she went into the kitchen.

The place was spotlessly clean. Still shouldering the child, she opened the refrigerator and recoiled. It was stocked with food, but everything was rotten or overgrown with mold. A head of lettuce had partially turned to sludge. Milk had separated in its plastic container that showed only a whitish-blue fuzz through its transparent lid. She swung the door closed. There must be something in the cupboards. She opened the one nearest to her—empty. The next was full of drinking glasses. Finally, in the third cupboard, she found some tinned food. She grabbed some baked beans down and put them on the counter. She put the baby on the centre of the kitchen table. Amused, bewildered, it gazed beatifically up at the ceiling.

She pulled open a drawer and grabbed a can opener. Working frantically, she managed to get the lid off of the tin.

It was empty. Or at least, not completely empty, for there were dried streaks of bean juice clinging to the sides of the tin, as if it had once contained beans, but a long time ago.

She reached for a can of pineapple slices and opened that. It was empty as well, except for the sickly sweet smell of old fruit. This was too weird. She picked up the baby, turned to leave, and immediately halted. There was a small girl in the doorway.

"Mum? Is breakfast ready?"

"S-Sophia?" she stammered.

"Mum, I'm hungry," the girl—she must be about seven years old—said primly.

"No time, come on, we're leaving."

"Where?"

Grabbing Sophia's hand, she dragged the girl down the hallway and out of the door of the flat.

"Mummy," the little girl said as they started down the stairs. "I don't want to go outside. It's cold and snowy."

"It'll be fine," Freya said, not at all convinced of this herself.

She felt the girl's hand pull away from hers as they reached the bottom of the steps. "I have to put my wellies on."

Freya tried the door handle, but it was locked. She pulled it harder and frantically looked around for the key. "Where is it? Where is it?" she muttered under her breath.

"It's on the windowsill," Sophia said, pointing.

Snatching up the key, she thrust it into the lock. It turned and in another moment, she had the door open. There was at least a foot of snow on the ground and she was barefoot, but she couldn't stay any longer. She pulled the key out of the keyhole.

The baby started crying. "Come on," Freya called over her shoulder.

"I need my coat."

"No time!" she snapped.

"Freya, darling?" came a voice from above her. "What are you doing?"

"Come on," she whispered, holding out her hand to Sophia.

"I don't want to go!"

The baby howled.

"Freya, where are you going? Come up and have some breakfast."

There was a rush of wind that slammed the door shut. Frantically, she flung it open again. Then with her foot outstretched to prevent the door from closing, she reached in and grabbed Sophia's arm. She heaved herself through the doorway and into the snow-filled front yard.

Only there wasn't any snow. And, suddenly, there wasn't a Sophia anymore. She stumbled and fell. She found herself lying on . . . grass. In the whole garden, there wasn't a flake of snow to be seen.

Freya looked down at herself and let out a long, strange cry of surprise and relief—she was dressed in the same pink blouse and jeans that she had been wearing when she first visited the Old Observatory.

Her head was clear now.

It hadn't been years after all, it had been . . . what? Days? She started laughing—it was all a dream, or an illusion. There were no children—she was now just clutching a dirty tea towel against her shoulder. There was no important work she was doing, translating that strange gobbledegook. All of it, since she met that weird little group—the militant Gerrard Cross, the odd Leigh Sinton, the rotund Brent Wood. She paused. She had an aunt who used to live in a town called Brent Wood. And the Reverend Peter Borough? *Peterborough?* And Felix. Felixstowe—that was a harbor town on the west coast. She'd caught a ferry there once. Those were names of towns, not people. But why? Were they illusions too? And her tutor . . . what did it mean?

Daniel. It had something to do with Daniel's disappearance.

Freya heard her name being called from inside. Stowe's legs could be seen at the top of the stairs. Scrambling to her feet, she flew to the door and pulled it closed. She still had the key, which she used to lock it.

Stowe's shape appeared dark in the frosted glass and he gave it a bang with his fist. Then, swift as a thought, he turned and dashed back up the stairs.

Freya needed no further prompting. She spun around and, as fast as her weak and malnourished body could move, she pushed open the front gate and ran out into the street.

4

Feeling uncomfortable in the fine Elfin clothes that the merchant Lokkich gave him, Daniel nonetheless tried to look natural. His sword was at his side, and a leather pouch, which seemed heavier than the weight it contained, bounced against his thigh.

He had become lost in his thoughts and had fallen behind Awin Kaayn, the musician he had met on the road. That was a stroke of luck. The merchant's plan had been a good one, but Daniel was able to refine it. To enter the feast hall as the minstrel's assistant was his idea and would remove much risk and attention from the operation.

By chance—or providence, or fate, for everything so far had gone unbelievably smoothly—Daniel had actually been introduced to Agrid Fiall. Returning to Kæyle and Pettyl's stall, he had encountered a small crowd of people clustered around it. He slipped in around them and edged to the back of the booth.

Kæyle was standing in the middle of the room, his powerful body at ease, and all the more threatening for his casual strength—he was taller than anyone else there. Before him was an elf, who was dressed in an outfit that was splendid, even by elfish standards. Thin black robes enfolded him, trimmed with grey and white lace—the one serving as an accent for the other. Pearls of varying sizes and brilliance were set into the black cloth, creating swirling patterns, as if depicting the sky on a hailstorm night. His face wore a thick, bushy beard that was jet-black and streaked with bright white hairs, which seemed to be a piece of the costume as well.

On either side of him stood what were obviously Elfin soldiers. They wore silver helmets and chest plates that were etched with woodland scenes. Everything else was covered with thick embossed leather. Short swords hung at their sides and long, thin spears rose over their heads. Behind these three were nobles and what appeared to be merchants of a higher class than those who owned stalls.

The eyes of all of these men turned towards Daniel as he entered, immediately pegging him as someone who didn't belong. "Who is this young—*man*?" the black figure asked.

"He is an unfortunate boy who fell into our world and came into my care. I have already made arrangements for him to return to his own world."

"It has been some time since I have seen a human. You used to see more of them about—when we used to steal them. Are you sure it is not a changeling? It's so hard to tell with those animals. My name is Agrid Fiall, young human. What is yours?"

"Daniel Tully, your lordship."

Fiall laughed. "*Daniel Tully, your lordship,*" he repeated in a mocking tone. "I'd forgotten how they sound when they speak. Marvelous, simply marvelous. One might almost believe that they were able to think as we do. There was that bard who managed it once, but I never saw him and believe reports of him to be exaggerated. Will you sell him to me?"

"No," Kæyle said once, with finality.

"Anyhow, where were we with the negotiations?" Fiall continued.

"The price is the price," Kæyle said firmly. "There is no changing it."

"Come now, it is your patriotic duty to supply us with charcoal for the fires needed to draw silver and gold from rock. It's what keeps many families fed and clothed."

"If ever I saw a grain of this gold or silver, then my consideration may be different. As I don't share in the fortunes of those who use what I make, I must set the price that seems fair to me."

"Do you want to own a part of a smelter's works? There is one I'm looking for a partner in," the moneylender asked with a raised eyebrow. Daniel had seen this expression many times before and had no doubt that even though the offer was in earnest, he'd find some way to cheat and ruin whoever took him up on it. Kæyle simply continued to gaze stoically at the minister.

"No matter, then," Agrid Fiall replied. He took a deep breath, as if regretting what he was about to say and wanting to put it off as long as possible. "I was trying to spare you some amount of shame, you see; the royal budget only extends to two barrels of your stock."

"That is no shame of mine."

"It means that we will have to requisition another nine."

Kæyle's face was impassive. "That is far less than fair," he said eventually.

"There is no need to tell me that," Fiall said in a plaintive tone. "It is how things are, and I feel as badly put upon as you do, no doubt. That is all I can offer, unless . . . unless you want to sell me the human. Go on, please . . ."

Kæyle did not respond, so the moneylender gave instruction over his shoulder. "Pay him."

"Are you taking the charcoal now?" Daniel asked Fiall.

Fiall had been about to turn away but paused for a final quizzical look at Daniel. Then, with a humorous chuckle, Agrid Fiall left, completely ignoring the question. However, an elf, apparently a clerk of some sort, stepped forward with a bag of money and while counting out silver coins said to Kæyle, "Delivery will be taken tomorrow morning. We want these five, and those five over there; no others. I shall mark them for you."

That was the whole of the interaction with the man that Daniel was supposed to kill, and he reflected on it as he stayed close to Awin Kaayn, drawing his new sky-blue cloak tighter around his shoulders—another piece of equipment from Reizger Lokkich—and struggling to keep Kaayn's enormous guitar on his back. He had offered to carry it, to make it look like he had a purpose there, but now he wished he hadn't. It was more strain in a stressful situation. Still, he supposed it helped to hide his nervousness. He was now suspecting that elves were far more perceptive and observant than most humans were—they seemed able to actually see emotions. Not just what was on your face, but perhaps what was in your heart as well. And fast—above all else, in Daniel's experience, elves were fast.

Things hadn't gone so well with Kæyle and Pettyl. He told them that he'd made another deal with Lokkich, which he wasn't able to tell them about, but it meant that they wouldn't have to pay anything and that he'd most likely be leaving tonight. Pettyl had started to ask questions, which Daniel wasn't about to answer.

Kæyle, who must have had some idea, said to him, "Daniel, don't do this new deal. Stay with us for the next few days and take the surer, more natural route home."

"No, I have to get back soon. I've heard my friend's voice calling me—twice now. I just feel—I need to get back as soon as possible, I know it. She needs me."

"It may not be in the plan that you reach her so soon."

"Plan? What plan?"

"The plan of the universe. The natural order that instructs all things, that guides the hearts of all living things."

"I shouldn't even be here, though," Daniel said resentfully. "If the universe had a plan to protect every living thing, then I'd have stayed where I belonged in order to protect Freya!"

"We aren't to know the plan," Pettyl broke in. "It is not for you to judge where you most belong."

"What does it matter what I do, anyway, if it's such a great plan?"

"Don't think of it as a plan—think of it as all of the created worlds working in an ideal state. Nothing is set, but things have a best course. Within this we may stay on our course, or travel a different one. If we go this other way, then we have made things disordered, and it may be difficult to correct after that. More, it may knock others out of alignment."

"But as far as I can tell," Daniel argued, "that sort of thing is happening all the time—at least, it is where I come from. And hearing here about the death of the true king and the exiling of the elves who followed him, as well as Agrid Fiall taking advantage of you and everyone else like he does—it seems to me like the universe needs a little helping hand to correct things. And if I can, then why shouldn't I? Is it the 'ideal state' that good people suffer?"

Daniel felt his blood warm and skin tingle. Things were falling into place now; it was getting clearer. "I was brought to this point by the universe—by God. This has happened to me before. Here I am, further away from my 'ideal state' than I've ever been. I've been put in an almost impossible situation, once again, and I know that I have the ability to win through and set things right. If there is a universal plan, then there's no way I'm not a part of it. I'm probably the only one in this world who can fix things and the universe knows it—that's why it brought me here. First I'll fix this problem and then I'll go back and fix my own."

"Sometimes a correction can swing out of control and cause as many problems as the problem it was meant to fix."

"I'll bear that in mind. Seeing as I'm the only one fixing things, I'm the only one who has to worry about that."

Kæyle left at that point, walking out of the tent with a sad face. Pettyl seemed as if she wanted to say more but didn't. Instead, she asked if Daniel was leaving now and he said he probably would. She gave him some food and he thanked her for everything—for looking after him, helping with his Elfish, feeding him, and more besides. He didn't want the last thing between them to be an argument. Then he left and said good-bye to Kæyle, who was standing at the entrance to the tent. He didn't say anything at first, he just shook Daniel's hand. Even after all this time, Daniel still found him hard to read. The collier didn't seem angry, though. He smiled as he gave Daniel a parting gift—a large, golden leaf.

"This is a leaf," he explained, "from the oldest tree that I know of in the forest. It has stood in the centre of the forest since before anyone started to count the years. It is very old, and yet every spring it produces new leaves. This is something of this place that you can take with you. It shouldn't weigh you down much at all, and it will point you in the right direction if ever you return."

Daniel had thanked him and put the leaf in an old schoolbook that he still carried around in his backpack.

The feast hall was an enormous building with wide, semicircular arches bowing overhead. From the rafters hung more of the brightly coloured banners and pendants with entrancing designs. There were two rows of benches running nearly the full length of the hall, which stopped before a long table that was raised on a platform overlooking the enormous room. This was the high table where the Elf Prince, his consort, and the most important members of his court were to sit. It is where Agrid Fiall would sit.

Daniel surreptitiously made his way to the back of the hall, behind the high table, and pushed past one of the tapestries. There were two large wooden doors that were standing wide open. Directly in front of them was the kitchen tent where cooks and servers were busily preparing the feast. The smell was unlike anything he'd ever smelt before—it was the rich, sweet smell of caramelizing glazes on top of roasting meat, of spiced breads and pastries, of freshly tapped casks of ale and wine, and a dozen more familiar and unfamiliar. They all mingled into a single overpowering aroma that made Daniel's mouth water and sent a sharp pain to his stomach, which had only had fruit and nuts for the last, to him, weeks, and now demanded something weightier.

With a regretful swallow, Daniel pressed on. He had to step to one side as a bevy of Elfin servers pushed past him, carrying wide platters of fresh fruit smothered in a dark syrupy sauce. Sighing inwardly Daniel turned to the right and entered a narrow corridor made up of the wooden wall of the feast hall and the canvas tent of the kitchens. This led to the flimsy wooden shack that served as a toilet for the revelers. It was nothing more than two long trough-like pits with a short, narrow, but sturdy bench-like railing before them. At full capacity, it could probably accommodate five on each side—ten altogether.

Daniel walked the length of this building where a disgusting stink that completely eradicated the pleasant odors of just a few moments ago hung like a mist and pushed against the far wall, which as Lokkich had assured him came apart at one end, just enough for him to squeeze through. He did this and found himself between the wooden wall of the latrine and the cloth of the tent around it. It was dark, damp, and smelled completely foul. Crouching, he tried as hard as he could to separate his mind from his circumstances and waited.

It was torture. The longer he stayed, the hotter and stuffier the tiny sliver of space became. He heard the feast start, as if from a great distance. The faint notes of a trumpet announcing the arrival of the prince and other nobles reached him, trickling like birdsong. There was a pause, a cheer, and then music, lovely and haunting, but which came to him in scraps and pieces. His mind tried to fill in images to match what he was hearing, but Daniel knew it was inadequate to whatever spectacles were being performed by the Elfin feasters.

Daniel pulled the gun from the leather pouch and held it before him, checking its mechanism every once in a while. It was at least an hour before anyone came into the privy to relieve themselves. Daniel had arranged himself to lie near a convenient crack, which allowed him to see the whole stretch of the room by moving his head with a very minute motion.

His hands had become sweaty holding the gun, so he placed it before him, constantly rejecting the almost constant impulse to check and reload it. He had no idea how old it was, though it seemed in good shape. Either it would work, or it wouldn't.

It had grown dark outside and a chill was creeping in. Daniel pulled his cloak even tighter around himself. It was quite dark, and Daniel wasn't sure if he would recognise Agrid Fiall when he appeared. He didn't know what would happen if he didn't at least try to fulfill his mission.

A shadow appeared in the doorway and uttered a disgusted oath. It raised its voice and demanded that a light be brought. A servant appeared with a lit lantern, illuminating the face of the self-important moneylender and treasurer. Daniel felt his pulse quicken as he lifted the gun—was it heavier than it used to be? It was certainly warmer—and rose silently. He shifted along the wall with stiff and aching limbs so that he was near the crack in the walls that he had entered by. He wrapped the fingers of his left hand around the wooden edge and gently pulled it wider. He stuck his right arm through and brought it up until he had dead aim on his target over a distance of about a meter. Practically point blank.

Daniel waited until Fiall had finished and turned his back, presenting a wider target. Daniel took a deep breath, paused for a heartbeat's time to make sure of his aim, and squeezed the trigger.

The gun exploded and kicked in his hand. Fiall twitched slightly and stood stunned. Daniel pulled the trigger three more times and the form slumped to the ground. He didn't know what it took to kill an elf, but he was pretty sure that the steel in the bullets would be toxic, if the wounds didn't kill him outright.

Daniel drew his sword and stuck it in the fabric of the tent. He jerked it down to rip a hole from head to knee and started to climb through it.

There was a shout from behind him and he saw another figure in the doorway, slightly hunched over the body of Agrid Fiall. Daniel raised his gun once more, sent the remaining bullets towards the silhouette, and escaped into the night.

5

Freya used the smaller side roads to move her way farther up into North Oxford. It was a winding, snaking path, but one that she thought would be hard to follow. She was banking on the hope that Felix hadn't been able to get out of the house fast enough to see which direction she'd gone. And so, tired and exhausted, she staggered past houses and parked cars—as well as people who duly ignored her—towards the place she had last seen Daniel, at St. Michael and All Angels Church. But she couldn't go there yet.

She limped into Summertown—little more than a busy hotspot of shops and restaurants along Banbury Road and a complex maze of terraced housing. She found herself wearing her jacket when she left Stowe's apartment, and in her pockets she found her cell phone and small purse that she kept her money and bank cards in—they must have been on her all along. She couldn't turn on her phone; its battery was probably dead. She thought to go to her apartment, but was afraid that Stowe would find her there—or worse, on the way there. She knew that she should go to the police, but she didn't know what would become of Daniel then. She had to at least make an attempt to rescue him. Then she would go to the authorities. If it really had been days that she'd been trapped, then there'd be another panic. She may have already made the media again—missing for the second time would certainly have a headline appeal.

Her clothes were dirty and smelly and her hair was an absolute disaster. She hoped that she didn't look so alarming that she would get thrown out of anyplace. She dug around in her purse for a ten-pound note and held it clearly visible before her as she walked into a small café. She put the money on the counter in front of her and ordered a baguette, some fruit, a packet of crisps, a coffee, and a bottle of juice. She took this food to a small table from which she could see the street without being seen.

She devoured her food as calmly and as slowly as possible under the circumstances, and waited. She got up to use the toilet a couple times, cleaning herself up as much as she was able to in the small sink and mirror, always returning to her table and keeping an eye on the street and the sky. She spent enough money to stop the staff from moving her on, gradually nourishing herself. She may not have eaten anything in days. It was vitally important that she didn't collapse. She needed to keep it together just a little longer.

At six o'clock a cautious waitress came over and told her the café was closing. Freya left and wandered the back ways and parking lots of Summertown until the sun was just about to set. Then, with her heart rising in her chest, she went to the church.

She stood outside the lych-gate. This is where Daniel had disappeared—she could still see him taking that first step into oblivion. She stared at the wooden frame and doorway and wondered what she had to do next. She wanted to bring Daniel back, not follow after him—but could she do that? And how?

There was a new feeling growing in her chest. It wasn't anticipation or nervousness—it was more like a charge that she was getting from the air. Something was happening. There was some sort of a . . . presence was the only way to describe it. Was it danger? She looked up and down the street. She was completely alone.

But, turning back to the lych-gate, she noticed something odd—it was darker inside of it than outside. She tilted her head so that the sky was visible through it and saw that not only was it darker, but whereas her sky was cloudy and overcast, she could see stars through the lych-gate.

"Daniel!" she called into the archway.

There was no answer. The darkness seemed to thicken. She tried again.

"Daniel!"

It now looked like full night through the lych-gate. She could see the churchyard through it, but it was like looking through a veil. She saw a light—at first she thought it was a trick of her eyes, but the flickering glow bobbed and grew in front of her.

"Daniel?"

6

Racing behind Reizger Lokkich, Daniel struggled to keep up just behind the merchant's swinging lantern. How could such a short, rotund figure move so quickly? It was a concept that scared him—however fast it was, a full rank of elfish guards would undoubtedly be able to move quicker, especially if they were on horseback. Behind him he could hear shouts and calls of alarm. Would they be able to track him in the dark? He should probably assume so.

Lokkich climbed a hill that stood outside the edge of the Fayre. He rose effortlessly up its side like a windblown beach ball, while Daniel staggered and gasped beside him.

"Ho there, *whisht!*" Lokkich called in a harsh whisper, closing the shutter on his lamp.

A light appeared from behind a clump of trees—a torch that was held by a thin, gaunt-faced being that looked less than human or elfish. It didn't seem to have any striking features apart from its plainness. It was bald, with a rounded, formless brow and long, sagging jowls. It reminded Daniel more of the face of a dog.

"There you are, you wretched thing. Give me that," Lokkich said, snatching the torch from its grasp. "Daniel," he said, "give him the cloak."

Daniel undid the clasp of the cloak that Lokkich had given him earlier and handed it over. When he looked up into its face again, he was so startled he let out a cry, quickly raising his own hand to muffle it.

"Shh!" Lokkich commanded, handing Daniel his own cloak and backpack back. "What's the matter? Do you want to make it so easy for them to find us?"

"I'm sorry, I just . . ." Daniel kept looking at the person in front of him. Its skin was no longer sagging; it was tightening, twitch by twitch, into features. It was making itself look like Daniel. A tuft of brown hair was even appearing on its head, and it seemed to be shrinking.

"That's enough, you," Lokkich said, angrily striking the thing on its head. "You don't want to give the game away completely. Take this again." He thrust the torch back to the thing. "Go that way." He pointed along the tree line. "Run. Your life depends on it. Now!"

It took off at a run, the blue cape and orange torch flames flapping behind it.

"What is it?" Daniel asked.

"It's a changeling. Vile member of a reprobate race. It has its purposes, though."

"What happens if they catch it?"

Just at that moment, there was a shout from below. "A light!" they heard someone call.

"If they kill it, they'll do us a favor. Quickly, this way." Lokkich hurried off again, with Daniel trying to keep pace behind him, deciding along the way that it would be a good idea to reload his handgun. After a while, Lokkich opened the shutter on his lantern again and slowed his pace.

"Are we going to get there in time? Is it too late?" Daniel asked, struggling for breath.

"We're here already," the other answered. "Now, take these." A small bag was thrust into Daniel's hands. It contained the items from his own world that he had killed Fiall for—the videotape, phone charger, comic book, and some odds and ends like the newer coins and mechanical pencils that Daniel had picked out. Daniel made sure to check that they were all there.

"Watch your step," Lokkich cautioned.

Daniel looked up and saw that they were standing on the top of a cliff. There was a large standing stone, about ten feet high, and then empty air—darkness.

The squat merchant put his hand out and moved it around, as if feeling the air. He muttered some words and the space in front of them started to . . . brighten. It was as if shadows of light were growing just above the cliff face.

"Daniel?" He heard Freya's voice call again, uncertain this time.

"This is it, just step through," Lokkich said. "I can't thank you enough for what you did."

"Wait, you want me to just walk off the cliff?"

"Yes, you must if you are to return."

"This is the way back home that you weren't sure was going to work the first time?" he asked, looking over the edge of the cliff and estimating a forty-foot drop.

"Conditions are ideal right now. What is more, you are being called. Summoned, if you like. You can't ask for better than that. Please, do it quickly. I cannot do it for you."

Daniel crept close to the cliff's edge. He was just about to take a deep breath to prepare himself for stepping out into certain death when a hand reached out of the darkness and grabbed him.

7

When the ghostly form of Daniel appeared within the lych-gate, Freya didn't hesitate. She leapt forward and grabbed him by the shoulder and pulled back with all of her strength. It was as if he solidified inside of her fingers. Suddenly she was falling backwards with him on top of her. They hit the ground together.

She lay, winded, looking up at the sky. Turning her head she saw Daniel, rolling gently onto his side. He saw her and smiled. "You saved me," he said.

Freya looked down. "What is it with you and clothes? You pick up something wherever you go. Where were you?"

"Elfland."

"What, are you serious?"

"It's a long story. I came back as fast as I could. I thought you were in danger. I thought I needed to save you."

"No, I managed pretty well on my own," Freya said.

"Really? I'm sorry. How long was I gone? It was weeks to me. More than a month."

"Not too sure on that point. It may have been just a couple days."

Daniel closed his eyes. Days. Only days. He rolled over and sat up. "Well, I'm not doing that again."

"No, me neither."

"Were you in trouble, really?"

Freya was just about to answer when a dark shape flew down from the sky and struck Daniel square in the chest. He went down, the black shadow—a human figure—on top of him. The attacking shape's face was bone-white and bald, its mouth full of sharp teeth. Luckily, Daniel had his arm up and under his attacker's jaw, or he would've had his throat already torn out. Slaver from those terrifying jaws was already dripping onto his collar. The thing's left hand was pinning Daniel's right, and its right was clutching at the side of Daniel's head.

Freya looked around for something heavy to hit the attacker with—a brick or a stick—but there was nothing in view.

"Fr'ya," Daniel uttered, half-choked. "Sw'rd . . . l'ft side . . ."

Freya rushed over and saw Daniel's sword glimmering at his

side. She reached for its hilt to draw it out, but the creature saw her. She felt its hand clutch her wrist as its face—disfigured and yet still perfectly recognisable—turned to her and snarled.

Freya didn't hesitate a second. She heaved with all her strength and pulled her arm away, still clutching the sword. She took a moment to find her balance once more, during which she saw the animal shift its weight towards her.

Then she heard five very sharp, tinny *bangs*. Something seemed to explode out of the thing's back, and she took another startled step backwards. It let out a death cry of "*Gah-ah-ahd!*" before keeling forward and falling on its face. It made no more movement under its own power.

Daniel shifted himself from underneath the corpse and together they rolled it over.

"So," said Daniel. "It's him. I was wondering if I'd see him again."

"You know him? It?" Freya said.

"I think so," Daniel said, looking closer. "He had hair and not so many teeth when I last saw him, but that's the guy I was talking to in the church just before I disappeared. He gave me some sort of enchanted leaf, then sent me out after you. It was obviously a trap."

"You carry a gun now?" Freya asked disdainfully. "I'm not sure I like that."

"Weren't you glad that I had it now?"

Freya handed Daniel's unused sword back to him.

"Do you know him?" Daniel asked.

"Yes. That was the . . . person that captured me. He was my tutor, Professor Felix Stowe. He tricked me into thinking I was married to him, that I had children with him. I think he meant to starve me."

"Huh." Daniel gave the body a kick. "You'll have to tell me more about that."

They stood over the body for a moment and then, without a word between them, turned and walked away.

"Freya," Daniel said, "about what we were talking about before all this . . . We need answers for this."

"Yes," answered Freya, although it wasn't an easy word to say. "I think you're right. We need to go back."

CHAPTER FOURTEEN

The Door and the Book

---------------- 1 ----------------

Before...

Daniel and Freya landed with a bone-rattling *thump* right in the centre of a large chamber filled with a light so bright they had to shield their eyes. When they were able to see once more, the first things they noticed was that Swiðgar and Ecgbryt were not with them.

"Daniel! Freya! Are you well?" came the voice of Swiðgar from the ragged opening above them.

"Yeah, we're fine!" shouted Freya, squinting around her, not used to such a glare. The chamber walls were high and straight with lots of faces, so that there were no dark corners in the room. The light fell from what looked to be a complicated type of chandelier in which flaming objects threw light on silver plates, which then reflected the light down into the centre of the room onto a large stone dais.

A large door made out of iron that had rusted into a dark brick-red took up one entire wall. It was covered with gears and dials of all sizes, some as big as the knights' shields. There were huge iron bars set into its iron frame that looked as if they might retract if the mechanism was worked properly.

Freya looked back up at the hole they had fallen through. It was right near the top of the ceiling, and it was not the only one. The whole top of the room was a honeycomb of tunnels that led down into the oddly shaped room.

"Can you reach back up to us?" called Swiðgar.

Freya said she didn't think so, but that the knights should try to find another way down. She described the room to them. "There are other tunnels leading in here—lots of them, and a door!" she said, still blinking in the light.

"Very well. Do not move from where you are, and we shall work to join you shortly."

"Worry not, æðelingas!" came Ecgbryt's voice. "Take heart; think on what King Ælfred would do in a situation like yours!"

Freya rolled her eyes at that and then felt Daniel's hand tug at her elbow. He was staring in apprehension at the walls and corners of the room. Shading her eyes, she looked around and drew her breath in sharply. Darkly clad, person-shaped bundles huddled together in the corners of the octagonal room. Some of them had faces—dull, nearly lifeless faces, in which pale eyes blinked and shifted. There were too many to count at a glance, and not one of them was looking their way; they stood disconsolately gazing at the floor. Freya shuddered.

She felt another tug at her elbow as Daniel directed her attention to the dais at the centre of the room. Looking closer, she saw in the centre of the dais a slight figure sitting cross-legged in front of a large wooden rack.

He looked like a young man, not quite old enough to shave.

His skin was smooth and so pallid it was almost white, but in the direct light of the chandelier, he seemed to shine brightly. He was very thin and wore clothes made from what appeared to be fine soft leather. His hair was long, a deep reddish-brown and swept back. He did not look up as they approached; his eyes were fixed on a large book that rested on the wooden rack.

His hands were busy with a regular, repetitive activity. In one hand he held a large rectangular stone. His other hand held nothing. The scraping sound came from his fingernails dragging firmly and steadily against the rough stone.

Freya looked closer—each fingernail was large, long, and bone white. In fact, they didn't look like fingernails at all, but more like horns growing from inside his fingertips. The strange youth was paying them no attention, only gazing in a detached, almost bored manner at the book in front of him.

"Excuse us," Daniel said in a small voice, clearing his throat.

Without any other sign of noticing his visitors, the boy put the stone to one side and picked up a thin length of embroidered cloth that lay across his lap. He placed it neatly down the centre of the book, gently closed it, and then raised his head, his expression not the least bit surprised at their appearance.

"Hello," he said in a soft, slow voice that flowed honey-thick. "Who might you be?"

Daniel introduced himself and Freya. The stranger's eyes regarded each of them in turn, running up and down their bodies. Daniel looked up at the strangely mirrored chandelier that was throwing light into the room.

"Is that daylight?" he asked.

"Of course," the stranger replied simply, turning his eyes to scrutinise his fingers once more.

"Does that come from the surface?"

"Yes."

Daniel and Freya exchanged a look of excited apprehension. "If we could climb through it, we could go home," Freya whispered urgently.

"But not before we kill Gád, right?" Daniel said in the same urgent whisper.

Freya twisted her lips.

"It's a long climb," the figure on the dais said absently. "And it spits you up in the middle of nowhere, but it does lead 'out,' as you have it."

"Where, exactly?" Freya asked.

"Oh, how should I know?" he said, dismissing the question. He placed an elbow on his knee and brought his chin to rest gently on his hand. "What realm are you from?"

"Er . . . ," said Daniel, not knowing what to say.

"England," Freya said. "We're traveling with knights named Swiðgar and Ecgbryt, from Niðergeard. Who are you?"

"What brings you here?" the boy asked, lightly brushing one of his boney nails down his cheek. "Why have you disturbed me?"

"We didn't mean to disturb you," Daniel replied, surprised by the coldness of the question. "We're looking for something . . . ," he said, then added, "but we won't tell you any more until you tell us your name."

The boy smiled. It was not a nice smile. "My name is Nemain, son of Credne; I am one of the Aes Sídhe."

"Who?" Daniel asked.

The boy smiled an indulgent smile. "There is a reason you've not heard of me. But come, tit for tat. Quid pro quo. Your names?"

"Hold!" came a bellowing voice that rolled around the room. Freya realised with relief that Swiðgar had arrived. There was a dusty *shlufff* sound and the knight's bulky form slid through one of the larger holes on the other side of the room. He fell next to a few of the silent, mournful figures in rags who lurched out of his way.

He rose and took large, swift strides around the dais towards the lifiendes, his eyes on Nemain and his spear raised. Ecgbryt slid into the room, glanced around quickly, and took his place behind him.

"Be careful, æðelingas," Swiðgar said in a low voice. "It is dangerous to deal with one of the cursed races. He is one of the *Tuath Dé Dannan*—the People of Danu—who are especially treacherous. They are descended of the same race as that of the Fær Folk, but with long life comes madness; their minds are not as they should be—cold and hard, where no light shines."

If Nemain even heard Swiðgar's barbed comments, he did not show it. He merely preened himself further, affecting an indifferent posture.

"They live so much longer than we," Ecgbryt continued, "that our lives seem as the span of a hawk's or other house-pet, and the best of them think little more of us than that."

Nemain yawned and threw a casual look around the walls where the strange people were standing in their dark, tattered clothes.

"Their minds are cold and hard places, like rooms of steel," said Ecgbryt, louder, directing his voice at the Tuath Dé. "Their passions are perverted, and they do not love what is good, only what is new, strange, and twisted. Some have said that they descended from the angels that were shut out of heaven when God first closed the gates. They live on the earth but a short walk from hell, with no knowledge of their homeland, and it has driven them mad." Ecgbryt spat.

"Quite," said Nemain, flipping his gaze up at them. Nemain grinned at him wryly, with something approaching genuine humour. "But enough about *me*," said the creature, flowing into a crouching position so quickly that Daniel completely missed the transition. "You say you are from England and your minders are from . . . Niðergeard? And whither go you all?"

"We told you . . . That is our own concern."

"So is it? Then why bother me and waste precious reading time?" Pouting, he casually pulled open the book's cover and idly started flicking through the pages. "I was in the middle of a thought that I had been thinking for thirty-two years—and to suffer such needless, pointless disruption—why it makes one's guts writhe."

"We've disturbed you," Freya continued deliberately, "because you are in our way. There is only one path downwards and it's led us here, to you."

She let the words hang in the air. Nemain made no movement or reply.

"Who are those people?" Daniel asked, pointing to the nearest wall.

"Do you know," Nemain replied airily, "I honestly have trouble remembering. I know that almost all of them were important to me at one time or another. Still, they *have* started to clutter up the place, but you know how one hates to throw anything out. You know that as soon as you do, you'll find yourself needing it. You think that you wouldn't possibly need a duchess, with several princesses at hand, so you dispatch her only to find within a week that the eyes of anything other than a duchess simply aren't penetrating enough for the purpose you need them."

Swiðgar leant down and said in a low voice, "These are the Faerie's prisoners—women he has tricked into lusting after him. Caught by his charms, they follow him willingly to the end of the earth and then pine away when he removes his indifferent affections from them."

"That's terrible," breathed Freya.

"What about this door?" Daniel asked, taking a step towards it.

"Don't touch the door!" Nemain yelled suddenly, crouching as if to spring.

Swiðgar's and Ecgbryt's hands went to their weapons, lifting them forward slightly. For a long moment, they were all frozen, on edge.

Ecgbryt was the first to move—at one moment he was still, and then he was suddenly in motion as he dashed towards the Faerie. But as he reached out to grab him, Nemain pushed himself upwards, springing over the knight.

Nemain's feet found Ecgbryt's shoulders and he perched there, hunching just above his helmet. The knight cried once in surprise at the thing's speed, and once again in pain as the razor-like fingernails dug into his upper arm, through the gaps in his chain-link armour. His axe clattered to the floor before he even realised that he had let go of it. Ecgbryt swung his shield arm in an upward arc to knock the Faerie off his shoulders, but the move was anticipated and he swung at empty air as Nemain slid down his back, its hands looping in the large leather belt and its feet gripping the sides of the knight's helmet. As he tumbled downwards, his feet lifted Ecgbryt's helmet off his head and flung it at the far wall where it smacked into the stone wall like a bullet. Two robed figures lurched out of its way as it fell to the ground.

Nemain now had two feet on the ground and two hands still in the large leather belt; he pulled at it with a mighty tug backwards, but Ecgbryt was too large and sure on his feet to fall at that, so he remained standing. A massive hand was now reaching around to grab at the Faerie, but the knight had to shift his weight to turn and Nemain took the opportunity to kick one of his legs from under him. Ecgbryt listed on his one leg, then fell slowly, like a tree toppling. He landed on his back, arms splayed outwards, and found Nemain standing on top of him, his feet pushing down just above the biceps with a calmly amused look on his face.

His shield still on his arm, Ecgbryt found movement nearly impossible, but his right arm was free and his natural strength served him well. He launched his arm forward in a swipe. Nemain lifted his left leg, but Ecgbryt was going for the right and he at last managed to lay a hand on his foe; his hand circled around the Faerie's ankle and he jerked the leg away, pulling Nemain to the ground like a rag doll. The fall stunned the Faerie and gave Ecgbryt enough time to pull himself up onto his knees. Crouching, he jerked the slight figure up in an arc and actually swung him once around his head and flung him brutally across the room.

Nemain flew half a dozen feet, twisting in the air so that his shoulders took the blow and not his head as he pounded into the hard stone wall. The Faerie collapsed in a heap at the feet of a catatonic grey lady and gathered his breath a while, spitting out some blood that had gathered in his mouth. When he had come to his senses and raised his head, he found himself looking at the metallic head of Swiðgar's spear. Smiling slyly, he flipped himself over gingerly and sat with his back against the wall.

"Well," the half-Faerie said as he dabbed at his bloody lip with the back of his hand, "that was fun."

2

"Stay, creature," Swiðgar growled. "One twitch and I shall ease the world of your burden upon it."

Nemain slumped to the ground. Freya saw that his chest was moving quickly, despite his calm manner. The awkward way he was sitting favored the left side of his body—he was probably in far more pain than he let on, and she felt strangely sorry for him even though Ecgbryt's blood still dripped from his fingers.

Ecgbryt had not come off much better. He stood with some difficulty and retrieved his helmet from the other side of the vault.

Daniel, seeing that Nemain was not in much of a position to move—but keeping an eye on him anyway—walked slowly over to the large iron door that was covered in gears and wheels of different sizes. Although it looked rusty from a distance, up close he could see the glimmer of grease and oil wherever two bits of metal touched. He gave the largest wheel in front of him a turn; although it was heavy, it moved easily. It was attached to a gear that moved with it and turned three other gears that turned another wheel, which rotated a quarter turn and then stopped. A small steel bolt shifted, locking this wheel into place, making it immobile. Daniel found that the bolt had fallen from another wheel, which was now able to move. He gave this wheel a turn, but nothing happened.

Freya came to stand beside him. "It looks like a puzzle," she said. "A clockwork puzzle—or a really big combination lock."

Daniel tried moving some of the other wheels, but most of them were locked. The solution seemed to lay in finding some way to shift the metal tumblers from one wheel to the next in order to withdraw the large metal bolts that fixed the door into the frame.

Freya turned and addressed Nemain, who was still lying against the wall. "This door—how does it open?"

The Faerie smiled slyly back at her. "Why do you suppose I would know?"

"He must know," Daniel said.

"Do it backwards," Freya suggested. "Find out which gears are connected to the large bolts."

They examined the bolts, but they were set far into the door underneath large panels and it was impossible to see where any of them started. They did find that under each one of them was a long rank of thin grooves that indicated a toothed gear might pull it back, and were further encouraged that they all looked well greased.

"If we can't follow it from the end, how can we know where to start?" Freya asked.

"It probably doesn't matter where it starts—like one of those sliding tile puzzles. We just have to make sure that everything's in the right place at the end. Ecgbryt, come over here and help us move this one at the top."

"Oh, for the wisdom of Ælfred," the knight muttered, when they had been working the problem for well over an hour. They had just found that the wheels could be moved inwards and outwards to connect with different gear chains, which put a whole other dimension on the problem.

"It's hopeless," moaned Freya.

"It's okay," said Daniel, "we're just learning the rules. Once we learn how everything works, then we'll be able to do it. We just need to be patient."

Freya looked over at Nemain, who was still being guarded by Swiðgar. Nemain gazed steadily at Daniel and Freya. When he saw Freya looking at him, he gave a casual smile. She turned back to the door.

"We're missing something," she said. "What about these little bolts, these tumblers? They fall from one wheel to the other, right? What if we're supposed to get them all to the bottom? They can't fall upwards, can they?"

"Maybe. But look." Daniel stuck his finger into one of the grooves and pushed upwards. "See, they have these little handles that let you move them back. If you turn them, it locks them into place just a little, then you can move the wheels back to how they were. If you do it right, you can move them between the wheels and probably right to the other side of the door."

"Oh, great. Perfect. When did you find that out?"

"Just now."

Freya sighed and sank into a crouch. "No," she said quietly.

"Come on, I'll bet we're on the right track. Maybe we have to get all the bolts up to the top."

"Or all the way to one side, or both sides, or all the edges, or only just the middle!" Freya snapped.

"We just have to keep trying. I refuse to let this puzzle beat me. We'll get the solution, even if I have to guess a million times."

"Yeah, okay. Whatever. I'm going to look around. Clear my head. Hunt for clues or something." She left Daniel standing at the door and turned around, rubbing her eyes.

"What about you?" Freya turned suddenly to one of the silent, motionless women. "Do you know anything about that door?" The figure did not look at her but drew away slightly.

"No, I thought not." Freya walked around the room, searching up and down for any markings or diagrams—anything that might give a hint on how to work the door, but she found nothing. This search took her near Nemain, who watched her so creepily she made a show of ignoring him.

Then she started to examine the stone dais that the Faerie had been sitting on when they first entered the room. She walked around the edges, then climbed up onto the dais itself. It was a plain, smooth surface with no designs or markings. She felt frustration rising in her chest again. She heard Daniel give instructions to Ecgbryt to turn certain wheels. She thought about the carvings that they had passed to get here. Perhaps one of those had some sort of directions or code for the door. Whoever designed a door lock so complex may well have wanted to keep the solution nearby. Or maybe the room itself was some sort of clue. She gazed around again, but she couldn't see how that could be. She looked up at the rays of sunlight that were being bounced into the room from some distant hole at the surface. Perhaps the door was there only to distract them and they had to climb now. Did the light seem to be getting dimmer? Why wasn't the air fresh?

What if it wasn't a riddle at all?

Weary and frustrated, she rubbed her eyes again and turned around. Her eyes fell on the wooden rack that held the large book the Faerie had been reading. The cover was plain leather with brass corner strengtheners attached to it. She stepped closer and leaned over the book.

"If you're going to touch that," Nemain said, "please clean your greasy hands."

Freya rubbed her fingers on the bottom of her skirt to remove the oil smudges from the door gears. Then she very carefully opened the enormous book to the first page. It was the size of a small poster and completely blank except for a short line of cramped writing in the centre. If it was English, she couldn't make out the letters; it looked like a lot of loops and long lines.

Freya started leafing through some of the pages. The first thing she noticed were the colours—bright, lively colours that tore across the yellowing pages like thunderbolts. There was also a mass of detail on each page—details of made-up figures, people, buildings, and landscapes. Each page was filled with pictures and scenes, usually showing people in some action. Words were written in the margins and in the pictures as well. Many of the pages seemed to be telling a story. She paused at two pages that each had six bordered images on them depicting a green-robed figure sitting in a forest glen talking to different groups of people as they apparently passed by. There was a picture of a king and a queen, a group of old men in brown robes, a beggar, the king by himself, two young maids, the queen and another young man, and others, including a demon with sheep's horns . . .

She turned more pages. One of them showed a stocky character in red wrestling with a man twice his size. One page had nine identical faces on it, all of them surrounded with the odd writing. One page had no writing on it at all—only a picture of two people performing an intricate dance, and the steps they took made it seem as if they were dancing across the page.

She turned the page again and heard a small "wow" from behind her. Daniel was standing there, looking at the book from over her shoulder, his eyes fixed on the two pages she had opened that showed a large, emerald, scaled serpent. It was lying on the ground, resting, its tail curled around its clawed feet. Freya felt her gaze travel along that tail to where it joined the ridged back atop large haunches where enormous emerald scales shimmered with tiny detail. Her eye continued along the back, over the crease in the book, and down the long, tapered neck of the beast to its long, horse-like face and vicious mouth. The beast was examining something that turned out to be a small person holding a torch in one hand and a sword in the other.

The detail was astonishing; each scale was rendered in precise detail. The rocks that the creature gripped were starting to crumble in its mighty talons. The wings looked veiny and tough. The night sky was above and the shadows cast by the moon and torch described massively powerful muscles beneath the thick scales.

Daniel took a step back and turned his face up to Nemain. "What is it?" he asked.

"It is a chronicle of our people—our history, our heroes, our knowledge, our genius . . ."

"It's beautiful."

Nemain gave a stiff-necked bow.

Freya turned back to the book and to Daniel, who was staring at the page showing the beast, his jaw slack and his face pale.

"Are you okay?" she asked.

"How does it end?" Daniel asked.

Nemain didn't respond. Freya turned some more pages, eventually coming to the end and the final spread. On the left-hand page—the next to last page—there were four pictures of a large group of people walking down a long slope, like a mountainside. As they descended, flames appeared. Each picture underneath showed the flames growing taller. There was no writing. The last page was a single image of a massive sheet of fire. Freya looked up at Nemain, whose smile now looked sad to her.

"How long have you been down here?" Daniel asked.

Freya, leafing back through more of the pages, felt her heart ache. It seemed so forlorn. She wished she knew the language the text was written in so that she could read it. She wanted to sit down with it and devour it—to get lost in its glorious pages for days, swim around in it. To find a work of such unimaginable beauty in a place like this, in the possession of a person like *that* . . .

"How should I be able to tell? Four years? Forty? Four hundred? Time isn't important when you're a prisoner."

Freya held her breath. She tingled with the sudden feeling that she was on the brink of understanding something important and that to move or even breathe might take it from her. She turned her gaze from the book to Nemain and then to the wretched figures standing against the wall.

"And you haven't had anything to read except this book?" Daniel asked Nemain.

"Why would I want anything else?"

"I—" she started, but choked. "I think I have it." She looked at the door and smiled. "I think I figured it out!"

3

"Think about it," Freya said to Daniel and the knights. "The door—Nemain—why would you need them?"

"Need them?" asked Daniel. "What do you mean?"

"I mean—" Freya forced herself to slow down. "I mean, why do you have them *both*? If you have the amazingly complex door that's almost impossible to open, why do you also need Nemain? If you have a clever Faerie with razor-sharp nails that can move as fast as a cheetah, why do you need an enormous iron door?"

"So?"

"I don't think it *is* a door at all. I think that it's a fake. Everything here is for show. Nemain isn't a prisoner—prisoners don't keep prisoners. And anyway, he can leave through the ceiling, the tunnels we came through, or, even more conveniently . . ."

Nemain's expression did not change; he just stared calmly at Swiðgar's spear point in front of him, raking long, bony nails against the ground. The large knight tightened his grip on the weapon.

Freya moved to the door. "Ecgbryt, hold the door right here," she said, tapping one of the larger wheels, "and give it a good pull—don't turn it, just give it a firm pull."

Swiðgar grabbed the wheel and pulled against it with all of his weight. It was a long moment before anything happened, and then, slowly and soundlessly, the whole door started to move.

"Yes!" Freya punched the air. "Ha!"

Daniel's jaw dropped and his eyes bulged as he saw the complex mechanism move away from the large bolts, which were revealed to be just metal stumps set into the stone. "It was never even locked."

"It didn't need to be, as long as everyone assumed it was. All these poor people—we thought they were prisoners, but they were just part of the illusion."

The next thing that anyone knew, Nemain was flying through the air towards Daniel, launching himself like a cat. Daniel registered the movement out of the corner of his eye and by the time he started to turn his head, Nemain was already flying towards him, his clawlike hands slicing the air in front of him.

Everything seemed to slow for Daniel. He tried to duck out of the way but could not move fast enough. He felt the burning pain of four razor-sharp fingertips rake across his upper arm. He screamed and fell.

He landed on the wooden bookrack, knocking it over and

sending the enormous painted book crashing to the floor next to Nemain.

The Faerie shrieked in horror and rushed over to the book. "You! You *creased it!*" Nemain picked it up, smoothed one of the bent pages, and shut it just as Swiðgar's massive hand clutched him around the neck and shoulders. With a fierce and brutal violence, he slammed Nemain's chest into the ground several times, the book bouncing in his hands. He was stopped by Freya's shouting.

"No! Swiðgar, stop! Please, stop!"

Swiðgar relaxed his hold on the Faerie, who gave a whimpering moan and crawled back to the book. He drew it close to himself and curled up into a ball, whimpering slightly.

Daniel writhed in agony on the floor. He would have been crying out with pain, but he couldn't catch his breath. His arm hurt terribly, and he was gripping it as hard as he could, not wanting to let go. He felt Ecgbryt's hands pull his own away and tug at the cloth of his shirt, examining the wound.

Freya stood above them as Ecgbryt untied the strings on Daniel's shirt and opened it slightly. He very carefully pulled Daniel's arm out of its sleeve. There was starting to be a lot of blood. Ecgbryt took the water pouch from his belt and washed the arm. Daniel found his breath finally and let out a howl of pain. Ecgbryt tried to sooth him with low words while giving his arm a few very careful prods.

"How is he?" Swiðgar asked.

"Not so bad for all of that. Do you hear, boy? You fought with one of the Tuatha Dé and will live to tell the tale. Not many can say as much." He asked Freya to fetch a small tin from his pack that contained a poultice—a dry, mossy substance with healing properties. He laid that to one side and then pulled a small knife from his belt; he cut a long strip off the bottom of one of the oilcloth blankets, then he placed the mossy material over the gashes on Daniel's arm and bandaged it up. "You know, Ælfred had his share of scars, and more besides. Did I ever tell you—?"

Ecgbryt's voice dulled to a pleasant murmur as Freya turned her attention to Nemain.

"Don't get too close to him," Swiðgar said. His spear was in his hand, angled downwards once again at the creature. Freya stood just next to the knight and looked down at the Faerie who was sobbing quietly. She frowned at his pathetic shape, chewing her lower lip.

"I don't think that you're a bad person," Freya said to Nemain. "You love the book because it's beautiful, and it's good to love beautiful things."

She crouched down and spoke in a lower voice. "But Daniel is worth more to us than the most expensive book in the world, and you damaged him. I think you know where we're going and what we're trying to do. We're trying to make sure that many more people are going to be safe from harm—we're going to try to stop someone from destroying a lot more than just one beautiful book—we're trying to save people. I don't know why you would want to stop us from doing that."

Nemain's sobs stilled to a broken, jagged breathing, allowing them to hear Daniel's gasps as Ecgbryt helped him sit up. Freya looked into the face of the Faerie for a little while longer and then stood. She walked over to the wall where the silent women were huddled. "You can leave now. The door's open. Follow us, if you like."

There was no response so she repeated herself with large gestures, and still there was no reaction to this news.

"Can they understand me?" Freya asked, turning to Swiðgar.

"Yes, but they will not listen. Come, let us depart. Their tale is not ended, and we can help them best by doing what we were sent to do."

Freya joined the others at the door. Ecgbryt packed up his

things, stowed his weapons, and then lifted Daniel to his feet. Swiðgar backed away from the now shuddering Nemain.

As they stood in the doorway, about to pass into the large, dry tunnel behind it, they heard a hacking cough and the sound of a weak voice trying to be strong.

"Everything will be destroyed in time. Nothing lasts forever. The only freedom is death—and the only escape is to hell!"

4

Freya's head was still spinning with the excitement of discovering the door's secret and Nemain's final attack, so she didn't notice the peculiar walls of the new tunnel until they had been walking for several minutes.

"Bricks!" she exclaimed. "It's a red-brick tunnel. Finally —civilisation!"

"Yeah," groaned Daniel. "And it smells *terrible!*"

He was right. In fact, the farther on they went, the worse the smell became. It was a decaying, sewage-like smell that stuck at the back of the throat, plugging the nose and burning the eyes.

And then something odd happened—the tunnel stopped. There was no wall in front of them, just a gap in the floor and beyond it a black emptiness that looked so thick you could almost reach out and touch it. They walked to the edge and held their lanterns out into the inky air and tried to make out any detail possible, but it was no good. The light was completely eaten up by the void.

"Listen," said Daniel, "do you hear that?" They all stilled their breathing and strained their ears. There was a distant *shh-shh* sound, like water falling a very short distance. It seemed to come from somewhere in the emptiness below.

"Look!" exclaimed Freya, as she glanced downwards. "Steps! Iron steps! It's a ladder!"

Below them were long strips of metal with griddle designs that had been fixed into the side to the sheer cliff face. The step had been joined by two sturdy handrails that ran alongside them. Before anyone could do or say anything, Freya had grabbed the lantern that Ecgbryt was carrying and had started down them.

"Does it go far?" Ecgbryt asked.

"It's hard to tell. I can't see the bottom," came the reply from the darkness. "I'll keep going until I run out of rungs. Oop—okay, that's it. I'm at the bottom. It's a drain or a sewer or something!" she shouted. "It's made of good old red bricks and mortar!" She held the torch above her head and found that she was standing on a ridge, below which ran a dark, murky water through a round channel. Torchlight glinted off of a part of the opposite wall, showing glazed tiles. "We're almost home," she said to herself. "We must be."

The man-made bank turned slightly, following the inside curve of the sewer. She followed it around a few steps to see if she could find anything else.

"Don't stray too far, lass," she heard Swiðgar call from above her.

Daniel's feet slapped down behind her and he picked up a torch and went towards her. "Freya?"

She turned to face him. "We made it, Daniel," she said in a low voice. "Look at these bricks! We made it back to the real world."

Daniel looked at Freya looking at the walls around her, her face eager. "Maybe one of these tunnels leads out—they'd *have* to, right? No one builds this without a way out—that's impossible."

"Freya," said Daniel, sounding more appalled than she thought he should. "We can't leave now. They *need* us. We're the mortals, remember? They can't destroy it without us. They—think of everyone in Niðergeard surrounded by the yfelgópes and think what will happen if we fail!"

"I know that!" Freya declared defensively. "I didn't say that I wanted to abandon them—I only meant that maybe we don't have to backtrack all the way back to Niðergeard to get home."

"Fine. But you have to, you know, finish something before it's over."

"*I know that*, Daniel."

"Okay."

"Okay."

"Lifiendes," Swiðgar said behind them. "Come now, don't wander off."

They regrouped. "Well," said Daniel, "where to now?"

The platform that created the ridge extended in two directions. There were no markings anywhere; neither way seemed any more promising than the other.

"On the one hand," Daniel began, "the river, or sewer or whatever, looks to be going that way. It leads somewhere, obviously. Another river or an ocean or wherever those things go."

"A water treatment plant, perhaps?" Freya suggested hopefully. "Isn't that where all sewers go?"

"The soul box won't be in a water treatment plant," Daniel said. "It's more likely to be somewhere away from anyone who could just stumble upon it. I think it's this way—against the flow."

"But we've been following the water all this time—it's what Ealdstan told us to do. Why abandon that now?"

The knights exchanged a look. Freya saw that a decision was made between them without even speaking.

"We must divide our party," Swiðgar announced. "One of us will go with one of you."

"What?" blurted Freya. "But that's the *worst* thing that we could do!"

"We are close—too close to go slowly. If we went the wrong way, our blunder could alert those guarding the heart and we would have lost the element of surprise that we desperately need for this to work."

"But we only got this far because we all stayed together! Would we have gotten past the gnomes and the Faerie if it were just two of us? What if there's an even bigger test coming up?"

"We'd either of us be able to handle it," Daniel said. "So long as we have the element of surprise."

Freya scowled. "If something happened, then the other two would be too far away to help. We could lose everything."

Swiðgar looked at her with an immovable expression.

"What if there are more splits? Is each of us going to end up going alone?"

Swiðgar shrugged. "It may come to that."

"It's stupid."

"It is what we are doing."

They decided that Ecgbryt would go with Freya, and Swiðgar with Daniel. They divided the provisions in their now very light packs and prepared to separate. Freya had a sad, reluctant look on her face, contradicted by Daniel's confident expression.

"We'll meet again," Daniel said, sticking out his hand.

Freya hugged him. "Be careful," she said.

They parted and, without backwards glances, went their separate ways.

5

Daniel and Ecgbryt walked down the tunnel, along with the flow of the sewer water. The walkway they were on took several sharp turns and sometimes the stream they followed moved fast, other times it moved slowly. A few times they passed a couple of deep, square pools of water, but the walkway never branched. They didn't go up, and didn't go down, just kept snaking through the darkness.

They had been walking for quite a long time when the section of the walkway they were on collapsed beneath their feet. It felt as if a rug had been pulled from beneath them—there was only the slightest sound of crumbling stone, and then they were falling. Daniel spent a frantic few moments clawing for handholds and kicking his feet against the shifting stone helplessly before they came to a stop.

"Are you hurt, æðeling?" Ecgbryt asked.

"I don't think so," Daniel replied. He had lost grip of his lantern, but it was lying quite near him. He checked himself for damages, but beyond the buzz of adrenaline, there was nothing. "Yeah, I'm fine."

He rolled over to pick himself up. Ecgbryt had already made it to his feet and was looking over the collapsed section of the bank. Coming to stand next to him, Daniel gazed up at a large scooped-out area where the path they were walking had been, and beneath it, a pile of rubble. It looked pretty impossible to get back up.

"It would seem," stated Ecgbryt, "that our best course would be to follow the burn with an eye to the path. If it wanders from us, then we will find a way to pursue it. But for now we must ensure our way is fast. I fancy that path fell by design, not by accident, and that our steps are not going unnoticed."

They gathered themselves quickly and moved on without a word more. They were walking along in the sludge now, so their progress was unsteady at first in the slippery canal but then more sure—the sewage water pulled at their feet, urging them faster and faster onwards.

6

Freya and Swiðgar crept up the tunnel, against the flow of the water. They walked in silence, alert to their surroundings—trying to be ready for anything unexpected. There was now more evidence of modern handiwork around them. The ledge they were on turned into a metal walkway that bridged the streams beneath them and led them under stone archways and through metal pipes, but their path never diverged from the narrowly railed walkway. Eventually, after about an hour, they allowed themselves to stop and rest.

"What's it like to be a knight?" Freya asked, more to break the silence than anything else.

"It's not an easy life," Swiðgar answered. "There are hardships and uncertainties. At the root of most events in the warrior's life is death. It is our stock in trade. For payment a merchant will provide goods, a nobleman will provide services for the tribute you give him. A warrior will deliver death."

"Were you always a knight?"

"Very nearly always. I was young when I entered into the service of my *dryhten*, my lord. I was just thirteen winters, but I had seen much already. My father was a scribe in Eoferwic, one of the capitals of Britain in my time. A wonderful city. He was a church man—a holy man. At that time, a great heathen army from the Danish lands arrived and settled in the area, promising peace and trade with those who lived there. The greedy men clamored to be the first to trade with them. They stayed there for a week. And when all the goods were sold, the Danesmen produced swords and started attacking the lands to the south.

"They raided Eoferwic, killing many, including our king, forcing the survivors to barter for surrender. The Vikings lived in my city, in the homes of the men they had killed. They piled the dead bodies in the wooden church and set fire to it." He bowed his head. "My father was one of those in the burning pile of the dead."

Swiðgar said no more, and after a moment Freya said, "I'm sorry."

"I had a choice, then," Swiðgar continued. "I could stay and help rebuild and fortify—perhaps take over my father's work, as

I had started to apprentice to him—but my heart was filled with anger. So, in despair, I fled south. I came across news that the king of Wessex, Æthelred, and his brother Ælfred were gathering forces to reclaim the land that was taken, and so I sought them out and joined their warband.

"I do not regret the road that I took. It has brought me honour of many kinds, and I believe I have brought honour to my land, my king, and my God with my service. But I have learned that a man cannot be just a soldier if he is to remain a man and not a monster. Destroying evil is never enough—you must also be willing to build good."

Swiðgar fixed his eyes on the tunnel up ahead. Glancing up, Freya saw a shimmering gleam in his eyes.

"That is my one fear," Swiðgar stated. "That throughout my life, I have not built sufficient good."

Swiðgar said no more, only rose and started gathering his things. Morosely, Freya joined him and they continued their journey.

The path gave a sharp turn along a wide channel that fed into an even larger river, and they were forced to walk away from the main waterway. There didn't appear to be any other choice. The large tile channel looked fairly unscalable and there was no visible walkway on the other side.

Freya's unease at this new tack quickly evaporated when she noticed a sparkle in the distance. "Swiðgar," she whispered, "lower your light for a minute."

He did so, and she shaded her eyes from the light it still gave. "I think that there's a light up ahead. It might be electric."

"Electric?"

"It's a sort of . . . light made out of . . . it's kind of scientific. It's a light made by machines."

"I see."

"Sort of enchanted."

"Yes."

They walked on, slowly drawing closer to the dim light. Freya's gaze was fixed on it as if it might disappear if she even shifted her eyes. It was a lightbulb—a single, naked, uncovered bulb. Her stomach was tense with what she supposed was anticipation—though it felt more like a giddy dread. Finally, they were standing underneath it and Freya let out a long, ragged sigh—and then found herself gasping in the cold, dank air.

"I can feel it too," said Swiðgar.

"What?"

"The power in this place. As if all things—the walls, the air, the water—as if they all wanted to hold you down, to pull you back. For whatever reason, these things are trying to keep us away from what lies beyond. Either trying to guard it or perhaps guard us. We will walk carefully from here onwards."

It may have been Swiðgar's words, but Freya did feel that her feet moved more reluctantly than before.

That lightbulb was the first of many; they could see more in the distance. They reached the next and found the others closer together, spaced maybe three or four meters apart in a single line above their walkway, that neither swerved nor branched off into other directions. Their presence was staggering to Freya. Not only was this a place where people had come, at least one person had come regularly enough to replace the bulbs when they burnt out. She walked beneath them, counting as she went, finding comfort in their spaced regularity. She sent her gaze farther along, counting the bulbs in the distance, when she saw something that stopped her in her tracks.

Gasping, she took a step back, falling against Swiðgar. "What is it?" he asked.

"I thought I saw someone—a person dressed in white. They just darted across the . . . the walkway up there. But they were so quick, I don't—I mean, I'm not sure what I saw. They startled me . . ."

"Stay behind me," Swiðgar said.

They continued more slowly, with Swiðgar cautiously leading a wide-eyed Freya, eventually coming to an intersection. There were two iron walkways that went to the right and to the left. Both were nearly identical and both led to enormous iron doors. "I think they're pressure doors," Freya said. "If the water gets too high, then they'll stop it from getting in. You open them by turning the wheel in the middle."

She stood looking at them critically. "Well," she decided, "the person I saw was moving from right to left, so I guess we should maybe take that door?" She pointed to the door on their left.

Swiðgar stroked his beard and then nodded. He put his large hands on the wheel in the middle of it and gave it a mighty turn. It gave and opened without a sound, revealing a man standing just inside, holding a large book open in front of him. He was dressed in a heavy cream-coloured robe that was slightly open to show a white robe made of some lighter, more comfortable cloth. He was old, with shoulder-length white hair and sharp features. He raised his eyebrows in surprise.

"Hello—?" he began, but was cut off by a cry from Swiðgar.

"Devil!" the knight shouted, leveling his spear and pulling his arm back, ready to strike.

"No!" The old man flinched and dropped his book. He leapt to the side just in time to stop being skewered by Swiðgar's spear, but not far enough to avoid it altogether. It tore into his side, causing him to cry out in agony. He dropped to his knees as Swiðgar brought his spear back again.

"Quick, lifiende," Swiðgar urged.

"Is it Gád?"

"It is!"

"Are you sure, I mean—"

"I'm certain! Hurry, now, before he can recover—before he can speak—*kill him!*"

"What? But that won't—Daniel has to—"

"He may have done so already; in any case, it'll keep him down. Hurry now!"

Freya looked down at the old man, blood seeping from his side. "No, I—I don't think— "

Swiðgar pulled his spear back and lunged for another attack, but it was the worst thing he could have done. He thrust the spear forward just as Gád leapt aside, missing him narrowly. With unbelievable speed, Gád gripped Swiðgar's spear, bent the top end of it back, snapping it off completely, and—gripping the head by its splintered shaft—thrust it back at the knight with incredible force. It penetrated his mail coat and lodged deep into his chest.

Astounded, winded, and now mortally wounded, Swiðgar made a grab at the frail old man, who ducked and dodged out of his way. Gád then delivered a blow to Swiðgar's chest, which drove his spearhead farther into him and caused him to fall backwards against the metal door opposite.

Freya cried out and dashed to Swiðgar's side. Swiðgar moved his lips, trying to speak, but only blood came from his mouth, exploding at first, and then in cascades as he fought for breath.

"What have you done?" Freya said, turning angrily. "What have you done?!"

"Hurry," Gád said, his hand moving back to his bloodied side. "I must talk to you. You are not out of danger yet."

CHAPTER FIFTEEN

Gád

---------------------------- 1 ----------------------------

Gád took Freya by the arm and pulled her gently across the doorway. She now found herself standing at the entrance to a large, luxuriously furnished room—completely out of place in a sewer and oddly unreal, like a movie set or a French palace. The room was several storeys high and square, with a multi-tiered floor. The walls were lined with bookcases and electric lights in extravagant sconces. Deep, red-patterned carpets were laid around the room atop white marble floors. Expensive-looking furniture filled the interior—grand armchairs, plush couches, wide tables, and a long desk—all beautifully carved and polished to a shine. There was a grand chandelier overhead, an enormous fireplace in one wall, and even an ancient TV set, the kind that looked like a small cabinet with a screen on it.

"Let go of me," Freya said, pulling her arm away from Gád.

"I really mean you no harm," he said, bending down before her. "I must talk to you for a few moments. Do you want to sit down? Are you hungry? Thirsty? I do so want to help."

"Then help Swiðgar. He's still alive. He—"

"Believe me," said Gád, standing up and moving to an armchair, "that no good would come of that. You saw his reaction upon seeing me. Is violence the first response of a reasonable man?"

"But you're evil . . . ," Freya said, uncertainty creeping into her voice.

"Yes," Gád said, sitting. "I assume that's what they would have told you. That's just one of the lies of Niðergeard. Please, sit down and allow me to explain."

Cautiously, Freya approached and stood near the chair opposite. She cast a look back at Swiðgar. "Please," she said, "before it's too late. Help him!"

"Yes, I will. But first I must see to the wound that he gave me," Gád told her, indicating the gash at his side. "Come inside, there are things I must talk to you about."

Reluctantly Freya followed him inside.

"I don't blame you for your trepidation," Gád said with a wince. He leaned forward and drew out a wooden box that was underneath the chair. "It's not your fault, I know. You've been told all types of lies about me—lies that left no room for question, lies that you thought could not be challenged."

"What lies? You control the yfelgópes. You've had Niðergeard surrounded for decades. I was there the last time you attacked. I was almost killed."

Gád brought the box up onto his lamp and opened it. It contained bandages and bottles. He shook his head. "Lies spun with the threads of truth are always the hardest to disbelieve. Yes, I control the yfelgópes, and with them I've surrounded and attacked Niðergeard—several times now, in fact. But *why* have I done so? For what purpose? Can you tell me? Do you know?"

"Because you're ev—"

"No!" Gád snapped, thumping the box with his palm. "The

exact, *specific* reason! No one is simply 'good' or 'evil' entirely. You can't tell me, can you? You have no idea!" Gád spat these words angrily, his face turning red. He jerked forward in his chair, causing Freya to flinch. "Stupid girl!" he spat at her.

Freya clutched the back of the chair, wanting to run but now afraid to. Gradually, however, Gád leaned back into his chair and placed a hand over his eyes.

"Forgive my temper," he said. "I have been unjustly imprisoned by Ealdstan for hundreds of years and I have forgotten my manners. It is unfair to you, I know, and I apologise."

He turned his attention back to the box and withdrew some sheets of sterile cotton and a bottle. He unbuttoned his shirt and shrugged it off his shoulders, then set about cleaning the wound.

"Yes, I've raised an army and intend to crush Niðergeard, but there is more than one reason that a man may revolt against the established order. They told you I was an oppressor, but under what circumstances would they tell you anything else? Authoritarian regimes need scapegoats to blame for their own mistakes. You've been there, you've seen what kind of place it is. The people are wasted, lifeless, spiritless. They want to die, but they keep hanging on. And whose fault is it? Not *theirs*, for the choices they've made. Not *Ealdstan's* for deceiving them. No, it's *mine*—the evil wizard's. Yes, they told you I was an oppressor, but what if I'm a freedom fighter? A revolutionary?"

Gád, satisfied that his cut was clean, rubbed some balm onto another sheet of cotton and removed a roll of bandages from the box. "Niðergeard is a hostile occupying force in this land, a malignant dictatorship. They want to control us, make us live in the past with them, give up our identities, our hopes and dreams—make us something less than human. Deny us of our basic humanity, our chance to be glorious."

"I know what you're try—" Freya began, but was cut off again.

"Would you help me with this?" he asked. "Could you hold this bandage, just behind the shoulder here? It's rather hard to reach . . ."

Freya cautiously rose and helped Gád bandage himself.

"Let me ask you a question. Was it *your* idea to come here? To go on some sort of mysterious quest underneath the surface of the earth?"

Freya didn't answer, but Gád didn't need her to.

"Of *course* it wasn't," Gád continued, winding the bandage around his chest with difficulty. "Imagine asking that of a *child*. They tricked you. They blindfolded you with their lies, told you all sorts of fantastic tales until your head started spinning, and when you were all mixed up, they took off the blindfold and pushed you where they wanted you to go. I do give them credit for their cleverness—but the fact remains that they perpetuate a sick, twisted, perverted doctrine designed to extinguish all of the brilliant and wonderful flames of humanity. The truth will always come out—I believe that. And *that* is why I stand against Niðergeard, for the sake of all the people in this world who are powerless to do so."

The two regarded each other silently. Freya sat staring at Gád, who had raised his hands and now held them steepled beneath his chin.

"It won't work," Freya said, now uncertainly. "My friends are going after your heart right now, as we speak. If you're trying to twist my mind around, or anything, it won't work."

Gád pinned his bandage down and settled back into his chair with a sigh. "Yes, I understand that." He shook his head. "Fortunately, I have prepared for all of this, and they are doing precisely what they must do in order to help me. Indeed, let us see how they're getting on."

A remote control appeared in Gád's hand and he pointed it at the antique television across the room. He pressed a button and there was a click, a hum, and a bluish-white picture appeared on the screen.

2

The canal that Daniel and Ecgbryt traveled along sloped down, down, and down, just as the banks beside them rose higher above their heads. The muddy, foul-smelling water rushed ahead of them, sloshing around their calves as it passed. So far the water hadn't risen, just kept getting faster. It was slow going, since the brickwork underfoot was slippery with sludge. Daniel wondered if they were on the right track, but this felt right. He felt a tug inside of him, as if an invisible fishing line were pulling his rib cage forward.

Then they saw the lights. At first they became aware of a blue glow growing around them. As they walked they saw the edge of a wall ahead of them come into sharp relief by the dim blue light. As they got closer, Daniel was aware of a kind of sizzling sound, and when they rounded the corner of the illumined wall, they could see where the light was coming from; in two long rows on each side of the wall were odd-looking orbs stuck on the end of black poles about a foot in height. They gave off a gentle radiance. Daniel stared into one of the orbs and could just make out the shape of a slowly moving flame, but nothing else.

"Enchantments," Ecgbryt stated.

"I'll say," Daniel replied.

They walked cautiously between the strange lights, which made an odd buzzing sound, but no heat. The glow seemed to get in behind the eyeballs and sit in the back of the head. Daniel shuddered but kept going, trying to find comfort by telling himself they were probably on the right track if they were starting to see magic lights guiding them.

They turned another corner and were met with an incredibly strong wind blowing across them. It forced Daniel to blink several times to close his eyes, and when he opened them again, he saw they were at the entrance to an enormous and magnificent cavern shaped like a pyramid. It looked almost half a mile to the other side. The stream they were following emptied into a pool of many levels—about a dozen concentric squares. They could see down almost to the bottom because the blue orbs of light were placed on each step, fizzing gently underwater and still giving off the radiant blue glow. On the ground around the square pool, tall buttresses and columns supported a roof that mirrored its depth and dimensions. Everything was covered in glazed tiles, mostly white but patterned with other colours.

At the far end of the pool, a large column rose like a lectern in a church. Unlike all the other surfaces they could see, this was pure blue stone that was tinged with ripples of white. Light from a hole in the ceiling fell upon its centre and upon a large, many-faceted box made of crystal that threw the light in all directions.

"This must be it!" Daniel said in an excited whisper to Ecgbryt. "That must be the soul box!"

Then came a scraping sound from both sides of the room. Daniel turned in horror as he heard the distinct and familiar scrabbling sound, and the first of the yfelgópes came into view.

"Hurry, Daniel," Ecgbryt cried. "We must run!"

They started around the pool at a sprint. Daniel's hand found his sword as Ecgbryt unslung his shield and hefted his axe.

3

"Ah, good," said Gád. "They've arrived. Let's see if we can . . ." He pressed a couple more buttons on the remote control and the image shifted, zoomed in, and panned to the right. Freya realised that she was seeing a fight taking place—inside of what looked like a giant pyramid.

She picked out Ecgbryt first, the enormous knight swinging his axe at a cluster of yfelgópes. He was mostly just knocking them into the pool in order to move forward as fast as possible. He was standing in front of and trying to protect Daniel, who was following behind him, sword drawn. Occasionally Daniel would stab or slash at an yfelgóp who had rebounded off Ecgbryt but not fallen into the pool.

"Well," said Gád, "that's going nicely."

"Nicely?" Freya asked, worried now. "What is it? Is that room some sort of trap?"

"No, not at all. If they do fight their way through my warriors and make it to the box, they will hold power over my soul."

"So aren't you worried about them getting through?" Freya asked.

"Worried? No, not in the least!" Gád said, smiling warmly at her. "In fact, nothing would make me happier. Do you think that I've truly, earnestly been trying to stop you? You were never in any real danger coming here. Did you think you were?"

Gád was wiping the blood off of his hands with a rag. "No, my dear, the truth is that I want everyone to succeed. That's the whole point of being on this earth, isn't it? To succeed? I *want* Daniel to be a hero. I *need* him to be one. The world needs heroes who are willing to fight and even kill for what they believe. His actions will help me to free millions of people all over the world. People just like you, who want to be free but don't know how to—who don't even know that they *aren't* free!"

"So it *has* all been a trap," Freya answered hotly.

"My dear, that's what I've been trying to tell you," said Gád. "But it's not *my* trap. You have been under *their* control far longer than mine. In fact, *my* control releases you from *theirs*. You've let

Niðergeard rule your life since before you even heard its name. But it doesn't have to be that way now."

"How can I trust you? How do I know you're telling the truth?"

Gád shifted in his chair and pointed across the room. "Do you see that door over there? It's just like the one you came into the room by. That door will lead you out of these caves—continue straight on until you see the light of day and feel the fresh air on your face. It's not locked. There are no guards on the other side. All you have to do is turn the handle and leave, at any time. That door will lead you home."

4

The blue column was now looming over Daniel. He could see a stone staircase that led up it. The yfelgópes weren't coming as fast now; the two had managed to create a little circle of protection around them, which the yfelgópes were reluctant to enter. Some had dived into the pool and were swimming across to try to meet them on the far side, but their weapons and scraps of armour made it hard for them.

They raced onwards. Ecgbryt dealt easily with the yfelgópes before them and then they had a clear stretch to the column. Sprinting as hard as they could across the tile floor, they sprang over the corner of the pool and made for the towering stone column at a dead run.

Daniel could feel something pushing him onwards—this must be how heroes felt when they were performing amazing deeds. There was no doubt inside of him; his thoughts were clear. He knew exactly what he had to do and how to do it, and as he reached the first of the stone steps, he knew that he *would* do what he came to do.

"Go, Daniel!" Ecgbryt shouted. "Get to the box!" He kicked an yfelgóp that was climbing out of the pool back into it.

Daniel's feet pounded up the steps, taking two at a time.

He arrived breathless at the top. The crystal box was nearly as big as he was. He could see something black fluttering around in it. There was a small doorway secured only by a latch. He flicked it open and peered inside.

In the box was a creature that had a bulbous, fleshy body, long spidery legs, and wide, flat insect wings. It had a stubby head and a long, pointed, needle-like mouth. It was jumping around like a fish out of water, banging into the sides of the box. Its legs weren't strong enough to hold it, and it was too heavy to fly. Its fleshy abdomen pulsed steadily, like a heart—exactly like a heart. This was Gad's heart—an ugly, black, fluttering thing. The sickness in Daniel's stomach deepened when he opened his eyes and looked down from the high tower to see Ecgbryt fighting some distance below him.

This isn't what heroes do, Daniel thought, pressing his lips firmly together. *They don't flinch at the last.* He seized control of his emotions, tensed his muscles, and turned back to the box.

Heroes are strong. He forced his hand to grip the door's latch.

Heroes fight against all odds. He sheathed his sword and drew the stone knife that Ealdstan had given him.

Heroes destroy anything that is evil. Without thinking about it any longer, he flipped open the door, spotted the fluttering heart thing, and plunged the knife into it.

5

Freya looked across at the door. "Do you mean it? This leads out of the caves?"

"Absolutely."

"What if we kill you?"

"Then you can still leave, obviously."

Freya turned and looked at Swiðgar, lying motionless just outside the door they came in by. "And what about Swiðgar?"

"It's too late for him," Gád said. "He's dead. I'm sorry. You may have thought of him as a friend, but in time you will come to realise that he was your jailer. You will have to leave him here."

"You said you'd help him!"

"I was not fast enough, I'm sorry. We talked too long. It was self-defense, if it helps to look at it like that."

Freya choked back tears. She could cry for him later. She thought about what Gád had said about sunlight and fresh air. She went to the door and tried the handle. It moved easily in her hand. "But what about the people in Niðergeard?" she asked, turning.

"Do you *really* care about them? Freya, you are free. Do you understand? This is what *you* wanted for this. Daniel gets to be a hero, and you get to go home. You both win. You both get what you—"

Gád jerked in his chair. His body tensed, rigid, his muscles fighting against each other, as if having a seizure, his head banging from side to side. It took Freya a moment to realise what was happening, and then it struck her—Daniel must have done it.

She stood, unsure what to do. Wringing her hands, she looked towards the large door that Gád had told her was the exit. Did she dare?

Gád made heaving, vomiting motions but expelled nothing. He looked in unimaginable agony. For long moments he rolled and writhed on the floor, and then finally became still, curled up in a ball, panting.

Exhausted, Gád pushed himself up and stood, swaying, just in front of Freya. His eyes were half-closed, and he seemed not able to see her. He turned and walked to a small table set next to the wall, which had a pitcher on it. He poured clear liquid from that into a small tumbler and took a drink—a few sips at first, and then the whole glass. He clutched at his throat as if it hurt him and then started to laugh.

"I forgot how painful living could be."

"What just happened?" Freya asked.

Gád turned to her with a smile and sweat on his brow. "Daniel has succeeded—he has destroyed the vessel that housed my immortality—and it has returned to me."

"I don't understand."

"I am mortal now—I'm back in the game. A long time ago I placed my mortality into the body of an undying beast, so that as long as it lived, I would continue to. In this way, I became much like your friends the knights, walking this world, yet always removed from it. Now, with the sands of my existence once again flowing, I can do anything."

Freya stood, blinking at him. "So . . . we lost?"

Gád shrugged. "Maybe from your point of view, but that's a rather simplistic view to take. This is just the movement from one state into another. It is neither better nor worse—just different."

Freya stood, confused. "So, what happens now?"

"That is for you to decide. You may attempt to complete the mission that Ealdstan charged you with—to kill me and then return home—or you may simply return home now."

"I—I don't know what to do," Freya said, and her eyes went to the body of Swiðgar, still lying dead.

"Do you *want* to kill me?" Gád asked her.

"No!" she cried, her eyes filling with tears at once. "I don't want anyone to die. I just want to go home! Wh-at—what am I going to tell the others?"

"I can help you with that. Follow me."

6

Freya walked as fast as she dared down the almost pitch-black corridor. The lamp from Niðergeard that she still carried with her seemed to be glowing dimmer now, and she couldn't always make out the ground in front of her.

She thought that she saw two spots of light ahead of her, like two dim stars. She dipped her lamp to see better and watched as the bobbing lights came nearer. She started to see outlines forming in the gloom, like the silvery outlines of a ghost.

"Freya?" she heard Daniel call.

"Ecgbryt, Daniel—" She hurried towards them.

"Are you okay?" Daniel asked after Freya released him from a hug. "I found Gád's soul and killed it! It's done, we can go back to Ealdstan and he'll let us go!"

"We don't need to do that. I think there's an exit nearby."

"Really? How can you tell?" Daniel asked.

"I passed it on the way to find you here."

"Where's Swiðgar?"

Ecgbryt was already standing over her and peering into the darkness behind her.

"He's . . . back there. Come on, I'll show you."

Freya led them both back the way she had come, to an intersection of pipes and ducts. And there, in the centre of the crossroads, lay Swiðgar's body, his broken spearshaft beside him, the spear's head still buried in his chest.

"Is he not sleeping?" Ecgbryt asked to himself. "Can he not be woken yet?"

He stepped forward and bent over the body and touched the cold face, then turned to Freya with an expression that nearly shattered her. She was already crying and through her misty eyes she saw a look on Ecgbryt's face like a wounded dog that had been kicked in the belly and it didn't know why.

"How did this happen?" he asked. "This should not have been possible."

Freya wanted to break down and tell him everything. She

took a deep breath and felt her stomach tighten till it was as hard as steel. She heard the words come out.

"We ran into Gád, and they fought. Swiðgar—he fought long and hard; I thought they would go on forever. Then Gád grabbed the spear and shoved it into his chest. And—it was over. I was terrified. Gád came up to me—I wanted to run, but I couldn't. And he stood over me, and then—then he grabbed at his chest and keeled over. He started spitting up blood and then—I think he was dead. That must have been when you—did whatever you did, Daniel."

Daniel and Ecgbryt just looked at her with impassive faces. For a while she couldn't tell if they were buying it or not. She held her breath and prayed for one of them to say something, anything.

"Where is Gád now?" Ecgbryt asked, looking around.

"He's back there," Freya said, indicating one of the paths. She continued hurriedly, "Swiðgar wasn't quite dead yet and he walked this way with me, but then he stopped and died."

"Did—did he say anything at the end?" Ecgbryt asked. "Anything about me?"

Freya felt a sweat immediately break out. This wasn't in the script. "I don't—no, he didn't. He was really weak, and we were hurrying to get to you. I'm sorry, Ecgbryt, I'm so sorry."

Ecgbryt turned back to Swiðgar's body.

"*Wela,* broðor, *wela. Án bealocwealm þu habbe. Caru ond ánlípnes is min.*" He sighed. "Did I fail you when you needed me most? My hand too slow to rise with yours? Did you want for me in your last moment? Did your heart cry my name, or was thought of me absent? I am sorry that I gave so much cause for you to speak against me in all the years we walked side by side."

Ecgbryt pulled the body of Swiðgar by its arms out of the rank and reeking sewer water and onto a dry stretch of paving and set about arranging the dead knight's clothing and armour.

"So your dear spear is broken. And where is your shield? Will you not fight again in this world? *Swa, swa*—continue the fight in the next world, and tarry there until I come join you.

"And I vow before you now never again to speak word of our past adventures. The uttering of them will taste always as stale water and dry ash if you are not to share such food of remembrance with me. No more will Ecgbryt drink to the health of dead kings or raise a horn to the memory of forgotten battles. My head will not again be warmed with thoughts of past glories and triumphs, but will be lit only with ideas of future conquest and the defeat of enemies—of returned bloodshed and vengeful violence.

"We have traveled many roads, you and I, long and dangerous roads, but the way always seemed shorter when I walked with you and burdens lighter." Ecgbryt placed a massive hand around the dead body's belt and hefted the enormous mass onto his back and across his shoulders. "So come with me a short distance yet and I will honour this which you have been left behind. You are not so heavy, for the greater part of you yet has gone on."

He turned to Daniel and Freya. "I would like to inspect Gád's body myself."

"No, Ecgbryt," Freya urged. "You have to help us get out of here first. There might still be yfelgópes around here."

"Very well," Ecgbryt said. "Which way did you think was the passage out?"

7

Swiðgar's body, though it would have been almost cripplingly heavy to anyone else, did not slow Ecgbryt down much at all. He walked silently behind Daniel and Freya as they moved down the new passage, which wound on with many curves and corners but was brick and piping all the way along.

This was the way that Gád had directed Freya to go, and she prayed that it wouldn't be another trap. The possibility that it was actually the way home, however, pulled her onwards, walking quickly ahead of the other two, pausing to wait for them at the turns so that they wouldn't lose sight of her. At one corner she paused long enough to talk to them.

"Do you see something up ahead?" Freya asked.

"I can't tell. Yeah, maybe. Something shining."

As they went farther, Daniel could start to see the ghostly image of a wall in the distance. "We're almost there," said Freya.

They kept their feet and moved onwards. White light was streaming past the wall—daylight, Freya realised with awe. For the first time in a month or more, they were seeing daylight, projected onto the brick wall of the corridor.

They rounded the corner and had to stop, their eyes dazzled by the light that fell through a large grille. They both gasped and shielded their eyes.

"The sun . . . ," said Freya, wiping tears off her cheeks.

"It hurts!" said Daniel, surprised.

Ecgbryt flinched and squeezed his eyes shut. "I have not seen the sun in over one thousand years. I do not remember that it stung so."

They moved forward, out of the direct path of the light, and stared up through the grille.

"Can you see anything?"

Daniel jumped up and down a couple of times to try to get a better view. "No, just the sky . . ."

"Feel that fresh air."

They stayed underneath the grille for several short seconds, fixated, before their fears pricked them onwards.

"Come on," Freya said. "It can't be far now."

But the next turning revealed a plain brick wall and nothing else.

They stared at it blankly and it stared back at them, just as blankly.

"It's like a bad joke," Daniel said.

Freya was in turmoil. Gád had lied to her. She had wanted to believe in escape so badly; she had wanted to put this terrible world and all that had happened to them far, far behind her. But now—now there was no telling what else they'd have to go through in order to get back home again.

"Maybe we can break through the grate," Freya said. "Maybe we can call out to some—"

A high, piercing scream cut through the air.

"Yfelgópes," Ecgbryt said. "We need to turn around and prepare ourselves. No good can come from fighting in a corner."

"Wait," said Daniel. "Where's the mortar?"

"What?"

"There's no mortar between the bricks. It's just a pile of stacked bricks. I think we can break it down."

Skittering footsteps and scraping clatter was heard from down the zigzagging corridor. Ecgbryt set Swiðgar's body down, propping it against the wall. He unslung his shield from his back and hefted his axe. He hunkered down, ready to meet any attackers.

"Be mindful," Ecgbryt said. "I shall protect you as best I can, but I may not be able to halt them all."

Daniel drew his sword and shoved its point in between the crack of two bricks. It slipped in easily enough, all the way down the long tip. He wriggled it gently from side to side, causing the wall to bulge towards him. "It's coming . . . !"

He pulled his sword back out, and with it, a stream of bricks and damp soil. He felt a hand on his arm and he was yanked backwards sharply, losing his balance and falling lengthways on the ground as the large old bricks fell to a crashing heap at his feet.

Freya was lying beside him. "Thanks," he said, picking himself up. Dust was billowing around them. The upper half of the wall had given way, turning into a large pile of bricks and dirt. Behind the wall was . . . more dirt. Dark, brown, muddy earth.

"No," Freya said quietly, despair finally sinking into her heart. "It's not fair."

"Never mind, Freya," Daniel said consolingly. "We'll find—"

"Hold on," said Freya, climbing forward on the dirt heap. "I can see light."

"What?"

"Up through here . . . it's—" She thrust her arm into the dirt and pulled. A small clump of mud and grass came with it, revealing a dim blue corner of sky. "Hurry, help me!"

They dumped their packs and leapt forward, clawing clods of dirt away. Freya's fingers dug into a mesh of fine white fibers, which turned out to be the roots of grass that hung like a curtain in front of her. She started ripping through it, tearing it apart as much as she could.

"Ecgbryt," Daniel said, turning to the knight who still stood, weapons at the ready. "Come on, help us!"

"Not today, young Daniel, young Freya. This is where our paths part."

Daniel also stopped. "What? Why?"

"Your work under the skin of the earth may be finished, but mine is not. I must toil in the darkness awhile longer yet."

"No, Ecgbryt—" Freya moaned, the image of Gád stabbing Swiðgar played over in her head. "If you stay here—" she choked.

"I'm not leaving!" Daniel exclaimed. "Ecgbryt, I want to stay with you."

"Daniel, you can't—"

"Shut up, Freya, this was always the plan. I was going to help you get home and then stay myself. I want to be a knight. I want to destroy evil!"

"Daniel, that's not—"

"I hate the world. Hate it! I'm not going back! I *refuse!*"

Ecgbryt knelt in front of Daniel.

"You must go," he said. "You do not belong here."

Those words cut Daniel to the heart. "Don't say that."

"I would not want you here."

"I don't care," Daniel said, eyes hot with tears. "*I* want me here."

Just then, the first of the yfelgópes rounded the corner at high speed, howling at them. Ecgbryt rose and with a swift motion brought his axe up and into its jaw.

"Go!" Ecgbryt commanded them.

Daniel drew his sword and went to stand near Ecgbryt. "You better hurry, Freya."

Freya looked beseechingly at Ecgbryt, who nodded at her and then turned his back.

Gritting her teeth, Freya dug up towards the light. She pushed with her legs and pulled herself forward just as a shower of loose dirt and pebbles fell upon her head. She was completely buried except for her forearms and ankles. She couldn't move her legs enough to kick herself forward, nor could she move her shoulders to pull herself out. Worse, she couldn't breathe—cool, damp earth completely covered her face. She flailed her arms as much as she could, trying to find something to grab, but found nothing.

Twisting, turning, and scrunching herself together and thrusting herself forward like an inchworm, she finally managed to get her head and shoulders out into the open air and blinding light. Her arms were next and then the rest.

She stood, blinking. Although bright to Freya, the sky showed it was only evening. She was in a field with a small clump of trees nearby and a large stone building just beyond that. She looked down at her feet on the ground and the loose earth that she had climbed through. She could hear nothing but the sound of the birds in the distance—no sound from Daniel or Ecgbryt.

And then with a lurch, the ground beneath her collapsed along the line of the corridor they had been walking down. It made an almost indescribable sound—a sort of muffled, *basso profundo crump.*

She watched the caved-in earth for any further movement and spied something pale and wriggling frantically. It was Daniel's arm.

Fast as a shot, Freya was over there and pulling at him with all her might. She wasn't strong enough to shift him much at first, so she started desperately to dig and claw away the dirt around him. She managed to uncover his face—she had almost been standing on it—which allowed him to breathe, with huge, grateful gasps, and from there they worked together to extract him completely.

"Ecgbryt—" was his first word, still spitting dirt from his lips. "Ecgbryt—"

"Is he still down there?" Freya asked, alarmed. She wasn't sure she had the strength to dig again. "Where do you think—?"

"No—" Daniel sputtered. "He pushed me. He pushed me away. When the walls started caving in . . . he could have pulled me towards him instead."

"Maybe not, maybe . . ."

As Freya searched for words, Daniel shook his head. "I saw his face, his eyes. He didn't want me with him. He didn't want me."

"Excuse me," came a voice from behind them. "But who might you be?"

They spun around and found a boy, a tall, lanky teenager with dusty-brown hair, staring at them in amazement. "Where did you come from?"

"Freya," Daniel whispered, "what do we do now?"

EPILOGUES

1

Now . . .

"So, Freya—where do we go?" Daniel asked, studying the board that had the train timetable posted on it.

"It looks like we take . . . this one, here," said Freya. "That's the village that the church is in, at least. We'll have to ask around after that." They stood, still staring at the map, both thinking the same thing. "I hope it works," Freya said, voicing the thought.

"The knights had to negotiate a labyrinth just to get to Niðergeard in the first place, remember?"

"Well, we'll just have to see. It may be a moot point anyway—we may not be able to get under the arch."

"We'll manage it somehow," Daniel said. "The other option I see is to head back up to Scotland and try to find where we came out. We'd have to navigate the Wild Caves again, which may be hard, but still possible . . ."

367

Daniel looked at the clock underneath the departures board. "We've got about forty minutes. Shall I grab some food for us?"

Freya nodded and gave him some money. "I'll be on the platform," she said. "Get me a coffee as well."

Freya stepped through the automatic doors and found an empty bench. She sat and bent over, putting her head in her hands. She squeezed her eyes shut and rubbed her temples, still not quite believing that she was about to do what they were doing—going back to Niðergeard. All the years of her life from now to the last time she was there were about trying to put it behind her—literally and figuratively.

And if it didn't work? She'd go back home. After seeing the date, she'd found that she'd been under Stowe's influence for over a week. No doubt she'd been reported missing. If, that is, she was even enrolled at Oxford University. She realised now that she wasn't sure where Stowe's enchantments started and where they ended. It was possible that every tutorial that she'd had with him, and every other student she'd shared them with, had been illusions.

She shook her head, trying to dislodge the dreadful thought from her mind. It'd be worth getting in contact with her parents somehow, though. She just couldn't think of a way to do it without jeopardising their mission—what she'd come to think of as her mission. Everything was traceable these days, and they were probably already on a dozen CCTV recordings, although Daniel had, he'd said, taken her along routes where there was less risk of that. How and why he'd come to consider and accommodate for that, she meant to ask him . . .

"Excuse me, miss?" a female voice asked.

Freya looked up, squinting at an officious-looking form silhouetted against the sunlight. She raised a hand to shield her eyes. "Yes?"

"Are you Freya Reynolds?"

Her eyes fell upon a badge that read Thames Valley Police. "Um, no, sorry, I'm not. Sorry."

The policewoman nodded. "Could you step this way, please?" She held up an arm, indicating the station forecourt.

"Um, what's this about, please?"

"Step this way, if you don't mind."

"I'm waiting for someone, and our train will be here soon."

"I understand. Step this way."

No options left to her, Freya stood with legs that shook like jelly. It would be a mistake to say too much without knowing what the police knew. She had to keep her story—whatever that would be— simple and opaque. It would be work, but she had spent most of her life keeping secrets. The trick was to always keep a few things in reserve, so it seemed like all her lies had been broken through when it was really just a single layer of them. If need be, she would throw them Stowe and the abduction. She would have to rewrite that, however, but she was certain that she could play the traumatised victim, in shock after her abduction, who was irrationally trying to escape to anywhere. It didn't have to make sense—she just had to stick to it.

She thought all of this in just the few steps it took to get back into Oxford's main terminal building.

Once inside, though, she stopped and drew a breath, trying to hide the plunging feeling that she felt in her stomach.

Daniel was standing in the middle of the forecourt flanked by two security guards, another jacketed policeman, and another, younger man in a cheap grey suit and short, military haircut—a police detective straight from TV. He was standing next to a man in a white shirt and tie with a nervous look on his face. Daniel wore a placid, resigned expression, but his clothes and hair were ruffled, showing signs of a struggle. His hands were behind his back, presumably handcuffed.

Freya felt the policewoman at her side grip her arm just under the armpit and at her elbow.

"What's this about?" she asked.

"Right this way."

"Who's that? I don't know him."

The man in the cheap suit turned to the nervous man in the necktie. "Is there a place we could talk in private?"

The man, his eyes wide and blinking at Daniel and Freya, nodded and turned. They followed him to a door marked Staff Only. This led them to a narrow corridor with many doors branching off. The nervous man opened one of them using a key. The detective put a hand on his shoulder. "It may be a little crowded in there," he said, with a slight Scottish lilt. "You all better wait outside. I'll call when I need you again. You two," he said, indicating Daniel and Freya, "inside, if you please."

Exchanging a glance, they entered the room, which was mostly bare except for a stack of chairs and two tables, one upended onto the other. A coffee vending machine that also advertised soup leaned dusty and in disrepair against the committee grey wall. All of this was lit by two luminous strip lights.

The detective pulled a couple chairs off the stack and placed them before Daniel and Freya. "Please, take a seat," he said, taking a chair for himself.

"It's hard to sit with my hands cuffed," Daniel said.

"Don't be a baby," the detective said. Daniel sat.

"Isn't this odd?" the detective asked. "All these sorts of buildings have odd little rooms like this. Would've been an office, in more prosperous times, or more likely a break room for the ticket tellers. But money gets tight, ticket telling becomes automated, and the room is forgotten about. I blame the Tories. Socialism is a small price to pay to keep everyone fed. What use is the free market economy if children go hungry? Economists don't know a thing about economy. Economy is feeding three children on the dole." He sniffed and looked around him. "Funny thing is, they can't even use this space for storage. Regulations only allot a certain percentage of space for storage and janitorial. If they wanted more space to store things, they'd have to build an extension or get an act of parliament. Isn't that mad?"

Daniel and Freya just sat looking at him blankly, Daniel sitting forward slightly in his chair.

"Sorry," the presumed detective said. "I do tend to rattle on when I get nervous. Gotta bit of Irish in me. Do you two still not recognise me?"

They stared harder at him.

"Are you a . . . detective, or something?" Freya asked, his face not even vaguely familiar.

"Ah, no, there you have me. I'm not a detective, but then I never said I was. But I *am* a policeman. Just a little outside of my jurisdiction. Ha, that sounded very Hollywood. But seriously . . . ," he said, reaching into his jacket pocket. He produced a flat black wallet and showed them the silver badge that displayed a thistle, which was clipped to the outside. "Here's my badge and my ID, which is going to give the game away, unless you have any more guesses."

He seemed to want an answer, so Freya shook her head.

The "detective" flipped open the wallet and held his identification card up close to them. They peered forward and read his name. "Think back, about eight years ago . . ."

"Alex Simpson," Daniel said. "Yes . . . yes! Of course! You!"

"Aye! I only bloody found you, didn't I? Wandering in our backfields, covered in dirt . . . the famous lost English schoolchildren. We all had to sit through a forty-five minute talk by a policeman about stranger awareness because of you two. I wasn't much older than you, so I'm not hurt that you didn't recognise me."

"But what are you doing here?" Freya asked.

"Been looking for the two of you, haven't I? And it's—here, Daniel, stand up; I can take those off of you now." He fished a key ring out of his pocket and unlocked Daniel's handcuffs. "Next time an officer of the law asks for a word, don't take a swing at him, alright? As I was saying, it's been bloody hard tracking you both down. Daniel, you were off the grid, naturally, but, Freya, you were in the system, but unlocatable. A week we've been hunting for you. I've managed to keep it quiet, but your parents are beside themselves. What happened to you?"

Daniel and Freya looked at each other.

"I'm sorry," said Freya, "*why* are you here, again?"

Alex slapped his head. "I'm sorry, I forgot. Niðergeard. I'm here about Niðergeard business."

"How do you know about Niðergeard?" Daniel asked, agog.

"It's a long story. I'll fill you in more later, but for now, suffice to say, I'm one of those above ground that exist to look after and care for the knights. I'm picking up where my father left off—like he did with his. It's one of those generational things. Goes right the way back to the Forty-Five."

Daniel and Freya's mouths hung open.

"Yes, secret society and all that. Well, it's a little more complex than that, but more about that later. First, I need to tell you that things are . . . developing. Listen," he said, and told them about Dunbeath, Morven, the trolls, and the dragon.

"That . . . sounds bad," Daniel said.

"It's worse than you think," Alex said. "Dragons . . ." He puffed out his cheeks and blew his breath out, shaking his head. "Anyway, what's happened with you?"

"Actually," Freya said, bracing herself. "There's something I need to tell both of you—"

"No, hold that thought," Alex said. "We should push on. You can tell me in the car."

"The car?"

"Aye. We've got a long drive ahead of us. Come with me. You're not under arrest, just 'helping me with my enquiries,' if anyone asks."

They left to find the two police officers still in the hallway. The security guards and the nervous man in the shirt had wandered off somewhere.

"Thanks, chappies," Alex said to the officers. "They've agreed to come with me and my associate. I owe you one."

The policemen just nodded and walked away. Alex shook his head. "The English . . . ," he muttered under his breath.

He led them out of the train station. They spotted the police car as they started down the steps. There was a man inside of it, in the passenger's seat, who made to get out when he saw them. The door opened and he stepped out, and as he did so, the car rocked with him—he was evidently very large. He straightened up to his full height, about seven feet tall, and looked at them from over the car's roof. Daniel and Freya stopped and looked at the man, hardly believing their eyes.

Alex flashed a smile. "Let me introduce my associate," he said. "Or have you met him already?"

"It can't be . . ."

"It's not . . ."

"Hello, young Daniel and young Freya."

"Ecgbryt!"

It was indeed the knight, but now dressed in a blue uniform and with a much tidier beard and closely trimmed hair that stuck out from a policeman's hat.

"*Swa swa*, it's Ecgbryt. Just so," he said, grinning. "What say you? Are you ready to rejoin the battle?"

2

Two Weeks Earlier...

Gád gazed down at Robin Ploughwright from the throne he sat upon. He didn't like elves, as a rule, and had plans to be rid of them for good. Although they could be relied upon, they were unpredictable. He had overcome his antipathy because they were perfect for just these sorts of jobs—distraction and detention.

Gád made a gesture, permitting him to leave.

Robin had walked a few steps when he turned.

"With respect," he said, twitching, "I know I shouldn't question—never have before, but I must ask . . . why not simply kill them, or detain them in a more conventional manner?"

Gád rose a hand to his chin. Kill Daniel and Freya? The thought truly hadn't occurred to him any more than removing chess pieces from his own side of the board halfway through a game. He liked them—they were so . . . manipulable . . . malleable.

"Really, Robin," he said, grinning. "Is that any way to treat a friend?"

A Short Note About Language

When the British monks first started to record the history and literature of their land, they wrote them in the Old English language but used the Latin alphabet instead of the pagan one. This was mainly for practical purposes, since Latin was spoken in nearly every European country at that time, usually by other priests and monks. The Roman system of writing was convenient, economical, and comprehensible to foreigners.

The problem, however, was that a few sounds used in English as it was at that time didn't exist in Latin and therefore had no letters to express them. To fix this, they decided to use the letters for those sounds that they already had, which came by way of the Scandinavians. A few of these letters and sounds were:

Þ, þ —called "thorn" and pronounced like the "th" in "thin"

Ð, ð —called "eth" and pronounced like the "th" in "then"

Æ, æ—also used to represent a vowel sound that was like the "a" in "ate"

Then England was conquered by France in 1066, and the English language went underground—all documents were written in Latin or French. When it started being used officially again several hundred years later, they didn't use any of the old letters or even most of the old words. This was the start of Middle English.

However, everyone living in Niðergeard and nearly all the knights who were already sleeping when this was happening didn't know of this change and a lot of them still use the old letters, which is why you'll find them in these books.

Ælfred - AYL-fred
Cnafa - KNAF-ah
Cnapa - KNAP-ah
Ealdstan - ee-ELD-stan
Ecgbryt - ETCH-(ye)-brit
Gád - GAAD
Godmund - GOHD-mund
Frithfroth - FRITH-froth
Kelm Kafhand - KELM KAHF-hand
Modwyn - MOHD-woon
Niðergeard - NI-thur-gayrd
Slæpismere - SLAYP-is-mare-eh
Swiðgar - SWIDTH-gar
yfelgóp(es) - EE-fel-GOHP(as)

Reading Group Guide

1. Freya and Daniel live with the knowledge that there is more to the world than what most people understand. How does this knowledge affect each of them?

2. "Black ops" officer Alex Simpson is committed to fighting the forces of evil. Do you believe that the presence of evil can physically manifest itself in the existence of malicious creatures? Do you believe, like Ecgbryt, that "there are places that are more enchanted than others"? Where and why?

3. Despite his grim situation in life, Daniel feels as if he belongs to another time, to a greater purpose. Do you believe a person can choose his or her own destiny or that it is chosen for him?

4. Though Freya declares that her time in Niðergeard was the worst thing she's ever gone through, Daniel fondly recalls it as the best thing that has ever happened to him. Why do you think two people, going through the same experience, have such different perspectives? How did Freya's and Daniel's experiences define each of them?

5. How are Freya and Daniel alike? How are they different? Why do you think they were each chosen for this task, and why were they chosen to do it together?

6. What parts of Freya's and Daniel's lives do you think were reality, and what parts were deceptions, meant to entrap them?

7. Daniel says, "I think I'd rather die doing something than die doing nothing." How does the ideal of being a hero affect Daniel's determination and course of action in the book? Does this ideal affect Freya's perspective?

8. Freya has the opportunity to kill Gád and falters. What prevents her from completing the quest set before her? Why do you think she lies to Daniel about what actually happened?

For more Reading Group Guide questions,
please visit www.ThomasNelson.com/RGG

Return to
Ancient Earth through

THE FEARFUL
GATES

BOOK TWO IN THE

ANCIENT EARTH TRILOGY

Available September 2012